# THE
# LAST
# SURGEON

# ALSO BY MICHAEL PALMER

MICHAEL PALMER

# THE LAST SURGEON

**Doubleday Large Print
Home Library Edition**

ST. MARTIN'S PRESS  NEW YORK

This Large Print Edition, prepared especially for Double-day Large Print Home Library, contains the complete, unabridged text of the original Publisher's Edition.

This is a work of fiction. All of the characters, organizations, and events portrayed in this novel are either products of the author's imagination or are used fictitiously.

**This Large Print Book carries the
Seal of Approval of N.A.V.H.**

To Sophie Love Palmer:
Such a short time in the world,
and you have already made so
many people so happy.

# ACKNOWLEDGMENTS

From concept to completion to publication, Jennifer Enderlin has been the shepherd of this book.

Meg Ruley, Jane Berkey, Peggy Gordijn, and the rest of the gang at the Jane Rotrosen Agency have each left a mark.

The Palmer guys—Daniel, Matthew, and Luke—have lent me their brilliance and creativity again and again.

John Roach taught me the politics of veterans' benefits and lack thereof.

Chef Bill Collins knows greyhounds and pad thai.

Chief Rick Towne, Hollis (NH) Fire Department, and Lonnie L. Larson CFI taught me about arson.

Dr. Joel Solomon helped my SUD score drop with his wisdom about EMDR therapy and treatments for PTSD.

Jeff Strobel and Peter Karlson know computer technology.

David Fulton knows kayaking.

Brilliant professor Katherine Ramsland is an expert in what makes killers kill.

Dr. David Grass is the doctor's doctor for all things neurological, just as Dr. Danica Palmer is for all things psychiatric.

Susan Reese and Susan Palmer Terry made me an almost expert in ICD and electronic medical records/billing systems.

Andrea Leers, as always, is my architect-on-call.

From Saudi Arabia and San Francisco, Dr. Abdel-Rahman Rabie and Ellen Rosenthal shared their friendship and knowledge of languages.

Sara Goodman, Jessica Bladd, Robin Broady, Ben Palmer, and my thirty-year pals Bill Wilson and Dr. Bob Smith were always there when the ship needed righting.

# THE
# LAST
# SURGEON

# PROLOGUE

"I know you can't believe this is happening, Ms. Coates, but I assure you it is. I have been paid, and paid very well, to kill you."

Belle Coates looked up at the intruder through a glaze of tears. "Please. Just tell me what you want," she said. "Just tell me what you want and you can have it. Anything. Anything at all."

The man sighed.

"You're not paying attention, Ms. Coates," he said with the accentuated patience of a third-grade teacher. "I am not here to bargain. I told you that. I'm here because this is what I get paid to do."

"But why? Why me?"

Belle made yet another futile attempt to stand. Her wrists and ankles were lashed to her kitchen chair by the sort of Velcro restraints she and other hospital nurses used so often on difficult patients.

"Those restraints look amazingly simple," the intruder said, "but I tell you they are a marvel of engineering and ergonomics. No pain, no marks. None at all. That's why I have a dozen or so sets of them in the drawer at home."

The man, six feet tall and wiry, had been hiding inside Belle's apartment, probably behind the couch in the living room, when she arrived home at nearly midnight. Her nursing shift—3 to 11 P.M. in the cardiac surgery ICU at the Central Charlotte Medical Center—had been a tough one, and she had relished every stair of the trudge that brought her closer to her apartment, a cup of tea, and a steamy shower.

She was just choosing a tea when he appeared in the doorway of her kitchen, an apparition in sky blue surgical hair and feet covers, latex gloves, black jeans, and a black long-sleeved tee. She was so fixated on his appearance that it was several seconds before she noticed the huge, gleaming knife dangling at his side. Her hesitation was more than enough. In two quick strides he was beside her, seizing a handful of her hair, snapping her head back, and pressing the blade against her throat. With just enough restraint to keep from drawing blood, he forced her down onto one of the oak chairs she had recently refinished, and in moments the restraints were on her. It had happened that fast.

**A dozen or so sets in the drawer.**

The statement was as terrifying as the knife.

Was he a serial rapist? A psychotic killer? Desperately searching for even the smallest inroad to understanding the intruder, Belle tried to remain calm and remember if she had read about such a man in the papers, or heard about him on the news.

"What do you want?" she said. "My fiancé will be home any minute."

He fixed her with pale, translucent blue eyes that were devoid of even the slightest spark of humanity.

"I don't think so. We both know about

your failed engagement. 'Celebrate Belle and Doug's love.' I'm very sorry about that."

Belle froze at the words, quoted from her wedding invitation.

"Who are you?" she managed again. "What do you want from me?"

"Now we're getting someplace." The man produced a vial from his pocket and set it on the table. "I want you to swallow these sleeping pills I found in your medicine cabinet the last time I was here. I have augmented what was there with some that I brought with me tonight, so there will be more than enough to achieve our goal. But before you take these pills, I want you to copy and sign a brief note I have composed explaining your despondency and your desire not to live anymore. And finally, I want you to undress, step into your tub, and go to sleep. See? Simple and absolutely painless."

Belle felt her breathing stop. This couldn't be happening. She wouldn't do it. He wouldn't be able to pry her jaws apart with a crowbar. She began to hyperventilate and shake, grabbing and releasing the arms of her chair.

"I won't do it."

"You will."

"I won't!" she began screaming. "I won't! I won't! Help! Someone help m—"

Her words were cut off by exquisite pressure around her throat. A hard rubber ball was forced expertly between her teeth and into her mouth. The killer remained absolutely calm during the insertion.

"That was stupid, Ms. Coates. Do anything stupid again, and you will be responsible for causing both yourself and your sister a great deal of pain."

Belle stared up at him, wide-eyed. The mention of her sister was a dagger. Hyperventilating through her nose, she still could not seem to get in enough air.

"That's right," the man said. "I know all about Jillian. Just like I know all about you. Now, refuse to do exactly as I say, try anything stupid again, and I promise, both you and Jillian will die prolonged and painful deaths. Understand? I said, do you understand?" Belle nodded vigorously. "I'm still not certain you do. Now listen, Ms. Coates, and for your sister's sake, believe me, I have no contract to kill Jillian—only you. With very rare exceptions, those I am not paid to kill, I don't kill."

He took out his cell phone, made a gentle tap on the screen's touch display, and held it up for Belle to see.

"I assume you recognize your sister's condo in Virginia—Arlington, to be exact, 489 Bristol Court to be even more exact. Nod if you agree that is the case. Good. I know how close you two are. You see, I read your journal, or diary, including entries from the trip to Nassau that Jillian took you on after you learned about Doug's . . . how shall I say . . . dalliance with your friend Margo. Surgeons. They are just so full of themselves, aren't they? I see you are having a little trouble breathing. Okay, here's the deal: I'll remove that ball if I get your assurance you will stay quiet and still."

Belle grunted her agreement and again nodded. The man pulled the ball out, keeping his fingers clear of her teeth, and dropped it into his pocket.

"Now," he said, "what you are about to watch is a live video feed—live as in *it's happening at 489 Bristol Court right this very instant.*"

Belle stared in disbelief at the full-color projection. The footage was unquestionably taken from her sister's tastefully and lovingly decorated condominium. She was certain that the woman sleeping alone in the queen-size bed was Jillian, also a nurse, and one of the main reasons Belle herself had chosen the profession. Following the automobile-accident deaths of their parents, Jillian had stepped in to raise her fourteen-year-old sister, often making major sacrifices in her personal life. Belle considered her to be the kindest, brightest, most centered person she had ever known. The camera had been placed above the valance in the bedroom. At the sight of Jillian, rolling languidly from her left side to her back, Belle began to hyperventilate again.

"Easy," the man warned. "Slow down. That's it. . . . That's it."

"Please. Please don't hurt her."

The apparition holding the phone leaned forward. Belle cringed as his empty eyes came level with her own. His pale white skin was tinted blue, a ghoulish illusion cast by her ecologically friendly halogen lights.

"You must calm down your breathing and listen, Ms. Coates. To save your sister's life, and yourself from a great deal of pain, it is essential that you believe I will do as I say."

"I believe. I believe. Turn it off. Turn that camera off and leave her alone."

"I'm going to make you a promise, Ms. Coates," he whispered, his lips brushing her ear. "I promise that if you fail to follow my instructions, Jillian will die, and die quite horribly. Do as I say and she lives. Want proof? Look here."

He held the phone at eye level.

"Enough," Belle pleaded. "Don't hurt her."

"I've placed small canisters of a potent nerve gas above the door frame inside the closet. Action almost instant. From this phone, I can control how much of the gas is released simply by tapping my finger. Incredible, yes? I am a virtuoso operating this setup. I put another camera in Jillian's bathroom because I want you to see what happens when just a smidge of this gas is inhaled."

"No, please. Please stop this. I believe you."

The intruder paid no attention. It was as if he had planned this demonstration all along. Belle's brain was spinning. How could she believe him? How could she not? What choice did she have? Would he really spare Jillian as he promised? Why would he? Why wouldn't he? The unanswerable questions roiled on and on.

"If I wanted to," he said as if reading her thoughts, "I could kill your sister—I could kill *anyone*—anytime, anyplace, and in any way I wish. But the point is I don't have to. I don't even want to. She seems like a nice woman. And as I said, there is nothing in her death for me."

He made two gentle taps on the phone's display, and Jillian's quaint bathroom came into focus, illuminated by a night-light beside the sink and a small diamond-shaped window above the tub.

"There are four levels of gas I can administer. The first three will cause increasing pain and the symptoms you are about to see. The fourth will kill . . . slowly. This is level one."

Within seconds, Jillian, wearing flannel pajamas Belle had bought for her, burst into the frame, fell onto her knees, and began retching violently into the toilet. Between bouts, she lay clenched in a fetal position on the tiled floor, shivering uncontrollably.

"Can you believe that's only level one?" the man asked. "I think I should patent this delivery system."

"Stop it! Stop doing this to her," Belle cried.

"Keep it down or I'll cut your larynx out and set it on the table. I'm sensing you need a bit more motivation, Ms. Coates. Allow me to oblige by upping Jillian's misery to level two. I'll keep it on level two until you start copying this note. Audio is really a must to get the full effect."

He tapped his phone's display again and now Belle could hear Jillian's grunting, labored breathing, interrupted by fits of gut-wrenching vomiting and sobs of pain.

"Please . . . stop . . . I believe you. I believe you."

He loosened her left hand and pushed the note she was to copy in front of her.

"Start writing your farewell letter, Ms. Coates. When you do, I'll stop killing your sister," he said.

Belle's face contorted in agony at the sound of Jillian's unrelenting anguish.

"Please . . ."

"Do you need more volume? Write the damn note!" the monster barked, pounding the table with each word. "You're dead regardless. But you can still save your sister's life—that is if you have the courage to do the right thing."

The man shut off the gas as soon as Belle began to write. In just a minute, Jillian's moaning stopped. Belle managed to pen the first four words before she began to sob.

"Finish," he said, "or I'll fire it up again."

"Why me? I haven't done anything wrong. I don't even know you. Why do you want me to die?"

"Not my call. Somebody in this great big world of ours has decided you have to go. And that somebody is paying me to make it happen. I can do it to you alone or to both of you."

"This is insane," she said, as much to herself as to the man who was about to murder her. "This is absolutely insane."

"I guess you enjoy listening to your sister scream. Allow me to show you level three."

The tormented retching Belle heard

could scarcely be described as human. On the tiny video display, Jillian's body convulsed more violently than before. As soon as Belle lifted up the pen again, the man pressed a button on his phone and her sister's screaming stopped. Belle found the strength to finish copying the note.

"I'm a man of my word, Ms. Coates. I'm also very good with handwriting and I have a large sample of yours from your journal. Mess with this and I'll dismember you joint by joint with that ball stuck back in your mouth. You'll still be alive to watch when I finally jack up the gas in Jillian's pad to level four."

"I did as you asked. Let her go."

"Sign it." The man studied the note with great care. "Okay, now the pills."

He shook the pills onto the table, motioning for her to take one.

"Please," Belle begged, still trying to make inroads into the utter helplessness she was feeling. "Who's paying you? Why do they want to kill me?"

"I'm running out of time and patience."

The man pressed a button on his phone like a puppet master pulling on invisible strings. Jillian's body again twitched with violent spasms.

"No! You promised!" Belle cried.

"You have the power to make this easier on Jillian. Think of all your sister has done for you. You owe it to her, don't you? Make me stop. I want you to stop me, Ms. Coates."

She could not listen to her sister's cries anymore. Her only thought was of the man's chilling proclamation.

**You're dead regardless.**

As though in a trance, her hand reached out shakily. Jillian's moaning abated as soon as Belle swallowed the first pill.

"Please . . . don't. No more."

"Keep swallowing and that's the last time you have to hear that nasty sound, Ms. Coates."

Belle tightened her jaw and nodded that she understood.

"Promise?" Her voice sounded like a child's. "I said, do you promise?"

"Ms. Coates, I might be a killer, but I'm a professional. You have my word. But I'm going to resume torturing your beloved sister unless all these pills are down the hatch."

It was too much to take. Belle raced to swallow the pills.

*What else can I do?* her mind kept asking. *What else can I do? . . . What else can I do?*

The action, in a way, was liberating. Her heart rate slowed and her tears stopped. In minutes, she no longer felt agitated or even frightened. The man's eyes, once haunting, now made her feel nothing at all.

"Good girl. You are simply going to close your eyes and go to sleep."

Her tongue already felt heavy. "You promised," Belle managed.

"You have my word."

After a while, he filled the tub, then undid her restraints.

"Clothes," he said.

Feeling the wooziness from the drug take further hold, Belle stepped out of her scrubs and dropped her bra and panties onto the floor.

Then she stepped into the tub.

"I love you, Jillian," she murmured. "I love you."

# CHAPTER 1

"Nick, Nick, throw it here! Come on, let it go!"

Nick Garrity cocked his right arm and lofted a perfect spiral to the gangly youth waiting across the yard. The boy, who would have been happy to keep playing until midnight, gathered in the pass effortlessly and immediately threw it back.

"Okay, that's it, Reggie. I gotta take Chance for a run and then get ready for work."

"One more pass. Just one more. After dinner I'll go over to your place and take Chance out. Promise."

Through the gloom of what was going to be a stormy evening, Nick could feel the boy's energy and see his enthusiasm. A drug-addicted mother, a long-gone father, time in juvenile detention for a crime no one seemed willing to talk about, seven years in a sequence of foster homes, and the kid was still upbeat and great to be around.

*How in the hell do you do it?* Nick wondered.

For most of the week, Nick's mood had been as somber as the prestorm sky. And as usual, there was no reason—at least not on the surface—to explain it. A night in the Helping Hands RV would improve his flagging morale. It usually did.

He made a final throw, handled as easily as most of the others, and then motioned for Reggie to come in.

"Come on, big guy. I've got to leave soon."

"So, where're you goin' tonight, Nick? D.C.?"

"I think so. Junie keeps track of that."

"Can I come?"

"It's a school night, and you promised to deal with Second Chance. Remember, don't let him off the leash or he'll see a squirrel and chase it to the moon. Greyhounds are bred to chase little furry animals. Use the long leash if you're going to throw him his Frisbee."

"How about I go with you tomorrow?"

"We'll see."

"I never get to do anything exciting."

"Yes, you do. Staying out of trouble is exciting."

Reggie punched Nick playfully in the side.

Nick put his arm around the youth's shoulders and walked with him to the back door. The modest one-family, with three bedrooms and a finished basement, was located in the Carroll Park section of Baltimore. Nick had lived there with June Wright and her husband, Sam, for a few months before renting the first floor of a refurbished two-family down the street, close to the park. Not long after the move, Reggie Smith, now fourteen, had taken over the basement bedroom.

A sequence of kids were constantly coming and going through the Wright household, including the six-year-old Levishefsky twins, Celeste and Bethany, who had been there for almost a year now. If one looked up "saint" in any encyclopedia, pictures of Junie, a sixty-year-old nurse, and Sam, a DPW worker, might well be there.

Since Junie would be working the RV tonight with Nick, her husband would be doing the cooking. The couple had children of their own, and grandchildren as well, but at every stage of their lives together, they had added foster children to the mix.

The Helping Hands RV was parked on the street by the Wrights' house. It was an aging thirty-four-foot mobile home converted into a general medical clinic. Nick loped past it on the way to his apartment. At six-foot-one, with broad shoulders and a solid chest, he still moved like the running back he had been in college before an illegal block had taken out most of his anterior cruciate ligament. Now the repaired knee was serviceable, but hardly ready to absorb a major hit.

Nick's father, once a football player himself, was a retired GP. The option of moving to the family home in Oregon was always available to Nick, but had never been one he had considered seriously. In

general, his parents were decent, understanding people, though not about their
only son. There was no reason to expect
they would be. In that same encyclopedia,
at least in their library, his picture might
have been inserted next to the word "disappointment."

"This is our son, trauma surgeon Dr.
Nick Garrity," they had introduced him on
more than one occasion during the years
when he was their golden child, "and this
is his sister."

Nearing his apartment, Nick heard the
low rumble of thunder in the distance,
sounding like a truck engine slowly coming to life.

He tensed at the sound.

He always would.

Nick's duplex would never be featured
in *Architectural Digest*, but that was fine
by him. Oak floors, a variety of posters
from the local art store, plus curtains and
a few plants gave the place an airy, comfortable feel. He was bent over beside the
mail slot, scooping up circulars and bills
from the floor, when he was hit from behind hard enough to drive his forehead
into the door. He turned, knowing what to

expect. Second Chance sat, head cocked, panting around the red Frisbee in his mouth.

"I'm running behind," Nick said, rubbing at his forehead, half expecting blood. "Reggie's going to take you out."

The dog pointed his snout toward the door and shifted his behind.

"No go, pal. Gotta shower."

They had been a team for almost two years, dating back to the first and only time Nick had ever been to a dog track. Lost in thoughts about Sarah, he had been on an aimless drive that ended at a casino in West Virginia. After an hour losing at the slots, he wandered over to the adjacent Tri-State track. He was in the midst of a particularly difficult time, when self-destructive thoughts had once again been seeping into his mind.

**Damn PTSD.**

Second Chance, a long shot in the fifth race and a natural bet for Nick, had been well in the lead when he suddenly slowed dramatically. Twenty yards from the finish, he was trampled by seven dogs as they passed over and around him, and was left nearly motionless in the dust.

An hour later, Nick and the greyhound had claimed one another at the adoption tent, where the dog's sleazy trainer tried to convince the Army trauma surgeon that Chance's uneven, lurching gait was due to nothing more than a minor concussion. Back home, the "concussion" responded dramatically when Nick, assisted by Reggie, Sam, and two Army buddies, cleaned densely packed dirt from each of the greyhound's ear canals.

Of all the therapies Nick had tried in his battle against post-traumatic stress disorder, Second Chance's presence in his life was the most consistently effective.

There were days when Nick was able to fit in some calisthenics and weights before going out on the road, but tonight, after playing catch with Reggie, there was just no time. He showered and was dressing in his usual work uniform, jeans and a faded work shirt, when he glanced over at a printout he had taped to the wall beside his bed listing the ten levels of SUDS— the Subjective Units of Disturbance Scale he used to estimate his mood at any given time. This evening seemed like a five: *Moderately upset, uncomfortable. Unpleasant feelings are still manageable with some effort.*

Progress, that's all he and Dr. Deems had decreed he should shoot for—just a little progress each day. Days like today, even after all these years, it was difficult to tell whether or not he was succeeding. He spent a minute patting and scratching Chance, and then pulled on a Windbreaker and headed out the door.

The thunder was louder now.

# CHAPTER 2

As usual, Junie Wright looked like royalty perched on the massive passenger seat, her iPod earphones in place.

"Let me guess," Nick said as he eased the RV down the street and toward the interstate south to D.C., "the Temptations."

"Nope."

"Sam Cooke?"

"Way off."

"Not more rap."

"Yup, it's my main man, Jay-Z. Pure sex through and through. Ummm-hmm." She punctuated the statement with a seductive shoulder shake and flashed him the smile that had raised so much money for various charities that it could have eliminated a chunk of the national debt.

An ample African-American woman with wide bright eyes and what seemed a perpetual smile, Junie was raised in the projects of Baltimore. After battling a thousand dragons on her way to a high school diploma, making it through nursing school was a relative breeze. She had been working for the Helping Hands Medical Foundation for some time when Nick returned to medicine and began volunteering first one night a week, then, after a half a year, two.

When the foundation went under due to mismanagement of their funds, Junie did what she often did in so many crises—she took control. First she formed a tax-exempt corporation with Nick as CEO and herself as chairman of the board. Then she mediated the sale of the RV to the corporation for one dollar. She proclaimed Nick the full-time, salaried medical director, and used his rugged good looks and history as a decorated combat surgeon to raise money and recruit volunteers. But by far her biggest challenge over the years—

especially since the disappearance of Nick's best friend, Umberto Vasquez—had been keeping the medical director afloat.

"We're gonna get wet tonight," she said, setting her iPod aside.

Nick nodded, keeping his focus on the road. Junie was good at many things, but making small talk was not one of them. The seemingly innocuous statement was her way of asking if he was okay and ready for their customary long night. One of the many symptoms that had gotten in his way since the horror of Forward Operating Base Savannah had been insomnia—fitful, perspiring, leg-cramping, nasty insomnia, coupled with more than one person's share of lurid nightmares.

"I can handle it," he replied. "I'm tough."

He turned the massive wipers on against the drops that were serving as reconnaissance for the storm that was predicted to hit full force by about eight. Junie, deciding that matters with him weren't dire enough to push, repositioned her earpieces and settled back into her seat. From the other side of the highway, lights flashed past hypnotically, summoning up, as they frequently

did, the vision of another set of headlights . . .

"That was some job you did in there,
Dr. Fury, sir."

Nick grins at the name, taken from
one of Vasquez's favorite comic book
heroes—Sgt. Nick Fury of S.H.I.E.L.D.
Now, after five months, most of the
hospital staff and many of the other
soldiers have picked up on it.

Dr. Nick Fury.

"You're the one who plugged that
sucking chest wound in that kid, Umberto," Nick says.

"Well, you're the one who taught us
how to do it."

"So, congratulations to us both. Listen, my friend, I have something I've
been meaning to give you for some
time. But before I do, I want your promise not to refuse it."

"But—"

"Promise."

"Okay, okay. I promise."

Nick reaches into the pocket of his
scrubs and hands over his Combat
Medical Badge, presented for medical
service during active combat. It is a

handsome award—oval, an inch and a half across, with a caduceus beneath a Greek cross at the center, overlaid on a field stretcher.

"I take this into the OR with me for luck," Nick says. "I want you to have it not only for what you do around here, but for the way you do it."

"I can't—"

"Uh-uh. You promised."

Umberto sighs.

"I'm honored, sir. I'll take real good care of it. Promise. In exchange, have a see-gar."

The stocky Marine staff sergeant, nearly half a head shorter than Nick but probably the same weight, produces two long cheroots, and the friends move to the front of the massive field hospital to light up. Nick is gritty with fatigue from what is now an eighteen-hour day. Vasquez never seems to tire.

FOB Savannah, one hundred kilometers southeast of Khost, isn't usually the busiest field hospital in Afghanistan, but today it probably has been. A convoy heading to the base along main supply road "Tiger" had been ambushed. Two deaths, twenty casualties. Four OR bays in continuous action all day. Bellies, limbs, heads, and the sucking chest wound in an eighteen-year-old named Anderson. Nice work by Umberto, who never failed to take one of Nick's combat emergency lectures. Nice work by the whole team, including Nick's fiancée of six months, Sarah Berman, also a surgeon.

She was career Army when they met. Nick, fairly new to a private practice in Philadelphia on September 11, 2001, had been hit hard emotionally by the tragedy, and had opted out of the reserves and into active duty. The two of them were as made for each other as they were fated to connect.

Nick and Vasquez lean against a Humvee parked in the dirt lot to the left of the main door and savor their cigars.

"You going to re-up when your tour is over?" Vasquez asks, his Dominican accent barely detectable.

"Maybe. I really love the work and the guys. So does Sarah."

"You've really hit the jackpot with that one, Doc."

"Tell me about it."

"The guys are crazy about her, and even more important, they respect her. She's still at it in there."

"Almost done. No need to save her a cigar, though."

Nick, a self-proclaimed "adrenaline junkie," has had three or four cigars in his life. This one, given his exhaustion, exhilaration, and the night air, is the very best. He warns himself against getting too fond of them. Sarah hates the way they make his kisses taste. It is nearly 3 A.M. A firm breeze sweeps across the desert, but provides little cooling. Far away, near the camp perimeter, a pair of headlights appears— twin stars jouncing toward them through the blackness.

"Who do you suppose that is?" Vasquez asks, inhaling deeply and exhaling through his nose. He flips on his radio and calls the guardhouse. "This is Vasquez at the hospital. Who's bouncing across the desert at us?"

"That'd be Zmarai from the clinic down the road, Sergeant. He's coming to check on his people from the firestorm this morning. Also, wants to mooch some supplies off you guys."

"Vasquez out," Vasquez says, turning to Nick. "Zmarai—now there's a scary dude. Beady eyes. Bad teeth."

"I'll bet he thinks the same of you," Nick counters. "He does a good job running that place and the little store. At least we have positive news for him this time. The two civilian casualties are both gonna make it."

The lights from Zmarai's truck move closer. The Afghani is a local leader who has his fingers in most of the area's pies, and often passes through security on his way to pick up supplies for the tiny clinic he runs. They know him well.

The battered, ancient Chevy pulls into the floodlit perimeter and stops fifteen feet from the massive wooden door to the hospital.

"Hey, Zmarai," Nick calls out as he approaches, "what's in the truck? I sure hope it's pizza."

Through the side window, the man looks off-kilter. His face is tilted skyward. His eyes are closed. All at once he opens his mouth and begins a chilling, screeching chant.

"Allah Akbar! . . . Allah Akbar!"

"Umberto, down!" Nick yells, now sprinting toward the driver's side. "Oh, my God! Get down! Get down!"

He leaps onto the running board and grabs the side-view mirror with one arm, pounding on the window with his other hand just as the engine roars to life and the truck surges forward, spewing sand.

Nick sees Vasquez appear at the tightly closed passenger window at the moment the truck shatters the main door with a fearsome jolt. It hurtles ahead toward the heart of the enormous tent—the operating and recovery rooms. Suddenly, Sarah appears, locked between the headlights. Nick barely has time to register that she is there, to see the terror in her eyes, before the grille of the truck hits her at the base of her ribs, tearing her nearly in half. Nick sees blood gush from her mouth as she flies backward toward the ORs.

Vasquez is slammed against a support

pole and driven off the running board. The truck bursts into the brightly lit space, scattering victims and hammering into patients. Zmarai hits the brakes, hurling Nick to the ground like a rag doll. Paralyzed by Sarah's gruesome death, Nick stares unseeingly at the floor. He knows the truck is going to explode and that he's about to die. The image filling his mind is Sarah. Suddenly, there is a blur of movement from his right side. Heavy arms wrap around his shoulders and drive him backward into the base of a massive refrigeration unit filled with blood and blood products.

Umberto!

Glass shattering, the refrigerator topples onto Nick and his friend, covering them both. Nick is semiconscious, facedown under the glass-and-steel appliance. Units of blood are torn open and their contents pour onto his head and torso. Then, amidst the chaos and screaming, Zmarai's ancient truck explodes. The roar is deafening. Blast-furnace heat floods Nick's face and arms.

Then there is nothing.

It is more than twenty-four hours before Nick begins to regain consciousness. His skin is badly scorched, his ears are ringing, and his hearing is muffled, but he can still hear the surgeon telling him that rather than leave the tent, Umberto had rushed back to Nick's side and saved his life. He is told that Umberto is still in a coma and there is only one other survivor, an orderly, who is still touch and go. There are twenty-eight fatalities. Some of the bodies, including Sarah Berman's, have not been pieced together yet. . . .

"Jeez Marie, Nick," Junie cried. "I just looked over at you and you weren't there. It's like the RV is on automatic pilot."

"I was here," Nick lied, flexing his shoulders and back against the chilly perspiration that was soaking into his clothes.

The rain had become a downpour, and the RV was blasting through it into the darkening night.

"You want to go home?"

"I said I was okay," Nick snapped.

Junie knew better than to react. Whatever had been going on was leaving him, and no one had gotten hurt. The episodes had been coming fewer and farther between. He'd be okay.

"On the highway, this here bus is like a battleship against a bunch of rowboats," she said.

"I . . . know. I'm sorry."

He slowed the RV to forty.

"You're going to be okay, Nick," the nurse said in what was half statement and half query. "You're going to be fine."

Nick's reply was a grim smile.

# CHAPTER 3

"Come on, gang. It's a simple question. An atom that loses one or more electrons becomes a what?"

Franz Koller bristled at the students' lack of respect for their education, and thought of killing them—every one of them. An aerosol blast of sarin, the nerve gas used in the Tokyo subway attacks, would do just fine. The glorious image brought a smile—twenty-two perfect teenage bodies, simultaneously tumbling from their chairs, writhing in seizure, soiling themselves as respiratory failure set in. His grin broke the tension between him and the tenth-grade chemistry class at Woodrow Wilson High in Coltin, California. The kids saw him brighten, and a few actually smiled back. Again, he pictured them squirming on the floor, their tiny backs arched in agony, mouths agape like fish on a dock, madly sucking for breaths that just wouldn't come. The visual made him laugh out loud. The students joined in and laughed with him.

"Oh, pleeeeasseee," Koller begged, kneeling in mock desperation on the scuffed linoleum floor. "Please take pity on your poor old substitute teacher and answer the question. I know we subs aren't supposed to actually teach, but I really know chemistry, and I'm determined to impart some of my knowledge to you."

Though he was born and raised in Austria, his speech was free of any accent—unless, of course, he wanted one to be there. On bended knee, praying before his class for some bright star to respond, Koller clasped his hands together and bowed his head. He paused for added dramatic effect before looking up and raising one eyebrow as if to add "pretty please, with sugar on top." It was a phrase he sometimes used when begging his victims to hold on just a little longer.

The class giggled, though somewhat cautiously. Little by little, he was winning them over. Koller was incredibly skilled at that—winning people over—especially those he was in the process of studying for what he called a non kill — murder that appeared not to be murder at all.

He laughed with the class as he rose, but his laughter was not at what they were finding funny. He was continuing the fantasy about their mass destruction— specifically the vision of their parents, cocooned in white chemical suits, coming to identify their bodies.

"One of you must know the answer. An atom that loses one or more electrons becomes?"

The only sound was the ticking of the wall-mounted clock. No wonder America's world dominance was on the decline, Koller mused. For years, in between contracts, he had protected his identity as a killer by creating new identities as a substitute teacher. He enjoyed the deception and the teenage girls, but until recently he also enjoyed making complex concepts clear. He had well-supported teaching credentials in California and Florida, where he also had residences. At last, a tiny hand, third desk from the back, tentatively came up. The killer's eyes flashed with delight. All heads turned toward the back to see who it was.

"Ah! Ms. Rebecca Woodorf."

The girl looked puzzled at his remembering her name. After all, what substitute teacher, without the aid of a seating chart, who had heard their names only once during attendance, could pull off such a feat?

"Please stand up, Rebecca. Stand up. It appears you are our only salvation. Now, prove to me and to your fellow classmates that America's tenth graders can stay with the Russians, Chinese, and Japanese when it comes to inorganic chemistry."

Koller rubbed his hands in anticipation. It was a game he enjoyed playing during the sometimes interminable periods between contracts—to win over the class so that he was all they would be talking about after school. He actually had never finished college, dropping out after he was recruited by a psychology professor to meet with the people who would eventually teach him how to kill for money. They were the ones who would supply him with unassailable teaching credentials. He was a quick study in every area. And while there was much to learn, he had a head start, because when it came to manipulating others and controlling their behavior, he already had a Ph.D. with high honors.

Rebecca rose. Her black sweater was tight against her slender frame, accentuating her burgeoning womanhood in a most appealing way. Koller noticed, too, that her lips were tight across her teeth. She was shy, though not too shy to show pride in her body. Interesting.

"Mr. Greene?" Rebecca said in a small voice.

"Yes. Go ahead. Give it to us."

"May I go to the bathroom?"

The classroom exploded in laugher. Rebecca glanced about, mortified. Koller kept his expression stern and his arms folded tightly across his chest. The laughter subsided.

"Only if you can tell me what an atom that loses one or more electrons becomes," Koller said, matter-of-factly.

There was an audible gasp and Rebecca's lips tensed even more. The students stared from their classmate to their substitute teacher and back, trying to get a read on each of them. Behind his deep brown contacts, Koller gave them nothing to fix on. In the next teaching gig, the lenses would be green or navy, covering his true eye color, a startlingly pale blue. His store-bought mustache would be on or off depending on his mood. Koller took pride in disguising not only his thoughts, intentions, and facial features, but his physique as well, which for this job, thanks to skillfully applied padding and latex, looked doughy and poorly maintained—anything but capable of snapping a human neck with the quick grip and twist of one hand.

"Are you serious?" Rebecca managed.

"The bathroom key in exchange for an atom that loses one or more electrons."

Koller paused just the right amount of time before breaking.

"Nah," he said with a broadening grin and a dismissive wave of his hand. "I'm just messin' with you. Of course you can go."

That did it. The students applauded and howled even louder this time, and Rebecca, who moments before had looked as if she were going to be sick, laughed along with them. Clearly still uncertain and off balance, she walked warily to the front of the class, past the substitute they knew as Mr. Robert Greene. Cautiously, she took the key attached to a model of a chlorine atom off his desk, and moved to the door. Once there, she paused before exiting the room, and turned back.

"Mr. Greene?"

"Yes, Rebecca?"

"A cation," she said simply.

Koller, though not the least surprised, gave her a playful bow and applauded, encouraging her classmates to do the same. She beamed then turned to go, the backs of her thighs taunting Koller as she closed the door behind her.

Playing head games with fifteen-year-olds. Ogling a child's ass. This day was becoming truly torturous.

In the past, teaching high school chemistry had been reasonably diverting, in addition to providing him with an effective cover. It was not a good idea to be a single man, leading a secret life, without having some sort of socially acceptable profession.

In addition, he had never done that well with too much downtime between contracts. But now, the queens of vapidity, YouTube, the Internet, and television, had taken their toll, and in most of the so-called students there was little mind remaining to mess with.

This was the end of the teaching, he vowed. From now on, when he needed a diversion, he would just drive out to the woods and kill something. It had been two weeks since the last contract. How long would he be made to wait?

He recalled with fondness the nurse from Charlotte, whom he had studied and then manipulated to ingest a lethal over-dose of sleeping pills, complete with a handwritten suicide note.

**Nicely done.**

You call, Franz Koller delivers. The CSI goofs would have given up searching for clues in the nurse's death before the first commercial. Koller heard the growing rest-lessness behind him and knew he was ignoring the class. Screw them. They were lucky he didn't go out to the local poison gas store for some sarin.

Sleepers and a suicide note. The woman was a magnificent non-kill—more intense

than screwing a hundred Rebecca Woo-
dorfs would have been. Belle Coates, first
in her class at nursing school, fluent in
three languages, was so exquisitely sexy,
lying there naked, helpless, and utterly
outmaneuvered, slipping away in the luke-
warm water of her bathtub. Just watching
her breathing slow and her head slip beneath the surface had given him a fearsome erection. He never even had to touch
her. Sex was all about control, and how
much more control could there be than—

The classroom door opened and closed.

Rebecca Woodorf returned from the
bathroom, less shy and more confident.

"You have some TP stuck on your shoe,"
Koller said casually as she passed.

The girl reddened, quickly glanced behind to see, then stared in confusion at
her teacher.

"Just kidding," Koller said. "Gotcha."

This time, the laughter from her classmates was directed at her. Koller did nothing to stifle it. The girl's shoulders sank
under the humiliation as she scuffled back
to her desk.

*Fun, fun, fun 'til her daddy takes the
T-bird away*, Koller sang to himself.

He sent a portly boy named Sommers to pass out a quiz left for them by their teacher. They were all quiet now, busily scribbling in their booklets, answering questions a sixth-grader should have known.

Ten minutes more . . . ten min—

His cell phone began ringing. The tone was AC/DC's famous guitar riff from "Back in Black." The students recognized the song immediately and looked up at Koller with surprise and reverence. Mr. Robert Greene was hip—the coolest chemistry teacher around.

Their delight did not come close to Koller's.

"Who is it, Greene?" one of the class toughs called out. "One of your biker babes?"

"I wouldn't be caught dead on a motorcycle, Harcourt," Koller said, flashing back to the contract on a surgeon from Chicago who rode his gleaming Harley into oblivion.

The bolts supporting the front and rear calipers, carefully modified by the master of the non-kill, disconnected simultaneously at the top of a long 10 percent grade on the interstate. Under the best of circumstances, investigators would probably never have spotted the modification. In the case of Lewis Leonard, M.D., a tractor-trailer saw to it that there was no modification left to detect.

**Nicely done.**

"So what's the call all about?" Harcourt asked far too loudly.

"It's nothing," Koller said, bursting to tell the truth to the arrogant little shits, but knowing he wouldn't. "Just an alert that an art dealer I like to buy things from has posted an item for bid on eBay. I get notified whenever he lists something new."

"What are you buying, a blow-up?"

"Ever hear of sarin, Stankowsky?"

"What?"

"Nothing."

"What is it, then? What are you buying?"

Koller glanced up at the clock. Four minutes before last bell.

"Want to see?" he asked.

Anything but chemistry.

The class begged him in unison.

He clicked a link in his e-mail and opened up an eBay product description and photo. Then he passed his cell phone around, allowing each student a chance to see the wooden desk lamp shaped like an old sailing ship that was now open for bids starting at $0.99.

"That's a piece of crap," one student exclaimed. "Wal-Mart wouldn't carry it."

There were guffaws from some of the others, but Koller didn't react.

"What do you think, Rebecca?" he asked.

Rebecca's eyes were fixed on her test booklet.

"I don't know," she mumbled.

"Take a look," Koller said. "You're the smartest one in this class—the only one whose opinion I would trust. The only one worth saving when the flood comes. I think it's simply beautiful. How about you?"

Rebecca glanced up at the phone as if half expecting something gross.

"It's a very nice lamp," she managed.

*What it is*, Koller was thinking, *is a job for Mr. Greene*—buckets of money for work he would happily do for free.

Last bell sounded, and Koller was out the door without even looking back at his class.

As soon as he was back at his apartment, he would decode the message encrypted within the picture of the lamp. Then, once he had all the facts, he would decide if $990,000 was enough for the job or whether $1,500,000—a million five— would be more appropriate.

Later that day, John Sykes, the principal of Woodrow Wilson High, called to say that the feedback from his chemistry classes was excellent, especially F block, the last period. Could Greene possibly come in and substitute again tomorrow?

# CHAPTER 4

The interior of the Helping Hands Mobile Medical Unit was straight out of a Norman Rockwell painting. Every inch of available space inside the 1996 Fleetwood RV was being used for something—notices, storage, medical equipment, office machines— creating a quaint, homespun feel, which was enhanced by the white honeycomb window shades, beige textured carpet, and incandescent accent lighting. The steamy windows and the grizzled, hardened faces of the three men at the center fold-out table, each in a different posture, each clutching a mug of coffee, completed the masterpiece.

It was a Wednesday, and at this stop— the muddy lot of Jasper Yeo's Dependable Used Autos—that meant Nick would be teaching his weekly class on obtaining VA benefits for post-traumatic stress disorder. Outside, the heavy rain was continuing unabated, pelting the roof of the clinic, and scrubbing the air clean after what had been an unseasonably warm day. The RV was crowded, so the seven men and one woman seeking treatment were using the covered bus stop at the corner as their waiting room. The inconvenience bothered them little. Most of them were near the bottom of life's totem pole, and quite used to being put on hold.

Inside the RV, the stakes in the tiny classroom were high. Benefit money each of the three men needed to survive had been denied by a VA review board. In fact, Nick's credential to run the course he had started was a protracted, ultimately victorious battle for his own benefits. It was a struggle that had begun with a rejection by the antichrist of VA claim evaluators, Phillip

MacCandliss, and ended with a high-level review board reversing the decision. Not long after that, possibly because of his heavy-handed opposition to Nick's petition, MacCandliss was passed over for promotion.

War.

"Sorry to keep questioning you, Doc," Eddie Thompson said. "It's just that this is my third go at trying to get my benefit pay. I'm running out of steam and I've already run out of cash."

Nick set his hand on the shoulder of the bullnecked ex-infantryman, whom he knew had witnessed inconceivable brutality—many of the victims, his friends.

"I know, Eddie," he said, not even attempting to cull the huskiness from his voice. "I know."

Given the flashback during the ride into D.C., it wasn't a great night for him to be doing the class. In spite of himself, Nick felt his concentration begin to slip. He glanced up past Eddie at the corkboard wall, festooned with job notices, lists of AA and NA meetings, nightly shelter possibilities, and other hints for survival on the streets. At the center of the announcements was the four-year-old poster requesting any information on the disappearance of Umberto Vasquez. The sepia photograph was slightly faded, but not enough to wash away the visage of the intensely funny, bright, compassionate Marine, who was the only other one to have survived the nightmare of FOB Savannah.

Vasquez, suffering from PTSD at least as debilitating as Nick's, had nevertheless helped him to grieve for Sarah, and had often held him for as long as it took for Nick to stop shaking, even as Umberto's own demons, and omnipresent cheap wine, were tearing away at his guts.

REWARD
For Validated Information Regarding
the Disappearance of Staff Sgt.
Umberto Vasquez
Last seen 2/20/06; Fort Stanton Park
Call Capt. Nick Garrity 202-966-9115

"Damn, they make it hard," Eddie moaned.

"For a reason. Three out of ten claims get VA approval. Three out of ten! That's millions, if not billions of benefit dollars that don't have to get paid out. They'll pay it if they have to, but they'll sure make you work for it."

"Ain't right," Corporal Matthew McBean added in his dense Mississippi drawl.

"But that's the way it is. When I was diagnosed with PTSD I made the mistake of asking the VA regional office and their lead benefits blocker, Phillip MacCandliss, to expand my claim to include that diagnosis. MacCandliss knew the rules and interpreted my request to mean that I had a claim previously denied. The proper wording for what I wanted to do would have been to 'amend my claim.' That misstep cost me four months of tedious paperwork. And that was just my first of a number of mistakes. MacCandliss counts on us caving in at some point and just giving up. He and many of the rest of them equate depression and PTSD with weakness. He underestimated me—at least in that regard he did."

"Shit, I'd give up all my bennies for one decent night's sleep," McBean said.

Nick nodded empathetically.

"Have any of you called the EMDR Institute yet?" he asked. "If not, let's make that your next homework assignment. Ask for Dr. Deems and tell her I recommended you call."

"You really think it'll help?"

Nick hesitated. Did he think it would help? The jury was still out on that one. Even so, the thought of ridding himself of his torment was enough motivation to continue experimenting with the relatively new psychotherapy tool. The idea of EMDR—eye movement desensitization reprocessing—was simple enough, and the technique had been used successfully for a number of conditions including performance anxiety, phobias, sexual dysfunction, and eating disorders.

Working with a therapist in D.C. once each week, Nick was now on phase four of an eight-phase EMDR program. By combining repetitive eye movements with varying mental snapshots of both positive and traumatic images, the treatment purported to eliminate most, if not all, PTSD symptoms. Nick was hardly a poster child for the technique, though.

Behind them, the floor-to-ceiling curtain opened a foot and Junie poked her head out.

"Got a minute to check this kid, Nick?"

If not for the class, both Junie and Nick would have been seeing patients from the beginning of the evening. In almost any situation, the nurse could match her skills and judgment against any M.D. or D.O., but it was Helping Hands policy—and that of the board of health—to have every patient checked by a doc, or else by a physician's assistant or a nurse practitioner, and tonight there were neither of those on duty, although frequently there were.

Nick passed out a sheet of instructions for the next class, and asked his three students to check it over while he was gone.

"What do you have?" Nick asked as he approached the curtain.

Junie did not pull her head back.

"I have a kid that I think has mono."

"Did you draw bloods?"

"A mono test, CBC and liver chems, plus an amylase and lipase."

"Throat?"

"Classic, if there is such a thing. I cultured it and gave him a supply of penicillin, a rinse, and some Motrin."

"Enlarged spleen?"

"I don't think so, but you know I'm not

the best at that unless it's the size of a football."

"You done good. Let's see him."

Junie did not move. When she spoke again, it was in a near whisper.

"I looked out a couple of minutes ago," she said, "and you were staring up at Umberto's poster. You okay?"

"Hanging in there. The class is a nice distraction—especially these guys—but that nightmare I had on the way here is still resonating. Good thing I don't have to hold a full cup of hot coffee."

"Have you tried your eye exercises?"

Nick kissed her on the forehead and motioned to the examining room.

"I'm doing fine. Now, let's go kick some mononucleosis butt."

Not surprisingly, Junie was spot-on in her assessment of the seventeen-year-old, whose residence was listed as the 24 Hotel—night-by-night cots for homeless men. With no major trouble swallowing, and no striking enlargement of his spleen, the youth was sent out with a "mono sheet" of do's and don'ts. As with most of their patients, the caregivers could only hope that he kept his follow-up appointment.

Nick was back giving final instructions to his class when the mono patient passed by them and left, followed moments later by Junie, carrying her umbrella.

"I'm going to grab the next victim," she said. "I'm thinking of stopping by Dunkin' Donuts across the street to see if they can donate a Box O' Joe to our waiting room out there. They've done it before."

"Like they have a chance against you."

A gust of chilly, wet air blew in as she opened and closed the passenger side door.

Just a few minutes later, the door opened again and a short, stocky, balding man entered. He was wearing a tan trench coat and shaking off an umbrella. He was followed immediately by Phillip MacCandliss.

"Good evening, Garrity," MacCandliss said, fixing Nick with dark narrow ferret eyes. "May I introduce Mr. Janus Fielding." He increased his volume so that anyone in the rear of the RV could hear. "He's with the D.C. Department of Health."

# CHAPTER 5

The sight of MacCandliss turned Nick's stomach. It wasn't the first unannounced visit he had made to the RV—two other times over the past few years he had "just stopped by to see what this operation is all about." But this was the first time he had arrived accompanied.

"We're very busy, MacCandliss," Nick said. "Why didn't you phone ahead for an appointment?"

"Now that wouldn't be a very good way to go about holding a surprise inspection, would it?"

The VA claims evaluator, infamous among

the GIs for his hard-nosed refusal to grant disability benefits, remained in the stair-well behind Janus Fielding. MacCandliss was swarthy and thinly built, and looked slightly ridiculous in a tweed walking cap, but Nick knew better than to take the man lightly. He was devious and unpredictable except in his unswerving drive to put him-self first in any situation.

Nick sized up the moment and con-sidered whether it was worth stalling until Junie's return. Still shaky, he wondered if he could control his temper, which was known to be hair-trigger when he was dealing with the confounding symptoms of his PTSD. He glanced out at the bus stop waiting area, but she was probably still in Dunkin'.

*Damn you, MacCandliss*, he barely kept from hollering out, *why tonight?*

"Okay, Mr. Fielding," Nick said instead, sighing audibly, "why don't we start at the beginning. Credentials?"

Fielding flipped open a dedicated leather case, revealing a Health Depart-ment badge and a photo ID.

**Facilities Inspector, Department of Health.**

"Exactly what is it you want, Mr. Janus Fielding?" Nick asked, recalling from a mythology course at Stanford that Janus was the Roman god of, among other things, doors and gates, and wondering how the man's parents could have come up with so prophetic a name.

"I have a list of complaints that have been filed against this medical facility, of which you are the owner."

"I'm assuming Mr. MacCandliss there is responsible for the complaints."

"The forms are all in order," Fielding said, pointedly ignoring the statement.

Behind him, MacCandliss was the very essence of smug.

"You know, we're very busy," Nick said, gesturing to the three men in the dining area, and out the window toward the bus stop.

Through the unremitting rain, he could see Junie approaching the shelter, carrying a large plastic bag and two ten-cup cartons of coffee. No surprise. Even if the staff at Dunkin' was resistant, which they had never been in the past, they were outmatched.

"To begin with," Fielding said, "I'd like to

do a walk-through and conduct an inspection of the way you are handling issues of cleanliness, as well as your equipment and pharmaceuticals. I am especially interested in assurance that the needles and syringes are properly locked."

"There's really only room for one of you," Nick said. "I'd appreciate it if Mr. MacCandliss stayed where he is, or better still, waited outside with the others."

Over the next few minutes, Fielding made his way down his checklist, without finding anything major amiss. He did suggest that the isopropyl alcohol swabs be kept locked with the syringes and needles, and that the file drawers holding the patient records be doubly protected against both theft and fire. Right from the beginning Nick could tell he was reaching.

*Bless you, Junie*, he thought, reflecting on the thoroughness with which she insisted they prepare the RV.

Fielding was certifying that the sharps disposal units and the trash receptacles were to code when the front door swung open. A thin, unshaven white man in a sodden peacoat entered and squeezed past MacCandliss, who took a decent soaking and looked as if being closer than a city block away from the fellow was too close. The man, whom Nick recognized from other visits, headed unsteadily toward the aft examining room. He was followed closely by Junie, who made enough eye contact with Nick to say several things at once, the most important of which was that she was worried about this latest patient.

Nick felt the same way. The man, who Nick recalled was named Campbell, looked sick. His eyes were dark hollows and he had an odd tick at the corner of his mouth. Nick watched as Junie followed Campbell to the examining room. Then she turned at the last second and glanced back.

*Don't wait long*, she silently urged.

Nick ushered Fielding back to where MacCandliss was waiting.

"Okay, guys, looks like I've got some doctoring to do. Feel free to wait . . . or not. Mr. Fielding, I can save you some trouble by telling you that we read the HIPAA manual as a bedtime story and that our board of directors makes surprise inspections of the RV all the time. Tell whoever filed complaints against us that they're wasting their time and yours. I'll be back when I'm sure this man is okay."

Without waiting for a response, Nick headed to the examining room. Campbell, who smelled like the streets, was still standing, shifting from one foot to the other. Had there been much more room, he certainly would have been pacing. His eyes, pupils wide, were darting from one side of the space to the other.

"Mike," Junie said, "sit down and let me get your coat off. I need to check your blood pressure. Nick, this is Mike Campbell."

"We've met. When was it, Mike, a year ago?"

"I don't know," Campbell mumbled.

It was an overdose of some kind. Nick felt almost sure of it.

"Mike, we want to help you. Give us a chance to help you. We're on your side. Have a seat up here."

Hesitantly, Campbell pushed onto the edge of the examining table. Junie was just beginning to help him off with his coat when Nick saw the wet stain six inches below his armpit.

"Glove," he said simply, to the nurse.

Without asking for an explanation, Junie slipped on a pair of latex gloves. Campbell reluctantly allowed her to remove his coat. The left side of his white Redskins T-shirt was soaked with an expanding oval of blood. At the center of the stain was a two-inch slit.

"Pulse one ten. Pressure ninety over sixty."

From the beginning of his medical training, Nick constantly had to suppress the urge to jump in and get to work when a patient was bleeding. As it was, unless there were obvious indications, he still could not bring himself to allow an injured person to continue bleeding while he took maximum, time-consuming precautions against AIDS, such as donning a gown, an extra pair of gloves, and plastic full-face shield.

"Mike, don't be frightened. I'm going to glove and then I need to examine you, and quickly."

"Where am I?" Campbell rasped.

Nick and Junie exchanged concerned glances.

"You came to the Helping Hands medical

van," Junie said. "I'm Junie and this is Dr. Nick Garrity. We're here to help you."

"Is this the hospital?"

"This is the mobile medical van."

Campbell looked wildly about.

"No hospital."

"We're on your side," Nick said, as Junie gingerly pulled off the man's shirt. "Anything we do will be to keep you alive."

Nick could tell immediately that there was no way this wound could be properly evaluated outside of an ER, and possibly an OR. The chest cavity could easily hold a lethal amount of blood if the blade had gone through the chest wall. A lobe or an entire lung could have collapsed. He was relieved to see that Campbell's trachea was midline—an excellent sign that for the moment at least, the lung was still inflated. His nail beds were fairly pink, another good sign.

"Systolic pressure is still ninety," Junie said, as if reading Nick's mind. "He's having a few extra beats."

"Hang in there, Mike," Nick said. "We'll explain everything in just a minute."

"No hospital," Campbell said again, his speech marginally thicker than it was before.

Nick carefully listened with his stethoscope. There were breath sounds out to the chest wall in all fields. He forced himself to take a step back. The knife wound could be nothing, or mortal. He knew that guessing at this point was a shortcut to disaster, but his clinical sense told him the wound was shallow. If so, the man's low blood pressure, confusion, dilated pupils, and irregular heartbeat were out of proportion to the severity of his injury. Something else was going on.

"Junie, could you get his record?" he asked, continuing his exam.

There was no question that Campbell needed transportation to the hospital, and quickly. The trick would be getting him to agree. Nick checked his blood pressure again. Eighty-five. Maybe there was more internal bleeding than he thought. Without asking, he slipped an oxygen cannula into Campbell's nostrils and turned the flow up to six liters. The man made no attempt to resist. Nick was preparing to start an IV when Junie opened Campbell's chart and pointed to a section.

**Known heroin and benzo addict . . . History of multiple overdoses, especially**

**meth . . . On probation. Terrified of going back to prison.**

"That explains why Mike is so reluctant to let us take him to the ER," Junie said. "Is that right, Mike?"

Nick could feel the tension in the man's body.

"Mike, I need to put an IV in your arm to give you fluid and medicine. Your blood pressure is really low."

Campbell's expression was that of a caged animal.

In seconds, Nick had inserted a two-inch IV catheter into a vein at Campbell's wrist.

"Extra wrap?" Junie asked.

Nick nodded. As usual, she was ahead of the game.

"Draw up one of Narcan and point three of flumazenil. Then hang a liter of saline and run it wide open," he said.

Junie unlocked the small crash cart and began drawing up the meds. At that instant, Campbell slid off the examining table and began turning frantically from one side to the other. Nick shelved his plan to anesthetize and probe the knife wound and instead tried to help the addict back onto the table. The exam could wait until the antidotes for the narcotics and Valium overdose were in.

However, before anything more could be done, Campbell bolted.

# CHAPTER 6

Mike Campbell, wide-eyed and beyond reason, bellowed and thrashed at invisible enemies as he charged from the examining room toward the front of the RV. Eddie Thompson, a hundred pounds heavier than the addict, rose to block his path, and was thrown aside like a child, stumbling against the table and down to the floor, sending coffee spraying from the mugs of the other two students.

Janus Fielding, moving with surprising quickness, reactively filled the spot vacated by Thompson, leaving Phillip MacCandliss exposed to the brunt of Campbell's onslaught. The claims evaluator, caught in the passenger-side stairwell, was slammed backward against the door with enough force to snap the latch and fling it open. Helpless, he disappeared into the pelting rain, landing on his back in the mire of Jasper Yeo's Dependable Used Autos sales lot. Campbell, naked from the waist up, stepped off the bottom stair and onto MacCandliss's belly, falling heavily next to him in the mud. Then he scrambled to his feet and lurched off toward the busy five-way intersection.

By the time Nick had taken the antidotes for overdoses of narcotics and Valium from Junie, Campbell was out of the van. Thank God she had taken the precaution of a bulky wrap around the IV, Nick thought. Thank that same God they had found a vein at the man's wrist—one of the best spots to protect a line. If he could catch Campbell, there was a good chance that Junie's maneuver might end up saving the man's life.

Eddie Thompson was awkwardly trying to return to his feet when Nick sprinted past. Two more strides and he was at the stairwell. Beyond the doorway, MacCandliss had managed to get unsteadily to one knee. Focused on Campbell, Nick leaped off the bottom step like a hurdler.

The scene ahead of Nick unfolded in slow motion. Campbell, still moving forward in a bizarre, uneven gait, was stumbling from side to side like a prizefighter about to go down for the count.

But he did not go down.

Instead, he stepped off the curb and into traffic. Nick, closing the gap between them rapidly, saw the bus that was barreling through the rain toward Campbell from the right. His instantaneous estimation told him that his patient was better than even money to be dead in a matter of seconds. But his mind's eye had locked on to something else as well—Sarah, coming from the OR, moving unaware across the path of a careening pickup truck, whose driver had no intention of stopping. The image of her being slammed in the midsection by the pickup froze him at the curb for what seemed an eternity.

Suddenly, he broke free of the paralyzing image. With no real plan, fully expecting to be killed, he charged into the street. Campbell was just about in the location between the headlights where Sarah had been when she was hit, but there was still a gap between the man and the massive bumper of the bus.

As he dashed across the road, Nick glanced to his right enough to see that the driver had spotted them and begun to react. She instinctively pulled the wheel to her left, just as Nick launched himself at Campbell, catching the half-naked addict by the waist. The two men pitched face-forward onto the rain-soaked tarmac and slid ahead half a dozen feet, past the speeding bus and into the next lane of traffic.

Brakes and tires screeching, the bus rose up on the driver's side wheels as it skidded sideways. For several terrible seconds, it hovered motionless, the front and rear wheels on the right side well off the road, its full length now at a right angle from the direction in which it had been headed.

Nick's chin snapped against the pavement and instantly split open. Dazed, he still managed to hold on to the two syringes. The SUV that had been following behind the bus spun out, with its passenger side wheels also lifting off the road. It smacked against the rear end of the bus. The impact kept both vehicles upright, and sent them skidding away from the two prone figures.

Nick rolled Campbell over. The addict was unconscious now, breathing slowly and sonorously. Drops of blood from Nick's chin landed on the man's chest and were instantly washed away by the pelting rain. On all sides, cars had managed to stop, forming a cordon around the two men.

Campbell's respirations were getting shallower and more widely spaced. It was possible the problem was internal bleeding and not a drug overdose, but as things were, in this spot, one condition was treatable, one was not. Nick doubted the man was getting effective ventilation, which meant the four-minute clock of brain death had started. Something had to be done. First, though, he had to get some air into Campbell's lungs. The addict's pulse was faint, and no more than twenty beats a minute. Tilting Campbell's head back, Nick closed off the man's nose and administered several mouth-to-mouth breaths.

The bus driver and a passenger had hit the street and were charging across to them. Many others were closing in as well, a number of them with open umbrellas. Nick took the syringe of Narcan and fixed it into the IV. The slight flow of blood from the end of the plastic cannula told him the line hadn't clotted off, or worse, been pulled out of the vein.

"Hey, what are you doing?" an onlooker called out.

Suppressing any number of snide responses, Nick emptied the Narcan and then the flumazenil into Campbell.

"I'm a doctor from the medical van over there," Nick said. "I need someone to grab his ankles and help me bring him back to our clinic. Keep your hands on his pant legs and away from that wound."

It was Eddie Thompson, breathless from his sprint across the street, who took the addict by the armpits and snatched him up as easily as the crazed man had knocked him down just a few minutes before.

"Just take care of that IV," Nick said, pressing his sleeve against his chin. "Sorry about your bus, ma'am. That was a hell of a piece of driving. I'll tell your boss."

# CHAPTER 7

The scene as comatose Mike Campbell was carried to the aft examining room of the Helping Hands Mobile Medical Unit would most certainly not have made the final cut in any Norman Rockwell selection process. Everything in the RV was wet—either with rainwater, mud, coffee, or blood.

Seated at their spots by the table, the two remaining students from Nick's small class looked considerably more sanguine than Phillip MacCandliss, who was slouched in the driver's chair, wrapped in a blanket that Junie had probably provided for him. His jaunty cap was gone, and his thinning, razor-cut hair was matted with mire. Janus Fielding stood to his right, leaning against the window, his expression appearing as if he might have dropped from the sky and landed in the Emerald City of Oz.

Comfortable with Junie's ability to handle this, or almost any other medical situation, Nick paused as he was about to head to the rear of the van.

"Sorry about that," he said to MacCandliss. "You okay?"

"No, I'm not okay. Do I look okay?"

"Nope. Now that you mention it, you don't look okay at all. Sorry I asked."

"Mr. Fielding is taking mental notes on all this, Garrity. He'll be filing a report on the bush league operation you two are running here. He knows, as do I, that every one of these unfortunate men and women would be better off in an emergency ward or a city-run clinic. I don't think that even in the weakest ER in the city you would find a doctor chasing his patients out into the street. You could have gotten any number of people killed. And for what? To save that . . . that cave dweller."

"Well, we can talk about this another time. I've got to get back there and see what I can do for our patient."

"What you can do, Garrity, is what you should have done when that wretched fellow first walked into this sad excuse for a clinic—you should have called nine-one-one."

Nick took several steps toward the rear of the RV, then paused and looked back over his shoulder.

"You know, that's an excellent idea, Mac-Candliss. I'm glad my nurse did it as soon as we realized how bad off the man was."

At that instant, the heavy night was pierced by the sirens of an approaching rescue squad and police cruisers.

"Well, doc," Junie said, "these Steri-Strips will hold until we can get you to a surgeon— maybe even a plastic surgeon. That is some impressive gash you gave yourself."

"Nonsense. This mug needs a plastic surgeon like a warthog needs a beautician. Let me dismiss my class and check on the people who stayed around in the bus stop. Then we can talk about whether or not I need to be sewn up."

"It's still oozing. Look, do what you want. There's just too much testosterone floating around here for me."

As usual, the paramedic and EMT had done a stellar job under difficult circumstances. In what seemed no time at all, they had gotten Campbell onto oxygen, cleaned up his old IV and redressed it while simultaneously starting a second one, evaluated and dressed the wound in his side, and begun treatment to raise his blood pressure and oxygen saturation.

"We're not going to have to intubate him at this point," the paramedic said. "I think you saved his life by getting the Narcan and flumazenil into him when you did."

"Aw, shucks," Nick said.

"And I agree with you that the wound doesn't look too bad."

"Stand over here and say all that again," Nick responded, gesturing toward the front of the RV where MacCandliss and Fielding were preparing for the arrival of a cab. "Nice and loud."

By the time the police finished at the accident scene and entered the van, the cab had arrived and the two men were gone. The cops, grateful that no one had been seriously hurt, and citing that they had more than enough statements to type up already, agreed to have Nick and Junie stop by the precinct house on their way to the hospital.

The eventful stop at Jasper Yeo's auto lot was almost over.

The van would be significantly late for the last two scheduled stops of the evening, but their patients would probably be waiting.

With no particular place to go, Nick's three students, Thompson, McBean, and Riddick, sprayed and wiped down the interior of the Fleetwood while Nick and Junie worked their way through the patients who had chosen to remain in the bus stop waiting room. Outside, the rain had finally begun to taper off, and inside, the tension generated by MacCandliss, Fielding, and Campbell had begun to dissipate. Lost in the pleasure of taking care of patients, Nick felt the unique, almost indescribable rhythm of the van settle back in. Finally, with the last of the cases tended to, and Junie readying the exam room for the trip across town, he came up to the front and sat down with his class.

"If we had tuition, I'd offer to refund it," he said, pouring himself a mug of coffee.

"If we had tuition, I'd double it," McBean said. "It was worth the price of admission just to watch that jerk try and shake you down."

"Don't ever underestimate MacCandliss; people who do end up with fang marks on their butts."

"No need to tell me. I know the man from way back."

Nick felt his interest immediately perk up. He knew that MacCandliss had not been the one who rejected McBean's request for increased benefits.

"What do you mean, Matthew?"

"I had a buddy named Ferris—Manny Ferris. You might have run into him."

"I don't think so."

"I'm a little surprised because he had—*has*—PTSD like the rest of us. MacCandliss rejected his petition for an increase in his benefits. Ol' Manny was depressed in the best of times. The ruling sent him onto the street and into the bottle. He went from a little room to a flophouse, and finally to a cardboard village. I used to visit him there from time to time. Then one day, after a couple of months had passed, I stopped by. The guys told me Manny was a new man. He had cut way back on his drinking and left the village. Kept talking about how the Marines had called him back and were planning to activate him for some sort of top-secret covert mission. Then he vanished."

**Top-secret covert mission.**

The words hit like a missile. Umberto had been sitting right there at that table when he said them to Nick. He was a man reborn, his countenance beaming.

**I've been called back by the Marines for a top-secret covert mission.**

That's what he said. Maybe those exact words.

Not long after that, like Manny Ferris, he disappeared.

"Matthew," Nick said, "has Manny resurfaced since then?"

"To tell you the truth, I don't know for sure, except that once, maybe a couple of years ago, one of the guys said that Manny was back on the street. I'm embarrassed that I never tried to find him, but for me life had changed. First I managed to get a job, then I met a terrific woman and we got a place together. Then I got into that eye therapy for my PTSD. I just sort of let Manny slide."

"Listen, don't be so hard on yourself. Life is all about living."

"I suppose."

"So tell me, how long has it been since you actually saw him?"

"Manny? A while. Let me think."

*Four years*, Nick was thinking. *It's been four years.*

"I know when," McBean said. "It was right after I got the job at the body shop. Four years. Give or take a couple of months, it was four years ago."

# CHAPTER 8

"The police ruled it a suicide. But could it have been murder? Hello, all you Charlotte Night Owls. You're tuned in to WMEW, 82.5 FM, home of the Rick Clemmons show, starring me, Rick Clemmons." The rotund DJ, draped in an orange-and-white Hawaiian shirt, wearing loose-fitting cargo shorts and a straw cowboy hat, pressed a yellow button on the eight-channel mixing board, cuing his show's signature heavy-metal guitar theme song. "For those of you just joining us, our in-studio guest this morning is Jillian Coates, from . . . Virginia?"

"That's right. Arlington."

"Jillian . . . do you go by Jill or Jillian?"

"Jillian . . . with a *J*."

"Jillian with a *J* is a photographer and the sister of Belle Coates, the Charlotte resident and nurse at the Central Charlotte Medical Center who died three weeks ago in an apparent suicide from a drug overdose."

"Nurse, Rick. I'm a nurse just like my sister. I just do photography as a hobby. Once in a while I sell a piece or have a show, but—"

"Yes. Well, the police called the death of Belle Coates an open-and-shut case. Our guest this morning, a nurse currently working at . . . ?"

"Shelby Stone Memorial Hospital in Washington, D.C."

". . . Shelby Stone Memorial Hospital, isn't so sure. Separating fact from fiction is what the Rick Clemmons Show is all about, and this juicy tale has more twists to it than a Twizzler. Bogus suicide? Botched investigation? Delusional sister? Psychic connection? You be the judge. But you know that Rick Clemmons always gets to the truth. So remember, our phone lines are open. Call anytime, boys and girls. Let's get to the bottom of this thing!"

Jillian balled her fists and reminded herself that media exposure was what she was after. *You lie down with dogs, you wake up with fleas*, her mother always said.

The weeks since Belle's death had been a living hell. With one terrible call from the Charlotte police, Jillian's life had come to an abrupt stop, and then made a sharp right-angle turn. Nothing would ever be the same. Not an hour passed that she didn't think about her younger sister and imagine what the final minutes of her existence must have been like. It made no sense that Belle, though hurt by her decision to break things off with the philandering jerk she was close to marrying, would be despondent enough to take her own life. She was all about adventure, discovery, and a love of people. Even in the infrequent troublesome times of her life, she had never even hinted at suicide.

Jillian was the volatile, eccentric one—the lone eagle with the spontaneity, the artist's eye, and the unpredictable temper. Belle was a warm breeze—a zephyr, making everyone's life she touched feel better.

**You lie down with dogs, you wake up with fleas. Who in the hell could have done this to her?**

When Jillian agreed to come to Charlotte for the radio show, Rick Clemmons's producer made it clear that the host, though genuinely caring, made his living by being outspoken and feeding the insatiable schadenfreude appetite of his audience. But at this instant, having to endure the man, she wished that he could know exactly what it felt like to lose somebody whom he loved as much as she did Belle. She wanted him to feel his stomach knot up at seeing his loved one's photograph—to endure a sadness so profound it threatened to stop his breathing.

Sadly, out of more than a hundred requests she had made to local, regional, and national media outlets, Rick Clemmons was the only broadcaster who agreed to air her story. Like it or not, she had to play by his rules. As desperate as she was, she probably still shouldn't have come. But she had to do something. There was no way she could just turn and walk away. This was her sister . . . her best friend. Somebody, someplace, had to know something. What else could she do but keep looking, even if it meant having to deal with a bottom-feeder like Rick Clemmons?

Clemmons pressed Mute on his mixing board, then turned to her and asked, "You ready to keep going, little lady?"

"I am," Jillian said, adjusting her headphones.

"We gotta share a mic, remember. The AKG is on the fritz. Means you gotta lean in real close, now."

His gaze traveled downward and Jillian could feel him unbutton her blouse with his eyes. She was used to men staring at her and flirting, but something about Clemmons made her itch. To distract herself, she again fiddled with her headphones and politely nodded.

Despite his show airing at the obscene hours of 1 A.M. to 6 A.M., Jillian had held out hope that Clemmons would actually have someone in his audience who could help her. Those hopes took a direct hit when she pulled her rental car into the station's dirt parking lot, abutting a barren, litter-strewn stretch of Highway 27 between Charlotte and Paw Creek. The producer had said nothing to prepare her for the ramshackle trailer from which WMEW broadcast.

When she first knocked on the rust-speckled trailer door, she half expected a crazed, toothless old man, shirtless in his overalls, to leap out and grab her. She knew going in that WMEW was small-market radio, but hell, this was bordering on microscopic. She wondered how a photographic study of the place would fit in with her current project on America's back roads. It wasn't surprising that Clemmons had to resort to tabloid radio to maintain competitive ratings, especially competing in such an ungodly time slot. But she was frustrated to the point of desperation, and it was either play this game, or don't play at all.

"Okay, Jillian," Clemmons said into the one working microphone. "Now, if I'm getting this right, some of the evidence you have that your sister was murdered is in her diary?"

Jillian paused to compose herself.

"Not exactly. After the police had completed their evaluation, I came to Charlotte to collect her things."

"What things?" Clemmons asked.

"Everything. Photographs. Clothes. Files. Her computer. I boxed everything up and hired a moving company to move all of her things to my place. I wanted to go through it all one last time before I . . . before I started throwing things away. The police didn't need any of it. According to them, there was nothing for them to investigate."

"Except maybe murder," Clemmons threw in.

"There was a diary—more like a journal, actually—but there wasn't much in it that I didn't already know. As you can tell, my younger sister and I were very close. Our . . . our parents were killed in an auto accident twelve years ago, when she was fourteen and I was twenty-four. We lived together until she started nursing school— the same school I had gone to in Washington. During vacations and summers, she stayed with me in the condo I bought with my half of the sale of our parents' place."

"Exactly what did you find in this diary that led you to believe the suicide note she left was somehow bogus or forced by an-other person?"

"First of all, I want to say that I am a psych nurse in one of the best depart-ments in D.C. I've been in that specialty for a long time. It's my job to know when someone is suicidal, and believe me, Rick, Belle was not suicidal. Not in the least."

"The diary?"

"It wasn't a deeply personal, from-the-heart diary; more like a journal of events in Belle's life. It wasn't locked up or hidden away. I found it on her nightstand while I was boxing up her things."

"So I'm guessing the diary—I'm sorry, *journal*—didn't say, 'I'm going to kill my-self.' If it did, you wouldn't be on this show."

"Exactly. There was nothing in any of her entries to suggest that she was even in a fragile state. In fact, I was planning on driving down in a week. All she said the last time I . . . the last time I spoke with her was that she couldn't wait to see me."

"But there was that broken-off engage-ment that she was depressed about, right? Her fiancé, Dr. Doug Dearing, an ortho-pedist at the Carolina Bone and Joint

Hospital, reportedly was having an affair with her best friend."

Jillian took some comfort in knowing that Clemmons had at least a cursory knowledge of the facts. She could handle him ogling her, but only if he gave Belle the respect she deserved. It was also great to hear Dearing's name and actions broadcast.

"Sure, she was depressed about it," Jillian answered. "Who wouldn't be? She had seen a therapist and gotten the sleeping pills that—that she took. But she was philosophical about the end of the engagement, and actually grateful she found out about what he was before"—Jillian paused and cleared the fullness from her throat—"they got married. There were passages in her journal where Belle wrote about feeling stronger, more like her old self again. She even referenced her upcoming diving trip to Cozumel with her girlfriends, and how much she was looking forward to it. That's not the writing of somebody who would take her own life."

Jillian had read the journal several times. It brought them closer, the way e-mails or talking on the phone had done. But it was also like experiencing Belle's death over and over again—traveling alongside her through years of hopes, joys, and disappointments, all the while knowing it would come to a tragic end.

"So, have the cops ever investigated this Dearing fellow?" Clemmons asked.

"They did. But he had an alibi. He was with his girlfriend and out of state the night Belle died."

"Then there's this wild psychic connection business. What was that all about?"

"I would prefer to avoid the implications of the word 'psychic,' and just leave it at 'connection.'"

"Go on."

"At what might have been the exact moment Belle died, certainly within the same half hour, three hundred and thirty-five miles to the north, I became as violently ill as I have ever been. It felt for a while, as I was getting sicker and sicker, on the floor in my bathroom, as if I were going to die. The horrible attack went on for half an hour or so, and then simply went away, just like that."

"Yes, okay. Well, the Night Owl listeners to the Rick Clemmons Show might believe in such psychic connections, but we're here to sort out the facts, and only the facts. And the facts in this case, at least as you have presented them so far, do not lend support to your contention that she was forced to write a suicide note and then forced to swallow a lethal dose of sleeping pills."

"I disagree. That's why I'm here."

"You'll excuse me for saying so, Jillian, but so far I'm not convinced. Tell me more about the journal. What about it made you think Belle was murdered?"

"It wasn't the journal so much as it was Belle's suicide note," Jillian said. "In both the note, when she told me she was sorry for what she had to do, and all throughout the journal, Belle referred to me only as *J*."

"So?"

"In the journal, that was just an abbreviation she used for me. She would never refer to me by an initial in something as emotional as that note. She'd write out my name, or at least 'Jill.' I don't know how, or why, but I'm sure she was forced to write the note and using just the letter *J* was her way of telling me so."

"Thin stuff, Jillian," Clemmons said, glancing down at the lifeless caller board. "I guess the police didn't make much of it."

"Actually, they didn't make much of anything."

"Well, did you notice anything strange about the things you found in her apartment? Anything at all?"

Jillian hesitated. She already felt foolish enough presenting the psychic connection, and hearing Clemmons talk about the journal made most of her points sound thin. But there was something else.

*I have nothing to lose by mentioning this*, she decided finally.

"In a box in the back of her closet, Belle had a stack of comic books—fifty or so different issues of the same kind, and they didn't make anything of those either."

"Comic books?"

"I feel I know—*knew*—my sister very well. I had no idea she was interested in any sort of comics, and I told the detectives how odd that was, but they just shrugged the notion off. In the box, right on top of the comics, were several printouts from the Internet. Belle had been researching them. I have no idea why, and as I said, the police just didn't care."

Clemmons glanced once more at the naked caller panel.

"Well?" he asked.

"Well, what?"

"What were the comic books?"

"Oh, I had never heard of them before, but they were all Marvel comics called *Nick Fury, Agent of S.H.I.E.L.D.* And on the cover of several of them she had written 'Doctor' or 'D-R period' right before his name, or 'Ph.D.' right after his name. Maybe that means something to your listeners."

"Well, it doesn't to me, except that your little sister may have been more eccentric than you knew. Maybe she had a secret life. Listeners, what's your opinion?"

As if on cue, a blinking light appeared on the studio's small call-in panel.

"There's one," Jillian said, forgetting for the moment that their mic was on.

"Thanks for the help," Clemmons said sardonically. "Hey! We got ourselves a caller. Hello to Troy from Weddington. You're on the Rick Clemmons Show, whatcha got?"

"Yeah, this here's Troy, from Weddington," the caller said in a dense, backwoods patois.

Inwardly, Jillian groaned.

"What's up, Troy? You're on air with Rick Clemmons. You got thoughts on the Belle Coates case?"

"Nah," the caller said. "I'uz just driving west on Seventy-four. Thought yer guest sounded hot. Figured I'd call."

Clemmons looked over at Jillian as though he were making an assessment, offering an apology, and issuing a warning, all at the same time.

"Hey, numbnuts," he said, "this isn't the dating game. We're doing real investigative reporting here. And yes, Troy from Weddington, for your information Jillian Coates is hot—tall and slender and absolutely gorgeous. But she ain't interested in you, Troy, and guess what, neither am I." Clemmons disconnected the call and cued the sound effect of an exploding bomb. "Look, folks, you got opinions, share 'em. You got information, especially about a Marvel comic hero named Nick Fury, or Dr. Nick Fury, give it up to us. You got a big woody like that idiot who just called, well, that's what your bedroom's for." Clemmons laughed.

Jillian was glad she wasn't holding a

weapon. Agreeing to appear on this show had clearly been a mistake. The time could have been better spent going through Belle's things again, searching for any kind of clue as to what might have happened that horrible night.

"As I was saying," she managed, "if you knew my sister, you'd know she wouldn't take her own life."

"Have you hired a PI? You know, some-body familiar with the ins and outs of po-lice work, who can review the case file with fresh eyes."

"I'm a nurse. The detective I called wanted a retainer that would have just about wiped me out. In the weeks since my sister's death, I've taken a leave of ab-sence and made finding her killer my life's purpose. I'm hoping somebody out there knows something and has the courage to come forward and help."

Clemmons clicked over to a second caller.

"Go, you're on the Rick Clemmons Show."

"Yeah, lady, why don't you come over to my apartment and I'll help you do some real detective work."

Clemmons disconnected the call and signaled for a commercial.

"Sorry. Even though I think it's true, maybe the tall and gorgeous thing was a little unnecessary. Ralph," he called out to the producer, a beanpole with a head resembling an ostrich egg, "what in the hell kind of calls are you letting through?"

"We ain't got a very big selection, Rick," the man replied from the tiny control booth. "Besides, you know as well as I do, that kind of call is why people keep tuning in. You're on in three, two, one . . . and . . . now."

"What happened to respect, people?" Clemmons barked at his audience. "There was a time when you callers at least had some sense of decency. Come on, Night Owls. How about some thoughts about the journal and Jillian's theory? You know, tonight's topic? How about some comments on that? How about those comic books she found? Doesn't it seem weird for Belle Coates to be collecting Nick Fury comics?"

Jillian looked again at the studio walls, adorned with pictures of Rick Clemmons glad-handing with celebrities she recognized. Maybe she had read him all wrong.

This wasn't a dream gig for him. He had mentioned getting fired from a much bigger station in Atlanta, but hadn't said what he did wrong. Rusted trailer or not, it was starting to sound as if his concern might be genuine.

"Sorry about these callers tonight, Jillian," he said on air. "Okay, everyone, the truth is what matters most on the Rick Clemmons Show, starring me, Rick Clemmons, broadcasting on WMEW 82.5 FM, where the weather is still the same as it was ten minutes ago when I last told ya', fifty-five degrees and dark outside."

Clemmons signaled to Jillian that it was her time to talk.

"I think whoever killed Belle knew her," Jillian said. "There was no sign of a break-in or a struggle."

"A young nurse with an obsession for comic books dies under at least suspicious circumstances. Her apartment is locked up solid from the inside. Theories, people. Theories."

A lone light on the phone bank began to blink, along with a message from Ralph on the small LED display announcing the caller's name.

"Hey there, Joe from Monroe," Clemmons said, "nice rhyme. You're on the Rick Clemmons Show, you got any four-one-one for us?"

The caller laughed. "For this cracker-jack? No. Nada. You're nuts, Clemmons, for having this whack-job on."

"Joe, get ready to be blown up. That your real name?"

"My real name is Officer You Don't Need my Name, of the Charlotte PD. And yeah, I got info. I was one of those who investigated this case. And I'll tell you this much. This lady is way off base. What are you trying to say? That we don't know how to do our job?"

"No. That's not what I'm saying at all. I just want somebody to listen to the facts I'm presenting," Jillian answered, her voice again husky with frustration. "My sister would never, ever have—"

"The fact is that comic books or not, your sister killed herself. Look, we got it bad enough out there with dopers and killings and carjackings, without you making things worse by questioning our ability. We investigated Belle Coates's death. We investigated it good. Those Internet printouts with the comics were years old. Years. She made the choice. She took the pills. She died. Case closed. Don't blame us for it, lady. Blame her."

"I . . . I . . ."

There was a click and a dial tone.

# CHAPTER 9

As she emerged from the dimmed lighting of the trailer, the morning sun took Jillian by surprise. Her focus during the broadcast had been so unwavering, she had completely lost track of time. Pausing in the weedy gravel parking lot, she blinked until her vision had adjusted to the glare. Then she checked her watch and sighed.

**The only four hours I could get you on any broadcast and I let you down.**

She tried, with some success, to convince herself that Joe from Monroe was nothing more than a twisted prank caller.

Cop or not, though, his words still cut and had hurt her deeply.

**. . . She made the choice. She took the pills. She died. Case closed. Don't blame us for it, lady. Blame her.**

In the studio, she had suppressed the urge to shout names at the callers that would have embarrassed Howard Stern. But she couldn't risk upsetting Clemmons and possibly having him cut the broadcast short.

When the morning crew arrived, Jillian was in a somber mood, still reeling from the horrific experience. Despite what had just transpired in the trailer, from Clemmons's wandering eye to his legion of moronic callers, she still managed to pitch the newly arrived morning show producer for more airtime. He politely declined.

It wasn't until Jillian reached her rental and unlocked the door that she heard footsteps behind her. Turning, she saw Rick Clemmons, straw hat in hand, hurrying toward her.

"You did great in there," he offered. "Thought maybe you and I could head on down to WaffleTown for some eggs or somethin'. Talk about the show and all."

Then he winked, as if he needed to make the subtext of his offer perfectly clear.

Jillian shook her head in disgust. "Clemmons, you really amaze me. You know that?" she replied. "I mean, don't you have any appreciation for what I just went through in there? And you're not making it any easier out here by hitting on me. My sister is dead and you were my best hope for catching her killer."

"Show still might help," Clemmons said, seeming not the least bit affected by her harsh words.

"Okay, I'm sorry for snapping at you. Your show wasn't exactly what I had in mind when I wrote and asked for a spot on it, but at least you gave me a chance. I owe you for that. But a thank-you—nothing more."

Clemmons's cheeks reddened slightly, and he was about to say something when the trailer door flew open and the pale, ovoid face of his producer poked out.

"Got a phone call 'bout the show, Rick. Guy says his cell ran outta juice afore he could get through. He wants to talk to our guest here. Won't tell me what it's about."

Jillian groaned. She knew the call would

most likely be crude or abusive, but she trudged back up the trailer stairs anyway. *For Belle.*

"Hello? This is Jillian," she said, slightly breathless from fatigue and the short climb.

"Ah, hey there, Jillian. Name's Roach, Kyle Roach, from out Oakbridge way."

"Yes, Kyle. Do you have information for me?"

Jillian tensed at what she was certain was going to be a crude retort.

"Tough callers t'night. Real bottom-feeders if ya ask me." He sounded like all the others, and Jillian was about to thank him and hang up when he added, "But I ain't one of them, I assure you. I have a wife and two kids at home. I listen to Rick Clemmons because I work the night shift at the Daimler plant, and those idiot callers he gets keep me laughing and awake."

"I'm listening," Jillian said.

"I would have called in to the show and all, but my cell phone here died on me."

"Yes, yes. The producer told me that. Now what is it?"

"I think we might want to get together and talk."

Jillian had had enough.

"Good-bye, Mr. Roach," she said.

"Wait. I said I was serious and I meant it."

Jillian was poised to cut him off but something made her stop. "Go ahead," she said, "but one crude word and you're gone."

"Okay. Here's why I think we should meet. I know who Dr. Nick Fury is."

"What?"

"I served with him in Afghanistan."

# CHAPTER 10

When Jillian arrived at the Calderwood Diner, Kyle Roach was right where he had promised he would be. He spotted her the moment she stepped inside the folksy road-side grill, and rose from his booth, farthest from the door. He was wearing a baseball cap, tattered along the rim, and a pair of faded olive green overalls that did little to mask his expansive girth. He was nothing like the crackpot Clemmons Night Owl she had been expecting, and his manner and aura immediately put Jillian at ease.

Despite her exhaustion, Jillian had spent much of the past day and evening awake

in her hotel room, pondering the link between Belle and Dr. Nick Fury. Finally, after
leaving a wake-up-call request for five,
she dozed off, twisting her brain into knots
over what sort of monster could have done
such a thing to such an incredible woman,
and how they could have done it. After a
brief shower, she stopped by Belle's apartment before heading for the diner.

Roach extended a hand to her as she
neared. His calloused palm was that of a
workman, his melancholy blue-green eyes
those of a soldier.

"Jillian Coates?" Kyle asked, in a logy
drawl.

"That's me."

"Kyle Roach, a pleasure to meet you."
He guided her back to the booth and
motioned the waitress for two coffees.
"First off, let me say how truly sorry I am
about the passing of your sister. I can't
imagine what you're going through. I lost
quite a few buddies in the war, and one
real good friend, but the years have taken
the edge off some. That's about the best I
can hope for. Same with you, I suspect."

Jillian thanked him for his understanding and especially for his honesty. After a

string of reflexive "I know what you're going through" sentiments from friends and coworkers, his remark was refreshing.

In hindsight, her decision to pay one last visit to Belle's apartment had not been a wise one. Seeing the dark windows from the street had been heart wrenching enough. Her last walk through the empty rooms, now filmy with dust, left her sobbing on the hardwood floor. The closure she had hoped for was absent, and she had trudged back to the street consumed by an insatiable hunger for answers.

"Thank you for taking the time to meet me, Kyle," Jillian said.

"Heck, it's nothing at all. I come here most every morning anyway, after I get out of the plant. I couldn't meet you yesterday because I was working a double. Sorry I troubled you to take an extra day here in Charlotte."

"It wasn't any trouble at all, really. As you can tell from the show, I'm desperate for information. Can I get you breakfast?"

"That's very kind of you."

"No limits."

"You should watch me eat before you say somethin' like that."

Roach ordered three fried eggs, sausage, bacon, two biscuits, gravy, and grits; Jillian, fresh fruit and yogurt. She felt herself shaking with the notion that she might be close to learning something, anything, that connected to Belle, even if the connection was a tenuous one. Forty-seven different issues of the same comic book, set in Belle's closet. No copies of even one other title. "Doctor" written in several ways on a number of the covers. Clearly Belle wasn't in it as a collector. The comics store around the corner from Jillian's place in D.C. had priced the complete issuance at just over a hundred dollars.

"Maybe we ought to talk before that breakfast arrives," Jillian said, "unless you can guarantee me you can stay awake after you eat it."

"Heck, I was thinkin' of makin' the grits a double order."

"Kyle, you know why I'm here. I'm here because I'm very interested in learning more about this Dr. Nick Fury."

"Well, what do you know so far?" Roach asked.

"Nothing really," Jillian confessed. "I spent a few hours in the hotel business center

Googling every combination of 'Nick Fury,' 'Dr. Nick Fury,' 'N. Fury' I could imagine. All I turned up were references to the comic book character."

"Well, that's to be expected. Like I said, I know only one Dr. Nick Fury and I doubt he's going to come up in any Web search," Roach explained. "See, Nick Fury, he's a comic book character, all right. But *Dr. Nick Fury*, heck, that boy is as real as these here menus."

"You convinced me it was important we meet in person to share what you know. Why? Is he some sort of criminal or something? Do you think he murdered my sister?"

Roach laughed in a deep, engaging way. "Ma'am, Dr. Nick Fury is a saint, not a killer. At one and the same time, he 'uz one of the most caring doctors and one of the toughest soldiers I've ever known."

The waitress brought over their food. Jillian studied Roach as he took a sip of his black coffee and a lengthy gulp of water before digging in. For a man of war, he seemed very much at peace—except for his eyes. She remembered the serenity in her own life before Belle died. Getting over their parents' death had been such a long climb for both sisters. Belle had been a constant source of strength throughout the ordeal and together they kept each other grounded.

"I want to know everything I can about him," Jillian said.

Roach paused and looked beyond her. She could see the years in Afghanistan cross his countenance like a cloud.

"I didn't join the army until I was twenty-eight," he began. "My skill wasn't with a gun much as it was with a wrench. But I was sent out on patrol more than once. Did HVAC work before, so naturally I eventually became an army mechanic. They shipped me all over the world fixing stuff."

"Did you enjoy it?"

"Yeah. Good work. Steady pay. Saw the world. I was in my midthirties when I got the call to go to Afghanistan—you know, right after nine-eleven, when we were turning up the heat on the country. Not that it actually needed any more heat."

He attempted a laugh, but this time

quickly gave up. No matter what, there was simply nothing amusing about the place.

"That's where you met Dr. Nick Fury? In Afghanistan?"

"Yeah," Roach said. "Only his name wasn't Dr. Nick Fury. It was Dr. Nick Garrity. 'Fury' was just a nickname one of the grunts gave him because of his first name, and it sort of stuck. He was like a water bug over there—all over the place, teaching Marines some basic combat medicine techniques that saved lives in the arena, volunteering at the local clinic, working more shifts at the hospital than assigned. The Energizer Bunny. Didn't have a patch on his eye, like the comic book Fury, but man, he sure was tough like him. Can you pass me the ketchup, please?"

Jillian slid the bottle across. Roach reached for it with his left hand. It was then Jillian noticed a long, jagged scar running from the tip of his index finger down past the base of his thumb and disappearing into his sleeve.

"What happened there?" Jillian asked.

"Well now, that there is my permanent reminder of Dr. Nick Fury," he said, speaking between bites. "Crushed my hand in a tool press. Fury was on duty. Spent hours repairing it. *A lot* of hours. People told me he saved my hand. I was flown to the hospital at Landstuhl in Germany for a revision of his work. They told me there was no revision needed, and sent me back. Didn't even change the antibiotics he put me on. It still aches a little when I do a double shift or stormy weather comes in, but I sort of welcome the reminder of how lucky I was to have that man on duty when I got hurt. Now you see why I wanted to meet you face-to-face."

"I do. So where is he? And why do you think my sister would be interested in him?"

Roach shook his head.

"No idea. I don't stay in touch with the old crew much. You see, something bad, real bad, happened on FOB Savannah where we were stationed."

Jillian saw the pain in Roach's eyes intensify. He set his fork down. Instinctively, she reached across and set her hand on his.

"Can you talk about it?"

"One of the locals turned out to be a terrorist—a suicide bomber. The guy's cover was running a health clinic for the people

just outside the wire. Fury was always helping him out with supplies, volunteering his
off-hours to treat Afghan patients and such.
Some thank-you he got."

"What happened? Did the terrorist kill
Fury?"

"Well in a way, maybe."

"I'm sorry, I don't understand."

"This bastard drives his truck onto the
base. Checkpoint has no problem letting
him in. He's a regular. But once inside, he
plows his rig right through the front doors
of the hospital. Blows himself and the truck
to kingdom come. Garrity was there, right
on the running board of the truck from
what we heard, trying to break the window
and get at the guy. He survived, by some
miracle. I heard that one of the guys he
worked with saved him somehow. The hospital was leveled. Most of the others didn't
make it, including his fiancée."

"Oh, my God."

Jillian wasn't certain she could continue
the conversation. She sipped some water
and stared at the wall behind Roach, suddenly spent. Images of Belle at her vibrant
best flashed through her thoughts. She

wondered what Nick Garrity's fiancée looked like.

"You okay?" Roach asked.

"No."

"Oh, I understand."

"I think you do. Any idea where Garrity is now?"

"Like I said, don't keep in touch with the old crew. But I wanted to give you this. Thought it might help you to track him down. It's been in my bureau drawer since he sent it to me."

Roach fished into his pocket, withdrew a folded newspaper clipping, and passed it across. It was an article from *The Washington Post* about the Helping Hands Mobile Medical Unit and its director, Dr. Nick Garrity. There was a byline, but no date.

"Nick mailed this article to me a few years back," Roach said. "He was trying to raise money to keep this RV on the streets. It's like a roving clinic, helping down-and-out folks get decent medical care. That's Nick."

"I've heard about this program—even thought about volunteering at one point."

"I sent him what I could. A hundred if I

recall right. I would have sent more if times weren't so hard."

"I'm sure he appreciated any amount you could manage. Is the RV still in operation? Do you think Garrity is still in Washington?"

"It's possible. Like I said, haven't been in touch with him since."

"I wonder what the connection between Garrity and Belle could be. She left D.C. right after she graduated. I can see her volunteering on something like Helping Hands, but she wasn't licensed yet when she left for—"

Jillian stopped mid-sentence when her cell phone began ringing.

"Excuse me," she said, retrieving her flip phone from her purse. Her brow furrowed when she didn't recognize the number.

"Hello?"

The reception was weak and between the bad connection and the din of the diner it was hard for her to hear.

"This is Scott Emberg."

"Who?"

"Emberg. Scott Emberg," he said louder. "I'm the president of our Oak Grove Condominium Association."

"Oh, jeez. Scott, yeah. Is everything all right?"

"Not exactly. There . . . um . . . was a fire last night. A big fire."

"Oh, God!" she exclaimed. "Is everybody okay? Was anybody hurt?"

"Everybody is fine, thank goodness. Two units suffered minor damages, but I'm afraid yours was where the blaze started. Much of it was destroyed."

"Destroyed?"

"Yes, especially the first floor. The fire inspectors are going over it now. I'm really sorry, Jillian. I would have called you sooner, but the cell phone number we have wasn't the right one. I had to wait until I could get it from the management company. I didn't see the second floor, but there's nothing left on the lower level. Nothing at all."

# CHAPTER 11

Jillian's heart sank as she stared in disbelief at the devastation that for six years had been her condominium—the first place other than her parents' that she had ever owned. The front door to her unit had been hacked away and the entryway marked off with yellow plastic ribbon.

She leaned against the scorched brick to keep herself from collapsing. If it weren't so tragic, condo association president Scott Emberg's assessment of the damage would have been laughable. The walls weren't blackened, as he had described. Most of them, on the first floor at least, were simply gone. Only the support struts remained, though those were transformed into something akin to the logs burned nearly to charcoal and ash in a fireplace.

Mountains of dark soot, littered with unrecognizable forms, created an alien landscape across the living room. Jillian's throat tightened as she gazed at the large pile of debris in the center—Belle's things, packed in carefully labeled cardboard cartons, and now just so much soot.

"I'm sorry, baby." Her words were a muffled whimper. "I'm so sorry."

Jillian's nostrils filled with the acrid stench of burnt plastic and vinyl. Her lungs felt raw. Bile percolated into her throat. For five minutes, she knelt on the ash and sobbed. Finally she rose and took several cautious steps inside.

The stack of Nick Fury comic books had been incinerated. It had been stupid not to leave them someplace safer. Jillian glanced about and laughed ruefully at the irony of that thought. There was nowhere safer—at least not in her world. The comics had seemed unusual for Belle to have, but not that significant. What else had been lost that might have shed light on

Belle's killer, she wondered. She felt no compulsion to sift through the charred remnants to prove what she knew in her heart—there was nothing left.

At the doorway to the combination sun-room and study—the only significant addition she had made to the place—Jillian spotted the V-shaped burn pattern just above the gnarled metal baseboard heater. According to Emberg, the fire inspector had pegged that spot as the source of the blaze. A subsequent call by her to the Arlington fire department supported that conclusion. According to the chief, it had taken investigators only a few hours to rule the conflagration accidental. The clothes inside a plastic bag left up against the electric baseboard heater had ignited, setting a nearby stack of similar bags ablaze, as well as a wastebasket and its contents. The telling signs, the chief explained, were the uniform V-shaped burn pattern and lack of any trace evidence of an accelerant.

Despite there having been a lot of green plastic storage bags around from the move, Jillian was almost certain she had not left any of them near the baseboard, and had turned off the heat before leaving for the airport. *Or had she?* She hadn't been thinking clearly since Belle's death, and in the rush to make the flight to Charlotte, who knew what details she might have overlooked? The weather had been unseasonably cool lately, and the study, beautiful as it had been, seemed to accentuate extremes in temperature. If only it had been warmer, perhaps this would not have happened.

Wondering if the damage to the upstairs had been as total as that around her, Jillian checked the ceiling. The panels had melted away, exposing blackened wiring and support beams. Miraculously, however, the exposed floorboards, though scorched and streaked black with soot, seemed intact in most spots. Perhaps the upstairs wasn't as badly damaged as Emberg had indicated.

Jillian was musing about the safety of what remained of the stairs when she heard footsteps descending from the second floor.

"Hello?" she called out.

"Hi there," a cheerful male voice replied from above. "I thought I heard someone come in."

The stairwell leading to the top floor curved to the right, making it impossible for Jillian to get a clear look at the man until he was almost to the bottom step. He wore soot-smeared tan coveralls with yellow and silver reflective tape wrapped around the arms and ankles, a bright yellow hard hat, and heavy, well-worn construction boots. He removed his helmet as he neared, revealing a mane of thick silver hair.

"I didn't realize anybody was going to be here," she said.

"Neither did I," the man responded. "Sorry about that. I hope I didn't startle you too much."

He navigated his way over a debris pile and pulled off his work gloves to extend his hand to her. "Name's Regis, Paul Regis. I'm a fire investigator with Atrium Insurance."

She took his hand, which felt smooth and cared for. His grip was firm.

"Jillian Coates," she said. "I live . . . *lived* here."

Regis quickly glanced about.

"I'm sorry, Ms. Coates. I really am. This is a terrible thing to have happen."

Jillian liked Regis for saying that.

"Worse than you could ever imagine," she replied. "But Scott Emberg, the president of the condo association, made it sound like the damage here had already been inspected."

"Oh, gosh, I apologize," Regis said, his hazel eyes earnest. "I'm a very trusting person, so that's probably the reason I'm always forgetting to show this. I should have it hanging in plain sight, but I never liked things around my neck."

He reached into the breast pocket of his coveralls. Pulling out an ID badge hanging from a metal beaded lanyard, he presented it to Jillian, who glanced at it. The photo didn't nearly do Paul Regis justice.

"Atrium isn't my insurance company," she said.

"I've been hired to perform an independent investigation of the premises," Regis explained. "You might not be an Atrium customer, but your condominium association is."

"Why did the condo association contract you to investigate? I've been told the cause was already established."

"Oh, yes, the burn pattern above the

heater in your office. It appears that they are right on the money. Arson investigators usually are. We're quick but careful. Atrium has several of us experienced inspectors on the payroll, mostly guarding against home or business owners who hire a pro to defraud their friendly neighborhood insurance company. Every once in a while, we find something the local department's inspectors have missed that points to arson. In that case, even if it's someplace modest—no offense—we've earned our keep."

"I see," Jillian said, feeling a great emptiness, and suddenly not anxious for Paul Regis to leave. "I didn't realize insurance companies had their own fire investigators."

"They all do. They'll double-check anything that's threatening to cost them money. That's why so many of the biggest buildings in so many cities have insurance companies' names on them."

Regis smiled, but Jillian abandoned a brief attempt to respond in kind. She had no relatives in the city, but half a dozen of her friends would be happy to take her in. Probably more. Most of them had already extended kindness to her by planning the funeral, bringing food, and staying over with her. It made her sad to think of having to impose on them again. It was hard to believe that before the horrible call from the Charlotte police, she was happy and fulfilled almost every minute of every day.

Regis seemed to have maturity and a genuine air of compassion. Maybe they could go and sit for a cup of coffee before she decided whom to call.

"You look a little pale," he said. "Do you need to sit down?"

"No, I'm okay. Actually, there's a bench on the lawn out front. If you have time, maybe we could sit down there for a bit."

Regis took her by the elbow and guided her out through what had once been the portal to her home. Twilight had nearly given way to a cool, breezy night. Jillian decided she would find a hotel and deal with everything else in the morning.

"I'm really sorry about your place," Regis said again.

"Thanks. It's just stuff, I know, but it was my stuff—mine and my sister's."

"I wasn't told that someone else lived here."

"It's just me. My sister died three weeks ago."

"Oh, that's terrible."

"She lived in North Carolina. I was storing all of her things before I decided what to do with them. Now they're gone."

"In my line of work," Regis said, "the first lesson you learn, and learn quick, at that, is things are replaceable, but people aren't."

"I'm grateful that nobody was hurt, or worse. It's just that—" Jillian's eyes began to well. She took a minute to compose herself. "These things were all I had to remember her by. Our parents passed away a few years ago in a car accident."

"It's a strange coincidence," Regis said, "but I lost my sister too."

"I'm so sorry, Paul."

"I'm not telling you this to make you feel bad for me or anything," Regis continued. "Just wanted to let you know that I understand how hard this must be for you. My sister's death has haunted me my whole life. In fact, she's the reason I'm a fire investigator."

"Was she killed in a fire?"

"Exactly," Regis said, staring off at the

condos across the walkway. "I was away at college when it happened. She was only sixteen, living at home. It was arson. Jealous boyfriend threw a gasoline bomb into her bedroom window while she slept. She didn't have a chance. Ever since that I've been fighting fires or investigating them—first for various fire departments, and for ten years now as an independent contractor."

"That's a horrible story. Just horrible."

"At least I can say Susannah didn't die in vain. I've helped police catch a bunch of arsonists. I'm very good at what I do. Lot of times I find evidence of arson that town or state investigators miss."

Jillian could see the man's eyes beginning to mist.

"That's good for you, Paul. And I'm sure what you do makes every day that much easier."

"It does."

"Somebody murdered my sister too. Forced her to write a note and then take an overdose of sleeping pills. And I'm not going to rest until I catch whoever did it. I don't want Belle's death to be in vain either."

"I'll pray that you succeed."

"Thank you."

Impulsively, Jillian turned and gave Regis a grateful hug. He returned the embrace, but broke it off when she did. His shoulders felt tight and powerful, and in spite of all she was going through, or possibly because of it, Jillian felt a slight spark.

"Well," he said, "I'm actually all done with my walk-through."

His voice rose as if he were about to say something further.

Jillian did not want him to leave and barely kept herself from saying so.

"I appreciate you taking the time to explain things to me," she said instead.

"You know, I'm really glad to have been here when you came."

Their eyes met, and for several moments, Jillian held his gaze.

"Thank you," she said. "You've made me feel much better."

"Look, it's getting dark out. I wouldn't hang around here much longer if I were you."

"Okay. I'll come back tomorrow and check the upstairs."

"Just be careful. The floor looks okay,

but there may be weak spots. I'd help you, but I actually have to drive up to Philadelphia for an inspection."

"I . . . I'm really pleased to have met you," Jillian said. "You are very empathetic."

"I left my cards at home per usual, Jillian, but I'd be happy to give you my number if you'd like."

**His eyes really are quite remarkable.**

"I would like that," she said, writing her cell phone number on the bottom of the notepaper he had handed her and passing that half back to him. "Expect to hear from me." She gave fleeting thought to kissing him then and there, but finally managed to pull her gaze away. "Thank you, Paul. Thank you for everything."

"Don't mention it," he said with an understanding smile.

Ten blocks away, after pulling his unmarked rented van to the curb, the man who called himself Paul Regis reached into the pocket of his coveralls to caress the smooth steel of the two small gas canisters he had extracted from their hiding place in the closet of Jillian Coates's upstairs bedroom. Beside them in his pocket were the top-of-the-line surveillance cameras and microphones he had also removed from the condo.

Jericho, the code name used by the organization who had hired him, had violated the most basic tenet of their agreement: no intervention.

**What a stupid thing for them to do.**

Rule number one—rule number everything: Franz Koller works alone.

Good thing the second floor hadn't collapsed onto the first. The canisters and spyware would be in an evidence bag, and someone would have connected the Coates sisters. Good thing he had been his usual professional self in concealing the V-gas and the surveillance cameras and microphones.

Koller pulled off the Hollywood-quality silver wig and removed his contacts.

"Jealous boyfriend," he said, laughing out loud.

The canisters of nerve gas and the surveillance equipment had been in a safe spot above the inside of the closet door frame and in the curtains. It would have taken an almost inconceivable piece of bad luck for Jillian Coates or anyone else to have discovered them before he had the chance to get back and remove them. Then whoever made decisions for Jericho had to go and nearly burn the place down. They would have hell to pay for doing something that stupid. Everything could have been ruined. If he had not been so busy, and had even remotely suspected Jericho might panic and break their agreement, he would have gotten out to Jillian Coates's condo right after Belle's death to remove the stuff he had placed there.

Good thing Paul Regis, insurance company fire investigator, had gotten mobilized to act and act quickly. Now, it was time to deal with the idiots who had nearly blown everything. From the beginning Koller suspected Jericho was connected in some way with the CIA, but in truth he didn't care so long as the payments made it into his accounts. Now, he cared. And Jericho, whether it was Agency or someone else, was going to pay.

Koller skipped to "Sympathy for the Devil" on the Stones CD he had been listening to, and breathed in a few more minutes of his success. Who knew, perhaps a roll in the hay with Jillian Coates was in his future. She was certainly good-looking enough—more than good-looking enough. Of course, thanks to Jericho's poor judgment, if she persisted in disbelieving the non-kill of her sister, she might earn a non-kill of her own somewhere down the line.

Reflexively, he stroked the canisters again.

"Nicely done," he said.

# CHAPTER 12

"I understand that you fell down."

The sloe-eyed ER doctor, whom Nick suspected was just a few years removed from her spring break party days, peered at the gash on his chin through thick magnifying glasses. After studying the wound from every conceivable angle, she still did not seem ready to make a stitch. It was as though his flesh were a block of uncut marble and one false tap would render it pebbles.

"Go ahead and sew, Dr. Baker," Nick said finally. "There's nothing to worry about. Besides, this is going to leave a character scar that will only enhance my reputation as a man of mystery."

The woman laughed uncomfortably.

"Whoever put those Steri-Strips on did a masterful job," she said.

"It was our nurse. She has that woeful condition where she's very good at everything."

"I thought about just leaving them on."

"I know, but she insisted, and she's very good at that, too."

The woman looked bewildered.

"Seeing as we're fellow doctors," she said, "you can just call me Amanda. And I'm sorry for seeming a bit nervous here. I'm rotating through the ER on my way to a residency next year in psychiatry. I don't understand why they insist we do a primary care internship except so they can fill in the coverage and on-call schedules and charge for what we do. Suturing up a trauma surgeon has never been a career ambition of mine. Feels a bit like baking a pie for Martha Stewart."

"Excuse me for saying this, Dr. Amanda, but you're not exactly bubbling with confidence here. How long have you been doing ER?"

"Two weeks."

"Then you're ready, Doc. Just think of me as a pillow and sew away."

Banter . . . lighthearted humor . . . *Who is this man and what have you done with Nick Garrity?*

Nick knew the answer. After four years a crack had appeared in the wall of frustration and uncertainty surrounding Umberto's disappearance. A GI with a story similar to Umberto's had disappeared and subsequently surfaced again. He had almost nothing by way of clues as to where Marine Corporal Manny Ferris might be, but whatever it took, if the man was alive, he would find him.

**I've been called back by the Marines for a top-secret covert mission.**

The statement resonated in his mind as Amanda Baker painlessly numbed Nick's chin. Four years. Four years without a word. Now, suddenly, there was hope.

By the time the second stitch was in, the future psychiatrist was utterly focused on the job and humming softly. Her hands, trembling slightly as she put in the local anesthesia, were bedrock solid now. The youthful innocence and uncertainty he had observed in her earlier were gone as well. Nick sensed that she was going to be a capable doc, whatever specialty she chose. During his own residency, he often questioned the absurd amount of responsibility thrust upon new trainees. Now, that thought segued into images of the soldiers he served with at FOB Savannah, many quite a bit younger than Amanda. The thought put a damper on his mood.

"Done," Baker chirped. "Fifteen stitches, seven-oh nylon, with three six-ohs thrown in just to secure the suture line. Looks pretty spiffy if I do say so. Now for some Steri-Strips to keep the tension off, and the real mystery about you will be whether or not you ever cut yourself at all."

"Told you not to worry."

"Five days. Sutures out in five days."

"Five days it is," Nick said, unable to fully cull Savannah from his thoughts. "Listen, Dr. Amanda, one of our patients from the medical van, Michael Campbell, was brought to the ER a few hours ago. I heard he had been transferred to the fifth floor of the Grossbaum Building, but I don't know which room."

"Of course," she said.

Nick followed Amanda over to her desk, where she dialed the floor's number.

"This is Dr. Amanda Baker in the ER. You have a patient named Michael Campbell. Could you tell me his room number? . . . Five-oh-two? Thanks."

"Ask her if any police have been in to see him," Nick whispered.

"Pardon?" Amanda shot him a puzzled look.

"Please ask."

"Have the police been in to see him yet? . . . No? Okay." She covered the receiver and whispered to Nick, "Apparently, a police officer is on the floor now."

"Thanks," Nick replied. "I gotta run." He headed out of the ER, then called back over his shoulder, "You did a great job, Doc."

Nick followed the signs directing him to the Grossbaum Building. The fifth floor was a step-down unit for intensive care patients being transitioned onto medical or surgical floors, or who would have been admitted to the ICU had there been space. Campbell's room was the last on the right. There was no police officer in the hallway, suggesting the officer was already inside his room. Nick knocked softly and entered.

Campbell, on his back, was restrained to the bed by all four limbs. A uniformed female police officer stood at his right. Nick was glad to see the addict hadn't required endotracheal intubation, but he did have a laryngeal mask airway in place, helping to provide some mechanical breathing support. The surgeons at City Hospital had done a CT scan and apparently decided the knife wound had not caused internal damage that would require an exploratory operation.

Campbell's eyes were open, but glazed. His expression was an intense mix of fear and confusion.

"Who are you?" the woman, a stocky brunette, asked.

Her brass name tag read SAMPSON, and her expression said there were an infinite number of places she would rather be than where she was.

"Dr. Nick Garrity from the Helping Hands Mobile Medical Unit," he answered. "Mike here is one of our patients."

"You the one who reported this guy's knife wound?"

Nick could see Campbell stiffen.

"Actually, no," Nick said. "That must have been someone here in the hospital."

"You know it's mandatory to report all stab wounds."

"Gosh, I thought it was more mandatory to save the patient's life. I did help to do that."

Sampson glared across at him. He had six inches and at least twenty-five pounds on her, but he had little confidence that he could have taken her in a fight, and no confidence at all that she would not like to try and find out.

"Can we remove this contraption?" she asked, gesturing at the airway. "I need to talk to him."

"I can't answer that question, Officer, except to say that I'm a surgeon, and if I went to the trouble to put a laryngeal airway in someone, I wouldn't want it taken out."

"But you're *not* the one who put it in, right?"

"Let me guess, Officer. You majored in community relations at the academy."

"I think it's time for you to leave, Dr. Important."

"And I think my role is to remain here with my patient."

Just as it seemed Sampson was about to leap across the bed at Nick, the door burst open and a bulldozer of a man, stuffed into a tweed jacket, wearing a crinkled blue shirt and red-striped tie, stepped inside. The veins on his tire-thick neck pulsated, and his face was flushed with anger.

"I'm Detective Lieutenant Don Reese, MPD. Which one of you idiots is fucking up my case?" The detective reached into his jacket pocket and flashed his badge. "Who are you?" he growled at Nick.

"I'm a doctor. I'm not from this hospital. I work on—"

"I don't care if you work on the good ship *Lollipop*. Did you have a hand in this mess?"

"Not really, I only—"

Reese, even more furious, cut Nick off again and turned back to Sampson.

"I want your district. I know every goddamn commander and captain in every police service area. Do you know what you've done?"

Sampson paled.

"Hey, I'm not talking to Dr. Eric the Red over here," Reese snapped, pointing his thumb at Nick. "You're the cop. I asked you a question!"

"I . . . I'm with the Four-oh-four," she stammered.

"The Four-oh-four. Commander Trudy Sandoval. She's not going to be happy with this. Not at all. Do you know what you just did?"

Sampson shook her head. "Lieutenant," she said, regaining an ort of her composure, "I'm just trying to make a report and probably an arrest here."

"Well, it'll be the last bust you make for a while if you do."

"Why is that?"

"Because this guy here with the knife hole in his side is an undercover cop working my case and you are about to flush two years of wiretaps and judicial hoop-jumping down the toilet."

"Shit," Sampson muttered. "Well, what do you want me to do now?"

"Either go get primped up because you are about to make the six o'clock news for blowing a major narcotics investigation, or just walk away and let me see if I can fix what you might have already broken."

The woman did not take long to decide.

"Thanks for not making a big deal about this, Lieutenant," she grunted on her way to the door.

"You can thank me for saving your career later," Reese replied. "That goes for you, too, Dr. Doolittle, out!"

Nick followed Sampson down the hall to the elevator. She made no attempt to keep the door from closing in his face before he could get on. He waited until he heard the car start down, then returned to Room 502, where Reese was waiting in the hallway.

"That was some performance, Don," he said, shaking the burly detective's hand. "Really impressive stuff. I guess we can finally call us even now."

"Hell no! You've got a long way to go and a lot of favors to collect before I'll call us even."

"What about that fancy GPS unit you fixed us up with after those kids heisted our RV and took it for a joyride?"

"Not even close. It's not every day a cop smashes his car into a rolling medical clinic during a drunk blackout. You saved my badge and maybe my pension by letting me sleep it off in the back room of that bus of yours and not reporting the accident."

"I did what felt right. Junie vouched for you, and you agreed to pay for the damages and to hook up with two of our AA pals."

"Three years now. I got my three-year medallion to prove it." Reese held up his key ring and let Nick squeeze the ornate bronze coin. He clasped Nick's shoulder and led him into the room.

"You just made it that much easier for me to do the same sort of thing for the next guy," Nick said. "Okay, we're not even. I own you forever. Isn't that how it is with the Chinese? No matter. I sure do appreciate you getting here so quickly. Campbell's on parole so it was important that Officer Sampson not bust him. I promised him, but one of the admitting staff here dropped a dime. Tomorrow, or as soon as he's with it enough to listen, he becomes that next guy I was talking about. I'm gonna try and make him the same deal I made you. Only he may have to go away for a couple of weeks if we can find a way to pay for it. Got that, Mike?"

Campbell nodded weakly.

"You're a good man, Doc," Reese said. "A hell of a good man."

"I'm glad you feel that way, Don, because I need another favor."

"Name it."

"Ferris, Manny Ferris. Marine corporal. Medical discharge maybe seven years ago. Around thirty-five. Five nine. Hair black. Eyes brown. Skin maybe some sort of brown-white mix. Has spent time in cardboard villages and flophouses. Last address unknown, but I'll be starting work on that as soon as I get home."

Reese checked his watch.

"I'm off tomorrow," he said. "Scheduled to go fishing with my cousin. Been really looking forward to it."

"I need to find him yesterday," Nick said.

# CHAPTER 13

Franz Koller waited on the edge of the bed for the girls to arrive. His Dell laptop glowed ghostly blue in the otherwise dark motel room. He had connected his PC to the Internet and even logged in to his eBay account, but he was not yet ready to contact Jericho. A phrase he once read in a *Wall Street Journal* article about unfortunate e-mailing incidents had stuck with him—it was headlined "Ready, Fire, Aim." It would be stupid, he knew, to message his employer while his emotions still ran hot.

The killer placed the pads of three fingers just below his wrist crease to check his radial pulse again. *Sixty beats per minute*—still way too high. When he was truly relaxed, truly in control of his emotions, his resting heart rate would be forty or even less. He expected the girls would help him to achieve that state.

*Patience*, he cautioned himself. *Patience.*

He would wait as long as it took for his anger to fully subside before responding to the ill-conceived, reckless torching of Jillian Coates's condominium. Only then, when he was in what he called his alpha state, would he compose his message, encode it within the pixels of today's eBay item—a tacky hand-painted nutcracker—and then post the nutcracker to his eBay auction account.

Steganography, the art and science of writing concealed messages. Documented examples of steganography dated back to ancient Greece, when wax-covered wooden tablets kept coded messages hidden from the enemy. Koller had first been exposed to it in a college course, but over the succeeding years, he had taken aspects of the craft to the point where he could have earned millions in licensing fees, had he not preferred to use his custom software to plan, execute, and be compensated for non-kills. The latest version of Koller's steganographic technique was akin to taking the most sophisticated coding technology available and dosing it with steroids.

He still couldn't wrap his mind around Jericho burning down Jillian Coates's condominium without consulting him first. He had made it clear when Jericho first approached him about a series of new contracts: Under no circumstances were his clients ever to engage, tail, touch, or even breathe near anybody associated with the job without his authorization—and that authorization was simply not going to be given.

Obviously, the sister of one of the marks fell into the "associated with" category. The more he dwelled on it, the more agitated he became. Where were the girls?

Wearing only a white terry cloth robe, Koller rose from the bed and powered through two hundred push-ups on the gritty motel carpet without breaking a sweat. He meditated fifteen minutes afterward before checking his pulse once again. *Fifty*. Better, but still not good enough.

He could not remember the last time he had lost his temper to this extent.

He was upside down and naked, performing a motionless headstand, one of the countless yoga positions he could execute to any yogi's satisfaction, when he heard a soft knock on the door. Dropping to the floor with catlike grace, Koller crossed the room without bothering to dress. A quick check through the peephole confirmed it was the escorts he had hired. The tall hooker with ebony skin he knew as Sandy. He had hired her before and offered to triple her usual fee in exchange for her cooperation this night. The short blonde accompanying her was a relative newbie, not yet out of her teens. She would be perfect, he decided.

"Good evening, ladies," Koller said, motioning them inside and turning on one bedside lamp. The cool evening air washed over his body, igniting his senses. The night smelled of action. Koller watched the blonde glance down at his penis as she passed. He closed the door behind them with a soft click, then double-locked it.

"Do you like what you see?" he asked the blonde.

The girl nodded and smiled with artificial shyness.

"Can't you speak, bitch?" Koller snapped.

"Darlene can speak just fine," Sandy said.

Koller crossed the room and kissed the tall, dark woman hard on the lips. Then he drew her hand down to help him become aroused.

"Did I ask for your opinion?" he said suddenly, grabbing her by the hair, but focusing on the other whore. "Did I?"

"No, baby," Sandy said, "you didn't ask me nothin'."

"That's right, I didn't," Koller said sweetly, releasing her. "Okay, listen up, ladies. The game is simple. I pay, you do. Sort of like Simon Says. You do what Simon says and the night is going to be very much fun. Mess up and fun will be a little more elusive. Either way, I promise you one thing; our evening's going to be memorable. Isn't that right, Sandy?"

"Simon ain't never hurt me bad, Darlene, honey. An' we been friends a long time now. Besides, whatever happens, he'll make it worth your while."

Sandy peeled away her knockoff Burberry trench coat, revealing only a black bra and panties. At Koller's request, she had on her stiletto high heels as well. The killer savored her long, toned legs, flat stomach, and sensual dark skin. In front of the closed drapes, Darlene held her own coat tightly across her slender frame. Sandy moved to where she was standing.

"Darlene, sweetie, you ain't got nothing to worry about, ya hear?" she whispered.

"He scares me," the blonde whispered back, but not quietly enough.

Koller heard her.

He grabbed her by the arm, hard enough to make her cry out in pain. Then he threw her onto the bed, as if he were tossing a pillow. The woman's overcoat flopped open, revealing, per instructions, only a garter belt and mesh stockings. Her breasts would need implants in a few years, he thought, but at the moment, they were schoolgirl perfect. Now it was time to see just what she was made of.

Koller was becoming more aroused. He sat down on the mattress next to Darlene and began to stroke the woman's fine, straw blond pubic hair, shaved in a landing-strip style.

"Sandy, baby," he said, "you go into the

closet and grab my black canvas bag and bring it to me. Don't open it, though. I got surprises inside."

Koller kept his eyes locked on Darlene. Her fear was easy to see. He could feel his pulse slowing.

Sandy returned, carrying the black canvas bag, and climbed onto the bed behind Koller. She placed her hands upon his shoulders and began to massage him, rubbing her long, delicate fingers down and across his bare chest, teasing his nipples. Darlene gazed up at them, unable to keep her body from shivering as though she'd just been pulled from a river.

"Whatchu freakin' about, girl?" Sandy snapped. "Take off your stockings and let's do our job."

"Hold on a second, love," Koller said. "Give me the bag."

Koller took the bag from her as he got up off the bed, then brought it to the small desk and opened it while keeping his back to the bed. From inside he withdrew four Velcro restraints. Turning, he showed the women. Darlene's eyes widened, but Sandy just giggled. Koller strode back over to the bed, now with a full erection. His eyes were a wolf's, locked on Darlene. The girl was beginning to hyperventilate. He checked his wrist for five seconds.

**Fifty. Maybe forty-seven.**

"Straddle her," Koller commanded Sandy.

Then he reached beneath the bed and pulled up a length of nylon rope he had earlier tied to the frame.

"Sandy . . . you didn't say . . . anything about . . . ropes," Darlene managed.

"Take it easy on her, baby," Sandy cooed to Koller. "Remember, she's sort of new at all this."

With his hand wrapped firmly around Darlene's neck, Koller bound the teen's wrist with the Velcro and tied the restraint to the cord. In seconds, he had repeated the maneuver with her other wrist and both ankles. The knots were impossible to undo without help. Koller nodded Sandy away, then he stroked the girl's breasts until her nipples responded almost in spite of themselves. The horror he saw in her eyes was blessedly pure, almost palpable.

**Forty-five.**

"If you scream, you're going to die," Koller whispered, his lips brushing her ear.

"Don't you dare move. Do you understand me?"

"Sandy, help me."

Koller raised a finger to keep Sandy from responding.

"I asked if you understood."

"Y-yes. I understand."

The master of the non-kill pulled a fifth length of rope from beneath the mattress at the head of the bed, then knotted it firmly about the teen's neck. Finally, he opened the black bag once more and withdrew a bowie knife with a nine-and-a-half-inch blade, a pair of large pliers, and three brown glass bottles, which he held up to the lamp to ensure they were full of whatever liquid they contained.

Finally, he rose and moved to his laptop computer. His erection was now fully tumescent, and his demeanor magnificently calm.

Koller could see Darlene's reflection in the three-foot mirror hanging above the desk. He watched unblinking as she tested the ropes. Her sobs and strangled breathing were a symphony to him. He checked his radial pulse again.

**An even forty.**

**Alpha state.**

The young whore had served her purpose.

He was ready to write.

He motioned Sandy down between his legs and made only the faintest murmur of pleasure when she took him in her mouth. Koller never averted his eyes from the mirror and the reflection of Darlene's terrified, tear-streaked face.

Opening a graphic file he had stored on his laptop, Koller ran a picture of the wooden nutcracker through his encryption program. His software, named Demaratus for the Spartan king known for his innovative use of steganography, was coded to his exacting specifications by some of the most powerful minds in computer cryptology. The application electronically prompted him to type his message. He no longer felt the compulsion to reprimand Jericho for its unacceptable behavior. He was far too relaxed for that. Instead he wrote:

**You broke the rules of engagement . . . mistakes will not be tolerated . . . the consequence is a new bid . . . post now . . . this is nonnegotiable.**

The words, he knew, were perfect— dispassionate, but accommodating. His demands would be met. Any alternative, as Jericho was well aware, was unaccept- able. Jericho would comply or find some- one else, and when it came to orchestrating murder that appeared to be due to acci- dent, natural causes, or suicide, there was Franz Koller, and there was everyone else.

Koller saved his message and instantly the image of the nutcracker reappeared where seconds ago his words had been. To decrypt the message required the matching key—a version of Demaratus that was customized for each client. Using his eBay account name, ChemLuv56, Koller posted the nutcracker for bid. Jeri- cho was instantly alerted that a message from the assassin was awaiting a reply.

Five minutes passed. Sandy worked vigorously to bring Koller to climax, while Darlene had acquiesced to her mattress prison. A message alert bubble popped up on the Dell laptop screen. Guvner- Poppins, the code name he assigned to Jericho, had listed a new item for bid. Koller clicked on the link and opened up an auction page on eBay. The item listed, containing Jericho's response, was a Stanley hammer and some nails. The irony of the chosen products was not lost on him.

The genius of his communication protocol was that every auction was authentic. Somebody would eventually be the highest bidder for the hammer and nails. It would then be shipped to the winner from a blind post office box.

Simple.

Koller downloaded the image and ran it through his decryption program. The return message read simply: *Understood*. Then Koller, bidding as ChemLuv56, made an offer for the hammer of $1.50. He smiled after placing it. He had just upped the fee for his next non-kill by half a million dollars. He doubted Jericho would make such a mistake again.

Koller pushed Sandy's head back, freeing himself from her mouth.

"Don't you want me to finish, baby?"

"No," Koller said. "I have some business to attend to."

He moved to the bedside and hefted the huge bowie knife in his hand.

"No!" Darlene rasped, the rope constricting her vocal cords. "Please, no!"

Sandy made a move forward, but Koller stopped her with a wave of the knife. Then, with his erection even larger than when Sandy had been performing fellatio on him, he straddled the blonde and with four perfectly placed strokes, severed the ropes.

Finally, he kissed each whore on the forehead and stepped back from the bed.

"Simon says, go home," he said.

# CHAPTER 14

Second Chance was asleep on the love seat in the study in his favorite position—on his back, with all four spindly legs pointing straight up at the ceiling. Nick had showered, dressed, and shaved, and was ready for the night's rounds in the RV, but mentally he was still scouring the city streets for Manny Ferris.

Initially, the possible breakthrough in his search for Umberto had dropped his SUD score to a rare two: *A little bit upset, but not noticeable unless you took care to pay attention to your feelings, and then realize, "yes" there is something bothering me.* Now, frustration had pushed his number up to a five.

Posters had been taken down, and maps of Washington, D.C., and Baltimore covered a good portion of the floors and walls of the study. In two days of dedicated searching, he had canvassed all of the most unsavory neighborhoods, back alleys, flophouses, and cardboard villages where Manny Ferris might be found. Dotting his maps were carefully placed color-coded pins, each representing a city street that needed to be searched again. He used a highlighter to trace the miles of pavement he covered, questioning every store clerk, loitering kid, and homeless person along the way. *Nothing.* Ferris was either the most determined hermit in the world or, in the four years since making his big announcement to Matt McBean, he had traveled on.

**But to where?**

Detective Don Reese had fared no better, even though he had given up his fishing trip to search.

"Manny Ferris is not in D.C.," was his terse conclusion.

That was when the bounce in Nick's

mood had leveled off and begun to slip. To his dismay, the Department of Veterans Affairs was as tight about disclosing last known addresses of their vets as it was about paying out PTSD benefit claims. They would not even comment on the status of the Marine.

Nick respected the agency's commitment to safeguarding personal information, given the PR fiasco and millions paid in damages after several highly publicized thefts of classified laptop computers. Even so, to keep vets from finding each other, when friends from combat might be crucial to a soldier's or sailor's well-being, seemed irrationally protective.

For some reason, Nick could not shake the feeling that Manny Ferris was alive. In a spiral-bound notebook, he kept a detailed log of every call he made to chief medical examiner offices in major East Coast cities, as well as to morgues in D.C., Virginia, Delaware, and Maryland. There were two instances of recorded death certificates for Manuel Ferris, one for a man in his eighties, the other a nineteen-year-old killed in Iraq. He even paid fifty dollars to a Web site purported to be a favorite among private investigators. The site searched newspaper articles and a multitude of court records, including incarcerations and name changes, but it was wasted effort.

Nick checked the time. He and Junie would be on the road in thirty minutes. He peered out at the pink-and-gold-cast sky, wondering if such sunsets would ever feel anything but empty to him.

The ever-present curse of PTSD was that everything reminded him of something he had lost—his bed of a restful night's sleep, the sun of his fiancée, the maps on the wall of his missing friend. Feeling another episode of melancholy coming on, Nick closed his eyes and balled his hands into tight fists, but relaxed them when he heard his front door open.

"Come in, it's open," he called out as Junie was halfway down the hall.

Chance, perhaps knowing the woman represented no possibility of play, remained in his upside-down-table position.

Junie entered the room, her broad smile fading the moment she saw Nick.

"Goodness, love, I guess I'm just stating the obvious, but you look like hell."

"Thanks for the compliment. I checked myself in the mirror and thought at worst I looked like heck."

The nurse spent a moment studying the maps tacked to the walls.

"That's a lot of walking you've done in two days," she said.

"Say, maybe, just maybe, that's why my feet are killing me. You know, Junie, truth is I didn't even consider not being able to find Manny Ferris. It's all a bit disheartening."

"It hurts me to see you so discouraged. I admire your dedication to finding out what happened to Umberto, but maybe it's time to let it rest."

"The man saved my life. I owe it to him."

"You owe it to yourself to live your life to the fullest, too."

"Well, maybe finding Umberto will let me do that."

"I'm worried you're chasing ghosts, Nick."

"What if he's not a ghost?"

"Then we better find him fast."

"We?"

Junie nodded and placed a comforting hand on Nick's shoulder.

"The night you learned about Manny Ferris, I don't think I've seen you so happy in all the time I've known you. I don't want to go on watching you suffer the way you have been. If finding our friend Umberto is going to take you even one step closer to health and happiness, I want to do everything I can to make it happen."

"Thank you, Junie. You're doing that. I honestly believe Manny Ferris and Umberto are connected. I've searched every street corner, morgue, and veteran's organization from here to Detroit, but I'm going to keep at it."

"Well, I know one person we haven't used who might help you."

"Oh, and who's that?"

"Reggie."

"*Our* Reggie? My football buddy Reggie? You-can't-ride-the-RV-if-you-don't-finish-your-homework Reggie?"

"The same. I promise that if anyone can help you find your Manny Ferris, he can."

# CHAPTER 15

With each stroke of his spoon-shaped paddle, Franz Koller felt a million and a half richer. What other job could he even think of where he could make so much money for doing something that he loved so much? Whatever this newest windfall of steady business was all about, he'd take it, no questions asked.

Maybe he'd buy another house.

Koller ignored the spray as he powered through three-foot swells, kicked up by a steady offshore breeze. The spray skirt kept the boat from flooding, and practice with the ocean kayak he kept at his estate near Panama City, Florida, had made him expert at steering with the foot-controlled rudder system. He would have preferred to work in less blustery conditions, but the fog, now beginning to blanket the iron-colored sea, provided additional cover he could not resist.

The rolling Chesapeake swells aside, Koller was delighted to be on the hunt again. Executing a non-kill was far more rewarding than executing a lesson plan. He was certified to teach in a number of states under a number of names. In past years, the profession had been tolerable, and occasionally even stimulating. If it weren't for being such an effective cover with flexible working hours, he wouldn't spend another minute trying to educate the insipid brats.

Unless Dr. Tightass, as Koller had come to think of the anesthesiologist whose life he was about to terminate, broke with his routine, he would be entering the water at the end of Parker Avenue within the next ten minutes. Koller had put in his own seventeen-foot, carbon-colored Looksha two miles to the south. He had bought the touring kayak in a mammoth sporting goods store outside of Newport, and later that night had slept with the salesgirl who had sold it to him. Life was good.

Rowing the extra mile to intersect the doctor's track was a precaution the killer had no trouble taking. It was best if the man believed he was alone on the water until the very end. Once the body was recovered, and once the time of death was established, there would be nothing suspicious for anyone to report to the police. Of course, that presumed there would even be a police investigation of any depth. But Koller knew there wouldn't be. Details and working through minutiae were at the core of the non-kill.

Even with the rough conditions, Koller was barely breathing heavily when he reached the eastern side of the Alexander Ledge Lighthouse. *The wonder of adrenaline*, he thought. Grabbing hold of the rusted ladder, which ran halfway up the ninety-seven-foot-high granite tower, he checked the time. Despite the chop, he had still made it four minutes faster than the best of his three trial runs.

**Details.**

In another twenty minutes, anesthesiologist Dr. Thomas Landrew would complete his early morning paddle out to the ledge.

"One mile to dead time, Doc," Koller said, checking his GPS and savoring the air, which was salty, but not as much so as at the ocean end of the largest estuary in the country.

He had shadowed Landrew for several days, deciding on the best way to dispatch him following the precepts of the non-kill. Early each morning, even when it was raining, Koller watched as the man embarked from the Parker Avenue put-in and paddled out to the lighthouse and back. The physician was fifty-seven, but his body could have been fifteen years younger than that.

The rigidity surrounding the man's schedule was impressive. He rowed, then left for work at precisely the same time each day, and made a leisurely walkabout of his substantial property each evening when he returned home. The non-kill at its best required using a target's weakness against him . . . or her. It was Landrew's obsessiveness about time that would be his undoing.

Chilly waves crashed against the rocks at the base of the lighthouse. Taking advantage of a brief interlude between swells, Koller reached into his dry bag, resting atop the cockpit tray, to confirm its contents. The two tools he would need were stashed safely inside nylon drawstring bags—a small hammer and a syringe. The latter was kept safe in a protective plastic case, and filled with four hundred milligrams of succinylcholine, or "sux" as many anesthesiologists and emergency specialists referred to the magical drug. Koller removed the needle cap and tapped gently at the base of the syringe, encouraging a tiny crystal drop of death to bead out. He imagined the onset of the paralysis of Landrew's muscles, especially the thick traps across the shoulder, and those chest muscles that were needed, along with the diaphragm, to breathe. A single shot of the massive dose he had chosen was all it would take to stop every muscle cold. Riding the swells, he rubbed his hands together vigorously, not so much to warm them, but to help contain his exuberance.

Over the sound of wind and waves, Koller heard the classical music Landrew

liked to play when he paddled. Mozart—
always Mozart. Hidden from view behind
the lighthouse, Koller gauged the distance.
He waited until the anesthesiologist tapped
his paddle against the granite boulders
before slipping out through the fog like a
mirage.

"Hey there," Koller called out.

Slightly breathless from his effort, Landrew did a double take, then shut off Mozart.

"I didn't know anybody else was out
here," he said. "At this hour there seldom
is. Where did you put in?"

Koller paddled toward the man's kayak,
keeping the syringe tucked securely under
his leg.

"Just a bit south of Parker," he said.
"This is my first time out to the lighthouse.
You?"

"Parker. I drop in at Parker every day."

The doctor sounded curious, but not
suspicious, Koller decided.

"Couldn't have picked a better morning,
eh?" the killer replied with a chuckle.

Drenched from ocean spray, Landrew's
silver hair escaped in spots from underneath his REI baseball cap. His distinguished

good looks and best-that-money-could-buy gear were, Koller thought, a perfect compliment to his type A personality.

"If you like fog, you're certainly getting the most out of the experience," Landrew said, sounding just a bit rushed.

"I certainly am," Koller agreed. "Mind if I anchor against your boat for just a moment? Mine's pretty unsteady in these swells and I want to secure my dry bag."

"I . . . suppose so."

**Okay, time's up.**

Koller pulled his craft alongside Landrew's, which was downwind and closer to the lighthouse. The mark, seeming slightly annoyed now, leaned over to help steady the other boat. Oh, how Koller loved it when his mark helped him to make the kill. The lighthouse, as he anticipated, shielded both men from the steady roll of waves, benefiting him with additional stability. The classic Three Dog Night song "Joy to the World" popped into his head and brought an audible chuckle.

"What's so funny?" Landrew asked.

"This is," Koller said.

With serpentlike quickness, he tipped his kayak to starboard, giving him the additional inches he needed to reach the base of Landrew's neck, focusing on a spot next to the spine. In virtually the same motion he drove the needle deep into the man's trapezius muscle and depressed the plunger, dispensing the sux. He pushed a few feet away and watched with undisguised delight as the nature of the attack registered in his victim's patrician face. Koller knew that beneath the man's Patagonia jacket, Landrew's muscles were already beginning to fasciculate—the individual fibers twitching and wriggling like so much spaghetti.

"What's wrong?" Koller asked with a grin. "Ocean beauty leave you breathless?"

"Why?" the physician pleaded, fumbling with his paddle but getting nowhere.

"You all ask that same question," the master of the non-kill replied. "Why is that?"

Then he laughed out loud.

With the sux working its magic, Landrew was motionless inside his kayak. His eyes were alert, though frozen in a horrified stare.

"Hey, fish got your tongue?" Koller asked, and laughed even louder.

Landrew's body, still upright, began gently

moving from side to side, lolled by the waves passing beneath his craft.

"Yes, that's the effect of your old friend sux," Koller said. "How many times in the OR have you used it on others? Hundreds? No, no, thousands. I'll bet you can feel your heart racing in a desperate effort to get oxygen to your brain. Don't bank on your brain winning that one."

Landrew's eyes remained fixed. Koller paddled forward and gripped the gunwale of the man's boat.

"You're a world-renowned anesthesiologist, Doctor," Koller continued, "but I'll bet I know succinylcholine as well as you do. Rapidly metabolized depolarizing neuromuscular blocker. Onset of action less than one minute. Half-life less than one minute. Breakdown product, succinic acid, won't be looked for—especially not in a drowning victim. And yes, even if you can't inhale, water will still get into your lungs passively, just from being submerged for an hour or so. So, who's the expert? Ah, but there's more."

Koller reached into his dry bag and took out the hammer.

"I still needed to figure out how you were

going to drown while wearing a life pre-
server," he went on. "Want to guess how?
Speechless? I understand. Okay, I'll tell
you, just like the police will tell the good
widow Landrew. There was an accident,
you see. A wave flipped your boat, or
maybe you fainted from an irregular heart
rhythm. Either way, you fell out of the kayak
and tried your best to get back in. But
then, gosh darnit, wouldn't you know the
kayak flipped over from a wave and the
gunwale came snapping down onto your
head. The blow knocked you unconscious.
Floating facedown in the water, kept there
by your life jacket, your lifeless body came
to rest amidst those rocks over there."

Landrew's eyes remained open, but
Koller knew he was already dead. He removed the REI baseball cap and tapped
the hammer against the man's scalp until
blood oozed out from a small gash. With
his gloved hand, Koller rubbed blood from
the wound against the gunwale of the
corpse's boat, augmenting the smear with
strands of hair ripped from Landrew's
scalp. He then loosened the spray skirt
before flipping the kayak over, spilling the
lifeless body into the sea.

"Nobody does it better," Koller sang softly. "Makes you feel sad for the rest."

He watched until the current carried the body and boat against the boulders at the base of the lighthouse.

Then, with several powerful strokes, he turned his kayak west and disappeared into the morning fog.

"Nicely done," he said to himself.

# CHAPTER 16

It was lunch hour. A steady flow of employees poured out from the Veterans Administration Benefits building, off to grab something to eat. Reggie Smith watched them leave from his position behind a hot dog pushcart on the other side of Vermont Avenue. Strolling leisurely to the next streetlight, the gangly teen crossed the road, then waited until another group had exited before entering the building. Junie and Nick had dropped him off a block away and were waiting there in the car.

The youth was only fourteen, and that worried his foster mother greatly, but he was physically ahead of the curve and had a survivor's wiliness born of his disjointed upbringing and several stretches in juvenile detention. Barring anything unforeseen, he had assured her, he would be okay.

Junie and Nick had misgivings.

Reggie was five and already in foster care when his remarkable sense of computers began to manifest itself. Initially, he was deemed cute and precocious, but that was before age seven when he began charging video games and CDs to his foster parents, intercepting the shipments to the house, and storing the booty beneath the clothes in his bureau drawer. By age nine he had been caught hacking into the computer at school and changing grades. By eleven, when he moved in with Junie and Sam, he had made another trip to juvenile detention for shoplifting and for frivolous, but disruptive, cyber crime.

"Reggie has the potential to change the world . . . or to rule a cell block," the judge had told his new foster parents.

With the Wrights' steadying hands on the tiller of his life, and Nick's role as a big brother, the boy was headed in the right direction. Junie's rationale in asking him to become involved in the search for Manny Ferris was that no one would be hurt, and someone they both loved would be helped. In all her years as a foster parent, caring for God only knew how many children, she had never used a kid or put one in harm's way as she was doing with this boy. But Nick was increasingly desperate to find Manny Ferris, and Reggie Smith, with an IQ measured in the 150s, was no ordinary teenager.

There was no metal detector. From yesterday's visit to the building, Reggie knew the lunchtime crowd would distract the lone security guard, making it easier for him to pass by. He was dressed conservatively, in tan corduroy pants and a blue collared shirt, over which dangled a perfect replica of the building's visitor badge.

Skipping yesterday's biology class, he had ridden into D.C. with Junie and spent several hours observing people and walking up and down the granite steps to the main doors. Using his cell phone camera, he snapped several quality shots of the building's visitor badge. It took him half the night to tweak the forgery using Photoshop, but before first light he printed his master-work, then had it laminated at a nearby Kinko's. It was virtually indistinguishable from the badge he had photographed, right down to the slight color fade and scratches on the laminate.

Perfectly calm, and relishing the chance for mischief, Reggie climbed the expan-sive steps and walked through the massive glass doors. Once inside the marble-tiled foyer, he marched purposefully, head held up, eyes solidly forward, toward the secu-rity desk. As he neared, he lifted his badge to eye level, then waved it in front of his body to attract the guard's atten-tion.

"My dad forgot his briefcase in his of-fice," Reggie said, again mindful to main-tain eye contact.

Suspicion was his greatest adversary now, and to counter it, he made certain his voice did not waver in the slightest. This was the gamesmanship he missed most about his hacking days. Hacking into a computer was so much more than just writing code, but only people like him understood that. It was certainly possible to enter a system long distance, from his personal computer, but the direct route, working from a computer already in the system, was so much faster and more convenient. To avoid getting caught when taking the direct route often required serious acting skills. The guard kept his face virtually buried in *The Examiner* while holding a roast beef sandwich in one hand and a Diet Coke can in the other. He barely glanced up to check Reggie's ID badge before waving him through.

Reggie exited the main stairs at the second floor, taking quick inventory of the layout, which he had studied on two different Web sites. It was just what he expected to find. He didn't anticipate having to search for long before finding a cubicle that suited his purposes.

There were only a scattering of employees who hadn't yet left for lunch. He had passed only half a dozen workstations before he found one with a yellow Post-it note taped to the side of the computer monitor. He checked inside the cubicle with the Post-it, looking for a jacket or anything that might suggest the usual occupant could be returning soon. Chances were that David Fulton, the name on the business card inserted in the plastic holder on the outside cubicle wall, was at lunch.

**Time to get started.**

Sitting down in Fulton's desk chair, Reggie gave a quick flick of the computer mouse to power down the screen saver. The computer was locked, as Reggie knew it would be, and required the right username and password to unlock it. He simultaneously pressed the Control, Alt, and Delete keys on the keyboard to activate the security prompt.

He couldn't help but laugh a little when he pulled the Post-it note off of the side of the monitor. David Fulton had written "Pword" on the yellow square and then just underneath, the characters "ABC123abc." Information technology departments that enforced top-notch security protocols were notorious for frequently mandated password changes. Often they made employees change their password every week or two. It was smart security, Reggie would agree, but it also made it difficult for workers to remember their passwords. Instead of dealing with a help desk to retrieve a forgotten password, the office drones, most of them dealing with nonclassified material, often simply wrote their passwords on a Post-it or slip of paper every time it changed.

Taking advantage of the Post-it technique was one of the oldest and best hacker tricks for accessing secure systems. If the password wasn't kept in plain sight on a Post-it note, chances were good that it could be found under the keyboard, or taped either to the side of a nearby filing cabinet or on the bottom of the upper desk drawer. Finding a valid password on his first attempt was a lucky break, but not an unexpected one. Still, Reggie's pulse rose a notch. He had promised when he moved in with Junie and Sam that he would keep his skills under wraps, but using them was always going to be a rush.

Next, the username.

If the security was typical, Reggie knew, he would have three chances to get the right combination of username and password before the system would lock up and he would have to find another cubicle. He typed "David.Fulton" in the username field—a common naming convention adopted by many information technology departments to uniquely identify each employee—and then he entered the password "ABC123abc." Bingo! It had taken less than five minutes from the moment he started his timer to access every system and file David Fulton's security profile allowed.

"I love it," Reggie whispered.

Seconds later, the teen had the VA intranet open and had clicked over to the bookmarked Veterans Information Search Web page. As Nick had instructed, he typed "Manuel Ferris" into the search field, then hit Return. Five matches instantly appeared on the screen, along with basic identifying information. Reggie downloaded each of the files onto his portable data storage USB key, which he had plugged into the back of Fulton's computer. Whatever information Nick needed, Reggie felt confident, was either now on that key or simply didn't exist.

Reggie slipped the small plastic unit containing the stolen files into his front pants pocket. Then, his racing heart nearly stopped. From down the hallway he heard a loud conversation, two voices, maybe three, followed by a burst of laughter. He was certain somebody had said the name Dave. Chances were fifty-fifty it wasn't David Fulton returning early from lunch, but if it was, Reggie's explanation regarding his father's briefcase would be of no help.

Time to leave.

He stepped outside the office with no more than a glance to his right, and proceeded to walk confidently away from the central staircase and what turned out to be two men in suits.

**Slowly . . . slowly . . .**

Somehow, he managed to resist the temptation to look back.

"Hey!" Reggie heard one of the men shout. "Was that guy just in my cube? Hey you, stop!"

Reggie had had enough close calls in his hacking life to know that sometimes the best option was not to try and talk his way out of a jam, but to run from it. With a sprinter's acceleration, he raced down the seemingly endless corridor, headed for the lighted exit sign. The commotion and shouts of the two men in pursuit encouraged several employees to poke their heads through their doorways or above their cubicle walls like prairie dogs.

Reggie risked a quick glance behind him to assess his advantage. The men trying to chase him down, both of them overweight and running in their suits, were not nearly as agile as he was in his loose-fitting corduroys and New Balance sneakers.

He was turning back to gauge the remaining distance between him and the exit door when a blond woman in a jacket and gray skirt, oblivious to the chase, emerged from her cubicle and stepped directly into his path. Shifting his weight in time to avoid a full-force collision, Reggie clipped the woman, spinning her sideways and down to one knee. She screamed loudly as the papers she was carrying flew up against the ceiling and then rained down on her.

"Sorry 'bout that, lady," Reggie said. "You okay?"

The blonde nodded, clearly confused by the collision and possibly the boy's congeniality. The delay was costly, however. Reggie's chances of making it to the exit without getting caught had all but vanished. Improvisation was often the hacker's best friend, and even in the worst of situations, he had never been one to panic.

Operating on instinct, he spun around to face the two men, who were now just a few cubicles away. Surprise was all he had. As he often did when playing tackle football in the yard with Nick, he dashed directly toward them. Their eyes widened.

Two doorways were all that separated them now. Reggie, arms pounding, was at full speed. The men raised their arms like Nick would have done, either protecting themselves or readying to make a tackle. Reggie waited until the outstretched tips of one man's fingers were almost to his chest before making his favorite move. Ducking and side-stepping simultaneously, he skidded to his right, shifting past David Fulton and his coworker. Instead of open lawn, though, he was looking at an empty cubicle. Moving instinctively, he leaped onto the desk. Then, grasping the top of the wall divider with both hands, he swung his legs around, vaulting himself up and over the divider and into the adjacent office.

Neither of the men was inclined or able to duplicate his maneuver.

"Help! . . . Stop him!" they hollered.

Reggie, smiling now, had already reached the stairwell door from which he had entered the second floor. There might have been enough distance between him and the men to take the stairs, but instead he launched himself over the stairwell railing and dropped onto the stone landing below, crying out in pain as his ankle rolled beneath him. Limping, he reached the main foyer just as the two men were entering the stairwell.

"Hey, slow down, there, kid!" the security guard barked as Reggie hobbled past his desk.

"Sorry, sir," Reggie shouted back. "Sorry."

He hurried as best he could manage out the huge glass doors and down the outside stairs. He was in pain and breathing heavily when he reached Junie and Nick. Behind him, he sensed more than saw the security guard racing down the stairs.

"Go! They're coming!" he managed, scrambling onto the backseat.

"Are you hurt?" Nick asked as Junie accelerated and turned at the next intersection.

Reggie patted the USB key in his pocket. "Not really," he said.

It was going to be hard to thank Junie for the rush.

# CHAPTER 17

Koller kept pace behind Jillian Coates, close enough to breathe in her apricot-scented perfume. His shadow, stretched long and thin by the midday sun, occasionally overlapped hers. He liked touching her that way. Sometimes he walked in perfect synchronized step. She of course had no idea that for blocks she was being followed. Wearing a different disguise, far more doughy Robert Greene than urbane, intelligent Paul Regis, Koller felt confident that even if she did make eye contact with him, he would be unrecognizable to her. At worst, she would think he was just a typical letch, testing how close he could get to her and thinking dirty thoughts.

How wrong she'd be.

The Landrew non-kill had been a masterpiece, flawlessly researched, planned, and executed. Now, Koller's bank account reflected his reward for that effort. There was no way of knowing how much more work Jericho intended on sending his way, but Koller had been in this business long enough to develop a sense for when a client's well was about to run dry. Jericho's pockets were extradeep, though, and he believed the work was far from over.

He decided it would be a wasted trip to return to the Panama City estate, his condo in Taos, or back to California to resume his life as a sedate but colorful substitute chemistry teacher. More jobs were bound to come his way and probably soon. Meanwhile, he was content to use the downtime to get to know Jillian Coates and see for himself how motivated she was to further investigate the cause of the fire that had ravaged her condominium. He applied simple mathematical logic to his plan on how best to deal with her: the pushier she was in her efforts, the less time she had to live. Even the students at Woodrow Wilson High could handle that equation.

Jillian left the crowded sidewalk and headed toward Anne Marie Cosco Hall, a nursing school dorm according to the sign-post Koller read. *Perhaps she's living there now*, he mused. His mind flashed on the chaos and havoc he could wreak if left to his own devices on a floor full of student nurses. The images, more horrible than any circle of Dante's inferno, aroused him.

Koller occupied himself with *The Washington Post*, which he read on a nearby park bench while waiting for his quarry to reappear. She did so twenty minutes later and proceeded to head off at a more accelerated pace. He liked her choice of clothes—not flashy or excessively tight, but not at all dowdy. Her breasts, beneath a cotton blouse, were totally enticing—a nice C cup, he guessed. But it was her behind, moving unself-consciously in her chino slacks, that he found most appealing. The way her hips swayed with each step was inspiring. Koller moved even closer to her than he had been before, wanting to take in another whiff of her intoxicating perfume. He decided then and there that he would have her, a willing sex partner or not, before he killed her. He considered it a bonus for a job well done.

The notion made him smile.

Jillian took a left onto Twentieth Street and walked a few blocks north, stopping underneath a green awning. Koller walked past her, but turned just in time to see her slip inside Madame Jessica's Psychic Readings Studio.

"Communing with the departed, are we?" Koller muttered to himself.

He wished it had been a private investigator she was visiting and not some medium who would take her money and toy with her emotions. Perhaps she could use someone to comfort her—someone like Paul Regis.

He was rock hard from following her, and from the taste of his last non-kill still fresh in his mind.

# CHAPTER 18

Of the five Manuel Ferris files Reggie Smith had obtained from his close call at the Veterans Administration building, only one seemed promising—a thirty-five-year-old with an address on H Street NW in Washington. There was no apartment number. The Internet and Nick's maps placed the address in D.C.'s compact Chinatown. As his cab pulled up to the curb, Nick stared at the structure and checked Reggie's printout again.

LUCKY BILL PEARL'S, the sign above the awning of a windowless, black brick building read. SERVING D.C.'S FINEST GENTLEMEN

SINCE 1949. Below the fringed awning, the entrance was moderately discreet, with three glass-encased glossy photographs of women on each side, presumably advertising the headliners in their roster of performers and exotic dancers. *Nikki . . . Sabra . . . Colette . . .*

Before he paid off the cabbie Nick checked the address a final time. Lucky Bill's hardly seemed like the residence for a man who had gone off for a top-secret covert military mission—unless the mission was here, in which case it hardly seemed likely the VA would be making the operative's identifying information available in its database.

The façade of the building was four stories high. It wasn't a stretch to imagine what the upper floors might be used for, but apartments were certainly one of the other possibilities. He scanned to the right and left, but there were no more entrances. Perhaps there was one on the far side of the building.

Nick tipped the driver 25 percent and went inside. He was carrying a small manila envelope containing several photographs of Umberto and one of Manuel

Ferris, enlarged by Reggie from a unit snapshot Matt McBean had come up with. The original photo was creased and grainy, and the enlargement only enhanced the deficiencies. In addition, Ferris was wearing some sort of a cap, further obscuring his appearance. From what Nick could tell, he was a narrow-faced, swarthy man with deeply set eyes, and was about the same height as McBean—five-foot-nine.

Nick had last set foot inside a gentleman's club with a group of fellow surgical residents. Bill Pearl's was considerably more upscale than that place had been. Just outside the barred ticket window, a bald muscleman sat perched on a wooden stool. Above the collar of his tux shirt, the tops of a kaleidoscope of tattoos circumnavigated his tree-trunk neck.

"How're you doing?" he asked the brute, who he realized had no eyebrows.

The man nodded without interest, and mumbled a reply. Nick fished a twenty out of his wallet, realizing as he did that he could have been much more subtle. The bouncer reached up a beefy paw and, instantly, the bill was gone.

"I'm looking for a man named Manny Ferris," Nick said. "I was told he worked here."

"Don't you think you're in the wrong club, sir?" the giant replied. "This is girls only."

"No, no. What I mean is . . . is there a guy named Manny Ferris who works or . . . or maybe even lives here?"

"What I mean is that I don't know," came the humorless reply.

Inwardly, Nick smiled. Here he was—a trauma surgeon, able to make life-and-death decisions in the hospital or in the field, fumbling for words with a man who threw people out of a bar for a living.

The club's interior was dark and loud, but smoke-free, and not yet very crowded. Someplace in the building, though, near the nightclub, he could smell that cigars were being smoked. So much for city ordinances, Nick mused. All hail King Cash. Several men sat at the bar, glued to the busty topless dancer on center stage slithering her athletic body down a polished brass pole. The stage lighting was professional, and Nick noted that it was synchronized to the dance music that was blasting out of an impressive stack of speakers.

In front of the arcing bar, plush, high-backed chairs lined the edge of the stage. There were a few men seated there as well, all dressed in business attire. Lucky Bill's was hardly the low-rent district of gentlemen's clubs. What business could such a place have with a burnt-out GI?

Nick had crossed to the opposite side of the club when he felt a gentle tap on his shoulder. A slender young woman in a slinky black dress was smiling up at him. Her elfin features were framed by stunning, jet-black hair, which flowed halfway down her back.

"You look lost, handsome," she said.

"I'm looking for somebody," Nick replied. "Do you know a guy named Manny Ferris? This is the address I was given for him. Are there apartments upstairs?"

The girl cooed playfully. "Hey, that's a lot of questions for a first date. How about a little champagne first? My name's Brandy, but champagne's my drink."

Nick wondered how much Bill Pearl's charged for a bottle of champagne, to say nothing of the services from Brandy. Even without her biggest-ticket item, it was doubtful his night-on-the-town ATM withdrawal was going to last long.

"So," Nick said, taking a seat at a corner table, "what about Manny Ferris, or Manuel Ferris?"

"You a cop?"

"Nope, not a cop. Just a guy who's looking for a guy named Manny Ferris. Do you know him?"

"I get paid to talk with the customers, Officer," she said.

"I told you, I'm not a cop. I've got a hundred I'm ready to exchange for information about Manny Ferris. It's very important to me."

"What if I don't know anything?"

"Forty just for trying."

"I'll take the forty in advance."

Nick reduced his stack of twenties by two.

"His name's Ferris," he said. "Manny or Manuel Ferris. The VA gave me this place as his address."

"The club? I think the owner may have an apartment on the top floor, and the girls use the second floor. But I don't know if anyone lives in the rest of the place. What's he look like?"

Nick produced the photo McBean had given him, and the girl studied it.

"He could be sitting right next to me and I might not recognize him from this picture. Height? Weight?"

"Maybe five nine. He's midthirties— might have been late twenties when this was taken."

"That's it?"

"That's it."

"Boy, I sure hope you're not a cop. If you are, you're not very good at it."

Without waiting for a reply, she turned, giving him one last look at her clock-stopping face and figure, and headed across the room toward a newcomer who looked strikingly like the cartoon mogul on Chance and Community Chest cards in the game of Monopoly.

Nick stood to leave. Another young, attractive woman, a redhead, approached him before he had made it to the men's room at the rear of the club. The VA record had to have been wrong, he was thinking, unsuccessfully trying the photo on the girl.

It certainly wouldn't be the first time they had bad information.

The restroom, with a swashbuckling cavalier on the door, featured orange marble countertops, neat rows of toiletries, hair combs in blue liquid disinfectant, and several small bowls of mints. Nick could not see under the stalls, but it seemed as if there was no one else in the washroom besides him and an attendant in a stained white collared shirt, askew bow tie, and faded red vest. He had a clean towel draped on his arm and passed it over as soon as Nick had washed his hands.

As the attendant turned toward him, Nick caught his breath. The man's face was deformed. Two thick flaps of skin were separated by several crisscrossing scars. It was as if someone had started a multi-step plastic surgery procedure and then stopped before it was completed.

"You have a nice day, sir," the man muttered.

Nick set a five in his jar. "Thanks. You . . ." He stopped mid-sentence. The attendant drying the sink and countertop in the strip club bathroom was Manny Ferris. Nick felt nearly certain of it.

"Manny? You're Manny Ferris, aren't you?"

Ferris looked away and mumbled a response.

"Manny, I've been looking all over for you! My name is Nick Garrity. I'm a doctor and a good friend of Matt McBean. I can't believe I've finally found you."

Ferris looked blankly at Nick. His rheumy eyes were empty and distant.

"Do you want a mint?" he asked.

His voice was flat—devoid of any emotion. His deformed face held no discernable expression.

"Manny, I'm a friend of Matt McBean," Nick said again. "McBean, from the service. I've been looking for you."

Nothing.

From his stack of pictures, Nick pulled out the enlarged segment of the photograph of McBean and Ferris taken years ago, and handed it to the man.

"Look, Manny. This is you right here. And this is Matt McBean. He told me you vanished four years ago. Where have you been?"

Nothing.

Ferris adjusted the combs and checked

that the towels were aligned. Then, without so much as a nod at Nick, he turned and inspected each of the three elegant stalls.

*Night of the Living Manny,* Nick thought.

Ferris did not protest being shown the photo a second time. There may have been a flicker of recognition, but then, just as quickly, it was gone.

"We have some new combs if you'd like to do your hair," he said.

Nick leaned in close to check the man's pupils for any sign of drug use. They were mid-position and seemed to react to light. Then he took hold of Ferris's wrist and measured his pulse. The former enlisted Marine offered no resistance and kept his wrist limp as Nick calculated his rate at sixty-eight.

"Manny, there's a good chance you know my friend Umberto Vasquez. It's been four years since I saw him last. He was signed on to do a top-secret job for the military, just like you were. Does that name mean anything to you?"

"How are you doing today, sir?" Ferris replied. "Do you need a towel?"

"Manny, please. This man served with

me. He saved my life in battle. Then a few years later, just like you, he disappeared."

No reaction.

Nick's enthusiasm at having found the man had vanished, along with his hope of learning Umberto's fate. He was wondering if it was worth trying to get Ferris into the RV in the near future for an examination and some blood work.

"Here, Manny," he said, with an edge of frustration and irritability that he knew was out of character. "Here's a twenty. Take a look at these pictures of Umberto Vasquez."

Ferris took the bill, but he would not take the stack of photographs, so Nick was forced to flip through them. He paused on one picture for a few seconds before switching to the next. Each time, Nick was careful to point out Umberto. Ferris kept the same dull expression throughout. Then, while Nick was showing him the penultimate photograph, something changed. Ferris's eyes widened. His mouth fell agape. He started to shake, and his face reddened. He turned away from Nick. Swinging him around by the shoulders, Nick held the photograph up to his face. The picture was of Nick and Umberto, standing in front of the RV with the Lincoln Memorial in the background. Nick could not remember with certainty, but he thought that Junie had taken the shot.

"Do you recognize Umberto in this picture? Do you?"

"Go away!" Ferris shouted, pushing Nick backward with force. "Go away from me!"

Nick stumbled against the counter and nearly fell. His eyes caught a blur of movement and he ducked, just as the glass jar filled with combs sailed over his head, shattering the mirror behind him.

"Manny, stop it!" Nick shouted.

"Can't stay. Must run!"

The man's eyes, once dead, had ignited with a feral frenzy. His strength was astounding. Stiff-arming Nick as he tried to follow him out of the bathroom, Ferris barreled into a cocktail waitress carrying a tray full of drinks. Nick managed three steps in pursuit before being grabbed from behind by the tattooed bouncer. Pinned face-first against the club's velvet-lined wall, Nick watched helplessly as his only link to Umberto disappeared through the fire exit door.

# CHAPTER 19

**The two biggest shortcuts to disaster in medicine are arrogance and everything else.**

Nick knew his focus was compromised. The warning about medical mistakes, from one of his former surgical professors at Brown, ran through his head like a Möbius strip. Arrogance wasn't the problem with him. It never really had been. But even under the best of circumstances, his thoughts had a tendency to wander. And twenty-four hours after his bizarre encounter with Manny Ferris, this was hardly the best of circumstances.

The RV was back in D.C., and the warming weather had brought with it a flood of patients. Routine . . . routine . . . routine . . . disaster masking as routine. The shattering of a medical career was as simple as a one-minute loss of concentration—a swollen lymph node missed, a rectal exam not done, an abnormal neurologic sign ignored, a telltale answer in the medical history passed over or not asked for at all. It was that easy. And for Nick, the danger increased in direct proportion to his SUD score, which tonight continued hovering around five.

They were on the third and final stop of the evening, parked on the street in the Anacostia section of D.C. Nick and Junie had the help of an experienced volunteer nurse named Kate, who was working beneath the lightweight canopy that served as their annex and at other times as their triage area and waiting room. Slowly but surely, the crush of patients had vanished, and not a moment too soon. Fatigue and Manny Ferris were taking over Nick's body and mind. For a few brief moments after entering Lucky Bill Pearl's, it had seemed some answers to Umberto's disappearance might be at hand. Instead, there were only more questions and more frustrations.

"So, have you had the chance to think about Ferris?" Nick had asked Junie during the ride in from Baltimore to their initial stop at Jasper Yeo's used car dealership.

"Booze," she said simply. "When in doubt, always bet alcohol. My money's on wet brain."

"Maybe, but for someone who is as much of a zombie as Ferris was, I didn't see too many of the stigmata that go along with alcoholism—you know, spider veins on the cheeks, a W. C. Fields nose, ascites, liver palms, weakness, impaired gait. Should I go on? Then there's those scars and lumps on his face. It's like he was the big loser in a gang fight."

"What, then?"

"I don't know. Probably alcohol. I also wonder if someone might have been preparing him for plastic surgery. But how do you explain his reaction to the photo of me and Umberto? It certainly wasn't me he was reacting to. You should have seen him, Junie. In about a second, he went from *Night of the Living Dead* to *Rambo*. Does that seem like wet brain to you?"

"Maybe drugs."

"I suppose."

Now Nick was listening to the chest of an anxious twenty-year-old woman who lived in the nearby projects. Junie cleared her throat and shook her head at him disapprovingly.

"Hear anything?" she asked—her way of telling him that he might want to start that part of the exam over again.

"Nothing yet," he muttered, and focused in.

Their patient had evidence of a loose mitral valve and no other good explanation for her recurrent chest discomfort. Nick asked Junie to run a cardiogram on her. They would have scheduled an echocardiogram and blood tests if she had insurance, but that was wishful thinking. Nick gave her a sheet on obtaining health coverage, and Junie promised to follow up with a phone call to see if she had any luck. That was the best they could do.

Running a clinic like Helping Hands involved compromises, especially when patient cooperation and follow-up were constant variables. Specialist involvement in their cases was more dependable.

Through study and courses, Nick was decent at reading cardiograms, but they had several cardiologists who donated their services to Helping Hands. Finally, there was the handout dealing with mitral valve prolapse that one of their heart people had prepared.

"Either of you want coffee?" Nick asked the nurse and patient. "It's going to be instant, but we have decaf and high test, and white stuff in the fridge."

Both declined.

"Is that woman out there on the driver's seat with you?" Junie asked their patient.

"Nope, just my boyfriend. He's the one sitting at the table."

Nick glanced toward the front of the RV. He had noticed the woman several times in passing. It was hard not to—very good-looking with short, sand-colored hair and a light spread of freckles across the tops of her cheeks.

"As far as I can tell," Junie added, "she never signed in to be seen. It's been like forty-five minutes. I thought she was here with one of our patients."

"I'll ask. She doesn't look like she's in

any trouble, but it is a little weird she hasn't spoken up. Maybe she's a reporter or one of MacCandliss's secret agents."

Nick, doing his best to appear nonchalant, stopped by the refrigerator for a Coke. Now that he could look directly at the woman in the driver's chair, he wondered how he had ever made it past her in the first place. She was wearing jeans and a white barn jacket with a brown collar— from L.L.Bean or Eddie Bauer or someplace like that, he guessed. She was facing slightly away from him, gazing out of the massive windshield. Then, as if sensing his attention, she turned and smiled—not a broad smile, but still enough to light up the whole front of the RV.

*Special.* That was the word that came initially to his mind, followed closely by *interesting*, *intelligent*, and *unusual*. As he approached her, Nick stumbled enough to slosh some Coke onto the carpet. *Nice start. Leave it, or mop it up?* Grinning sheepishly, he went back to the galley and returned with some paper towels.

"Hi," he said, looking up from one knee and sensing he was speaking an octave higher than usual.

"Hi, yourself," she said, seeming totally at ease.

It felt awkward to be so close to her. As incredible as was her smile, her eyes, an unfathomable blue-green, were even more so. He made it to his feet and braced his leg against the console between the front seats to gain some breathing room.

"Are you here to be seen by the medical staff?" he asked.

*Medical staff! Give me a break!* he chastised himself. *Just tell her you're the doctor.*

"Nope," she said. "Healthy as a horse. But you can help me with this." She reached into a thin brown paper bag and held up a copy of *Nick Fury and His Agents of S.H.I.E.L.D.* "My name's Jillian Coates. I'm a psych nurse at Shelby Stone Memorial. Got a moment to talk, Dr. Garrity?"

It took forty-five minutes to pack up the canopy and wipe down the interior of the van. Jillian pitched in and got to know Junie as she did. Nick stayed close to the women and entered the conversation when he could. "Special" was right. There was a femininity and wisdom to her, coupled with a sharp wit that he found totally appealing. Nick, who hadn't really broken through his PTSD enough to become interested in any woman since Sarah, was surprised to find himself making some comparisons. Junie exchanged enough glances with him to make it clear she was thinking the same things.

Finally, with the nurse, Kate, off to her home in the suburbs, and the shades pulled, Nick and Junie sat at the fold-out table and listened with empathy and quiet astonishment to the sad story of the death of Belle Coates, and her odd connection to the medical director of the Helping Hands Mobile Medical Unit through an almost forgotten nickname.

"You say your sister had actually written in M.D. and Dr. and Ph.D. next to Nick Fury's name on the covers of these comics?"

"She seemed to be trying out every form of doctor."

"Like she *heard* it rather than *read* it."

"I wish I had the issues to show you," she said, "but they were destroyed when my apartment burned down a few days ago."

"Your sister was murdered and then

your apartment burned down? Do you think the two are connected?"

"How can I not, Nick, except the arson people didn't find anything."

"Well, unless you're incredibly unlucky, it seems suspicious to me," Nick said, wishing he could come up with something, anything, to help the woman. "Wait a minute," he said suddenly, "I have a friend, a detective with the D.C. police. He is incredibly well connected. I wouldn't be a bit surprised if he knew the arson people in Arlington, or at least here. Can I put you in touch with him?"

"That would be great. I have the number of one of the insurance inspectors who looked at my place. Maybe I can get a copy of his report over to your friend."

"I'll get a hold of Don first thing in the morning," Nick said, feeling his knees beginning to go to Jell-O from the woman's eyes.

In the end, it seemed obvious that Belle Coates had come across a reference to the name Umberto Vasquez had given to his friend a million miles and a hundred thousand years ago—not just *come across* the name, but had been impressed enough by what she had heard to go out and buy more than forty different copies of the comic book.

**Dr. Nick Fury.**

At one o'clock, Junie encouraged them to keep talking and wandered off to lie down in the aft examining room.

"Even before our parents died, Belle and I were reasonably close," Jillian said, "but there was a fairly wide difference in our ages, and I really didn't know all that much about her and what she was into. By the time of the accident, I had already been married for like a year and divorced, and was out there in the big, wide Washington world making up for the time I lost by getting married so young. The truth is, I was living on the edge a great deal, partying, always first in line for anything that would provide a rush, and chasing my passion for photography to some pretty dangerous places."

"Then suddenly you were the parent of a teenage girl."

"It sounds like that would be the case, and that's what I expected when I somewhat reluctantly agreed to stay home with Belle. But that's hardly what happened.

Belle was the most centered, spiritual person I had ever met. Yoga, flute, painting, athletics, gardening, cooking. Whatever there was to experience, she wanted to try it. She didn't care if she ever became the best at anything, except maybe nursing, but she wanted to know things, to feel them in her own way, not necessarily to master them. And she was without a doubt the best listener I ever knew."

"She sounds pretty incredible."

"She was. Even at fourteen it was like being around some sort of advanced lifeform. In the end, before she chose nursing and moved into the dorms in D.C., she was the one who was teaching me how to live—I mean really live. Not loud or big, but softly and passionately, with a delight in the details of things and of people."

Jillian's eyes filled, then overflowed. She made no attempt to wipe aside her tears, nor was she at all embarrassed by them.

"I never tried to stop the tears when I used to cry over Sarah," Nick said. "I felt they might be, I don't know, cleansing. Then the PTSD took hold and all of a sudden I wasn't crying anymore. I just stopped."

"I don't think that's good."

"I guess. As devastated and grief-stricken as I was, I don't think I even felt sad."

"Just empty."

"That's right. I can't believe you said that. Just empty. It's an almost indescribable feeling. Umberto used to say that as long as I could cry, there was hope. More than anyone else, including my therapist, he was upset when I stopped. At some point he also told me that he hadn't cried a single time since his discharge from the hospital after the explosion. He went from being the best soldier I've ever known—a man who ran back instead of running away, and risked his life to keep me from being blown to bits—to being an aimless alcoholic. He didn't have any physical wounds like I did, so they refused to consider his PTSD reason enough for a Purple Heart."

"I'm so sorry."

"Thanks, I can tell you are, and that really means something to me."

"Then he disappeared."

"Then he disappeared," Nick echoed, shrugging helplessly.

"Listen, Nick," she said. "I want to help you find Umberto. Meeting you, and thinking about the strangeness of all those comic books Belle wrote on, makes me believe there has to be a connection. Somehow or other, her path and Umberto's had to have crossed. And if getting through to this Manny Ferris will move you closer to finding Umberto, then I want to help you with that as well. I've got ten years as a psych nurse that says I can help there."

"I'd love the help," Nick said, wondering if he should have delivered the words more forcefully.

"You told me that Manny Ferris had an almost violent reaction to one of the photographs of Umberto."

"Not almost violent. He went berserk. It was nothing special—just a photo of me and Umberto standing by the RV. There was at least one other of Umberto and me. But Ferris took one look at that picture, heaved a jar at me, and bolted."

"Do you think I could see the photos?"

Nick retrieved the envelope from one of the drawers in the galley and passed it across. Now, instead of her eyes, he became fixated on her hands—smooth, pale skin, nails not too long, with a clear coating except for the ends, which were quarter moons of white polish. He studied the movement of her long, delicate fingers as she went from photo to photo.

"Umberto has a very kind face," she said.

*He would love yours*, Nick thought.

"That's the photo," he said, "the one that set Ferris off."

Jillian appraised it with the concentration of one used to examining art.

"I self-published a book of my photos of the great buildings and monuments of D.C. Gave it to friends for Christmas. The shots of the Lincoln were my favorites."

"I'd love to see it."

"You may get your chance," she said, this time lighting up the galley with her smile. "I wonder . . ."

"What?"

"Maybe it wasn't the clinic or you or

Umberto that upset Ferris so. Maybe it was the setting—the Lincoln itself."

"How could we ever prove that?"

"Well, how about we do a little photo shoot of our own. Interested?"

# CHAPTER 20

Nick paced along the crowded walkway in front of the Lincoln Memorial waiting for Jillian to arrive. The afternoon sky was crisp and bright, with only a few passing clouds to block out the three o'clock sun. If Jillian's analysis of the photograph was accurate, it was around this time, four years ago, that Junie snapped the picture of Nick and Umberto that sent Manny Ferris running for the exit door.

It was after three that morning before Jillian had left the RV. By then, Junie was asleep in the back examining room, and

Nick was entangled in a mesh of bewildering feelings surrounding the intense, engaging new arrival in his life. It was Jillian who came up with the idea to take photographs from every conceivable angle around the Lincoln Memorial, then observe Manny's reaction to each. Maybe there was something to her theory that it wasn't who was in the picture that so upset the Marine, but what.

To be certain they did not confuse Manny any more than he already appeared to be, Jillian wanted to get the time of their shoot as close as possible to the actual hour the photograph had been taken, in case time of day factored into his intense reaction.

It took some careful study of the photograph's light and shadow for Jillian to determine the hour. Nick was astounded by her ability to deduce information from a single picture, right down to her figuring out that it was also taken in the springtime, based solely on the clothes worn by pedestrians in the background. He was certain if she had chosen a career in radiology, she would have been a star.

Jillian spotted Nick and called out to him as she hurried over. The last time Nick had experienced anything remotely close to a crush, he and Sarah had just met and were going out on their first date. Now, it was Jillian who had invaded his thoughts. They were supposed to meet by the stone bench, but Nick was too anxious to sit and wait. He tried to attribute his nervous energy to a desire to solve the Manny Ferris mystery, but he knew better.

"Hey you," she said, "are you ready to be my assistant?"

"You look professional."

*And stunningly beautiful*, Nick wanted to add, but fought the urge.

"I thought we were meeting at the bench," she said. "I was waiting for you there."

"I guess I got antsy," Nick said. "Figured I'd start scouting potential shots."

"Well, I would have brought my Nikon D300 and wide-angle lens, but then I remembered I'm a nurse and about two grand short of being able to afford one, so you'll have to settle for my Canon Rebel XT. It's a little like a beagle next to an Irish setter, but they're both pedigrees."

"Hey, for all I know about photography, you could have pulled out a shoe box and told me we're doing this with a pinhole camera. Consider me your loyal assistant, ready and willing to serve."

"Is that a promise?"

There it was again. That flirtatious blink of her eyes and infectious smile that seemed to add ten degrees to an already warm spring afternoon.

"We better get started," he said. "We've got a lot of pictures to take and not a lot of sun left."

They finished the shoot in just under two hours. Jillian had stashed a portable printer in her camera bag, so they were able to print out twenty or so quality shots, representing every conceivable vantage point. The pictures from the east exterior captured the monolithic temple columns, palatial staircase, and expansive cause-way. A few shots were from the temple in-terior, as well as one of Lincoln himself.

"So, if it's the Lincoln shot that sets Manny off, does that just tell us he's states' rights and not an abolitionist?" Nick asked with a wry grin.

"Either that or he's scared of statues."

"That would make him staurophobic," Nick replied.

"Now, how did I know that you'd provide

that information?" Jillian asked, punching him teasingly on the shoulder. "I feel like I've been set up."

It was childish, he knew, but Nick beamed inwardly at having impressed Jillian with his knowledge of phobias, the subject of a psychology term paper in college. What else could he impress her with, he wondered. But as quickly as that thought arrived, it left. This woman just wasn't the type.

They continued sorting through the photographs, picking the very best shots to print from the hundreds stored in the camera. There was a picture of the Washington Monument across the Reflecting Pool, taken from the very spot where Dr. Martin Luther King, Jr., delivered his "I Have a Dream" speech. Another captured the north wall of the Washington Monument through the Lincoln Memorial's towering side portico. There were a couple shots of the back of the memorial as well, including one from the walkway along Parkway Drive Northwest and another rear shot taken from the bike path across the Potomac, which ran parallel to the George Washington Memorial Parkway.

"Looks like we're ready to go," Jillian said,

zipping up her tripod bag after they printed the final shot. "Are you sure Manny will be at the club?"

"Manny Ferris seemed as much a fixture in that bathroom as . . . the fixtures in that bathroom," Nick said. "He'll be there. I'm sure of it."

# CHAPTER 21

By the time they arrived at Lucky Bill Pearl's, the April sun had long ago set. A cool night wind chilled their skin. The two descended the dimly lit carpeted staircase with Jillian leading the way. Nick kept a few paces back, wanting to see if the bouncer who had pinned him up against the wall was again working the door. As luck would have it, it was another bald gorilla, although he was equally adorned in ink.

Maybe because the weekend was approaching, the club was more crowded this time than last. Nick watched with amusement as Jillian took in the scene. Her mouth hung just a little agape as she stared in bewilderment at the arcing bar, the high-backed chairs lining the edge of the stage, the brass poles, and the women— spectacular-looking by almost anyone's measure.

"You guys do this for fun?" Jillian asked, leaning in close and speaking directly into Nick's ear so she could be heard over the techno music blaring in the background. Nick enjoyed the sensation of her lips against his skin and wished the music were even louder and her question a little longer.

"I'm going to go find Manny. Do you think you can handle it here until I get back?"

"Sometime soon you've gotta come and see where I work," Jillian said.

Nick waited until Jillian was settled at the bar before making his way over to the men's room. When he glanced back, a heavyset man in a light blue suit was sitting down next to Jillian and starting his rap. Jillian waved to Nick, assuring him with her eyes that she had the situation well in hand.

It wasn't until Nick had pushed against the swashbuckling cavalier on the restroom door and called out Manny's name that he realized Jillian had the prints they had made.

"Manny?" he called out again. The orange marble countertop was dry and the toiletries were still in neat rows on top. Leaning over, Nick scanned underneath the stall doors, but they were all empty.

On his way over to the box office to check and see if Manny was even scheduled to work that night, Nick spied Jillian seated at the black lacquered bar, flanked by three leering men, each ignoring the girls on the poles as he vied for her attention. As if sensing Nick was watching her, Jillian turned and waved across the club.

*Not to worry,* her playful look said.

Stepping into the dim, carpeted foyer of the stairwell landing, Nick peered into the box office window, but the room was empty.

"Hello," Nick called out. "Is anybody there?"

Then he felt a strong grip on his shoulder. Nick turned.

"Hey, buddy," a surly voice growled, "remember me?"

It was the same bald heavyweight who just yesterday had pressed him against the club wall like an ink stamp while Manny Ferris made his escape.

"How could I forget," Nick replied, more calmly than he was feeling. "Isn't your name Dick?"

The bouncer's massive hands grabbed Nick's shoulders, then spun him around and began shoving him up the stairway.

"When I toss someone out of here, it's permanent. Didn't I make that clear?"

"I'm sorry, I don't speak gorilla. Must not have understood you," Nick said, struggling futilely to hold his position.

"Well, maybe you'll understand this."

With a hard push, he launched Nick into the club's blackened glass front door. Nick crashed into the frame shoulder first, knocking the heavy hinged door open as if it were part of a doll's house, and cracking the glass. With his arms and legs flailing, he spilled out onto the sidewalk, rolling into a somersault as he fell, and continuing to roll until he was off the curb and onto one knee. Then, hoping he didn't show the pain he was feeling in half a dozen places, he forced himself to his feet.

The bouncer, hands on hips, stood glaring at him.

"Look," Nick said, "my friend is still inside. At least let me go down and get her."

"Sorry," the bouncer answered with a toothy smile. "But I don't speak asshole."

Jillian checked her watch and frowned. Nick had left to find Manny Ferris nearly twenty minutes ago. Now she was starting to worry. To make matters worse, the gentlemen crowding her end of the bar were getting restless.

**Where is he?**

With no small effort, she managed to handle the quartet of admirers strutting about her bar stool like peacocks. When they weren't inspecting, they were preening. When they weren't preening, they were jockeying for position. Of course, she acknowledged, this *was* a men's club—*their* men's club. She could deal with matters so long as she didn't run out of small talk and synonyms for no.

One of the men, with sloppy-drunk eyes and a sagging face that could have passed for a Rorschach inkblot test, was becoming a problem.

"So, baby mama, are we going to dance or not?" he slurred.

"I'm sorry, but I'm a customer, not an employee," she answered him, stone-faced.

He turned with a huff and Jillian smiled to herself. Again, she checked her watch. Nick seemed resourceful, but that did not stop her from worrying. Years in nursing had turned concern into a sort of sixth sense that was impossible for her to shut off. Even so, she knew her feelings for Nick were shaped by more than a professional instinct for his well-being. There was an attraction to him she simply could not deny.

"I'll pay you double whatever he offered," a man was proposing, leaning close enough to give Jillian a lungful of Old Spice.

Jillian was readying to rebuke the advance when a tall man, dressed in a black turtleneck and a tailored Brooks Brothers jacket, stepped between them.

"Hey, what gives?" Old Spice snapped. "The lady said she wanted to hang with me, so back off."

"I said no such thing," Jillian shot back.

The two men glared at each other and

Jillian would not have been surprised if they started to growl. The tall man, who had thinning black hair, an aquiline nose, and confident dark eyes, reached inside his blazer, pulled out a toothpick, and slipped it into the corner of his mouth. His narrow face was pocked by acne scars that were ill concealed by his rough five o'clock shadow. The diamond studs pinned on each ear had to be two carats at least.

"Hey, friend," the newcomer said, "why don't you take a hundred Pearl Bucks and go hang with a lady that wants your company."

With his Jersey accent he could have easily passed for one of Tony Soprano's henchmen. He pulled out a roll of fake bills.

"You think you can buy me off with toy money because you're big into jewelry?"

"No. I think I can buy you off because I own this place."

Jillian watched with amusement as Billy Pearl padded the Spice man's sweaty hand with a wad of colorful Pearl Bucks.

"Sorry about that," Pearl said, turning to Jillian. "We love it when women stop by at the club—especially beautiful women."

"Thank you," Jillian said, feeling no threat from the man.

"Our patrons come here and pay a good deal of money to behave like sharks. Sometimes innocent guppies become part of their feeding frenzy. You have my apology."

"No need, but accepted. I'm a very fast swimmer."

"Have you been here before, Miss—?"

"Jillian."

"Miss Jillian. Buy you a drink?"

"Thanks, but you'd better have a lot of Pearl Bucks on you to do that."

"I appreciate the feedback. I'll make sure to tell the boss. I know this sounds like a line, but what's a pretty girl like you doing in a place like this?"

Jillian laughed. She liked Pearl.

"Actually, I'm here with a friend, whom I can't seem to find at the moment. We came in to talk to one of your employees, Manny Ferris. Do you know him?"

Pearl's eyes narrowed and his lips tightened. She was being assessed by him, but for what and why, she did not know.

"Know him? Yeah, I know him," Pearl said finally. "Manny's my cousin. What do you want with him?"

"He's not in any trouble, Billy, if that's what you're wondering."

"Maybe your business with Manny isn't any of my concern, but seeing as he's family, and he's, well, not all there, if you know what I mean, I kinda need to make it my concern."

"I'm a nurse on the psych unit at Shelby Stone. I need his help, is all. We think Manny may have information about a man we're trying to find."

"I promise you, Manny Ferris doesn't have information about anything, at least not information he can get in touch with."

"What does that mean?"

Billy studied her for a time, as if deciding if she should be trusted.

"You're a nurse," Billy said. "Maybe you can help."

"Help with what?"

"What do you know about brainwashing?"

"We studied it in a psych course," Jillian said. "The modern version goes back to the fifties. It involves breaking down a person's sense of self so they can build a new one."

"Manny was a sharp kid, even when he

came back stressed out from war and was drinking all the time. Then he disappeared for a while and one day he showed up here. He looked as if someone had cut up his face and he seemed to me as if he had been brainwashed."

"How sad. What makes you think he was brainwashed?"

"It was like the old Manny was gone, but replaced with nothing. He couldn't tell me where he was, or what he had been doing. Only that he needed a place to stay and something to eat. Drugs? Pain? I don't know who did it or how, but somebody wrecked his mind."

"My friend went to find him in the men's room. I don't think he found him there."

Pearl laughed.

"Manny doesn't have much range. If he isn't in the bathroom, then he's in the basement storeroom sleeping on the job. When you can't rely on your bathroom guy, you're really in trouble."

"He sleeps in the basement?"

"It's not as bad as you'd think. In my more colorful youth, I used to store other stuff besides toilet paper and cups down there. The space had to be comfortable and roomy enough to work in, but also well concealed, if you get my drift."

"Can I see him?" Jillian asked.

Pearl considered the request.

"Well," he said finally, "if you don't mind following me into the men's room, I'd be happy to give you a tour."

"What about my friend Nick? I'm getting a little worried. He hasn't come back."

"I'll check with the guys out front and find out where he is. I'm sure that if he's not in the washroom with Manny, then they're downstairs. Come on, I get a kick out of showing off the room anyway."

Billy Pearl knocked on the men's room door, waited less time than Jillian would have liked, then escorted her inside and made a quick assessment of the situation.

"Okay, so Manny's not here. That means he's downstairs. Here's the deal; I'll give you two hundred Pearl Bucks if you can find the secret door."

"Pearl Bucks. Tell me the truth, Billy, did you plan on naming your money after the writer, or was it a coincidence?"

"Next to the location of the mystery door, that's my biggest secret. But I will tell you that my eighty-nine-year-old mom still has my diploma from James Madison High up on her wall."

"Got it. But what would I do with two hundred Pearl Bucks anyway?"

"Okay, make it three hundred."

Jillian groaned, then began to walk the elegant black-and-white bathroom perimeter, observing that it was hospital clean and blessedly odorless. As for finding a door to some secret chamber, she knew at the outset that she had no chance. Pearl watched with keen interest as she continued to look in all the wrong places. He kept his arms folded tight across his chest and his face etched in a know-it-all grin.

"I give up," Jillian conceded quickly. "I'll have to pass on the Pearl Bucks."

Beaming at his own ingenuity, Pearl marched over to the row of bathroom sinks and wrapped his hand around one of the opaque plastic soap containers.

"Showtime," he announced.

Turning the container clockwise a full 180 degrees, Pearl pulled the stainless steel mount out three inches from the sink backsplash. A spring-held door next to Pearl, camouflaged to look like part of the black-tiled wall, popped open without making a sound. Jillian, who was standing only a few feet away, stepped back in surprise.

"That's amazing," she said.

"We used to have some pretty serious business going on down there."

Pearl eased open the hinged doorway with his fingertips, then flicked on a light switch on the upper wall of the stairwell. Jillian followed him down a short flight of well-built wooden stairs that descended into a dimly lit antechamber with a cement floor. Proceeding cautiously, she had to duck low to avoid colliding with the exposed lightbulb dangling by a dust-covered cord. Through a small alcove she emerged into a much larger storage room. Boxes of paper goods and other bar supplies were neatly stacked on plastic shelving units that lined the jagged stone walls. Abutting the only wall without shelving, Manny Ferris lay sleeping on a thin mattress resting atop a rusted metal bed frame. Jillian was grateful she had been prepared for his disfigurement.

"Hey, sleepyhead," Pearl said with surprising gentleness, "customers are wondering where you at. Did you forget to set an alarm?"

Manny jumped up, rubbing his eyes, mumbling something Jillian could not understand.

"Did you hear it?" Pearl asked. "Did you hear him speak Arabic?"

"What?" Jillian said.

"Arabic. He can barely put two words of English together, but every now and then the poor bastard blurts out sentences in Arabic."

"How do you know?"

"We have a lot of Arab clients. One day, one of them heard him. Said he didn't have much of an accent either."

"Amazing," Jillian said.

"That's one of the reasons I think he was brainwashed. Maybe the Arabs did something to him when he was over in Iraq, fighting. Who knows?"

Manny's eyes were glazed from sleep, but Jillian suspected they would not become more lucent even after he'd been awake for hours. Nick was right, vacant was the best description for Manny Ferris.

**Nick.**

"I'll go find out about your friend," Pearl said, reading her thoughts. "You stay here with my cousin. Don't worry, you're safe."

Pearl hurried up the stairs before she could respond.

"Hello, Manny," Jillian said, keeping her voice intentionally calm and nonthreatening. "I've been looking for you. I wanted to talk to you about some pictures that I took."

Manny gazed at her blankly.

"Got to get to work," he mumbled.

"Of course," Jillian said, walking over to him, "but before you do, I have some pictures I want to show you. They're of the Lincoln Memorial. Do you know that building?"

She could see the color begin to drain from his face. He took several cautious steps backward, pinning himself into a corner.

"No . . . yes . . . no."

"Don't worry, Manny. Nobody is going to hurt you. I just want help knowing why you don't like that building. Can I show you some pictures? They won't hurt you. I promise."

"No! Don't want to help." Manny's voice was hoarse and strained.

Slowly, Jillian reached out and took his hand. He made no attempt to pull away. After a minute his tension began to abate.

"Come," she said. "Sit down here next to me."

A few more seconds and the frightened Marine did as Jillian asked and stared at the photos she had printed earlier that day at the Lincoln Memorial.

"Is there anything about what is in these pictures that upsets you? Think, Manny, it's important."

Nothing.

Jillian began to lose hope, but when she arrived at the pictures taken from the rear of the memorial, Manny's tension returned and he began to shake. She showed him the final shots of the day, taken from the bike path across the Potomac. Manny looked at the first picture and began to sob.

"Please . . . no more . . ."

Jillian felt her pulse quicken as she studied the man.

"It's this shot, isn't it, Manny? This one from across the river. This is a view you remember. Did something happen to you out there?"

"Please . . ."

"Tell me, Manny," she implored, "What was it? What happened to you there?"

Manny Ferris could not or would not

answer. Then the connection between them was broken by footsteps descending the wooden staircase. Billy Pearl appeared, grinning broadly.

"My bouncer, Felix, remembered your friend from the last time he was here and threw him out. He's across the street. Felix says he was a real troublemaker—a pain in the butt. You sure he's a doctor?"

Jillian laughed. "He drives around in a huge RV clinic taking care of poor people."

"Bad Felix. Well, at least that's one mystery solved. Did you get what you needed from Manny?"

"I'm not sure," Jillian replied. "But I think I know where to start looking. Let me check my hospital and see if there are any doctors who might be able to help Manny."

"Thanks. I'd appreciate it. Come back anytime. I'll have Felix bring your friend back in. Drinks are on me."

"Thanks," Jillian said, "but I think he'd be just as happy with a few hundred Pearl Bucks."

# CHAPTER 22

Phillip MacCandliss hated the zoo. It wasn't the notion of captive wild animals he hated, it was the specific place itself— the National Zoo off Connecticut Avenue. He hated the commotion and the bratty children. He hated walking on an unending bed of peanut shells, and the overpriced crap food and cheap souvenirs. But mostly he hated the smell—the odiferous stench of beasts, pissing on straw beds, buzzing with flies. Something about the rank smell reminded him of the majority of the vets who relentlessly harassed his office begging for handouts.

He assumed that his intense distaste for the place went back to the trips he had taken there with Denise and the girls before she had left and poisoned them against him. But it really didn't matter. He hated the place and that was that.

Why his CIA contact had picked the zoo as his meeting point he had no idea. An unfortunate coincidence was his best guess, but by no means his only one. They had ways of knowing things—everything. It was what they did.

Apart from receiving a mysterious iPod, delivered to him via interoffice mail the day after taking the assignment, this meeting was the most spylike thing he'd done. The device came with a single preloaded song, titled simply "Play Me." By listening to that track, MacCandliss learned how to use the iPod as a two-way radio, as well as how to arrange a rendezvous with his contact in the event of trouble. The song vanished from the iPod after one listen. It was very *Mission Impossible*, and Mac-Candliss loved being a part of it all, even if only a peripheral part. Now, though, there was legitimate trouble.

MacCandliss had never had reason to

use the emergency number before. After dialing, he hung up at the sound of a tone and synced the iPod with his computer, as he had been instructed. The sync operation added a new track to the iPod playlist. It wasn't a song, but a computer voice detailing the specific location at the zoo, and the time when his contact would be waiting. He synced the iPod again to erase the track.

His instructions were to proceed into the zoo from the Lot B entrance at precisely eleven o'clock, buy a box of Cracker Jack, and then take Olmsted Walk past the Reptile Discovery Center. At that point, he was to put the iPod headphones on and await additional instructions. Mac-Candliss wondered about the early hour. He had heard that crowds were the friend of the Agency. To his surprise, there were already hordes of people strolling the paved walkways, along with field trips that included what seemed to be every grammar and middle school student within fifty miles of the city.

Coincidence? Doubtful.

This was the first time in over five years that MacCandliss had set foot inside the place. Not coincidentally, it had also been more than five years since he had seen, or even spoken to Melissa, seventeen, and Cassie, now fifteen. La Bitch had made certain of that. Years of bad-mouthing him and accusing him of abuse had the girls acting as if he was a cobra. His only regret now was not having smacked Denise more often when they were married. At least then the girls would have something to get over with their therapists.

Feeling as uncomfortable as if he were trying on new shoes, MacCandliss continued to walk the park. The heat was forecast to be near record high and he wished he had dressed lighter. He saw a boy, about six, standing in front of the glass-enclosed gorilla yard. The child clung to the string of his red balloon with one hand while slurping down a slush he held with the other. The toxic neon blue drink had stained the bottom half of his face. Mac-Candliss had little patience for children—even when his daughters were small. As he neared, the boy ducked under the guard railing and banged on the glass.

"Hi, gorilla!" the boy called out. "Can you say hello?"

The boy's mother, a modestly dressed, somewhat frumpy woman in her late thirties, knelt down beside the youth to encourage her child's exuberance. Mac-Candliss cringed.

"It's not a parrot," he said to the child. "It's an ape and apes don't talk."

The boy spun around, but moved too quickly and accidentally let go of his balloon. MacCandliss watched as the diminishing red dot shrank into the cloudless sky.

*Another reason to hate zoos*, MacCandliss decided. *Balloons.*

"That wasn't very nice," the boy's mother snapped.

"But it was nevertheless, madam, the truth," he said, handing her a ten. "Good day."

**The truth.**

His job was all about sifting through a dung heap of lies searching for it. How many vets had embellished their psychiatric symptoms just to steal from the taxpayers by way of the government, MacCandliss wondered as he strolled off in victory. What he hated most about his job at the VA were the times when he was forced to be the liars' enabler. It sickened him. What he enjoyed most was blocking PTSD benefit pay and watching how fast a seemingly helpless, hapless vet found sustainable work.

Of course standing up to the PTSD sissies was an unpopular position within the VA, though he knew of other bureaucrats who secretly felt the same way he did. Support for crooks left the best impression with his superiors, along with the highest probability for promotion. The key was doing things by the book . . . but precisely by the book. As long as the denial of benefits appeared to fit within regulatory guidelines, the claims administrator who paid out the least was the one who got the most.

But the call from Jericho, now years ago, had shown him that there were possible shortcuts if a man were willing to take some chances, and accepting Jericho's proposal had been a no-brainer.

Now, for the first time since becoming part of the operation, his future was under attack. There had been a security breach at the Vermont Avenue VA office. He adjusted his iPod headphones.

"Hello?" he said softly. "Anybody there?"

Silence.

He continued along Olmsted Walk, listening for his contact. He wasn't entirely sure what to expect. He was just passing underneath the heavy overhead wires by which the orangutans traversed the road from one cage to another when a man's deep voice spoke to him.

"Look up," the voice said.

MacCandliss did as instructed and immediately spied three hideously ugly orangutans, traveling hand over hairy hand across the O Line from the Think Tank to the Great Ape House on the opposite side of the walkway.

"Beautiful creatures, aren't they," the voice said. "I didn't want you to miss that."

"Where are you?" MacCandliss asked.

"I'm here. That's all you need to know."

"Jericho?"

"Call me that if you wish. Just keep walking. You don't have to speak so loudly. Your iPod was put together by people who know what they're doing. Don't move your lips too much and you'll appear as though you're singing to yourself. Understand?"

*Cloak-and-dagger,* MacCandliss thought.

*These guys love cloak-and-dagger.* He couldn't tell if this was the same man who had initially contacted him on his unlisted home phone, offering him a chance to help his country and his bank account. In exchange for his services, MacCandliss was promised a significant jump in job grade and salary level. A no-brainer. Two days later, he was called into his supervisor's office and informed he'd been promoted.

"Proceed to Lemur Island," the voice said.

"Aren't those the animals that would follow each other anywhere, even off a cliff?"

"That would be a lemming, Mr. Mac-Candliss, and it's a myth that the rodents commit mass suicide. Clearly, you're not much of an animal lover."

"Only if they're grilled medium rare and smothered with onions."

"Very well, Mr. MacCandliss. Assume that I can see you. Stop when you reach Lemur Island and look at the exhibit while we talk. Under no circumstances are you to turn around. Do not try to figure out who or where I am. Is that understood?"

MacCandliss felt a surge of anger. He

was treated like one of them, but only when it suited their purposes. Well, they were anonymous and he was set to take a fall if the security breach wasn't straightened out. All he could do was to follow Jericho's instructions and supply them with some names. Perhaps it was time to up the ante on his services.

When MacCandliss was in position at Lemur Island, the voice again spoke to him through his headset.

"You sent word you needed to speak with us?"

"At the weekly staff meeting at my office, we discussed security measures in the wake of a breach at the Vermont Avenue building."

"I wasn't aware."

"Neither was I. Then I read the official report."

"And?"

"A man—a young black man from what we can tell—using a bogus ID, hacked into the desktop computer of a low-level account specialist, then almost got caught getting away. Computer forensics traced the specific files that had been compromised and included that information in their report. The intruder was looking for Manny Ferris, one of our guys." There was a prolonged silence. "Are you still there?"

"I'm here. Do you know who the person was?"

"No. But I did get a copy of the security tape. It looks like a boy—a teenager—but I don't know who he is. As usual with the stone-age equipment they buy from convenience stores and allocate to the VA, the camera didn't get a clear shot of his face."

"Do you have the tape with you?"

"Of course."

No "nice job" or "great work."

"We have ways of figuring those things out," the voice said. "Now listen carefully. I want you to put the tape in your Cracker Jack box and drop it into the trash receptacle to your left. Then leave the park the way you came in. We'll be in touch."

"That's it?"

"Yes. That's it."

"Look, I'm not comfortable with this anymore. Unlike most everyone in the VA system, the computer forensics people actually know what they're doing. I did a lot of research for you. There are ways to connect me to Ferris."

"I said we'll be in touch."

"That's not enough anymore," MacCandliss snapped, aware of a sudden flush of nervous perspiration. "I want information. I want to know exactly what I'm putting my neck on the line for."

"We promised you promotions and you've gotten them."

"Well, that's not enough anymore. My job security might be shot. If these forensics people keep digging, I may end up in front of a judicial hearing. I want to know what I'm involved in. I don't know how deep this thing goes, but I'm guessing deep enough." MacCandliss could not believe what he was hearing his own voice saying. "Forget the promotions," he went on, "I want cash and I want information, or I'm going to dial forensics' number before they dial mine."

"I . . . see. And what sized . . . bonus do you think would be appropriate?"

"Half a million should cover what I would stand to lose from my pension if this situation blows up and I have to run," MacCandliss replied, the uncertainty now gone from his voice.

"Thank you for bringing these matters

to our attention, Mr. MacCandliss. I understand your position and I will see that your concerns are addressed. Please rest assured that you will be well taken care of."

"I'm deadly serious," MacCandliss said.

"Oh, so are we."

# CHAPTER 23

When his phone rang—the Bach Organ Fugue in G Minor Koller had programmed for that number—he knew Jillian Coates was calling Paul Regis. He answered on the fifth ring, already in character.

"Yes," he said, as his mind traveled back to that day in her condominium, seizing upon the details that made her put so much trust and faith in the insurance investigator.

"Hello, is this Paul?"

"Yes it is," Koller said. "Can I help you?"

"Paul, it's Jillian Coates. You were at my condo last week."

"Jillian, of course." Koller made certain his voice revealed both surprise and delight at her call. "What can I do for you?"

"Well, I was speaking with a friend of mine. Well, not really a friend. We just met actually."

Naturally, she was talking about Dr. Nick Garrity. Koller had followed her to the Helping Hands Mobile Medical Unit, but had tired of waiting for her when an hour passed after she disappeared inside the RV. He had returned to his hotel and done some research on Garrity's operation, and knew enough about the onetime army doctor and his shoestring-budget medical RV to feel certain that the man was hardly a threat.

"So," he said, drumming his fingers on the desk, "does this new friend have anything to do with me?"

"No," Jillian said, her laugh sounding somewhat forced. "I went to see him because . . . because we have some friends in common. In passing, I happened to mention the fire and my persistent suspicion that having my sister being murdered one day and my apartment burning down just a couple of weeks later seems like more than a coincidence. He agreed with me, and promised to speak with a friend of his who is a detective on the Washington police force."

"Do you know this detective's name?"

Koller was bouncing the eraser more rapidly and forcefully.

**Stupid Jericho!**

"I don't know his name," Jillian said, "but I was wondering if you might send me a copy of your report so my friend Nick can take it to him?"

"Of course. Where are you staying?"

Jillian gave him the address of the nursing school dorm, which he had already written down.

"I'm so grateful to you, Paul. Do you expect to be in D.C. any time soon?"

"Not that I know of, but I'll see what I can do."

"I'm still busy trying to find a lead on Belle's murderer, and I've used up most of my vacation time at work, but as soon as things slow down for me, I'll call, okay?"

"That would be terrific," Koller said, wondering why she almost certainly was lying about how she knew Garrity. "Listen, I'll get a copy of the report and get it right off to you tomorrow."

"Thanks, Paul. You're the best."

"No, Jillian Coates, you are."

# CHAPTER 24

"This is easy. How about giving me something really hard to do."

Reggie shifted his gaze between the two computer monitors crammed side-by-side on his makeshift board-and-cinderblock desk, as his fingers deftly worked two keyboards simultaneously. It was hard for Nick to believe that he had known the kid for more than two years, during which Reggie Smith's remarkable intellect and abilities had never been disclosed.

With Jillian's guidance, Manny Ferris had managed to break through whatever had damaged his brain enough to single

out a view of the rear of the Lincoln Memorial as being particularly disturbing to
him. Now, it was crucial to determine precisely where he had been and, at least as
important, why he had been there.

Nick, Jillian, and Junie stood clustered
behind the gangly teen, who was nothing
short of a digital maestro, conducting his
symphony from the comfort of his well-
worn swivel chair with no small flair for
showmanship. Nick was aware of Jillian's
closeness—the pressure of her shoulder
against his, the fresh scent of her hair. He
knew what was happening, but after so
many years, he had trouble believing it.

The photograph that Ferris had selected
provided more than enough information
for Reggie. He began with Google Maps
and brought in some software of his own.
There was an air of tense anticipation as
he worked. In all, after re-creating the trees
lining the Potomac, it took him no more
than three minutes to locate what he said
was the only building from which Manny
Ferris could have a view across the river
to the rear of the Lincoln Memorial.

"Voilà!" the teen announced triumphantly.
"This is it."

With a flourish, he struck one more key and the monitors simultaneously changed their displays to show the same image. Nick and Jillian leaned close to get a better look as Reggie used his mouse to zoom in on the building.

"So explain to me how you figured this out?" Nick asked.

"Basically, I used Google's massive database of images, which can be overlaid with different views like street detail, terrain, trees, even satellite imagery. When I typed the landmark, Lincoln Memorial, into the search field, I was able to use the hybrid map and satellite view to pinpoint buildings on the same latitude. Based on distance, I wrote a custom software program to calculate the number of stories high a building would have to be in order to get that view. That narrowed it down to this building here in Arlington, Virginia. That's all there was to it. Did you follow me?"

"Of course I did," Nick said, his tongue firmly in his cheek. "I am, after all, an M.D."

"I live only a few miles away from there," Jillian said. "I think I know that building."

With another touch of his computer

mouse, Reggie changed views so that instead of looking down on the building from the satellite perspective they could see it from the street level, as if they were looking at it head on.

"Oh, the Web is a beautiful thing," Reggie sang softly, "a beautiful thing, a beautiful thing."

"Amazing," Nick said now. "I used to think I was traveling on the cutting edge of information technology. Now this stuff is like elfin magic to me."

"Nah, you just didn't grow up with it, is all," Jillian said.

"Right. For me Pong was revolutionary."

"Pong?" Reggie asked.

"Never mind," Nick and Jillian answered in unison, exchanging amused glances. Nick could not help but continue to look at her. She was vibrant and at ease, and carried herself with a natural energy and grace. As quick as the urge to take her into his arms came, images of Sarah invaded his thoughts.

*I'm just not ready*, he told himself. Somehow, though, the words seemed more hollow than usual.

"Reggie, can you zoom in any closer?"

Jillian asked. "I think I know what that building is for."

"Right on," Reggie said, again changing the view.

"I do know it. I've ridden my bike past there a bunch of times. It's a medical spa. I think they also do plastic surgery there."

"Plastic surgery," Nick said. "I'll bet Manny was a patient there."

"Hang on. Let me get the address. Then I should be able to look up the business name."

In seconds Reggie had found not only the business name and address, but also the company's Web page.

"Singh Medical Spa and Cosmetic Surgery Center, 167 Andover Avenue, Arlington, Virginia," Nick read. "It says on the Web site the business is owned by the world-famous—that's what it says, world-famous—plastic surgeon Paresh M. Singh."

"Look at his picture," Jillian said. "He's sort of cute. I like the granny glasses."

"So what's next?" Junie asked.

"I could get that nose job you've been telling me I need," Nick suggested, "and then scope the place out."

Junie and Reggie laughed.

"Wait, that might not be such a bad idea," Jillian said. "We do need to get into that building and have a look around. Scheduling some sort of a tour of the place seems like the right thing to do."

Junie nodded.

"And you would get that tour because . . ."

"Because I'm going to have major work done and want to visit several of the best plastic surgery centers before deciding where to have it."

"And your husband, Dr. Deeppockets here, of course wants to accompany you," Junie said.

"Husband?" Nick replied.

"I've always said you're a great catch."

"Very cute," he said. "Thanks for the suggestion."

There was a brief silence before Jillian said, "She does have a point, Doc. If we want to pull this off we really should go in as a team."

"Not just a team, as a couple," Junie corrected. "A rich couple with a husband who wants his trophy wife to get some buffing up. Ninety percent of the women who have plastic surgery don't need it, so that won't be an issue. Don't you think, Reggie?"

She gave a light tap on the leg of Reggie's chair, startling the teenager, who actually jumped a bit.

"Oh yeah," he stammered. "Absolutely. You should definitely be a couple, for sure. But you gotta be the part if you're gonna play the part."

"What are you getting at, Reggie?" Nick asked, shooting the teen a reproachful look.

"I mean you guys better like, you know, be all coupley—kiss and all that to make it real, you know."

"Oh, that's good thinking, Reggie," Junie said, scooping up the baton. "The lad's right. If you two can't convince us you're a couple, you're certainly not going to convince the plastic surgeon that your intentions are real."

Nick glared at Junie, who in turn just smiled and gave him an impish wave of her fingers. Then he glanced over to Jillian, who was shifting her weight from foot to foot with nervous energy. But she also made no attempt to put the suggestions to bed.

"You guys are ridiculous," Nick said. "Just ridiculous. We don't need any practice to—"

Without warning, even to himself, he took Jillian by the waist, bent his knees, and dipped her backward toward the floor, ballroom style. Then he leaned down and kissed her on the lips. For a moment, Jillian's eyes were open wide. Then, slowly, they closed as the kiss gained momentum. Her lips parted just a bit and his opened in response. He slid one hand up her back and supported her head. Her hair felt like silk between his fingers. Two seconds, ten, a minute—Nick would never know how long that kiss lasted. He did know that any sense of self-consciousness vanished in the first instant. With some reluctance, he eased Jillian upright, and with his arm still set around her waist, he turned to Junie.

"There. Was that believable enough for you?" he asked.

"It was for me," Jillian said, brushing her hair from her forehead and regaining her breath.

"Look," Reggie said, with no regard for the subject he was changing, "they have a virtual tour of the building on the Web site. The place seems pretty fancy."

Junie took a close look at the panoramic photomontage of the Singh Center lobby that Reggie had put up on both monitors. It was a massive sparkling white marble foyer, with a working fountain in the center and several gold-framed pieces of art hanging on the walls, including a large portrait of Singh himself.

"Just in case they're watching," Nick said, "we'll probably need to pull up in some sort of high-end auto, certainly not the junker I drive."

"There are rentals," Junie said. "It'll be my treat."

"First, we need to make an appointment," Nick said.

Jillian fished her phone out of her purse and dialed the main number. She put the cell on speaker and brought her finger to her lips to remind the others to remain quiet. A woman answered on the third ring. She had an educated British accent.

"Good afternoon. Thank you for calling the Singh Medical Spa and Cosmetic Surgery Center. This is Daintry Calnan speaking. How may I be of service?"

"Yes, hello. My name is Collins, Mrs. . . . Jefferson Collins," Jillian said. "I'm planning to have some plastic surgery and I'm calling to schedule a tour of your facility and hopefully to arrange to meet Dr. Singh."

"Referring physician?" Daintry asked.

"Oh, a doctor I met at a cocktail party at my friends the Bronsteins'," Jillian replied, now comfortably in touch with her skill at improvisation. "I can't for the life of me remember his name. When I told him what my husband— I mean what *I* wanted, he told me your spa was the only place to go."

"Few would argue with that," the receptionist replied. "We do have availability for a consultation with Dr. Singh in three weeks. That would include a tour of our facility."

"Oh, three weeks is simply too far away for us. I'm afraid that won't do. I was hoping to see your surgical center tomorrow, actually. It's the only time that works for my schedule. I do a great deal of volunteer work at the children's hospital, you know. If not tomorrow, then I'm afraid I'll simply have to look elsewhere."

"As your doctor friend at the Bronsteins'

said, this is the top-of-the-line facility for any sort of plastic surgery. Would you mind my asking what specific procedure you were thinking of having done?"

"Well, several of them," Jillian said.

"Several?"

"Yes. I'm considering some extensive work. I'd rather not discuss it over the phone."

"Mrs. Collins, you are aware that plastic procedures done here usually cost tens of thousands of dollars, none of which is likely to be covered by your insurance? Plus there's a week or so of residence in our very exclusive spa hotel."

"Yes, I'm quite aware of the cost. I would expect nothing less from a facility with your reputation. This is a gift from my husband. He invents software, you know, then builds a company, then sells it, then builds another one. This next sale will be the fifth— no, no, the *sixth* time he's done it."

Silence.

"Um . . . well, then, in that case, hold a moment, please."

Classical music piped out from Jillian's cell phone speaker. She put a finger to her lips again to remind everybody to stay quiet.

Fifteen seconds later, Daintry came back on the line.

"Well, I have some good news," she announced. "It appears we had a schedule cancellation that wasn't in our computer system yet. Tomorrow afternoon will work just fine. Shall we say three?"

"We shall say that," Jillian replied, giving her audience a thumbs-up.

She clicked her cell phone shut after finalizing the tour time and getting specific directions from McLean, Virginia, where she lied about living. The three standing around her looked at one another in stunned disbelief.

"You were incredible," Nick said finally. "Absolutely incredible."

"I was Blanche in our school production of *Streetcar*. Reggie, please write down 'Jillian and Jefferson Collins' so we don't forget our names."

"You can borrow my wedding band," Junie said.

# CHAPTER 25

Franz Koller's mood brightened as soon as the surgeon began to stir. The gamma-hydroxybutyrate, one of the newer of the so-called date-rape drugs, was wearing off. It had been easier than he expected— much easier—to orchestrate her non-kill. The main problem he needed to overcome was that except for her surgical practice and teaching obligations, Dr. Abigail Spielmann lived a virtually monastic existence.

He had followed her for five days and had entered her East Side brownstone three times, each time easily disabling the antiquated security system. He had rigged up microcameras in her second-floor study and her third-floor bedroom, searching for any secret life—any deviance—on which he could build his kill. What he found was a dull woman of fifty, unmarried and, as far as he could tell, asexual. She returned home every evening at about nine, poured a large glass of a high-priced Syrah, and went to her study to write. At ten, having finished the wine, she repaired to her bedroom, read for ten or fifteen minutes—currently an Indira Gandhi biography—and drifted off to sleep. Somewhere in the early morning she awoke briefly, went to the bathroom, and then turned off the bedside light.

Dull. Unbelievably dull.

And soon, dead.

On his second visit, inspecting her kitchen, Koller hit pay dirt. A corked half-filled bottle of the Syrah on the counter, and a bee-sting kit with an epinephrine auto-injector in the refrigerator.

World-famous Abigail Spielmann, the foremost authority on surgery involving cardiac tumors, had an Achilles' heel.

Koller wondered if he had made some sort of error in his calculations of the amount of GHB he had dropped into her wine. The half-life of the magnificent drug was just half an hour. It was a Friday evening, and she wouldn't be discovered until there was nothing in her body left to detect. But by his estimate she should have been lucid an hour ago. Koller was confident the delay would not derail his plans any. The bees in his mason jar were doing just fine.

Spielmann could not sit up, although she was trying now. Koller had lashed his mark's ankles and wrists to the posts of her mahogany bed frame using his beloved Velcro restraints. He had carefully inserted his little red ball into the woman's mouth before she could scream. He found the confusion and fear exploding in her eyes intoxicating.

"Good evening, Doctor," he began. "My name is Koller. Franz Koller. It's a pleasure to meet such a distinguished physician."

Spielmann's attempt to talk, or scream, came out a muted, choked sob.

Once the security system was disabled, handling the lock on her front door was child's play—for a very experienced, creative child. When he first started his research, while seated behind her in the vast hospital cafeteria, Koller slipped her key ring out from her purse, made clay impressions, and dropped it back. Later, using the molds, he created duplicates of the keys from flattened soda cans and used a tension wrench to insert and turn them. He had learned the trick years ago from a locksmith friend, who suggested that bringing a clay impression to a locksmith was asking for a report to the police.

The doctor kept up her struggle against the restraints, valiantly but without success. Koller, dressed in his surgical garb, placed a gloved hand on her shoulder to calm her. Clutched in his other hand was the bee-sting kit he had just taken from her purse. He made certain that she saw it.

"You know what this is, Dr. Spielmann," Koller said in his calmest voice. "The kit, itself, isn't at all frightening. This, however, would be worthy of a scream if you could."

Koller leaned over the side of the bed and retrieved the mason jar containing eight large honeybees. Spielmann's body shook violently. Beads of sweat formed on her brow then dripped into her eyes. Each bee had a white thread tied neatly around its body. The threads dangled down the outside of the mason jar like octopus arms. Holding one thread, Koller opened the top of the jar, extracting one of the bees, then quickly sealed the jar before any others could escape.

"Have you ever seen a man fly a bee before, Dr. Spielmann? A funny little sight, isn't it. It's blessedly simple to do, actually. You place the bee inside a film canister, then freeze it for about ten minutes. The cold knocks the little fella unconscious, allowing its keeper—me—to tie the string around its little body without getting stung myself, though that would only hurt me.

"You, of course, are a different story altogether.

"Without your EpiPen, this guy would kill you."

Spielmann thrashed against her restraints. Koller pulled down on the thread, guiding the buzzing bee hovering above his head onto the exposed skin of Spielmann's right arm.

"I wouldn't struggle much if I were you,"

Koller said. "Might piss him off. And you'd best not scream when I take out that ball. Bad things might happen."

As usual, Koller was careful to avoid her teeth as he plucked the red ball from her mouth. The bee, perhaps tired from its brief flight, walked in a circle on her arm. Abigail's respirations were labored, close to hyperventilation.

"What . . . what . . . do you want?" she breathed.

"I want to talk a moment," Koller said. "But if you try to scream, the ball goes in, followed by the stinger. Understand?"

"Yes," she whispered hoarsely. "What do you want from me? I have money."

"I'm well paid to be here," Koller said. "But thank you anyway. First, I want you to know just how truly impressed I am with you and your accomplishments, Doctor."

Abigail stammered, "I . . . I don't understand. . . ."

"You've pioneered techniques for robotic surgery that I am certain will be a lasting legacy. You're going to be well remembered, Dr. Spielmann. I do hope you know that."

The bee floated off her arm and danced erratically above her head before coming to a rest on the comforter. Spielmann traced the insect's path with frightened eyes as it slowly crawled up her shoulder, inching across her neck then onto her face before taking flight again.

"Please . . . stop . . ."

"See, we have a lot in common, you and I," Koller continued. "Our life is our work. Neither of us has any children. We've never bothered with marriage. No, our passion has been our careers and you've done a marvelous job with yours."

"I'll pay you to leave," Abigail sobbed. Her tears rolled unabated down her cheeks.

"Our work, I guess, is our children. Our labor of love. Isn't it, Doctor? But have you ever stopped to truly appreciate each moment of your day? I mean, when you're cutting out those nasty cardiac tumors with that robot of yours, have you ever asked yourself if this could be the last surgery you'll perform? If you knew it was to be the last, would you treat that procedure any different from the others? Savor each cut and stitch in a way you never had before?"

"Why are you asking me this?" Her voice was weak and shaky. The bee was airborne again. This time it landed on Koller, who didn't even flinch.

"You see, I think about these things," Koller continued. "I constantly ask myself, is this the last time I'll ever do this again? Most parents can't remember the last night they carried their tired little munchkin off to beddy-bye, but sure as sunrise and sunset, that night does come. It's a shame when such a monumental moment passes without proper acknowledgment. I won't let that happen to me."

Koller slipped the ball back into her mouth. Using the thread, he guided the bee onto Spielmann's arm, then pinned the insect onto her flesh with his thumb and index finger. Despite trying to be gentle, he used too much force and crushed the bee before it could sting.

"Dang," Koller said, wiping up the small mess with a tissue. "Good thing I have some backups with me."

Koller retrieved a second bee from the mason jar, marveling a moment at the artful way the thread traced the bee's erratic flight path.

"I mean, I have killed surgeons before—a couple of times, in fact. But I don't know if I'm ever going to be hired to kill another surgeon again," Koller continued. "Think about it, that would mean you would be the last surgeon I ever kill." The assassin paused a moment, clearly deep in thought. "I have to really, really embrace this moment. You can't record these feelings, the smell of your apartment, your fear. But if you believe it might be the very last time you do something, it's best to approach it with deserved reverence. You might not be the last surgeon, but then again, you might."

Koller pulled the string tied around the honeybee until the insect came to a rest on the fleshy anterior triangle of Spielmann's neck. She tried frantically to flick it away by tilting her head and flexing the muscles of her neck, but Koller held the bee in place. He agitated it. The wings were a blur of motion. Its legs marched helplessly as it tried to free itself.

Then, probably fearing for its life, the honeybee stung.

To escape, it tore away part of its abdomen, leaving behind its stinger and deadly venom sac, where the medical examiner would certainly find it. Koller knew the muscles of the sting apparatus continued to pulsate, injecting more venom deeper into Spielmann's skin.

A three-inch swollen welt materialized almost instantaneously on Spielmann's neck. Her eyes were the size of silver dollars. Within seconds, more hivelike bumps started popping up all over her face, arms, and legs. It was what Koller expected would occur in a systemic allergic reaction. Her lips and eyelids began to swell too and it was clear to Koller that the ball in her mouth wasn't helping her breathing any. He waited a few minutes before taking it out. By then her airway had swollen closed, enough to make screaming impossible. Next, he undid her restraints. Then he watched as she rolled off the bed and landed hard on the Oriental rug. She was crawling on her hands and knees in a desperate attempt to get to the stairs leading to her kitchen.

"I wish I was a betting man," Koller said, smiling down at her. "Because I would bet when you get to your refrigerator you won't find your prescription allergy kit there. Then again, maybe you will."

With her strength failing rapidly, Abigail Spielmann reached the head of the stairs. Then she fell, tumbling over and over before coming to rest twenty feet from her gourmet kitchen. Incredibly, she still managed to get to her hands and knees again. Inch by inch, as her body continued to swell and redden, she made it to her refrigerator. Pulling open the door required a Herculean effort. Her eyes were swollen shut now. Her breaths came in sporadic, wheezing fits.

Koller watched unblinking, absorbing her every move. There were no glass jars to crash on the floor and disturb the neighbors. Koller had already removed them and would break a few in a plastic bag to scatter about the kitchen floor before leaving. The only items to spill out in her frantic search for the kit, were those he put within her reach; a head of lettuce, a plastic bottle of ketchup, and two sticks of butter.

Spielmann collapsed face-first onto the cold tile floor, the cool air from the open refrigerator bathing her now lifeless body. Koller placed the prescription allergy kit a foot away.

**Nicely done.**

"Any moment can be our last, dear doctor," he said. "Sadly, this is yours."

# CHAPTER 26

Mr. and Mrs. Jefferson Collins arrived at the Singh Medical Spa and Cosmetic Surgery Center at precisely three. Earlier in the day, Daintry Calnan had called with the news that Dr. Paresh Singh had been called out of town for an emergency consultation. She tried to reschedule their appointment, but Jillian told her that for the time being, it would suffice if they were able to tour the facility.

"It will save us time when we do get to come in and schedule my surgery with Dr. Singh."

The novelty of their plan had worn off

and the reality was sinking in. Despite her theater background, Jillian had never had any talent for lying or deceit. Now, she used mental images of Belle and memories of their last conversation together to keep her focus under some modicum of control.

Nick was at least a seven on the SUD scale: *Starting to freak out, on the edge of some definitely bad feelings. You can maintain control with difficulty.* He had not shared the fact that he had suffered through another bad night. Restlessness, insomnia, nightmares, free-floating anxiety, even leg cramps—the works. Brain chemistry run amok. As usual, there was nothing transpiring in his personal life to correlate with the flare-up—nothing, of course, except the sudden arrival in it of Jillian Coates. As exciting as it was to feel himself falling for a woman, it was also as frightening as his PTSD episodes themselves. How could he ever even consider bringing someone into the bog that was his recurrent mental turmoil? Perhaps when—*if*—they caught up with Umberto. Perhaps then.

The receptionist, Daintry, was posted

by the massive glass doors, watching their approach. She was a statuesque blonde in her early forties, although Jillian had trouble being certain about that fact due, she suspected, to the artistry of the woman's employer. By the time they had exchanged handshakes, the receptionist had obviously sized them up and decided they were the stuff of which patients of the Singh Medical Spa and Cosmetic Surgery Center were made.

The combination lobby and reception area was even more imposing than the Web site had led them to expect. The vast space—nearly all marble—featured an eight-foot-high fountain in the center and huge, original artwork on three walls.

Seated behind a marble counter to one side of the lobby, wearing a dark suit tailored to show off his linebacker's build, was a security guard with a square jaw and a plastic ID around his neck.

"That's a Shelby Stone ID," Jillian whispered to Nick. "I guess this place is directly affiliated with the hospital."

Nick and Jillian were both wondering about Manny and Umberto. At this point, the connection between the two soldiers was tenuous—identical somewhat casual remarks made four years ago by each man regarding their return to the military, and their enrollment in a top-secret covert mission. In addition, Manny was much more of a candidate for plastic surgery than a product of it.

Still, both Nick and Jillian had seen Manny's powerful reaction to the vista they believed he had seen from high up in this building. Looking around at the opulence surrounding them, it was hard to believe either Manny or Umberto ever had anything to do with the place. But now it was time to home in on that possibility.

"So," Daintry said, passing a price list across to Jillian, "I will check once you have given me your insurance, but it is doubtful they will provide coverage for any of our procedures."

"I'm sure that won't be a problem," Jillian said.

"Yes, yes, of course." Daintry passed over a tastefully done brochure and encouraged the Collinses to visit any floors that were available by elevator. "I have a patient coming in for preadmission," she said, "otherwise I would be glad to accompany you."

"Can I please see one of the suites where I might be staying for my recuperation?" Jillian asked.

"The actual suites are locked or occupied, but I'll unlock the sixth floor where some of them are located. Once you're staying here, you'll need a room key to access your floor. I can't imagine you won't be totally pleased with your suite. It will have all the amenities you could ask for, plus a spectacular view of the city. Some very famous Hollywood personalities have stayed there, and they have had nothing but praise for it."

"I would like to see the operating room or rooms," Nick said. "I once had a bad outcome with knee surgery, and I prefer to be as careful as possible around hospitals."

"Our two operating rooms are not in use at this time, but the elevator will take you to the observation balcony one floor above them."

There was something about the receptionist's expression that made Nick uneasy—a look of mistrust, perhaps. Had they already said or done something wrong?

Jillian took his arm as they headed for

the elevator. Her closeness did away with much of the anxiety he was feeling.

The two operating rooms were located underground—floor B-2. The button was at the bottom of a column that went down to B-2 and up through L to 6. A row of five keyholes across the base of the stainless-steel plate confirmed that some of the floors could be closed off or accessed only after being unlocked. The security measures were no surprise. Privacy was the watchword of the rich.

B-1 opened onto the observation balcony above the ORs themselves. Viewed through glass or Plexiglas from the overhead walkway, the rooms were gleaming spaces with state-of-the-art operating microscopes and monitoring equipment, along with screens most likely used to display projections of the befores and afters of noses, jawlines, chins, wattles, eyes, lips, and the like.

Both Nick and Jillian were impressed with the scene below them. It was impossible not to be. If plastic surgery were a religion, the Singh Medical Spa and Cosmetic Surgery Center was the Mother Church.

Jillian turned and headed back to the elevator. Nick was about to follow when he saw movement through the small glass window in the door to the operating room just below him. A moment later, the door opened and in came a tall, thin figure—a woman, it appeared—with a hair cover, surgical mask, maroon scrubs, shoe covers, and latex gloves. Nick pulled back from the edge of the balcony so he was probably out of her line of sight, and watched as she went directly to a floor-to-ceiling steel cabinet against one wall, retrieved a large, sterilized, cellophane-wrapped instrument tray, and quickly made her way back out of the room.

Nick waited a few seconds for her to return and then gave up and followed after Jillian. His thoughts were spinning. The woman might have had something to do with a central equipment supply room, but why would she be coming—rushing was a more appropriate word—into an unoccupied OR, dressed as if she had just left an active OR? And why would she need a sterilized instrument tray if, as Daintry had said, there were no operations taking place that day?

More likely, she was a nurse—possibly a circulating nurse, specially trained to oversee all aspects of patient care and nursing performance during an operation. There was a haste and purposefulness to her movements that suggested she needed to get the tray back to an ongoing procedure.

But there were no surgeons in the building . . . and no operating rooms in use—at least not on this floor.

"The second floor is the gym," Jillian said, studying the brochure as they walked on excessively plush carpeting past the closed mahogany doorways of the offices of Paresh Singh, the nursing supervisor, and the business manager. "And the lap pool is also on two. At the end of this hallway is the family waiting area. Pretty amazing place."

"Pretty amazing," Nick echoed.

He scanned the corridor, noting the security cameras at each end. The medispa, for all of its elegance, gave him the creeps. There was something cold and lifeless about the place. He was anxious to share with Jillian what he had seen in the OR, and the conclusions he had drawn, but he sensed that they hadn't really been alone for a moment.

They took the elevator to the sixth floor. Suites 6A and 6B were locked, but at the end of the corridor was a sitting area enclosed by huge plate-glass windows. The vista was an unobstructed panorama over the treetops to Washington. The view, including the back of the Lincoln Memorial, was spectacular, but hardly unexpected. They had seen something almost identical on Reggie's computer screen.

Nick's jaw was clenched.

He felt almost certain that Daintry Calnan had lied to them when she said there were only two operating rooms and no surgery going on. He wanted more than anything to get down to level B-2 and see if there were other operating rooms, and if one or more of them were in use. More likely, judging by the size of the two operatories they saw, there was a B-3 floor, probably accessed by one of the key slots in the elevator. Of course, he thought, there also had to be a stairway down from B-2. Maybe he could find it somehow.

The image of the broad-shouldered se-

curity guard, plus the plethora of monitoring cameras they had passed during their
tour, argued for restraint. Any unusual
movement in the building would be noticed immediately. Bad idea.

"Can you imagine either of our two
friends basking in this place?" Jillian asked.

Nick wanted to warn her to say as little
as possible, but she seemed to have picked
up on his concern, and conveyed that fact
to him with her eyes.

"Only as our guests," he replied.

"Can you think of anything else we
should be looking for, darling?"

"Just our car."

The security guard in the lobby looked
as if he hadn't budged since their arrival.
Daintry appeared to be expecting them.

"Quite a place," Nick said.

"I'm pleased you like it."

Jillian took the woman's hand. "All we
need to do is meet the doctor and plan the
surgery," she said.

Daintry seemed pleased.

Once at the car in the rear parking lot,
Nick stood beside his door, and then asked
Jillian to join him and gaze back at the
medi-spa.

"What's the deal?" she asked.

"The deal is that this is a bad place."

"Daintry Calnan is certainly a bit on the chilly side, I'll give you that."

"More like an iceberg. But there's more. She's also a liar—either a liar or the most uninformed receptionist imaginable. I'll tell you about what I saw in the OR when we're on the way home, but suffice it to say that I believe Dr. Paresh Singh is not only in the building, but performing surgery at this very minute."

"Performing where?"

"When we're away from here we can speculate. First, take a look at the place. Gaze at it lovingly."

"Okay. I'm doing lovingly."

"How many floors do you remember from the elevator, not counting the basement ones?"

"Seven, counting the lobby."

"Okay, now count up starting from L. Quickly, though. I'm certain the Dragon Lady is watching, and I don't want her to suspect what we're doing."

"One, two, three, four, five, six, seven, eight, nine. But—"

"Exactly. I counted on the way in. I'm

quirky about numbers. There are two floors that no one, not even the elevator, wants to acknowledge even exist. Let's talk on the way home, Mrs. Collins."

"I don't think I want to trust this place with my body," Mrs. Collins replied.

# CHAPTER 27

The psychiatric wing of Shelby Stone Memorial Hospital was overcrowded and understaffed, which for Jillian meant it was business as usual. She was halfway through a grueling twelve-hour shift, the second in as many days. Still, for her, work had always been a refuge, and getting outside of herself, taking on the challenge of caring for the sick, the sad, and the confused had almost always given her strength. Since Belle's death, it seemed that she needed work and her patients more than ever.

This had been an especially challenging afternoon. Beds on the psych unit, and throughout the hospital, for that matter, were filled. The interns and residents on the ER were nearing the end of their training year, and were shipping patients up to the wards with minimal workups. Jillian's feet had begun swelling beyond what her white canvas work shoes could comfortably contain. And now she had been assigned a new admission for whom there would not be a bed available for several hours, if that. A somnolent, jaundiced, alcoholic man, probably in his sixties, he should have been admitted to a medical floor. His right eye was discolored and swollen almost shut. Diagnosis: *Acute and chronic alcohol intoxication. Possible impending delirium tremens.*

*Typical.* The diagnosis of alcoholism of any kind would not have gotten the fellow past the managed care gatekeepers and off the ER, but "impending DTs" would, despite the fact that the condition only occurred *after* cessation of drinking. Technically, every active drinker had impending DTs. Now, instead of offering him privacy, Jillian had no choice but to treat the poor guy in the hallway. It was not that Shelby

Stone was a bad hospital. The nursing service had won many awards and national acclaim. It was more that the sprawling institution was just unwieldy much of the time, and the patient population was so ill.

She had taken the man's vital signs and was in the midst of changing his IV bag when Nick, wearing jeans, sneakers, and a plaid Western shirt, appeared at her side. He reminded her of Trapper John, M.D., from *M\*A\*S\*H*, with his bushy reddish brown hair that seemed extra wild today. Actually, she acknowledged, she liked that look. A lot.

"Hey you," Jillian said, "this is a fun surprise."

"We brought the RV in early to pick up some supplies and have it serviced at a place that does it for free."

"Sign me and my Honda up."

Nick nodded down at her patient, lying quietly on his hospital gurney. Jillian had pushed the rolling bed up against the wall so at least they weren't blocking foot traffic.

"I always believed that if there were no alcohol, there would hardly be any hospitals," Nick said. "I haven't worked inpatient for a while, but I'm guessing triage to the hallway isn't exactly HIPAA compliant."

"It's not exactly Joint Commission sanctioned either. But we had our JCAHO certification approved last month, so I think we're all safe to behave badly for another year. What brings you to paradise?"

**I haven't stopped thinking about you since we met, that's what.**

"That bizarre tour we took of the medispa just won't clear out of my head," Nick said instead. "I'm just not sure what our next move should be."

"It's been haunting me, too. Between Manny Ferris's freak-out, Daintry getting her signals crossed about the whereabouts of the surgeons, those mysterious unaccounted-for two floors, and the nurse showing up in the deserted operating room, I think there is cause for concern. Besides, Daintry just seems like someone with secrets."

Nick was paying attention, but he was also reflexively checking the battered man's pulse at the wrist and neck, then pulling open his lids and examining his eyes with a penlight he had plucked from Jillian's breast pocket. Next he gently palpated his belly. Finally, he glanced at the plastic ID bracelet on his wrist and bent close to his ear.

"Ray, it's Dr. Nick Garrity. Can you hear me? Open your eyes if you can hear me." He put some uncomfortable pressure on Ray's breastbone with the knuckle of one index finger. "Ray? Come on, Ray, open your eyes. Jillian, have you or any of the docs examined him yet?"

"I assume they looked at him down-stairs. Maybe not as carefully as they might have. I heard it's a zoo down there. I was getting ready to go over him when you got here. Something the matter—I mean other than the obvious?"

"Dunno for certain," Nick said, "but I think his right pupil is slightly larger than the left."

"Subdural?" Jillian asked, referring to the life-threatening collection of blood ex-panding between the skull and brain that often followed head trauma.

"A lot of folks have gotten CT scans of their heads for less indication than this," Nick said. "I think he could certainly use one, and I would say sooner rather than later."

"If you're right, Doc, you didn't just drop by to see me, you were sent by a higher power."

"Nonsense. We're a team. The Jefferson Collinses. If a subdural's there, you would have picked it up."

To the hospital's credit, within five minutes of Jillian's call, residents from psych and neurosurgery were on the scene, and ten minutes after that, Ray Goodings was on his way down for a CT scan.

"When this place works, it works," Jillian said, looking up at him with an expression he wanted to capture and bottle for future use. "How about you wait in the lounge if you have time? I have some reporting to do about how poor Ray could have just made it off our service before he was ever really on it."

Thirty minutes later, she entered the lounge, unable to contain her excitement.

"Subdural," she said simply. "Pretty big one, too, according to the psych resident who went down with him. Ray's on the neurosurgery service now. What a man you are. Five minutes in this hospital and you save a patient's life and make a heroine out of one of the nurses. No wonder they call you Dr. Fury."

Mentioning the words sent a shadow across her face.

"Hey, nice going," Nick said, clasping her shoulders and hoping he could soften her thoughts of Belle. "You were connected to that guy. That's what this caregiving stuff is all about. Connection."

Jillian glanced about, then stood on her tiptoes and kissed him gently.

"There's more where that came from," she whispered. "Now, where do you want to start?"

"Well, let's step back some and look at what we already know. We think poor Manny might have some connection to Umberto, based on what McBean told me, and we believe Umberto has some connection to Belle based on the Nick Fury comic books you found in her apartment. We also believe that Manny's reaction to the photographs is a result of his having been a patient at the medi-spa."

"And?"

"Umberto is between Manny and Belle. He's the one linked to each of them."

"So what are you getting at?"

"I think we need to take a close look at

what happened at the medi-spa around the time Umberto and Manny disappeared."

"By that you mean . . ."

"Check out the patient records from four years ago. See if we can learn anything."

"Do you think Umberto was also a patient there?"

"I don't know, but it's worth investigating to see if the timing might be a missing link."

"Four years. Excuse me for saying so, but that's a stretch."

Jillian rose and walked over to the single, narrow window. The panoramic view of Virginia and the Potomac from the seventh floor was breathtaking. She followed a sailboat skimming across diamond ripples. When Belle was a child, the two of them loved to go out together on their family's Sunfish. Then, suddenly, they were orphans, and now, Belle herself was gone. Jillian felt completely adrift. When—if—they found Belle's killer, would it really put an end to the profound emptiness she battled each day? The possibility gave her hope and, at the moment, that hope was all she could really ask for.

Fighting the fullness in her throat, Jillian returned to the table.

"I agree it's worth looking into," she said.

"Okay. I spent a little time on the Internet. The Singh medi-spa is a joint venture between Paresh Singh and your employer, Shelby Stone Memorial Hospital. Remember that badge on the security guard?"

"I do. One of the brochures in the medi-spa lobby said it's been that way since before I started working here ten years ago."

"So, since you're an employee of Shelby Stone Memorial, you should be able to access the electronic medical records for the spa, assuming the two facilities share the data. We can start by looking at medi-spa patients from four years ago and work our way back from there."

"We have a computer near the nurses' station. Let me see what I can do."

Jillian exited the lounge and followed the circular corridor to the nurses' station, where they had recently installed a computer kiosk. She parked herself in front of the kiosk, which was really just a laptop computer locked inside a black metal case, providing employees access to various

applications including shift and medication schedules, room assignments, and of
course, electronic medical records. The
psych floor was one of the first to get
trained on the new EMR system, affec-
tionately known among the nurses as the
Even More Redundancy application.

Jillian logged in to her account, but
accessing records other than those of her
own patients was clearly an ethical breach.
She launched the EMR application and
clicked on the pull-down menu for "Facility
Name." As Nick had suspected, there was
an entry for the Singh Medical Spa and
Cosmetic Surgery Center, in addition to
other facilities connected to Shelby Stone
Memorial. When she tried to access those
records, however, Jillian got a PERMISSION
DENIED pop-up dialog box, followed by a
loud and somewhat startling error beep.
Logging off quickly, and smiling sheepishly as if she had made an inadvertent
mistake, Jillian returned to the nurses'
lounge.

"I can't get access."

"So much for Plan A," Nick said.

"But wait, there actually is a Plan B.
Let's go down and check on Ray. Then I

can scrounge maybe twenty minutes if the floor is still quiet. We can take a trip down to the records room and see if we can get those files the old-fashioned way."

"There still *is* an old-fashioned way?"

"Last I heard."

Within the hour, the neurosurgery resident told them, Ray Goodings would be in the OR having a drainage procedure. Then the hard work would begin—finding a way to get him off booze and into recovery.

"Turns out shipping him to the psych ward in error may have saved him," Jillian said.

"Maybe this experience will scare him into sobriety, providing he even remembers it."

"Every time an alcoholic stops drinking, there's a possibility that this will be it, and he'll never have to stop again."

"I like the way you think, nurse."

Taking the patient elevator down to sub-basement level two, the pair emerged into a windowless, dank, and eerily quiet hallway.

"Makes Manny Ferris's bedroom seem like a suite at the Four Seasons," Jillian muttered. "This area used to be the very center of the hospital. I have to come down here less and less as the changeover to EMRs progresses, but I really hate it when I do. I think the records room—what's left of it—is the last door on the right."

They proceeded along the dimly lit corridor with their eyes adjusting to the gloom as they went.

"Who on earth works down here?" Nick asked.

"I've only met him a couple times. The Mole, they call him," Jillian said, "but his real name is Mollender. Saul Mollender, I think. I heard that when the whole EMR unit was created and moved to the top two floors of the Corwin Building, he just stayed."

"A dinosaur."

At the corridor's end was a classroom-style door with a frosted-glass window-pane, upon which, painted in peeling letters, were the words RECORD ROOM. Jillian opened the door without bothering to knock. It was a cavernous space, made somewhat claustrophobic by a drop ceiling and row upon row of stacked cardboard storage cartons and tall metal shelving units, a number of which were still packed with color-coded patient records. The only other furniture in the room was a slate-colored fiberboard desk, positioned directly in front of the entrance.

Saul Mollender sat in his chair behind the desk. There was a large stack of records piled neatly on top of the otherwise uncluttered surface. No photos, no pictures on the wall, no calendar. The topmost patient record folder was flipped open and Mollender, cadaverously thin, with graying hair and wire-rimmed glasses, appeared to be entering data from it into his computer.

"Can I help you?" he asked, not bothering to look up from his work. His voice was nasally and his tone unfriendly.

"Yes," Jillian said. "I'm sorry to trouble you, but—"

Mollender cut her off. "No, you're not really sorry. You're here, aren't you? If you were really sorry, you would have acted on that fact and left me alone."

For a moment, Jillian was speechless.

"Well, yes, but what I mean to say is that I'm trying to access some records, but the system won't allow me."

"Name?"

"Of the patient?"

At this Mollender groaned and closed the file he was examining. As he looked up at Jillian, he took off his oval spectacles, the lenses nearly as large as his owl-like eyes.

"*Your* name."

"Jillian. Jillian Coates, R.N. Seventh floor."

Mollender put his glasses back on and keyed her name into his computer.

"What records?"

"The patient?"

Again, Mollender groaned.

"Do you see this stack of paper?" he said. He tapped his index finger repeatedly on the file of folders. His tone seemed even more annoyed than before.

"Yes."

"Well, these aren't going to key themselves into our system, despite what the optical character recognition software people seem to think. So, I don't really have time for your lack of clarity, Ms. Coates. *Facility*. What facility's records are you trying to access?"

"Oh, right. The records are from the

Singh Medical Spa and Cosmetic Surgery Center. It's jointly owned by—"

Mollender cut her off again. "I know what it is. But you can't see them."

"Yes, I know I can't see them, that's why I'm here."

"No, by 'can't see them' I mean not *authorized* to see them. Do not have the proper permission—that kind of can't see them."

"But aren't the records in our system?"

"Well of course they are," he said, as though she had just asked if air was necessary to breathe. "They're in our system assuming they're not more than ten years old, and my dwindling staff and I haven't keyed them in manually yet. Manual data entry, if you didn't already know, is very error prone. Which is why distractions are deadly, or did you not read the sign." He pointed behind them, where a handwritten sign taped to the door read precisely that: DISTRACTIONS ARE DEADLY. "But despite our archaic methods of record management, we have what is known as a firewall. Ever heard of it?"

"Computer security," Nick said.

"Who's the boy genius?" Mollender quipped.

"Dr. Nick Garrity," Jillian said, no longer bothering to disguise her growing irritation. "So what can I do to get access to the files?"

"Well, you could go get a job there. I hear they're hiring."

"Cute," Jillian countered. "Now I understand all those employee-of-the-month awards on that empty wall over there."

She found herself purposely leaning over Mollender's desk, getting into his personal space. The man really was pathetic. She had never hit a person before, but the Mole was inspiring such thoughts.

"What else can we do?" Nick asked.

"It's a firewall, sir," Mollender reiterated. "That means no access unless authorized. So unless in your spare time you or Ms. Nurse here are hobbyist computer hackers, you're S.O.L."

"S.O.L.?" Jillian asked.

"And I thought you medical types were acronym happy. That means shit out of luck."

"You've been very helpful, Mr. Mollender," Nick said.

Jillian shot Nick a confused look. Leaning in close, Nick whispered a single word into Jillian's ear.

"Reggie," he said.

# CHAPTER 28

The follow-up appointment for Mr. and Mrs. Jefferson Collins was on a Friday, three days after their initial tour. They picked up the S-Class Mercedes at the rental agency at the last possible minute, and Nick took on the payment. At four hundred dollars per day, plus tax, he could not allow Junie to rent the car again. But he did admit to Jillian that he was going to miss driving it. Beneath a somber sky, he guided the machine to a butter-smooth stop on the brick driveway in front of the Singh Medical Spa and Cosmetic Surgery Center.

"I'm terrified, Nick. I'm not sure I can pull this off."

Nick himself was so distracted and anxious about what was to ensue at the medi-spa that at first he did not even respond.

"Hello? Are you with me, Nick?"

"I'm here," Nick said, gently patting her knee. "I was just going over the plan in my head. We'll do great. I promise."

Nick put the car in park, but kept the engine idling.

"Check the bag again," he said.

"I did that just before we left."

"We only have one crack at this, Jill. Check it again. I mean, *please* check it again. Dammit, I'm sorry. I am really crazed that we're doing this. I have no idea what will happen to us if we get caught, but I suspect whatever it is will involve the suspension of our licenses to practice. We can back out now if you want."

Jillian thought about it.

"I would give up everything to find Belle's killer. If we're right about the Singh Center somehow being connected to her death, what choice do I really have?"

Nick simply nodded. He felt the same way about Umberto. The debt he owed the man could never truly be repaid. There were times since the nightmare of the explosion when he found himself wishing that Umberto hadn't raced back that morning to save his life. But over the years since his involvement with Junie and Helping Hands and EMDR, those instances had all but vanished. And now there was Jillian. Everything that was good in his life, everything that lay ahead for him, he could link to his friendship with the Dominican. If something sinister had happened to Umberto that could be connected to Paresh Singh, then getting to the bottom of it was worth any risk.

Jillian must have sensed Nick's growing concern because she took hold of his hand and looked deep into his eyes.

"We'll be okay, Doc. Besides, I loaded up on Pepto before we left and then did something I almost never do. I took a beta-blocker to combat all this adrenaline and keep my heart from exploding out of my chest."

Their anxiety was understandable, but their plan had a decent chance of working, despite Junie's objections to it for being overly risky. The entire scheme hinged on getting Jillian alone with the computer in

Paresh Singh's office. For better or worse, almost everything depended on Nick being able to sell a bogus injury, severe enough to frighten Daintry Calnan and have her make her boss come to his aid.

Reggie estimated they would need Jillian to be alone in Singh's office for five minutes. Nick's acting job would be a delicate one. Daintry had to be upset enough to call Singh down to the lobby, but not so frightened that she dialed 911. Nick had no desire to be calling Don Reese begging for another favor. If things came to that, all hope of penetrating Paresh Singh's computer would be lost.

Jillian unzipped her bag and peeked inside. She sifted through the contents, mostly cosmetics, before extracting the small, two-gig USB key Reggie had given her earlier.

"It's here," she announced. "What's on this thing again?"

Nick tried to recall Reggie's exact words, but when he was unable to do so he opted to read them. From his jacket pocket, he pulled out the folded piece of paper containing the instructions the teen had printed out.

"It's called a rootkit," Nick said. "It's used to disguise the fact that a computer system has been compromised. Remember, all you have to do is plug that USB key into the USB port you locate somewhere on the computer and double click the program icon on the screen to launch it."

"Sounds simple enough. Put the key in the port and double click the icon."

"Best laid plans," Nick muttered to himself.

Unfortunately, he spoke loud enough for Jillian to hear and she shot him a distressed, panicky look.

"I'm sorry. I shouldn't have said that. We'll be fine," Nick said, though his words failed to reassure himself.

Nick reread Reggie's detailed instructions one last time. For Jillian's benefit, as well as his own, he tried to summarize the technical aspects of the plan.

"I guess what's on here will install some sort of backdoor access, allowing Reggie to create, as he wrote here, a VPN—a virtual private network tunnel—into the system through a proxy server."

"I don't know anything about VPNs and proxy servers. You really trust him with this, Nick? I mean, most kids his age spend their free time shooting hoops, not hacking computer systems."

"Actually, he does that, too. Pretty well, to tell you the truth. But I trust him. If he says it will work, all we have to do is our part. Okay, then, we're ready. Let's sync our watches."

It was imperative that Jillian know exactly when Nick planned on initiating his diversion. She had to be ready to move the instant Paresh left her alone in his office. Being even a minute off schedule could result in failure . . . or worse.

"You just sell it," Jillian said. "If I get my chance, I'll do my part. That's a promise."

"I've had this injury for years and my knee still really does lock from time to time. I'll sell it, no problem. Are you ready, Mrs. Collins?"

"Ready, Mr. Collins."

Nick eased the Benz around to the spacious, partially filled parking lot at the rear of the building.

"To luck," Nick said, touching her lips with his, but not forcefully enough to disrupt her perfectly applied makeup.

**Delicious.**

He exited the Mercedes and walked around to her door.

"You look beautiful," he said as she stepped out of the car.

Jillian's ruby lips flashed a movie star smile worthy of any red carpet, but Nick could feel the tension in her grasp and see it in her eyes.

The rear of the Singh building was nearly identical to the front. Their figures reflected handsomely in the eleven-foot windows that ran the width of the structure. The security desk was to the right, just on the other side of the glass, but there was no sign of the militialike guard—a definite break, provided the man stayed away.

They felt the sudden drop in temperature from the air-conditioning as they stepped into the resplendent marble foyer.

Daintry, austere behind her marble desk, rose to greet them. "Welcome back, Mr. and Mrs. Collins," she said, taking first Jillian's hand, then Nick's.

Her grip, like everything else about her, seemed rehearsed and controlled.

"Thank you for fitting us in the way you have," Nick replied, reminding himself not to lose sight for a moment of the fact that the woman had things to hide.

As was the case with their previous visit to the spa, it surprised and slightly embarrassed him that acting rich and arrogant wasn't totally unpleasant.

"Dr. Singh is upstairs in his office. He shouldn't be long."

"No security man today?"

"Garth? No, he's here, but at the moment he's off making rounds."

"I'm impressed that you take security so seriously."

*Careful*, Nick warned himself. *You may look the part and even act the part for short spurts, but this woman is used to the real deal. Mess with her and she'll sniff you out as a fraud in a heartbeat.*

Nick took Jillian by the waist and guided her over to a towering work of art that filled half of the rear wall.

"Ready to roll?" he whispered.

She took a deep breath and exhaled slowly. "I confess I'm glad I won't be here to watch."

"You've still got the tough job. But there is one encouraging sign."

"Yeah, what's that?"

"My knee is actually starting to ache."

# CHAPTER 29

Nick and Jillian spent the first ten minutes of their second visit to the medi-spa fidgeting in the sitting area to the right of the receptionist's desk.

"I do apologize for the delay," Daintry said, seeming genuinely concerned. "I'll ring the doctor and see if he'll be much longer. I know that he is very eager to meet you both. I'm sure he'll be here soon."

As if on cue, Nick heard the chime of one of the elevators as it arrived at the lobby level. The polished brass doors glided open and out stepped Paresh Singh. The surgeon, slightly built with a thin mustache

and wire-rimmed spectacles, was singu-
larly unimposing, except for his eyes,
which were piercing and dark, and his
smallish hands, expertly manicured and
featuring a number of rings that were probably worth more than Nick claimed on last
year's tax return. He was no more than
five-foot-seven, and although his jet-black
hair was razor cut, and his suit finely tailored, Nick found it a stretch to believe that
the man was world renowned and the
master of this glass-and-steel palace.

"So," Singh said, after the formalities of
introduction, his accent clipped British with
a modest amount of Indian. "I apologize
for the delay and hope that Daintry has
taken good care of you. She has been
with me since the beginning, and I would
be absolutely lost without her."

"She's been wonderful," Nick said.
"You're lucky to have her."

"Dr. Singh," Daintry said, "as you requested, I've had the solarium prepared for
Mrs. Collins's private meeting."

Nick and Jillian immediately exchanged
sideways glances. They had seen the solarium on their tour—plants, sculptures,
and waterfalls, but no computer. All Nick

could do was shrug. The plus of having the security guard off on rounds had just been trumped by this latest turn. Why had he thought for even a moment that their plan would come off without a hitch? But this hitch was potentially fatal.

Jillian meeting with Singh in some Luddite heaven, devoid of the one thing they needed, was certainly not part of their strategy. If Nick's SUD score had been hovering around a six, it just shot up close to an eight: *Freaking out. The beginning of alienation.*

He calmed himself with thoughts of a Buddhist quote from a college philosophy course that had stuck with him throughout the years: *There are two mistakes one can make on the road to truth—not going all the way, and not starting.* Now, he decided a third mistake needed to be added: Not possessing a backup plan.

Jillian, perhaps sensing his panic, stepped in for the save.

"Well," she said, clearing her throat, "I hope the solarium is equipped with a computer. I wanted to show you pictures of movie stars and models with the sort of features we would like me to have, and I'll need Internet access for that."

"Most understandable," Paresh Singh answered. "We can just convene in my office."

**Bless you, Mrs. Collins.**

"That would be perfect," Nick said. "I'll be waiting here with Daintry. Take as long as you need."

He glanced down at his watch, and, unseen by the others, Jillian checked hers. Precisely ten minutes until showtime.

Jillian air kissed Nick near the cheek and then, spinning around, accompanied Singh toward the elevator.

"I'm so looking forward to getting to know you," Jillian said as they walked away.

Nick mentally ticked off one minute for Singh and Jillian to settle into his office. He had no doubt she would come up with the names for the surgeon to check out online. He knew she was nervous—probably as nervous as he was—but she was handling matters with incredible cool.

Praying that the security guard stayed away just a little longer, he made several laps around the massive center fountain, on occasion making eye contact with Daintry, smiling warmly whenever he did. Anxious husband. Nick checked his watch again. Five minutes down. He vowed to keep from looking too many times.

The succeeding minutes were an eternity. Finally, it was time. Nick made one last stroll around the fountain, until it was directly between him and Daintry. Then he shouted out and dropped to the floor, groaning in pain.

"Are you all right?" Singh's receptionist called out, rushing around to him. "What happened?"

"Oh, dammit. It's my knee. It's locked. It's happened before, but not for a while."

*Do it, but don't overdo it*, he was thinking as she knelt beside him.

He kept his left leg bent at a forty-five degree angle and rolled from side to side.

"What can I do?" Daintry asked, genuinely upset.

"There's loose cartilage floating in my knee," he said, groaning every few words. "A piece has gotten caught."

"You didn't slip or anything?"

Nick nearly smiled, imagining her wondering when she'd have to call their lawyer.

"No, no. I didn't slip. Dammit, but this hurts."

"I'll call nine-one-one."

"No!" Nick responded. "Like I said, this happens every few months. You can do what needs to be done, Daintry. Believe me, you can. Just take my foot and point the toes upward while you gradually turn the whole leg to the right, pulling it toward you as you keep pressure toward the floor."

Daintry paled at the notion, and clearly could not visualize the instructions, which Nick was making as complicated as he dared.

"I . . . don't feel comfortable with things like this," she said.

*Okay*, he decided, *it's time*.

"Dr. Singh can do this. It will only take him a minute." Nick moaned and writhed from side to side for emphasis. "Please hurry and call him. This is killing me. . . . Oh, shit! . . . I'm sorry I cursed, but this really hurts. Man, I should have had it fixed."

"I'll call Dr. Singh."

**Atta girl.**

Nick remained moaning on the floor behind the fountain as she raced back to her desk. He managed a glance at his watch. Jillian had to be ready.

"He'll be right down," Daintry said before she had even returned to him.

Nick imagined Jillian speeding into the sequence that Reggie had taught her. Three minutes to find the USB port, plug in the key, locate the rootkit application, and double click it. From there, the installation process should only take a minute.

To his left, the elevator chimed and, in seconds, Paresh Singh was kneeling at his side.

"I understand your trick knee has locked," he said, totally calm. "Are you in much pain?"

Nick groaned the answer and mumbled something that required repeating. The trick now was not to make things too easy.

"It usually pops back pretty easily," he managed.

"Wouldn't you rather we called nine-one-one?"

Singh didn't say the word "liability," but Nick could tell he was thinking it.

"Please," he begged. "People help me with this all the time. Just pronate my foot and slowly straighten the leg and the cartilage will pop out of the joint space. I guarantee it will work. If it doesn't you can call the rescue squad."

Singh sighed, clearly still weighing his options and the risks. Finally, he stood and took Nick's foot in both his hands. No sooner had he begun to move the leg than Nick cried out and the knee straightened.

"Bless you, Dr. Singh," Nick gasped. "Bless you."

"That was easier than I expected," Singh said. "Can you stand?"

"There's only one way to find out. Give me your arm, please. You're a wizard."

In moments, Nick was on his feet, testing the knee.

At that instant, the elevator chime sounded. It was everything Nick could do to keep from cheering.

"Not the knee again," Jillian said, squeezing his hand twice to say the job was done. "Jeff, we're going to Dr. Gavryck right now. You could have been really hurt."

"But did you and the doctor finish? He did an incredible job unlocking this knee."

"Thank you, Doctor," Jillian said. "The rest of our session, I'm afraid, will have to wait. Daintry, I'll call to reschedule."

"That would be fine," the woman said, still pale. "Call me as soon as you have matters straightened out."

Jillian Collins took her husband by the arm and helped him to the door.

"Don't count on it, Daintry," she whispered.

# CHAPTER 30

"We're in."

To Nick, Reggie's words were all he wanted to hear. The Singh Medical Spa and Cosmetic Surgery Center held secrets, dirty secrets. He felt certain of it. Now, thanks to Jillian, they might have the means to prove it. Much as Nick wished that Buddha's road to the truth was just a stroll down easy street, he had long known better. There was plenty of risk and disappointment, pain, and even death along the way. But now, there was hope.

Once again, Nick, Jillian, and Junie stood behind Reggie and his well-worn swivel chair. It took the teen hacker all of five minutes to access the computer on which Jillian had installed a rootkit. She recognized the desktop configuration now displayed on Reggie's computer monitor as belonging to Paresh Singh.

"That's amazing," she said.

"With the rootkit, we can access that computer from right here," Reggie said, "same as if we were sitting in his office."

"Won't they see us moving the cursor around?" Nick asked.

"Stop your worrying, Dr. G. It's a zombie computer now."

"Oh, that makes me feel so much better. But won't they notice their PC eating the flesh of the living?"

Reggie laughed. "That's a good one."

"Once in a blue moon, I'm funny," Nick said. "But this might not be it. What the heck is a zombie computer?"

"Well, basically, it's just a computer that's been compromised by a hacker, but the owner isn't aware it's being used by anybody else. The only clue they'd have is an unfamiliar IP address appearing in their access logs, provided they even had a reason to look."

"IP address?" Jillian asked.

"It's like a phone number for the Internet," Reggie explained. "It can be traced to a home computer, same as your phone number can be traced to your address, or wherever you're calling from. That's how I got caught the last time, if you want to know the truth. But I think I know what I did wrong."

"Reggie!" Junie said.

"Okay, okay. Just to be safe, though, I'm using a proxy to access the machine so nobody can trace the IP address back here."

"Oh, I feel so much better now that you've explained," Nick said. "Junie, how old did you say this terror on two legs was?"

"Too old and not nearly old enough," she answered, bringing her fist down lovingly on the teen's head.

Jillian leaned in closer.

"So what we're looking at now is actually Dr. Singh's computer desktop?"

"Yup. Thanks to you, we're in control of his machine. For the time being we can access whatever applications Singh can, using his security credentials."

"Amazing," she said again.

"Not really. Computers get way too much credit—usually from people who don't know how they work. Still, you have to know what you want them to do. Do you?"

"I think so," Jillian said. "I didn't have time to see what application they use for their electronic medical records, but seeing how they are a joint venture with my hospital, I'll bet they use the same software we use at work. May I?"

"Be my guest."

Reggie bowed to Jillian and motioned her to his chair. She bowed back respectfully and took his place. A connection had formed between the two of them. Nick had noticed it before.

Jillian went straight to the applications menu.

"I feel like I'm fifteen, sneaking out of the house to see my boyfriend."

Nick, too, felt the thrill of the illicit—the adrenaline coursing through him as they closed in on secrets they were never meant to know.

"Do you see the EMR program?" he asked.

"Yes! This is it. It's the same application

we use at Shelby Stone. Eat your heart out, Mollender."

Having been in one of the first groups trained on the software, Jillian was easily able to navigate through the various screens and prompts.

"Okay, from here I can search records by year. I'll start from four years ago until now, yes?"

"Beginning in April. You got it," Nick said.

He crouched low beside her, breathing in the intoxicating scent of the woman who, without his permission, seemed to have set up permanent residence in his thoughts. Jillian worked the application effortlessly.

"Okay, so it looks like the clinic has a database of about twenty thousand patients."

"Is that substantial?" Junie asked.

"Not for a major hospital like Shelby Stone, but for a private practice it certainly is. According to this billing summary tab, the medi-spa's gross income last year alone was over twenty-five million."

"I'd call that respectable," Junie said. "Just wait until next year's Helping Hands

fund-raiser. I think Dr. Singh will enjoy getting to know me."

"Fear the Junie," Nick said. "Listen,
guys, we've got to keep moving. It's possible someone could stumble onto the
strange IP number, right, Reggie?"

"Ladies and gentlemen, he *can* be
taught."

"You wait, Smith; the next pass I throw
goes right through your chest. Jill, can you
search by name?"

"Of course."

"How about we start with Manny Ferris
first."

Jillian typed "Manuel Ferris" into the
designated search box. The query returned no records. Subsequent searches
using variations of his name also yielded
no results. The same was true when she
tried "Umberto Vasquez," and even "Belle
Coates."

"Dead end," she sighed.

*Damn*, Nick thought. *Mistakes on the
road to truth . . . Number three, not possessing a backup plan, and number four,
not bringing along hiking boots.*

"We had no right to think we'd hit it on

the first try," he said. "Let's get a look at all those records."

"Um, listen," Reggie said, "it may be hard to detect our IP address, but it isn't impossible. Fifteen or twenty minutes, then we can try another time."

"Got it," Jillian said.

She switched screens and quickly filled in the required fields to generate patient reports from four years ago. The request took only a minute to run and when it did, the system returned a list of more than five thousand entries.

"Looks like every patient that walked through the doors of the place," Junie said. "That's a lot of information. Forget about fifteen or twenty minutes. We could be here for days."

*Damn*, Nick thought again.

The screen displayed one record per row, listed by patient name, ID number, and ICD code. The ICD code, or International Classification of Diseases, Jillian explained, was used by physicians and hospital data entry personnel to label patients' diagnoses such that procedures could be itemized and billed appropriately.

Five thousand entries for one year at the Singh Center.

"Each record is a mouse click away from more detailed information," Jillian said. "Physicians' notes, photographs, X-ray images, plus procedures performed, products used, and amount billed. Every scalpel, every box of gauze pads, every IV bottle. They're all here."

"Incredible," Nick said, not bothering to mask his discouragement at such a vast amount of data on such a vast number of patients.

"Welcome to the wonderful world of electronic medical records," Jillian said.

"Try the first one just so we can get an idea of what things look like."

Without gathering any information on the patient in row one, Jillian clicked on the image tab and opened a photo of the frontal torso view of a naked woman. Reggie caught sight of the picture before she could remove it and quickly leaned in for a better look.

"Darn, but that chick's got some mighty big—!"

"Reggie!" Junie snapped.

"And anyhow," Jillian added, removing

the photo and glaring at the youth with good humor, "she had them reduced. That's this procedure code here."

Nick sensed Jillian's mounting tension as she opened the next record on the list. Her apprehension was understandable, he was thinking. Thanks to Reggie's skill and the vulnerability of the electronic records system, they were committing an almost inexcusable invasion of privacy that would, quite possibly, cost Jillian and Nick their careers should they get caught. For the first time, he began to question his convictions.

**Please, give us something. Anything.**

Jillian merely sighed and began to scroll down the list. Nick did not recognize any of the names or most of the ICD codes as they flowed past. In his medical practice, he never dealt with lifts, reshaping, body contouring, liposuction, or breast work, so the unfamiliarity of the codes was understandable. Then, after a hundred or so patients, one ICD code caught his eye: 929.9. As a trauma surgeon, he knew that code well. *Crushing injury of multiple sites.*

"That one, Jill," he said. "Please click on that one."

The name of the patient was Giuseppe Renzulli. Nick remembered reading something on Paresh Singh's Web site about his world-renowned reputation for tackling difficult reconstructive procedures, specifically shotgun wounds to the face. From what Nick read in the file and observed in the pre-op images, this particular case would have required a mastery beyond compare.

According to the physician notes in Renzulli's record, the 929.9 was elaborated as a shotgun wound to the face. Most impressive were the stunning three-dimensional CT scans, each showing a sea of floating bone fragments and shotgun pellets, sandwiched between a cracked mandible and a remarkably intact frontal bone.

"Oh man, that's gross!" Reggie exclaimed. "That dude dead?"

"According to this, he's very much alive," Nick answered.

He leaned over Jillian's shoulder and read aloud from one of many physician dictations—the conclusion of the admission note by Paresh Singh.

The patient is a twenty-eight-year-old Caucasian male, with massive trauma to the neck and face from a self-inflicted shotgun wound. Definitive reconstruction and repair of nasal, orbital, maxillary, mandibular, and ethmoid fractures feasible, requiring multistaged reconstructive maneuvers. Primary access to fracture sites will be via transcutaneous vertical Lynch incision. 70% of fractures appear to be Type III.

Jillian turned away as he read. It was then Nick realized the man's suicide attempt was another painful reminder of Belle. How could he be so insensitive? He placed a hand on her shoulder. She in turn reached across her body to take his hand in hers. The moment was brief, but the emotions within it were intense.

"How could somebody shoot themselves like that and not die?" Junie asked.

Nick flashed on one such case he had treated in Afghanistan, but before he said anything about it, he turned to Jillian.

"Talking about this okay?" he asked.

"Yeah, it's okay," she said, her tone bittersweet. "Thanks for asking."

"A self-inflicted gunshot wound to the head is almost always fatal," he explained, "that is, assuming the victim puts the gun in his or her mouth or presses it hard against the temple. But when a gun—a shotgun especially—is placed under the chin, the recoil can actually redirect the muzzle, causing massive trauma to the face, but avoiding any vital structures in the brain."

"That's gross," Reggie said.

Nick took the mouse from Jillian and continued reviewing the file.

"For this guy, no doubt, fixing him was a massive undertaking. From these reports it looks as though he went through several multistep reconstructive events, totaling about thirty operations."

"That's not the only total that was massive," Jillian said. "Take a gander at the bill this case generated."

Nick looked at where she was pointing and whistled.

"Half a million dollars for this work alone. No wonder Shelby Stone formed a partnership with these guys. Even if the patient defaults on their share of the bill, the insurance company owes a hefty six-figure payday for Singh, and a percentage of that goes to the mother hospital."

"Well, that does explain how Paresh Singh can afford that marble fountain."

"If they're so well known for this type of work, I wonder how many shotgun injuries they reconstruct in a year?" Nick asked.

"I can tell you," Jillian said. "I'll just look it up by that ICD code."

Jillian entered the numbers, keeping the scan limited to the twelve months beginning the approximate date Umberto disappeared.

"Keywords shotgun . . . and . . . face . . . and there you are."

Four seconds after she hit the Enter key, twenty records were identified.

"Amazing," Nick commented. "Maybe that's what the J. Geils Band meant when they named their album *Blow Your Face Out.*"

"Who's the J. Geils Band?" Reggie asked. "If I ain't heard of them, they must be old."

"With you, anything that wasn't recorded last month is old."

"Twenty cases in that one hospital doesn't surprise me very much," Jillian said. "Between fifty and fifty-five percent of all suicides are caused by guns, but there are over fifteen hundred attempted suicides in the U.S. alone each day."

"That's an incredible number," Junie said.

"Sad, but true," Jillian said.

Nick thought through the math.

"So, if Paresh Singh is world renowned for his ability to reconstruct faces after a shotgun blast," he said, "it's not inconceivable there could be at least a hundred such cases in the U.S. each year—probably more worldwide."

"One-fifth of them sent to the best of the best makes sense to me."

"Let's look at these twenty," Nick said, "but we'd better move quickly. Sooner or later someone's going to catch on to the breach."

Behind them, Reggie kept touching his face, as though trying to visualize how the gunshot wounds Nick described could actually be survivable.

The first five files they reviewed were grisly but also well documented. The skill of Paresh Singh was undeniable, although the residual facial damage in each case was still fairly striking. Nothing in those files

jumped out at them as being out of the ordinary. Something troubled Nick about the
sixth case, though, a patient named Edwin
Scott Price from Plano, Texas.

The majority of suicide attempts with a
firearm were males, thirty to fifty years old.
Edwin Price was forty-five. But although
he fit the profile, there was a feeling Nick
could not shake while he was scanning
the X-ray images, photos, and CT scans
attached to Price's file. Something about
the record was familiar—not possible
given that the electronic chart was one
he'd never seen before, and the patient
one he'd never heard of. The echoing concern nagged at him.

**Why?**

Nick was about to abandon the CT
scans and move on when Reggie leaned
over and exclaimed in his ear. "Dang! That
dude is just as messed up as the first poor
sucker we saw."

"What do you mean?"

"I don't know. I'm good at figuring out
patterns, and those pieces of bone look
almost exactly like that first guy you showed
me."

"That's it!" Nick exclaimed.

"That's what?" Jillian asked.

"Why I've been feeling like Price's record was familiar. Let's go back to that twenty-eight-year-old Caucasian male we looked at first."

"Giuseppe Renzulli?"

"That's the one."

Jillian pulled up Renzulli's file.

"Can we see both side by side?"

She opened a new window and soon had the two patients' three-dimensional CT scans displayed next to each other.

"Well, I'll be . . ." Junie's voice trailed off.

"They're identical," Jillian said.

"Told you," Reggie boasted.

Nick studied both pictures intently, his brow knit.

"I'm not a statistician," he said. "But I'm willing to bet the RV that two identical bone fragment dispersals from a shotgun blast to the face is a statistical impossibility."

"Are the procedures done on the men the same?" Junie asked.

"Doesn't look like it to me," Nick said. "Renzulli had some pretty significant complications that Paresh attributed to his anesthesia and local infection."

"There's something else we're missing," Jillian said. "I can feel it."

Nick went back through Price's and Renzulli's notes and films. The only thing in common between the two records was the CT scan.

"Didn't you just say that these procedures cost hundreds of thousands of dollars in hospital billing?" Junie asked.

Nick's focus was locked on trolling through Price's file, such that he almost missed the question.

"Yeah," he said absently. "Why?"

"Well, take a look here," Junie said, tapping her finger on the screen.

"Hey! Fingers off the monitor," Reggie scolded.

"Well, I'll be . . ." Nick had to blink to make sure he was reading it right. "Jillian, as a joint venture with Shelby Stone, doesn't that mean Singh operates his medical practice himself, but combines his purchases and billing for supplies with Stone?" Nick asked.

"I think so. That way he gets the benefit of Stone's purchase power. He probably sends Stone a percentage of his collections for the procedures he performs."

"Well, according to this, Edwin Scott Price had almost a million dollars of reconstructive work done."

"And? What am I missing?" Jillian asked.

She turned around in the chair to face both the others.

"What you're missing and what Junie just pointed out," Nick said, "is that none of Singh's profits that were shared with Shelby Stone from Edwin Scott Price's million-dollar new face came from an insurance company."

"That would mean Singh didn't want Price's insurance company to even know he was doing the work. Why would that be?"

A devilish smile crossed Nick's face.

"I don't know. But let's give our little implanted rootkit a rest and then when Reggie tells us it's safe, we start looking to find other identical CT scans and take a real close look at Singh's billing practices when it comes to fixing shotgun wounds."

# CHAPTER 31

Franz Koller sat on one of the recently installed benches at Poplar Point and watched the moonlight dance across the Potomac. The plan was for his client to take the bench directly behind his, facing toward the woods, so they could keep their backs to one another as they talked.

The cloak-and-dagger bullshit was cumbersome, Koller thought, but he had done business with the Agency before, and like the golfing gorilla who hit a four-hundred-yard drive and then followed it with a four-hundred-yard putt, this was the way they operated. He knew whom he was dealing with and they knew that he knew, but that made no difference to the way they did things. The only question that remained unanswered for him, and in truth he didn't really care whether he ever knew, was the precise identity of Jericho, the individual or group within the Agency who had the resources and clout to authorize the cancelation of at least six people. And at the going rate for the master of the non-kill, that was some serious clout.

There was a chill in the air, a bit unusual for this time of year, and Koller was glad he had opted for his heavy jacket, not only for warmth, but for concealing his favorite direct-kill weapon—a Ruger bull-barrel .22 with an integrally suppressed silencer. The gun provided him with an emergency escape option, and given that this meeting breached several protocols he lived by, he considered the precaution a wise one.

Koller wasn't bothered by the meeting place so much as he was by the time. Late at night, in a public park, any passing patrolman worth the tin on his badge would be wise to question any bench sitter.

**I just want to ask you to be very care-**

**ful, sir. Muggers like to hang out here late at night. . . .**

Koller grinned at the notion. For a time, he closed his eyes and indulged himself, imagining what it might be like to have a mugger actually approach him here. The direct kill his mind created was swift and silent—one hand up, through the flesh of the throat, and fully around the larynx. After the initial thrust, before death, his imagination allowed him to pluck the would-be assailant's eyes out with his thumbs.

*Somewhat messy, but nicely done*, he decided. *Nicely done, indeed.*

Koller suspected that he was about to meet Jericho the person, or else the head of the organization calling itself by that name. He was curious why this client was so insistent on rendezvousing with him in person. A face-to-face meeting was potentially dangerous for each of them— lethal for one of them if it were Jericho's intention to kill him. But killing him at this point—at any point for that matter—made no sense. It had to be that once again, as was the case when Jericho elected to burn down Jillian Coates's condo, established protocol was about to be broken. Only this time, his client had wisely decided it was easier and safer to ask permission than it was to seek forgiveness.

The killer sensed movement and sound, and slid the Ruger onto his lap. A full minute passed before he actually heard the voices of a man and woman, approaching along the walk to his left. Koller inhaled through his nose and began the process of slowing his pulse. They sounded harmless and intoxicated, but professional killers would. He followed the couple out of the corner of his eye as they emerged from a dense grove and approached along the walk from a hundred feet away. At the same time, he scanned to his right. *Nothing.* If the couple were good enough to fool him, it was going to be a hell of a fight.

He buried his pistol beneath his jacket.

"Hey, there, buddy. How're you doing?" the man said.

He was an absolute house, six five, two-eighty or more, and if he had anything less than a 0.2 blood alcohol level, he deserved an Oscar. The girl on his arm was petite and quiet.

"Have a good one," Koller said, still on

red alert, but now for anyone whose presence the couple might have masked.

"You betcha," the bear said.

He hiccuped, stumbled once, and then proceeded on.

Koller holstered the Ruger and checked his watch. Always arrive late. Another unnecessary CIA gorilla shtick. In exchange for the tax-free million or more they were paying him for each kill, he'd give them five more minutes. The Jericho contract had already brought him millions. With luck this meeting would end up adding to that haul.

From behind him, Koller heard footsteps on the grass. Two people, almost certainly men, one of them, like his previous visitor, quite large. He did not turn around, but again prepared himself for action. If they were pros, they were either clumsy pros or meant him no harm. Jericho and a bodyguard, he decided.

The heavier footsteps stopped fifty feet away. The smaller man continued forward, then sat down on the bench with his back to Koller.

"Thank you for meeting me like this," the arrival said.

*That voice.* Now Koller understood why his client had shown up with security.

"It's my pleasure. Who's the muscle back there?"

"How did you—?"

"Look, you pay me what you do because I'm the best. If you have any other plans aside from a chat, you'll soon regret that."

"Killing me would make quite a story. Perhaps since you're so astute you already know who I am."

"I watch TV," Koller said. "You the head of Jericho?"

"This isn't a quiz show. Form your own opinion about that."

"I'm not wearing a wire."

"I know that already. We scanned you ten minutes ago."

"The drunk and the girl. They're good."

"My whole team is good. That's why we hired you."

"So, let's get down to it, then. We didn't need to meet in person to arrange a job. You already know how that's done."

"There have been some changes. What I need now is to know that I can trust you."

"An ironic request of somebody in my line of work, don't you think?"

Koller began to relax. There was no way the future vice presidential nominee, with his ticket already well ahead in all the polls, would set himself up to be killed. It also went far to explain Jericho. Before his recent selection, Lionel Ramsland had been the deputy director of the CIA.

# CHAPTER 32

For several minutes Lionel Ramsland remained silent. He had already been chosen to join the ticket with John Greenleigh, his party's leading presidential candidate, well in advance of the August nominating convention. Popular and respected defenders of democracy, few expected they would lose.

"I know that we erred with that condo fire," Ramsland said finally.

"Do you remember what I told you about my marks?" Koller asked.

"Refresh me."

"Under no circumstance are clients ever

to engage, tail, touch, or even breathe near anybody associated with a mark without my authorization—and that authorization is something I would simply never grant."

"Okay, you've made yourself clear."

"I had materials well concealed in the place that I hadn't had the opportunity to remove. If the police had found them, it could have gone poorly for me—and you."

"Our mistake."

"And you paid me for that mistake. So?"

"Well, it seems Operation Jericho has a few new and unforeseen stress points. Nothing I'm that worried about, especially with you on our side. But then again, I didn't get to where I am by being passive."

"You know I'm a professional and I always deliver. Customer satisfaction guaranteed or your victim back," Koller said with a chuckle. "Maybe I should have that slogan printed on my business cards."

"Maybe you should."

"Go on, sir."

The man many considered more powerful and decisive than his much younger, more intellectual running mate cleared his throat. Koller noted for the first time the fatigue in his voice.

"I love this country," Ramsland said, "and consider myself a patriot, someone who would do anything in his power to protect her. Anything. It's important to me that I believe you would do the same."

"Country love is your business, not mine."

"The people who have hired you in the past told me I could expect that answer from you."

"Then you shouldn't have brought the subject up."

"As the moving force behind Jericho, I could not in good conscience address our latest concerns without meeting you face-to-face and at least asking."

"Detachment is a valuable asset in my work, but so is loyalty."

"To the country?"

"No, Mr. Ramsland, to my clients."

"I see."

"Why don't you cut the cloak-and-dagger bullshit and come sit next to me?"

Ramsland did as the killer suggested and for a few pregnant moments, the two men locked gazes and sized each other up.

"You're not what I pictured," Ramsland said.

"I try to stay out of the papers. Sweet to think you were fantasizing about me, though."

"My sources told me that you had a—how did they put it—an *eccentric* sense of humor."

"I don't really enjoy being talked about. Go on. I think you should get to the point."

"Ah yes, I was told about your bluntness, too. Okay, let me begin by saying that we have a responsibility, you and I. A great and important responsibility."

"If you say so."

"I can tell a lot about a man by his eyes. But yours tell me nothing."

"That should bring you some degree of comfort," Koller offered. "It means I have no agenda other than the one you pay me to have."

"And if somebody were to pay you more money to have a different agenda?"

The man, closing in on the end of his sixties, close to being a heartbeat from the presidency, was uninspiring. But then, to Koller, most people of stature and power were. Ramsland was a throwback to the days of détente and domino theory back-room politics—a saggy-skinned prune with puffy eyes who overfilled the blue power suit peeking out from underneath his London Fog trench.

It amazed Koller that the balding, silver-haired fool stirred up emotions in anybody other than his mother, let alone a majority of the free world. Koller kept his eyes fixed on the man, and had a brief flash as to what he would look like with his lungs full of sarin. Still, underneath Ramsland's doughy exterior, Koller sensed toughness, and warned himself not to lose sight of that observation. Guys who played chicken with tanks and missiles tended to have balls.

"I might not be a patriot like yourself, but what I am is a professional. A consummate professional with my own set of laws. At the moment, you are protected under those laws. Whatever you have to say here you can say in confidence."

Ramsland took a deep breath and exhaled slowly.

"Okay, Mr. Koller. I know that by torching Jillian Coates's place we violated one of your laws and placed you in some jeopardy. But she had gone on air with some potentially damaging information, and we felt we had to act quickly."

"I know much more about the woman than you do, believe me. All you did was make her more determined than ever to keep investigating things. I've had to start following her to make certain she doesn't make any progress."

"We had intended to follow her, but with what you're costing us, and the small size of our group, we just didn't have the resources."

"What you did was panic."

"Okay, okay. We panicked. But I need to tell you that our concerns about Ms. Coates weren't entirely unjustified."

"Oh?"

"A week or so ago there was a security breach at a downtown VA facility. A kid, a black kid in his early teens, no less, accessed the computer system and started digging around for information about an individual connected to Jericho."

"How is Coates involved?"

"The kid's name is Reggie Smith. He's fourteen. He has a decent-sized rap sheet from his habit of hacking computers. He lives with a foster mother and father in

Baltimore. Living near them is a family friend, a doctor named Garrity."

"Nicholas Garrity. I know, I know."

"Jesus, you *are* good."

"So let me get this straight. A fourteen-year-old kid got information from the VA computers that you couldn't have deleted?"

"Actually, the truth is we couldn't find it. That goes back to what I said about manpower. We don't always have the resources to bypass proper channels."

"Go on."

"So, Garrity. He's in the VA system as having severe PTSD. That's—"

"I know what it is," Koller cut in. "Is Garrity part of Jericho's concerns?"

"Indirectly, yes."

"Is Jillian Coates?"

"She wasn't, but she became a player once she began sniffing around for her sister's killer. That's what led her to Garrity."

"So, you want me to kill them?" Koller offered up their lives with the same emotion he would have used to order a Grand Slam breakfast at Denny's.

"No," Ramsland said, "I've got our people

watching Garrity and his partner, June Wright, and their medical bus. Wright is Reggie Smith's foster mother. There aren't enough of us to follow them all twenty-four seven, but we are keeping an eye on them. Your assignments for Jericho have been geographically arranged to keep the media spotlight away from any pattern in your marks. We can't risk igniting curiosities by having anything happen to Jillian Coates or people close to her, which Garrity has now become."

"If she gets in the way, she's dead," Koller said. "That's what you get for stirring her up."

"Okay, then let us handle Garrity. I'm betting he's a patriot like myself. He'll understand what we're up against here and back off."

"If not?"

"We'll cross that bridge when we come to it."

"Whatever you say. So if it's not Garrity or Coates, why did you bring me out here?"

"The kid has caused one of our people to go squirrelly. The guy's a small cog in our machine, but he's become a weak link."

*I hate mixed metaphors*, Koller thought. *I can't believe you were a big shot in the CIA for all those years, let alone that you're going to be vice president.*

"It will cost you a million two," he said, "an extra fifty if you want the job done quickly."

"Quick as possible."

"Your call. Same rules apply. I can get what information I need about the mark off of eBay."

"Don't you even want to know who it is?"

"In time."

"I'll just give you his name so you can get started."

Koller sighed. "As you wish."

"He's a VA claims processor named MacCandliss. Phillip MacCandliss."

# CHAPTER 33

Nick had never set foot in Lieutenant Detective Don Reese's office before that day. Given the circumstances surrounding their initial meeting, discretion was always an unspoken agreement between them. But when Nick phoned, already en route to the second district's station house, Reese did not bother asking what he needed. Nick's request to meet was reason enough for the detective to rearrange his schedule.

The uniformed officer assigned to reception duty, seated in a closet-sized room behind four inches of Plexiglas, was in her early twenties. After phoning Reese, she instructed Nick and Jillian through the intercom to take seats on the molded plastic chairs lining the foyer.

Tucked securely under Nick's arm was a large manila envelope, thick with confidential records from six different Singh Center patients. Over a one-year period, four years ago, each of them had been treated for a self-inflicted shotgun blast to the face. Examined individually, there was nothing that stood out about any of the cases except for the violence and utter destruction of their trauma. However, beyond the differing names and Social Security numbers, these six cases were identical, right down to the CT scans, cardiograms, and progress notes. In addition, the lists of hundreds of supplies and medications, obtained through Shelby Stone purchasing, were also identical. The likelihood of even two cases having such similarities was probably akin to the odds of winning the Powerball lottery seven or eight times in a row.

Nick and Jillian knew they had stumbled upon something illegal, but they suspected much more was behind the charts than mere larceny—even larceny on a fairly grand scale. Who were these patients and did they have anything to do with Manny or Umberto? Those were questions Nick hoped Don Reese could help answer.

A buzzer sounded to their right and the large steel-reinforced door securing the entrance to the inner sanctum of the precinct station slid open. Reese greeted them with warm, enthusiastic handshakes. He wore a white button-down shirt and red-striped tie, his imposing stature made even more so by the holstered gun tucked beneath his left arm.

"Thanks for taking the time today, Don," Nick said after introducing him to Jillian. "I really appreciate it."

"I gave you permission to tell your friend about us when you told me how special she is to you. Did you?"

"He did," Jillian said, "but my memory's been horrible lately and I already forgot it. I was intending to call you about the fire that destroyed my condo, but I've been waiting until I get the report from the fire investigator for the insurance company."

"Sorry to hear about your place. I'm here for you anytime."

"I appreciate that."

"Like I said in the hospital, Nick, we've got a long way to go before I'll call us even. That goes for your friends, too. Let's talk in my office."

Reese escorted the pair through the high-tech, temperature-controlled dispatch center, pointing out details along the way such as the raised floor, necessary to keep the computer systems from overheating the room. There was also a bank of television monitors, broadcasting a grim version of reality TV—the lives of the prisoners locked in the nearby detention cells.

"The heart and soul of nine-one-one," Reese said, gesturing around the communications center. "Over three hundred thousand calls handled last year alone."

Nick could feel the detective's pride in the force as he explained the dispatch process. Coming here had been the right way to begin. With Reese's help, there was a good chance they'd soon have some idea of just how big a fish they had on the line.

They exited the dispatch center and were directly in front of the door leading to the detention facilities.

"How many are in lockup here?" Jillian asked.

"Like the heart of an enlightened man," Reese replied with a wry grin, "the chambers are full."

Nick was impressed by Jillian's knowledge of police procedures and her familiarity with the jargon. It was knowledge, she had explained, honed over years of dealing with mentally ill patients, whose lives were often inextricably linked to the judicial system. After they had failed to explain the six identical cases, it was Jillian who suggested they use a police database to conduct a more comprehensive investigation. That was when Nick had phoned Reese.

The lieutenant detective's modest office was on a third-floor corner, and so had windows on two walls. The desktop, shelves, and windowsills were filled with framed photos of his children and grandchildren, as well as volumes of forensics and police law. The walls were decorated with various memorabilia highlighting a twenty-five-year career of distinction. A cop's cop.

Nick and Jillian took seats across from Reese, and Nick immediately launched into a detailed explanation of recent events, including their history with Manny Ferris and his possible link to Umberto, as well as their growing suspicions of the Singh Clinic's billing practices following Jillian's installation of a rootkit into Paresh Singh's computer.

"Mother of God, Garrity. Talk about playing fast and loose with the law. You guys make Dillinger look like Little Miss Muffett. I'm beginning to feel the return-favor jar filling up."

"That's fine by me," Nick said. "We can call this the last one. But I tell you, there's some nasty stuff going on here, Don. Take a look at these medical records."

Nick pushed the manila folder across the desk, but Reese was clearly reluctant to review the contents.

"Do you have any idea what a sharp DA could do to us for just having these in the room?"

"Jillian will help decorate our cell."

"Silk flowers," she said.

"I like her," Reese said.

"Join the crowd."

Unable to keep his detective's curiosity in check, Reese softened, unhooked the envelope, and leafed through the printouts. After a few minutes he locked eyes with Nick.

"Enlighten me, Nick. I got a gift B minus in college bio, so most of this medical jargon is like Sanskrit. I'll buy what you said, that we've got a bunch of rubber-stamped records that have never been billed to any insurance company for reimbursement. But what does that mean?"

"It means Paresh Singh is hiding something."

"Such as?"

"Well, that's what we need your help figuring out. The patient IDs on these files are actually Social Security numbers. From what we've been able to learn, if they're not valid numbers, the system won't even allow the patient record to be created. But when we tried to look up these six individuals by their Social Security number, we didn't get anywhere."

Reese leaned back until the two front legs of his worn wooden desk chair lifted off the floor. Then he stared down at his hands, processing.

"The Singh Center would have to bill an insurance company to recoup the cost of labor and supplies, right?" he asked finally.

"That's right," Jillian replied.

"So technically, Singh would be out a lot of cash if he did the work but didn't bill."

"Well, that's what's even more peculiar about it," Nick said. "It looks like they were paid for these jobs. Look, here's the column of charges for each case, and here's the one for receipts. They balance out. Either somebody paid for these operations, or Singh's books have been cooked."

"What are you suggesting? I thought you said the insurance companies weren't billed."

"We took advantage of the rootkit access to take a closer look at their billing and financial records."

"Great," Reese groaned. "Say, did you also get a glimpse of those tiny detention rooms across from our dispatch center?"

"Stick with us, Don," Nick pleaded.

"Okay, but you guys better be ready to treat my ulcer when it erupts."

"We did some quick math on what the average total bill for a shotgun wound to the face would be. It was anywhere between five hundred thousand and a million dollars."

"And?"

Jillian took over for Nick. "And I had some friends at Shelby Stone who work in accounts receivable do some more digging for us. They were able to tell me how much the hospital earned from their share of the Singh medi-spa's net profits from four years ago. If we assume these six procedures here are forgeries that generated no revenue for Paresh Singh, then Shelby Stone's share of the take that year should have been substantially less than in subsequent years."

"But I'm guessing that wasn't the case."

Both Jillian and Nick nodded.

"The profit Shelby Stone made from their joint venture with the Singh Center had to have included revenue from these six bogus procedures. At least our accounting people suggest that was the case."

"But if that was true, then somebody, probably Singh, paid Shelby Stone out of his own pocket because no insurance company reimbursed them for the procedures. Why would they do that?"

"We agree it doesn't make sense," Nick said. "Maybe they were concerned some astute comptroller at Shelby Stone would notice that Singh's supply orders and purchased inventory were significantly out of proportion with what they claimed to have earned in profit."

"Singh buys his supplies from Shelby Stone?" Reese asked.

"Yes. It's part of their joint venture agreement. Singh gets a good price on supplies because Shelby Stone Memorial buys their inventory in larger quantities. In exchange for that perk, and of course patient referrals, Shelby Stone takes a cut of the Singh Center profits."

"But if somebody notices they're buying more supplies than their profits suggest they need . . ."

Reese's voice trailed off as he thought through the significance.

"It might suggest to somebody that Singh was hiding money from Shelby Stone," Nick concluded.

"Interesting theory, but what about proof?"

"We have nothing useful at this point. And we don't want to bag these guys on some money-laundering scheme either. We're looking for Umberto."

"And my sister's killer," Jillian added.

"So you want me to look up these people

by the Social Security number on their medical records to see if I get a hit in our system?"

"You are the police. We're assuming you have access to more resources than we do. Things that a pedestrian Google search might not turn up."

"Supposedly, these patients shot themselves in the face with a shotgun," Jillian said. "You'd figure somebody would have reported the incident to the police."

Reese rose from his chair, laced his fingers together, and stretched his interlocked hands skyward until his knuckles cracked. Then he groaned and took his seat again.

"I try to remind myself to stretch every couple hours. These days, my bones have more creaks than an old mattress. . . . Okay, you convinced me. I agree there is something going on here. I'll run these Social Security numbers through our database. But Nick, what you guys have done, up to and including compromising their computer system, isn't just crossing the line, it's drawing a damn new one. And stealing medical records seems like a shortcut to both of you losing your licenses."

"Then call us even," Nick offered.

Reese just shook him off.

"Nah, I'm famous for my shortcuts. I just don't want to see you get in trouble."

Reese keyed in the patient ID from the first record on the pile. His eyes were focused and intense as he typed.

"Damn . . ."

Reese's voice trailed off as his fingers continued tapping away on the keyboard, searching.

"What is it?"

"I ran this first Social several ways. No matter what, it keeps coming up classified—restricted."

"What does that mean?" Jillian asked.

"Ever since nine-eleven, local police departments have been sharing data with federal law enforcement agencies. That cooperation has helped to nab not only a bunch of would-be terrorists, but your run-of-the-mill crooks as well. These days, if you get a speeding ticket in Orlando or a federal gambling charge in Vegas, I'll see it here." Reese poked his computer monitor for emphasis. "That's how conjoined all these data have become."

Nick thought for a beat before asking, "So, what did that first patient tell you?"

"That you guys are into some deep yogurt, my friend. I've never been restricted before."

"Tough time for a first," Nick said. "What about the others?"

Reese keyed in the next ID. His intense expression returned. Again he shook his head.

"Same thing. Classified. I'm starting to think we need to bring the captain in on this."

"I don't want to put you on the spot, Don, but can you wait? I'm sure you trust the captain not to sit on us, but we're just not ready to chance it. We don't know who is involved or what Paresh Singh is really up to. If we jump the gun, we risk exposing ourselves and perhaps losing the only link we have to Umberto and to Belle's killer. Who do you think could have this sort of clout?"

Reese shook his head in disbelief. "Who do *you* think? FBI? CIA? NSA? One of those agencies that doesn't even bother with initials? You're already in deep, my friend, and I'm not sure when all is said and done, I'll have enough rope to pull you out."

"Maybe they're making new identities. I mean, it *is* a plastic surgery center," Jillian suggested.

Nick appreciated her stepping in and breaking the escalating tension between him and Reese.

"Possible. But I've been able to access personal information about other people in federal witness protection before. Why not these guys?"

"Maybe they're just bigger fish," Nick said. "More difficult to hide."

Reese continued searching the other IDs. Gauging by his expression, Nick figured something about the fifth patient ID might be different from the preceding four.

"Hey, look, this guy here seems to be a real person."

"You got an address?"

"Forget the address, I got a name, a name we all know," Reese exclaimed. "This Social Security number is registered to a Manuel Jimenez Ferris."

"Manny! We were right, Nick."

"Well, put away your party hats, folks. I

looked up this Social when you asked me to search for the guy, but it was a dead end. I couldn't track him after his last address in Richmond, Virginia."

"We met him. He had found his way to his cousin's place in D.C."

"Did you see his ID?"

"No, but that wouldn't have helped much. His face was badly scarred. We had a picture, though, and we're both sure the man we saw working the men's room at Billy Pearl's gentleman's club was him."

"Billy Pearl's," Reese mused. "I know that place. Know *of* it, I should say. So why was your Manny Ferris's face messed up? You think he had plastic surgery?"

"With that result, not by Paresh Singh he didn't."

"Unless Singh never finished the job."

"Or that wasn't the real Manny Ferris."

"I don't know what I think yet. Let's see what this last record shows."

Reese keyed in the patient ID of the sixth record in Nick's stack. A few seconds passed, then Reese's eyes widened and a look of amazement washed over his face.

"Another restricted file?" Nick asked.

The cop shook his head. "Nope. We got ourselves another hit."

"Yeah? What's the patient's real name?"

"According to this database, that Social Security number is registered to Umberto Vasquez. Your missing friend, Nick."

"So why didn't they change his and Ferris's Social Security numbers like all the others?" Nick said, his jaw now tense.

"I think you know the answer," Reese said. "These guys don't leave loose ends. They didn't change the Socials because they didn't need to. My bet is that neither of them were slated to survive."

# CHAPTER 34

Nick knew he was shaking and bathed in sweat. His sheets and T-shirt were soaked. Still, his eyes refused to open. As had happened so many times, with so many different nightmares, release would not come. He was the helpless captive of the terrifying sequences of his dream.

**Sarah. Once again he is kissing Sarah. He can taste her lips, intoxicating and familiar. Her eyes are the same emerald green that had possessed him the first night they met. With her arms around his neck, her body moves against his in a desperate, pleading**

rhythm, crying out for what they both desire.

Suddenly, Sarah pushes herself away, but now, it is Jillian who has been kissing him. Her face glows with an angelic light that grows brighter and brighter still, until Nick can no longer discern her features. But the glow is no longer human—it is a truck barreling toward them through the night. Jillian moves first, shoving Nick aside. He falls hard to the ground. Precious seconds are lost—seconds that he needs to reach her before the grille of the truck does. He scrambles to his feet and charges toward her, but it is too late. The sound of the impact as the vehicle slams into Jillian's body echoes like a thunderclap in Nick's mind.

Flames erupt all around him, and within them he sees the driver's sharp silhouette applauding the carnage. Nick's legs are on fire. The pain of his searing flesh is unlike any he has ever known. The man in the truck laughs at his agony. Through the billowing smoke, with the fire swelling around him, Nick

**sees the driver's face and gasps. It is his own.**

The alarm clock was Nick's savior. He sat bolt upright, staring out his bedroom window at the gray dawn. *Guilt.* That was how his therapist had explained the recurring nightmares. Guilt for Sarah's death. Guilt for the skill he had used to save so many other lives. Guilt that he had helped Zmarai earn a trusted status on the base. Guilt that Umberto, who had saved his life that morning, had surrendered his own life to the bottle, and then vanished.

The recurrent horrors were his punishment for not having done more.

Before this latest variation, it had usually been Sarah who died in his nightmares and Nick the one who drove the truck that killed her. Now Jillian was his victim too. It didn't take a Freudian scholar to work out the significance of that change. He simply wasn't ready to take a woman hostage in a relationship—probably never would be—even a woman as genuine and special as this one.

He was carrying too much baggage. True, Jillian was toting baggage of her own.

No adult could make it this far in life without a goodly load. Perhaps having her entering his nightmare meant they were closing in on some truth. He just needed to find a way to relax and let things happen between them if they were to happen. The Freudian wouldn't have worked up much of a sweat over that one either.

On his feet, Nick shook off the last vestiges of this latest trip to hell, stretched, and headed to the bathroom, reminding himself of Junie's most constant teaching: *Time is nature's way of keeping everything from happening at once.*

The plan for the day was to meet Jillian at Shelby Stone and to try the Mole one more time. Thanks to Don Reese, the stakes were increasing. They had Paresh Singh dead to rights in terms of his counterfeit records, although given the illegality of the way Nick and Jillian had obtained the information, dead to wrongs was probably a more appropriate term.

But they needed more—specifically, the connection between Singh's surgical satellite and the mother hospital. Somehow, Saul Mollender had to be convinced to try to search for medical records pertaining to

Umberto, specifically any from four years ago. Jillian had attempted a search of her own, but was electronically denied access. Without the Mole's help, they were at another dead end.

Nick hooked Second Chance to a short leash and headed to the park. He followed the mile walk with a half hour of intense EMDR work that helped get him from a SUD score of seven down to six. Then he showered and headed into the city.

Jillian met him in the Shelby Stone lobby, dressed in a pair of dark slacks cinched with a broad leather belt below a simple beige silk blouse. He kissed her gently on the cheek when they embraced and held her close a few seconds longer than might have been appropriate given their surroundings.

"Somebody missed me," Jillian whispered in his ear. "I like that."

"I like that you like it."

For the briefest moment, he flashed on the dream and her face, afire in the headlights of the truck.

"You okay?" she asked.

"Fine," he said dismissively. "I'm fine."

It was then that Nick noticed the package

tucked under her arm, wrapped in brown paper with a small white card taped to it.

"Aw, you shouldn't have," he said.

"I didn't. At least not for you." Jillian's smile was enigmatic. "Call it a little Mole softener. I thought I'd try bribing our friend into helping us rather than beating us out of his office with a broom."

"What could possibly accomplish that?"

"You'll see," she answered.

"It seems to me it would help to have a sense of what makes the man tick before we barge in and ask him to stick his neck on the line for us," Nick said in the elevator ride to subbasement level two. "You're the shrink nurse. Any ideas?"

"Well, maybe it's obvious, but my guess is he feels left behind, abandoned, and disrespected after the hospital administration stripped him of his power and influence when the electronic medical records project was completed. He seems bright enough, but his sour personality couldn't have helped him when they made the final decision on the position."

"Sort of a chicken-egg thing," Nick said.

"Exactly. Did he get bypassed because

he's miserable or has he become what he is because of what they did?"

"Probably a little of each. Is there anything we can do about it?"

"Dunno. Empathy and trust are usually good places to start when trying to get through to anyone."

"With a pinch of bribery thrown in."

"Who said surgeons have zero insight?"

"Hey, that's my specialty you're talking about!"

They proceeded down the dimly lit corridor to Saul Mollender's mausoleum: MEDICAL RECORDS.

"I hope you got him new window stencils," Nick said, pointing to the eroded lettering.

"Be brave."

Jillian winked at him and then opened the door. Though their lives had changed dramatically since the last visit here, time stood still in the Mole's world. The man was seated as before, at his neatly kept desk, behind a tall, carefully maintained stack of records. He groaned when he glanced up and saw the visitors.

"Oh goodness," he sighed. "I must remind

myself to be even less hospitable next time. What on earth inspired you two to come back here again?"

Nick saw Jillian's cheeks redden, and remembered her warning him about her hair-trigger temper. Just a few seconds in the man's gloomy office and trust and empathy appeared to have been cast into the industrial shredder beside his desk. Without the Mole noticing, Nick gently wiggled the package Jillian carried. *Trust and empathy . . .*

"Yes," she said, quickly regaining her composure. "Well, since we took up your time and you were so gracious to consider helping us, I wanted to give you a little something in return."

Jillian set the wrapped package down on the desk. The Mole stared at it with a perplexed scowl, as though a bomb squad might now be needed.

Begrudgingly, he unwrapped the package, tearing the paper thoughtlessly and ignoring the card taped to the outside. It was a framed saying, which he lifted up to study.

"Thank you, but I already have one of these," he said, gesturing to the wall behind them.

He turned the frame around and Nick saw for the first time what Jillian had done. Printed in marvelous calligraphy was the mantra of Mollender's bleak operation, DISTRACTIONS ARE DEADLY, done on parchment, matted in black, and tastefully framed. Nick wondered how much of the job Jillian had done herself—most or all, he suspected. Now, it was his turn to fume.

"You know what, Mollender?" he said. "You might not appreciate what Jillian did for you, but you could at least, for a moment, pretend to care and, God forbid, to act civil."

The Mole lowered his oval glasses to the bridge of his nose and peered at Nick—perhaps the record keeper equivalent of rolling up his sleeves for a fight.

"Why should I?" he asked defiantly. "It's obvious she did it only because you want something. If you believed a framed aphorism would make me your friend, then I'm sorry to say you were sadly mistaken."

Mollender set the gift on the corner of his desk, glass side down, and went back to studying a file.

"We need your help, Saul," Nick said.

The record keeper hesitated, leaned

back in his chair, and looked thoughtfully at his visitors.

"What is it you need?"

It was working! The Mole sounded less hostile, even vaguely interested.

"We need to know if a friend of mine was a patient here four years ago," Nick explained. "That simple."

"Oh, is that all? Well, why didn't you just say so?"

"Then you'll help us?" Jillian asked.

"No, of course not. Obviously, you tried and were denied access because that's how the system works. Now you come down here wanting me to violate a rule of my department—hell, of the U.S. government! Listen, Ms. Coates, why don't you take this work of art and hang it where you work so you can remind yourself not to bother me again. Now, good day, ma'am."

"Good day nothing!"

Jillian snatched up the plaque and stormed out of the records room, leaving the door ajar, expecting Nick to follow. Nick, however, stayed where he was. Standing alone in the hallway, she looked back at him incredulously. He held up a finger, silently asking her to give him a minute alone with the man. Her response was to slam the door hard enough to rattle the frosted glass.

Nick let a minute pass before speaking. Mollender did not even acknowledge, let alone question, the surgeon's continued presence.

"Why are you so angry, Saul?" Nick finally asked.

"I'm sorry. I thought you had left."

"I'm guessing it's not because of this job. No, I work with broken people all the time, and I know a shell when I see one—something a person builds around himself to keep from getting hurt. I have one of those shells, Saul. And it's a whopper, too. Hard as diamonds, impenetrable. Do you know why?"

"Do I care?" Mollender shot back.

"Because in the Army, I nearly lost my will to live. I'm still not sure I've gotten it back, but a day at a time, I keep trying."

At that Mollender stopped looking down at his file and actually made eye contact with Nick.

"You served?"

"Captain Nick Garrity, of the 105th Forward Surgical Team, at your service."

Training prevented Nick from saluting the Mole, even though such action might have been considered playful and friendly by a civilian.

"What branch? Where?"

"Fifty-sixth Combat Support Hospital in Forward Operating Base Savannah."

"Afghanistan," the Mole said in a near whisper.

"Yeah. About one hundred kilometers southeast of Khost. I lost my fiancée and all my staff except one in a terrorist attack. Suicide bomber drove his truck into the hospital. I could have been blown to bits if my friend hadn't raced back in front of the truck and pulled me under a steel refrigeration unit. I came home more or less shattered. Gave up my surgical practice to drive around in an RV—a rolling clinic— providing health care to those who can't afford it, and helping vets like myself get their PTSD benefit claims approved. It's been all the medical work I can manage."

"Sad story," Mollender said without cynicism.

Then the Mole did something Nick did not expect. He opened the top drawer of his desk and took out a blue velvet box.

Lifting the lid, he turned the box around and held it up. Nick immediately recognized the medal inside, a small silver star centered within a much larger bronze one. The medal was attached to a broad ribbon with five stripes: two blue, two white, and one red.

"Silver Star," Nick said. "Yours?"

Mollender shook his head.

"My younger brother Andy's. He enlisted at thirty because he believed in what we were doing over there."

Nick immediately understood the significance of Mollender's possessing the medal.

"How'd it happen?" he asked.

"Roadside bomb on his second tour to Iraq," Mollender said, his eyes misting with the memory. "He was a terrific soldier. The medal was for something he did before that day. Andy's life is just a statistic now. Was his sacrifice worth the cost? I have to believe it was. Andy was all about sacrifice."

Nick grabbed a pen and blank piece of paper off the desk and began to write. "Will you help us, Saul?" He passed the note across.

"You asked me that already."

"My friend is a solider. His name is Umberto Vasquez. He was the only other survivor of that suicide bomber. I wrote his Social Security number—his hospital ID—on that piece of paper. My phone number is on it as well. Umberto was all about sacrifice, too. Until that night he was the best soldier I had ever known. My closest friend. After the explosion, he was just a mess." Nick flashed on an early morning soon after he had taken over Helping Hands, when he had searched for Umberto, one of many times, and found him wedged against the stone support beneath a bridge, comatose from booze, filthy, unshaven, and soaked in urine. "He was a basket of nerves and booze," he went on. "PTSD at its worst. One day not too long after that, he disappeared. Said the military wanted him back for a special assignment and just vanished. I think he may have been here in this hospital after he went missing. I need to know what happened to him, Saul. Four years ago. Was he a patient here? What was he treated for? Just think about it, is all I'm asking."

Nick turned and opened the door to leave.

"Hey!" Mollender called, stopping Nick just before he stepped into the corridor. Turning, he saw the man holding up the piece of paper. "Your phone number here—is that a six?"

# CHAPTER 35

"We're going to get them, Nick. I can feel it now."

Jillian clenched her fist for emphasis. The fierceness of her anger, kept fairly dormant for most of the time Nick had known her, was almost palpable.

"That calligraphy was a great idea," he said.

"Thanks. Belle taught me how to do it," she said, her eyes dimming at the mention of her sister's name. "But it was you. Mollender is the key, and you somehow managed to get through to him. I have been so damn frustrated since Belle died that I've been having trouble hanging on to my faith, and that's never been an issue for me. Now, I'm beginning to feel hope. Whoever did this to her, and Umberto, and poor Manny—we're going to get them."

"Hey, easy on the optimism. Mollender didn't promise us anything."

"I know. But you accomplished what seemed impossible—you got through to him."

Nick shook his head.

"He's a sad, bitter guy. It didn't feel all that great to see him have to connect with his pain. Much as the new-agers might disagree with me, I feel like sometimes it's better to keep that stuff packed away."

With a few hours before Jillian was due at work and Nick had to ready the RV for a night of servicing the mean streets of Baltimore, they had driven out to Nick's place in separate cars. The day was warm, and Nick suggested a picnic in the yard with Second Chance, or perhaps in the lush park at the end of the street. Within a short while the idea was forgotten.

As they sat on the living room sofa sipping tea and sorting out the significance of Saul Mollender's change of attitude, both of them were sensing a growing tension—a tension born of the feelings that had been evolving between them, the tension of opportunity and desire. The greyhound had taken to Jillian immediately and now sat beside her, his muzzle resting on her leg.

For a time, neither of them spoke. Then Jillian reached across and covered Nick's hand with hers.

"Would it scare you to death if I asked you to take me to your bedroom?" she said.

"Maybe not to death, exactly, but it might scare me."

"Then I won't ask."

"Okay, let's do that over again. Take two. Second chance. Pretend you just asked if it would scare me to death if you asked me to take you to my room."

"And your reply?"

"If you can pry yourself free from my pooch, I think it's a terrific idea."

"Me, too."

Chance started to follow, then, perhaps thinking better of it, hopped up on the couch and rolled onto his back. Nick held Jillian's hand and led her down the hallway to his bedroom door.

"You sure?" he asked.

She looked up at him and held his gaze with hers. "As sure as I need to be," she said finally.

"Be it ever so humble," he said, guiding her inside.

"I like it. I feel you in here."

The room was spacious and airy, with bookcases covering one wall and two large windows another. Nick's library, neatly arranged, featured huge medical tomes, historical biographies, the complete works of Poe and Shakespeare, and a large array of paperback novels, most of them adventure stories or thrillers. Interspersed throughout were framed photos of his family.

"No photos from your army days?" she asked.

"I have them, but they haven't made it out of the box yet."

"I understand."

Nick sat on his mattress and watched as Jillian scanned the titles in his bookcase.

"I never was a huge reader," she said, pulling out a copy of *Two Years Before the Mast*. "Not like Belle. I always want to be around people or out experiencing nature.

When it gets late, I'm usually so beat that instead of picking up a book, I just conk off."

"If you were subject to recurrent nightmares like most of us with PTSD, you might become more of a reader. Sleep is definitely not our friend."

Jillian scanned the list of SUD scores taped on the wall beside the bed.

"You have the nightmares often?"

"I never used to before the explosion and Sarah's death. Since then it's like the event got branded into my brain. I have variations of the same bad dream almost every night, and so far there's not been a damn thing I can do to keep them from happening. Last night, you were in there."

She sat on the bed beside him, her expression playful.

"Me, in a nightmare," she sighed like a starstruck teen. "Now that's something a girl doesn't hear every day. Tell me about it."

"I don't think so."

She caressed his face, and again looked deeply and seriously into his eyes.

"It's okay to tell me," she said.

"All right, but it wasn't pretty. It started off as a dream, a really nice one actually.

But then it ended with the same truck that killed Sarah hitting you instead, cutting you in two. I'm not always the driver, but last night I was."

If the mention of Sarah's name or the horrific outcome of the nightmare upset Jillian, it did not register in her expression.

"Tell me about the nice part of the dream," she said.

She leaned her body against his. He tingled at the feel of her skin pressed against his own.

"We were kissing," he said.

"Like this?"

She held his face in both her hands. First their lips met, then parted. Their tongues explored with increasing urgency. The feel of her hands caressing the back of his neck and the gentle pull of her fingers through his hair sent shivers through him. Still kissing, she eased him onto his back and nestled in next to him.

"Yes," Nick breathed into her ear. "We were kissing just like that."

Nick had dozed off, perhaps only for a few minutes, when his cell phone startled him awake. Images of their lovemaking refused to leave. He could not believe that it had happened and could not wait for it to happen again. Reaching across Jillian, he answered the phone and set it on speaker.

"Hello, this is Nick Garrity," he said, having to clear his voice after the first word came out as a croak.

"Three years ago, Umberto Vasquez was transported by ambulance from the Singh Medical Spa and Cosmetic Surgery Center to Shelby Stone Memorial."

"Go on," Nick said to Mollender.

"Three years and one month ago to the day, to be exact. Vasquez was brought by a private ambulance, Littleton Ambulance Services, it looks like. I've tried Google, Yahoo, and a couple of other places, but I can't find them, and I've never heard of them."

"I can't thank you enough for doing this, Saul."

"Maybe not. But I will take that gift your friend Ms. Coates was kind enough to make for me—that is if she hasn't incinerated it."

Jillian nodded vigorously and gave Nick a thumbs-up.

"Nope, she still has it. She's an optimist.

You're a good man, Saul Mollender," Nick said.

"Not really. I'm a bit of a dud. I know that. I did it because I believe Andy would have wanted me to. And I trust you. Not really sure why. I guess when you spend your day reading medical records you forget the humanity that goes into those pages. Perhaps you reminded me of that."

It was then Nick realized Jillian had started getting dressed.

"Saul, hold on a second." Pulling the phone up to cover the receiver with his hand, Nick asked, "Where you going?"

"That date. Belle was a nursing student at Shelby Stone on the day Umberto was brought there. I'm going back to the hospital before my shift to see if I can catch up with Nancy Lane at the nursing school. She's been like a mother to each of her students for over twenty years, and she keeps incredible records. There's a chance that she'll be able to figure out where Belle was working that day. I'm certain that's where her path and Umberto's crossed and that's how she knew about Nick Fury."

"Good idea. Saul, sorry, you still there?"

"Yeah, I'm here."

"So, what floor did Umberto go to after he was dropped off at Shelby Stone?"

"Well, that's where it gets really interesting," Mollender said.

"How so?"

"There are no other entries in his record."

"Nothing?"

"Not a word. According to all I've been able to find, Umberto Vasquez was delivered at Shelby Stone Memorial at ten o'clock that morning. Then he just disappeared from our records. It's as if he simply dropped off the face of the earth."

# CHAPTER 36

On the way south, Jillian phoned Nancy Lane, dean of the nursing school at the Shelby Stone Institute of Health Professions. She had seen the woman at Belle's funeral, and then received several concerned calls from her after that.

During the horrible days following the fire in her condo, when it appeared as though Jillian was destined for an extended stay in a Residence Inn or crashed out in a succession of friends' guest rooms, Lane had come through for her as she had in so many situations for so many students. One phone call was all it took to secure a room for Jillian indefinitely in Anne Marie Cosco Hall, the nursing school dorm.

Lane was not in her office when Jillian called, but her secretary felt certain she would be back before leaving for the day. In addition to all her help, the dean was one of the few who did not discount that Belle had been murdered. Hopefully, knowing that Jillian's request to meet pertained to her sister would be enough to keep Lane in her office.

With time to think during the sluggish drive to D.C., Jillian's mind wandered to the beautiful and entirely unexpected afternoon spent in Nick's arms. Her desire to take their relationship to the next level had, she acknowledged, been there almost from the start. He was a beautiful, deeply caring man, with demons that were keeping him somewhat at bay. But she felt ready and anxious to help him drive them from his life. All the two of them needed now was time.

Belle had once likened Jillian's dating life to the Oregon Trail, joking that it had begun along the smooth tracks of the hopes and desires of her admirers, only to become littered along the way with pieces of their broken hearts. If only her sister could be here to meet Nick. Jillian's feelings for him were unlike any she had ever experienced before, and after they had made love, her mind flashed like neon with a giddy, but also panicky thought—*this was it*. Nick Garrity was the one.

Logjammed by the heavy afternoon traffic, Jillian grew increasingly anxious about her chances of catching the dean in. By the time she had parked and trekked from the garage to the office, she had all but given up. She had also given up intellectualizing her feelings for Nick, and was ready to let emotion guide her.

Lane's office door was closed and there was no light spilling out from underneath it. Jillian cursed softly. Thanks to Saul Mollender, they had taken a huge step forward in connecting Belle to Umberto Vasquez, and possibly learning more about why she had been killed. Armed with the bewildering information that Umberto's medical record had him going by ambulance from the Singh Center to Shelby Stone, where his arrival was never documented, Jillian wanted to move as quickly as possible.

Something was very wrong with Singh's clinic, and now it seemed quite possible that something was rotten at Shelby Stone as well.

She made a tentative knock, then sighed with relief when she heard movement from within. Nancy Lane, in a charcoal business suit, embraced her warmly. In her early sixties, the dean had grayed over the years, and with her granny glasses and jovial laugh, reminded some of Santa's wife. But she was a force. She had almost single-handedly built the nursing school into one of the top in the country, and was showing no signs of slowing.

"Thank you for waiting," Jillian said.

"Everything all right in the dorms?"

"Perfect. It seems like lately I'm always thanking you for something, but thank you for that one. Staying here has made a huge difference. The insurance company has come through, so now I'm looking for a new place."

"Take your time, dear. Stay here as long as you need to. So, come into my office, sit down, and let's talk."

"Thank you . . . again."

Jillian followed Lane into her office suite, accepted a cup of tea, and settled in on the sofa beside her.

"So tell me now, what's going on?" the dean asked. "I understand it's about Belle?"

"Yes."

"You know, I think about your sister all the time, Jillian. Nothing about her death makes any sense. I wrote a recommendation for her when she moved to Charlotte, and she called me so excited when she got the ICU job. She was already such a shining star in our profession. Her loss has affected us all deeply."

With effort, Jillian used her anger to help her maintain composure.

"I know that," she said, "which is why I came to see you. Many people admired and loved Belle, but you are one of the few who truly understood and believed in my conviction that she would never ever take her own life."

"I did then and I do today."

"I've formed a friendship with a doctor named Nick Garrity. He runs the medical van that drives around caring for the homeless people around D.C. and Baltimore."

"Yes, of course. I have heard wonderful things about him and the marvelous nurse who works with him."

"Junie Wright. Actually, they are partners in the van."

"They do such good for so many."

"Well, there's a connection between Belle and Nick that I'll tell you about when I have more time. For now suffice it to say that Nick and I might be closing in on finding her killer."

"Oh, my God. Please be careful," Lane said.

"So far we're just feeling our way along, but we're not taking any chances," Jillian replied, smiling inwardly at the recent events in the Singh Center. "We don't have all the facts yet, so we're not ready to make any claims, but Belle's death might be linked to the disappearance of Nick's close friend, a soldier named Umberto Vasquez."

"So, what can I do to help?"

Jillian withdrew a folded piece of paper and handed it over.

"I need to know where Belle might have been on that date."

"Three years ago?"

"She was a senior nursing student back then. I think that date might be very important somehow, but I can't be sure."

"Let me check. Our record keeping for student schedules is a bit haphazard, so this could be tough. I'll start by pulling up her transcript from student services."

Lane crossed the office and settled in at her desk. Jillian took the black spindle-backed chair catty-corner to her. The search did not take long.

"Well, I may have something here," the dean said after no more than two minutes.

Lane motioned for Jillian to look at her computer screen. Seeing Belle's school photo in the upper right corner of her digitized nursing school transcript brought a now familiar mix of sadness and intense anger to her chest. Intuitively, Lane took hold of Jillian's hand.

"Your sister was a beautiful woman," Lane said. "Inside and out. We have all her awards, faculty recommendations, and certifications listed here. She was a standout member of our community, admired by her peers and revered by our faculty."

"Anything on or around that specific date?"

"No, not on the date you gave me, though I thought it reminded me of something. Then I saw this here." Lane pointed to an entry in Belle's transcript. "It was an honor we gave Belle for being one of our top students. She was allowed to observe, as part of her rotation in surgery, the operation for Aleem Syed Mohammad."

Jillian drew a blank on the name, though it sounded familiar.

Sensing her former student's puzzlement, Lane helped her out. "Mohammad was a terrorist—one of the highest ranking we have ever captured. Our troops found him in a cave—somewhere in Pakistan, I think. I don't remember the exact details, but I recall that his men defended him to the death. He was turned over to the CIA and was brought back here."

"Of course. I remember now. Belle told me about what happened. I was away, but she saved me the newspaper articles."

"Exactly. Not long after he was captured, Mohammad became progressively ill, and was found to have a rather large tumor in his heart—quite a rare tumor as I recall, although I'm blocking on the name. He needed major open-heart surgery to remove it. Our hospital was selected for the operation because of our proximity to where he was being held in Virginia. Plus, we've handled this sort of high-profile thing before."

"As I said, I was away at the time. Friends and I were climbing in the Rockies. Belle was the only nursing student in the OR, yes?"

"There was also a medical student."

"She told me the operation, what there was of it, was a nightmare."

"Mohammad was the second-most-wanted terrorist in the world behind Bin Laden himself. Capturing him was quite a feat. I'm glad I don't know what methods were being used to interrogate him, but that all came to a halt when he became ill. A team of experts was assembled from around the country to perform the surgery. Then, as they were transferring Mohammad from the stretcher to the operating table, he had a cardiac arrest. Never made it to the surgery."

"How was Belle chosen to observe the case?"

"It was very last-minute who got picked because we weren't sure right up until the day of the operation if the government folks were going to allow it. As I recall, there was no doubt about choosing her."

Jillian was truly dumbfounded by the news. The day after Umberto disappeared, after he had been delivered by ambulance to Shelby Stone Memorial Hospital, Belle witnessed the operating room death of one of the world's most feared and reviled terrorists. There had to be a connection. But what? And were those events in any way tied to Belle's murder three years later? No matter how she twisted that thought in her mind, Jillian could not see how they could be.

At the moment, though, Umberto Vasquez, Aleem Syed Mohammad, and Dr. Nick Fury were all they had. Despite the lack of an obvious scenario that connected the three, this was going to be exciting news to share with Nick.

"Do you have any idea who else was in the operating room that day?" she asked finally.

"I don't have a clue. I'm sure some of the names are in the man's hospital record. We could check there, or we could see if the case was recorded."

"Recorded?"

"Yes. Did you know about the cameras hooked up in the operating rooms?"

"No, I didn't. Do you record every operation?"

Lane shook her head. "We don't have the resources to do that because each operation has to be edited down to a manageable length and then transferred to DVD for storage. But selected cases—the ones of teaching or legal or historical importance—are recorded now."

"Where do we get the funding for that?"

"As part of a grant—federal, I think. Shelby Stone was one of the first metropolitan hospitals to install video equipment in all twenty-four of our operating rooms. We use the videos in our teaching curriculum, and so do the medical school and residency programs. In addition, I've heard of a couple of malpractice suits that have been squashed because of the recordings."

"Do you think Mohammad's operation was filmed?" Jillian asked.

"Well, I suppose if they're going to record any case, they'd have done that one."

"Then there should be a DVD of his operation archived somewhere," Jillian said.

"I think you're right," Lane said. "We request them by the surgical procedure or even by the surgeon, and the record room transmits it to us or maybe sends a disc over. I could ask one of our instructors how it all works."

"Don't worry about that," Jillian replied. "You've been an amazing help already."

"But how will you find out?"

Jillian flashed on the Mole. "I have someone I can call," she said.

# CHAPTER 37

Phillip MacCandliss knew the Jericho people would come to their senses. Given the level of exposure and risk thrust upon him following the Manny Ferris breach, they had actually gotten off easy. In addition to Vasquez and Ferris, he had delivered three other worthless vets to them over the last four years. The three, like Vasquez and Ferris before them, were near duplicates for the photos Jericho had provided him—seven-out-of-ten-point matches for the facial characteristics they had insisted upon, one of them an eight.

Five hundred thousand for that kind of

judgment, resourcefulness, and loyalty was a small price to pay, especially when he revealed the precautions he had taken to back up his demand for a bonus. Jericho was CIA, and it would have been foolish to make demands of them without some sort of protection. Despite Jericho's reassurances, the hacking of the computer system at the VA had him edgy. If he needed to bolt suddenly, he would need a solid escape plan and the money to make it work.

True, he could not come up with that much incriminating evidence to put in the safe-deposit box he told them about. But they had no way of knowing. True, he had no idea who Jericho was, but he did have the photos and the names of the men he had turned over to them, as well as the reasons for his suspicions that Jericho was a unit within the CIA. A tape of the conversations with his contact would have been nice to have, but assuming it was the CIA, they had ways of telling when they were being recorded. The bottom line was that his Jericho contact seemed impressed enough with the steps he had taken to ensure they didn't mess with him, and that was all that mattered.

Humming an off-key rendition of "God Bless America," MacCandliss maneuvered his dented and rusting Subaru Impreza through D.C.'s downtown stop-and-go afternoon traffic, en route to the designated meeting place, a room at the Crescent Hotel. The car needed a new timing belt and the transmission fluid was leaking, but that didn't matter now—at least it wouldn't in a little while. His first move with the money would be to replace his junker with something sexier—much sexier.

Money was power and he was about to have a lot more of both. A half a million dollars, by his accounting, would net him many thousands more given how he planned to invest it. How he was going to hide this newfound wealth so his ex wouldn't get her grubby paws on any of it was a detail he had yet to work out. But he would.

MacCandliss had been warned that the Crescent was a dump—rooms by the hour. But such a place meant no security cameras. Once inside the seedy hotel lobby, he proceeded to the front desk as per plan. He was carrying an empty duffel bag.

"May I help you?" the attendant asked.

The man behind the dimly lit counter had a cherubic face and a hapless, burnt-out smile.

"I've misplaced my room key."

"Not a problem. Name and room number?"

"Phillip MacCandliss. Room seven-twenty-seven," he replied, citing the room number provided him by his contact. Mac-Candliss then handed the desk attendant his driver's license and, just like that, he had a key to the hotel room that suppos-edly he had already procured. MacCan-dliss chuckled to himself while waiting in the lobby for the elevator to take him up to seven. These guys just couldn't get enough spy shit. It was all a game to them—a big game.

As he marched along the threadbare corridor carpet, he wondered why they bothered going through the missing key bit. Wouldn't it have been just as easy if he made the reservation himself and then checked in to the room before the meeting? The ruse made him only a little curious.

They had their reasons. His expertise was in selecting perfect candidates for Jericho. Theirs was in playing spy games.

There was a DO NOT DISTURB sign around the handle of Room 727. MacCandliss removed it and slipped his electronic key into the slot. *Payday*, he thought. He entered the room, putting the sign back where it had been. The television was on. Probably something connected with the illusion Jericho was creating that he had checked in earlier. The door connecting with the adjoining room was locked. The bathroom door was ajar, and the light was on. Except for half of the stall shower, which was covered by a featureless plastic curtain, he could see no one was there.

"Hello?" he said, tentatively. "Anyone in there?"

Feeling suddenly ill at ease, he flipped on the light. The room was as he had expected—gloomy and tawdry, with frayed curtains and a faded bedspread. It was impossible not to wonder how many sexual engagements had been consummated on the queen-sized bed over the years. He lifted the hem of the spread. The mattress was up on a wooden platform.

With a sigh designed to slow his pounding heart, he rounded the bed and stepped into the bathroom. The toilet and rust-stained sink had to be at least fifty years old, and the tiny institutional hexagonal tiles were probably even older than that.

"Hello?" he said again.

A tidal wave of apprehension swept over him as he grasped the edge of the curtain and jerked it open. The stall was empty except for a black overnight bag sitting on the drain. *The money*, he thought excitedly. *Goddamn game players!*

MacCandliss felt his tension begin to abate, and actually managed a tight smile. Then, as he reached down for the bag, he realized that it was his—name tag and all. Not a replica—his, taken from the hall closet in his apartment.

*Damn them!* Give him the money he had asked for, but make sure he never took them for granted. Good move. He had to hand it to them. A really good move. He hefted the bag up, reentered the bedroom, and gasped.

His heart stopped completely, then decided to beat again.

A man was standing at the foot of the

bed—tall and well built, with a narrow face and dark hair swept back. He was dressed completely in black, wore wire-rimmed glasses, and was carrying a black brief-case.

"God, you scared the shit out of me."

"Sorry for that," the man said. "I knocked, but there was no answer."

"You what? I didn't h—"

The man tossed the briefcase onto the bed.

"Here's your money."

"Then what's in here?"

"What do you think? This *is* a hotel."

"With what I have on you, you guys are real jerks to play a stunt like this. Whoever broke into my apartment and took my stuff out ought to be canned."

"Actually, that was me. Name's Koller."

"Like the toilet," MacCandliss snapped.

"Different spelling," Koller said with an unsettling grin.

MacCandliss opened his bag and pulled out clothes for an overnight stay, toiletries—*his* toiletries—and an inch-thick packet of photographs, secured with a rubber band. He snapped the elastic getting it off and stung his fingers. Cursing, he let the photos—colored snapshots and black-and-white professional jobs, pristine and well-worn—fall out onto the bed. Then he shuffled them around. They were all of children, dozens and dozens of naked boys and girls, from toddler to teen, all races, in all manner of poses and postures and angles, many of them quite unsettling.

"What the—?"

"Not yours?"

"No, they're not fucking mine. I've never been into this sort of thing."

"Oh, my mistake," Koller said, happy to see MacCandliss touch a number of the pictures. "Let me make it up to you."

He snapped open the briefcase and flipped up the lid. Hundred-dollar bills—stacks of them.

"That's more like it," MacCandliss said, greedily snatching one of the stacks.

Beneath the single hundred, there was only blank paper.

"You can count it," Koller said calmly. "It's all there."

Before MacCandliss could straighten up, he felt a sharp jab at the base of his neck. In that same instant, with just a small amount of pressure, the succinylcholine was in his body.

Koller's powerful arms had him before he could even mount a struggle. Less than twenty-five seconds later, restraint was unnecessary.

"You're a very stupid man," Koller said.

MacCandliss, terrified, felt the muscles in his body begin to quiver as though insects were burrowing below his skin. The man let go of him and he dropped to his knees, then toppled over onto his back.

"What have you done to me?"

"Did you really think your little safe-deposit box would protect you? It took me ten minutes to find the key you taped under your bureau drawer. Ten minutes. Your lawyer's name was all over papers in your desk. We'll have no trouble getting him to cooperate with us when we reason with him and he learns about the perversions you've been involved in."

MacCandliss was wide awake and alert, but nearly helpless. His chest was tightening, squeezing on his heart.

"I'm dying . . ."

Did he say that aloud, or just think it?

"You're not dying, but you will die," Koller said. "I didn't inject enough sux to over-dose you. I wouldn't want you to miss your fall. You see, you're going to jump out this hotel window and splatter. I do hope no-body is underneath when you land."

MacCandliss's lips felt like stone, un-movable. The quivering of his muscles had stopped.

"Why?" he mouthed before he could no longer move his lips.

"I love it," the killer said. "It never fails. Always the same question from you guys. *Why?* Well, hell, I honestly don't know why somebody paid me to kill you. But I do know why you will kill yourself. You see, although you don't know it, you called the help desk at work yesterday and had your laptop sent to the IT department for some routine maintenance. Shame on you for having so much kiddie porn on it. Grue-some stuff, really. Somebody tipped you off about the find. There's an e-mail to that effect, which you apparently read last night, so you know the noose around your neck was starting to tighten. They were going to bag you on child porn. Do you know what they do to short eyes in prison?

"So you checked into this hotel last night. Brought only a few of your things, which you've already seen here. Nobody is going to question why Phillip MacCandliss jumped out the seventh-story window of the Crescent Hotel. The sux will already be metabolized, so your autopsy won't show any drugs. 'And he had two little girls,' everyone will say. 'Such a shame.'"

Nearly effortlessly, Koller lifted MacCandliss off the floor and turned so that his mark could get one last look at the money.

"Easy come, easy go," Koller said. "My advice is to just relax and enjoy the ride."

Phillip MacCandliss felt himself being maneuvered over the windowsill. For a moment, as he hung down, his lids fell open, giving him a view of the scene seven stories below. Then he felt hands pushing on his bottom, and he began to slide forward.

*It's not going to happen*, he thought.

But it was.

He slid off the sill and was instantly airborne. The wind whipped past his face as the world rose up to meet him. Despite what he had read on several claim filings from vets who had near-death experiences, his demise wasn't painless and beautiful, or filled with a warming, beckoning light. There was only pain, brief and beyond excruciating. Nearly every bone in his body shattered at once. His skull erupted against the hood of a parked car. Fragments of his brain exploded onto the windshield like a spattering of bugs.

Seven stories above, Franz Koller mussed the bedspread, scattered the pornographic photos about, set the toiletries on the sink, and left Room 727 through Room 725, pausing only to check that the door between them was locked.

**Nicely done.**

# CHAPTER 38

"If there ever was a DVD recording of the Aleem Syed Mohammad operation, it's gone now."

Saul Mollender sounded bewildered, but also more energized than Nick had ever heard him.

It was nearly half past midnight, and the Mole had just returned the call Nick had left on his machine at seven, giving him details of Jillian's meeting with the nursing school dean. Patient volume on the four-stop Baltimore loop had been unusually light, and Nick and Junie were already parked on the street by her house, nearly done cleaning up the RV.

"Does that make any sense?" Nick, now slouched in the driver's seat, asked Mollender. "We're talking about one of the most high-profile cases that Shelby Stone has ever had. Since they had the capability to do so, how could it not have been recorded?"

"I don't have any record of the surgery in my database either."

"That's crazy."

"But there's more. When can we meet?"

"Now?"

"Of course now. Do you want to know what's happened here or don't you?"

Nick rubbed at the gritty fatigue stinging his eyes. The day had started early, and the ecstatic exhaustion from his time with Jillian had never gone away.

"You can't tell me over the phone?" he asked.

"If I wanted to tell you over the phone, I would have told you over the phone," the Mole said, suddenly sounding like his old testy self.

Junie, who had finished restocking, waved

that she was done, and motioned Nick to lock up.

"Jillian won't be off duty until one," he said after Junie had left. "I want her to be there."

"Does she have my plaque?"

"If she does, she'll bring it."

"I don't want to meet in or near the hospital."

*Are you going weird on me?* Nick came close to asking.

"Okay, we'll meet wherever you want," he said instead. "But remember, I have to drive in from Baltimore."

"Should be fun without any traffic for a change. There's an all-night coffee shop, Mike's, on South Dakota near Eighteenth. One thirty?"

"Make it two," Nick said.

Just as he hung up, Junie startled him with a knock on the passenger side door.

"This folder was on the kitchen table with a note from Reggie for you," she said, passing it over.

"He's an artiste on the Internet," Nick replied, "so I asked him to do a little research for me. Thanks."

"Next time, ask him to do some homework. Good job tonight."

Junie winked at him and headed to her house. As the quiet closed in, Nick flipped through the articles Reggie had put together, then closed the folder and sat staring through the darkness at nothing in particular. Quickly, his thoughts homed in on Umberto—clear images of the man as he was at FOB Savannah, working in the base clinic during his off-hours, taking vital signs, straightening up the waiting room, smiling and joking with the patients. Always smiling. Always joking.

What in the hell had become of him? Why was Mollender suddenly acting so secretive? What was the connection between Belle and Dr. Nick Fury? Had she really crossed paths with Umberto, or did she hear the name from someone else?

Hopefully the answers to those questions would not remain elusive for much longer.

Finally, with a prolonged stretch and a deep sigh, Nick flipped open his cell phone and called Jillian.

"Hope you can stay awake a little longer,"

he said. "We've been summoned by the Mole."

It seemed as if the owners of Mike's L.A. Diner and Coffee Emporium had tried and failed any number of times to find an iden-tity for the place. There was neon and more neon, framed black-and-white gloss-ies of Bogie, Bacall, and Betty, and a grease-stained menu that was a cross be-tween a railroad car diner's and Starbucks'. There was also, at almost two in the morn-ing, a decent-sized crowd that included college students from nearby Catholic Uni-versity, street people, and a few affluent suburbanites, but did not, to this point at least, include Saul Mollender.

While waiting for the man, Nick ordered a black coffee and Jillian an iced tea, fries, and a grilled cheese sandwich. There was no overt discussion about their afternoon lovemaking. Both felt comfort-able simply being together, holding hands underneath the table, and proposing dif-ferent theories that would fit the bizarre, trun-cated medical record of Umberto Vasquez, and the absence of any videorecording of the Aleem Syed Mohammad operation.

"Maybe they didn't record it for security reasons," Jillian suggested.

"Possibly. But I would think the CIA or whoever was in charge of questioning the dude would have wanted to show the world how enlightened and compassionate we were, even to one of the archenemies of our country."

"Any idea why Mollender would have said he wanted to meet us out here?"

"I still don't know him well enough to say. He sounded a little, I don't know, disconnected on the phone. Sort of squirrelly—sensitive and tuned in one moment, brash and confrontational the next."

"The keys to everything are the hospital records and the video of that operation, Nick."

"Then I guess we'll just have to wait and see what the Mole found."

"Hopefully we won't have to wait long."

She gestured behind Nick. Saul Mollender approached their table with his head down and his gaze shifting from side to side as if he were part of some clandestine operation. He skipped the formality of shaking hands and quickly sat himself down on the empty chair across from them.

"People have been talking," Mollender said.

Nick thought the man seemed agitated and anxious.

"Talking? Who's talking? What about?"

"About me," Mollender said. "One of my two employees noticed I was doing some research for you. He spoke to the other of my employees and they both started asking questions."

"About our investigation?" Jillian asked.

"Heck no," Mollender snapped. "My team doesn't gossip. That's against my policy. But the two of them are wondering if I've turned over a new leaf and decided to become more helpful to people—God forbid, friendly even."

Nick shook his head in disbelief.

"You made us come all the way out here at two in the morning just so you could protect your reputation of being a grouch?"

Mollender remained tight-lipped and serious.

"Do you know what would happen if word got out that people could just barge into my office and not only demand attention from me, but actually get it? By the way, do you have my plaque?"

Suppressing a smile, Jillian passed the framed calligraphy across, mentally adding the records room head to the list of the most eccentric people she knew.

"So you're worried that maybe people might actually, I don't know, use your services?" she asked.

"Funny, very funny. But yes. First of all, our services, such as they are, are dwindling with each record we make electronic. Ever hear of a position whose job it was to make itself obsolete? We're literally working ourselves out of existence. The only way we three can stay employed is if no one knows we're there."

"Easy, Saul. Easy," Jillian said gently. "You can only do what you can do."

"I guess."

"Now, can you tell us what you found out?"

Mollender motioned the waitress over and ordered a tall glass of skim milk, warmed on the stove, not in a microwave.

"And don't try and trick me," he said to the girl. "I can tell." He turned back to Nick and Jillian. "What I found out is that Fred

Johnson is even more of a jackass than I originally thought."

"Fred Johnson?" Nick asked.

"Before I delve into him, can you tell me why somebody would have wanted to steal the DVD of that operation?"

"Did you say steal? I thought you just said it was gone."

"And that's the truth. If it ever existed, it's gone now."

"Why am I not surprised," Nick said.

"I personally supervised setting up the video camera system in the ORs over six years ago. For that reason, let alone everything else I've done for my unit over the past twenty years, you'd think I'd be the one selected to run the electronic medical records department. But no. Smarmy Fred Johnson gets the position over me, just because he's the CTO's nephew or cousin or something."

"That true?"

"That's what I heard. The personnel lady told me I was lacking people skills, whatever those are, but I never believed her. Smarmy. I think the word was invented for Fred."

"Do you have any proof that somebody

stole the DVD of Mohammad's operation?"

"We have three cameras in each of our
twenty-four operating rooms on three separate floors—a direct overhead shot into
the incision, one up from the foot of the
table, and one that continuously pans the
room, including the anesthesiologist's station at the head of the table. Each camera
is attached to a DVR machine by cables,
like a supercharged TiVo."

"Amazing," Nick said, pleased to sense
that the Mole had regained much of his
equilibrium.

The waitress returned with the stove-
warmed milk, and Mollender sampled it
like a wine connoisseur before nodding his
approval.

"Supervising the recording process," he
went on after a few sips, "is one of the few
functions my little department still has, but
I've heard rumors that it might not be for
long. Damn Johnson. Anyhow, as things
stand, the OR supervisor tells us which
operations they want recorded, and we
push the buttons—well, my assistant Annette does, anyway. She has a booth in

the operating suite and works from there. At the end of each day, she burns the cases onto DVDs because we can't store all that data indefinitely on the DVR machines.

"We also keep a registry of the discs, which is what the instructors use to look up operations they want to show their students. We catalog them not only by date and time, but also by IDC code and keywords. I checked after you called, Doctor. There is no entry anyplace for Aleem Syed Mohammad's surgery."

"Could somebody have taken the DVD and deleted the entry in your database as well?" Jillian asked.

"Anything is possible, I suppose. But why would somebody do that? Actually, I asked myself that very question any number of times. Tell me about this Mohammad fellow. What do you know about him?"

Nick produced the folder of articles Reggie had printed out during the evening.

"Mohammad was born and raised in Jordan," Nick said. "He was in his late forties when he was captured in Karachi by U.S. and Pakistani Special Forces in a joint operation code-named Shining Star. There's no telling how many deaths he was responsible for. He was a prime suspect in several major bombings, including the massacre at the United States Embassy in New Delhi."

"What's his affiliation?" Mollender asked. "Are we talking Al Qaeda?"

Nick shook his head.

"I haven't had time to go through all this yet," he said, "but I think not at first. Apparently at some point after the Iraq invasion, his organization, Islamic Jihad in Jordan, merged with the Al Qaeda terror network, making him one of the most powerful and wanted terrorists in the world."

The Mole thought for a few beats. "Yes, I remember now. His capture was touted as a major victory in the war against terror."

"Correct," Nick said. "The controversy that erupted when word got out that Mohammad required surgery to remove a dangerous cardiac tumor, and that a team of doctors had been assembled for the operation, was intense."

"I guess there were those who felt the famed Hippocratic Oath phrase 'Do no harm' applied to the doctors, but not to the patients," Mollender said, chuckling at his own humor.

"There were threats made by extremist groups who wanted him saved, and others who wanted him not treated at all," Nick added. "They promised retaliation against anyone who helped keep Mohammad alive, which they believed would have made it possible for us to torture him some more. That's why the location where his surgery was scheduled to be performed was kept a closely guarded secret, right up until the day of the operation."

"According to Nancy Lane at the nursing school," Jillian said, "a lot of people felt justice had been served when Mohammad died on the operating table that day. Autopsy results indicated he suffered a massive brain aneurysm and subsequent cardiac arrest from chronic high blood pressure."

"Tough way to go," Mollender said.

"That's why we need to see the tape of his operation. Maybe Belle's death was some sort of retribution for his death, even though it's hard to understand why they waited three years."

"But why her?" Nick asked. "Saul, that operation is all we have at the moment. We need to know everything we can about it. I can't believe you, of all people, don't have a backup."

Mollender snickered. "Hence my statement that Fred Johnson is a jackass."

"What does he have to do with any of this?" Nick asked.

"Before Johnson took over, I would send the DVDs by mail to my friend Noreen Siliski, who runs a disaster recovery business in Sutton, Virginia. She would then copy the files to her servers and mail the DVDs back to me and, bingo, we'd have our backup. Noreen is a wonderful person. Very bright, very unique. We were once quite close. Now we're just . . . good friends."

"You don't sound so pleased about that."

"I'm not, really. But like you said, what can you do?"

"Sorry. Can you go on?"

"So when Fred Johnson takes over and sees this minuscule payment we're giving Noreen each month, the guy decides to flex his muscles, make it a point to the hospital administrators that he's looking after every nickel and dime. Meanwhile his EMR department is a million over budget. I was told to stop sending backups to Noreen."

Jillian frowned. "I'm afraid to ask when Johnson made you stop using your friend for disaster recovery."

"Four years ago. A year before Mohammad's operation."

"So that's it, then. No video. Even if we *were* able to find out what personnel were in the OR that day, it won't tell us anything about what happened during the operation."

For the first time, Jillian noted a glint in the Mole's eyes.

"Well, all might not be as bleak as it seems, my friend," he said. "You see, if Mohammad's surgery was ever recorded, then there is a copy of that video nobody knows about. That's why I asked who would want to steal it and cover their tracks by deleting it from my database log, and the real reason why I wanted to meet here. If someone's stolen the original DVDs, I didn't want to meet anywhere near the place."

"But you just told us there wasn't any backup," Nick said.

"I told you there wasn't *supposed* to be any backup. Well, with Fred Johnson being so self-righteous about Noreen, and at the same time being so wrong, I guess I forgot to put in the paperwork to shut down our little disaster recovery operation."

"You mean . . ."

"Yup. Fred Johnson assumed, as did everybody else, that we stopped sending DVDs to Noreen. But as with most things, the pompous jackass was wrong. Buried in that massive budget of his is one tiny line item that he wouldn't find unless he went through the whole thing ten times with a fine-tooth comb. You see, I changed the name of Noreen's company but I never canceled her contract with us."

"Saul, let me buy you another milk," Jillian said.

# CHAPTER 39

Better Safe Than Sorry Electronic Storage, Noreen Siliski's data backup and recovery business, was located in an isolated three-story brick business center on the outskirts of Sutton, Virginia. It was ten in the morning when Nick pulled into the nearly deserted parking lot. Rush hour traffic away from the city had been intense, although he suspected it was not unusually so. Nick had the entire day free. Junie would be working the RV with one of his backups, a seventy-year-old retired professor of medicine from Georgetown—a brilliant, caring woman, who was beloved by the patients and utterly devoted to the evening each week she spent on the roads with Helping Hands.

The drive across the river and south was made in virtual silence. Mollender, sitting in back with his hands folded tightly in his lap, stared out the window of Nick's 1995 Cutlass Cierra. In the front, Nick and Jillian were each engrossed in the same gnawing question: Would the recording of Aleem Syed Mohammad's ill-fated surgery shed any light at all on the strange one-way ambulance trip of Umberto from the Singh Center to Shelby Stone, or on Belle's subsequent murder three years later?

"Just pull in there a couple of spaces left of the Dumpster," Mollender said, breaking the prolonged silence. "The chute is coming out of Noreen's office on the third floor. She's always remodeling."

"You got it," Nick said, easing into the spot.

Down on the seat, where the Mole could not see, Jillian squeezed Nick's hand. Then they followed Mollender into a rather stark, tiled lobby and up two flights of stairs.

At that instant, a gunshot rang out from

within Noreen's office, then several more in rapid succession.

Nick pounded once on the door and grasped the knob. The door flew open.

The woman's outer office, which was about the size of a two-car garage, had been stripped down to the studs. On a stepladder at the center of the room, wielding a hefty cordless nail gun, was Noreen Siliski.

"This is what one can do when there is almost no human traffic," Noreen said, making no mention of Nick's rather sensational entrance as she stepped down to the floor and shook hands heartily with the new arrivals. "Business was good when I petitioned the owner to add storage space. When he finally approved the changes, business was bad. But I love building things so I'm doing it anyway."

Half the office was covered by bedsheets, sprinkled with a fine misting of sawdust. The smell of freshly cut wood hung pleasantly in the air. In the center of the main room next to the ladder was a wooden rolling workbench, underneath and on top of which were an assortment of tools, including a circular saw and cordless drill.

Noreen Siliski was a pleasant-looking brunette, slightly on the muscular side, with her dark hair pulled back in a sizeable ponytail. Nick sensed that her jeans and white denim work shirt might be the central elements of her wardrobe.

"It's wonderful that you're doing this all yourself, Noreen," Jillian said.

"It's sort of learn as you go, but I've always been able to handle most tools."

Finally, Mollender stepped forward.

"I like what you're doing here, Noreen," he said, seeming somewhat cowed.

"That's nice of you to say, Saul."

"So you have the recording?" Jillian asked, anxious to break the negative vibes she sensed were building between the two.

"I believe I do. Saul told me the date. I digitize and archive all the video files he sends me, so it was easy to find. I burned it to DVD so we can watch it here in the office. Can you pull the shades over there?"

Noreen went to the back room and quickly returned, struggling some to push a steel AV cart over the threshold and into a free corner of the room, in front of a quartet of folding chairs. On the top of the cart was a forty-inch HD television set with a DVD player on the shelf beneath it. As the door she came through began closing, Nick caught a glimpse of the work space that lay behind it—one with a raised floor, similar to the call center at Don Reese's precinct headquarters, and racks that he figured were used to house her computer equipment.

Nick proceeded over to the wall housing three double-hung windows. The chute to the Dumpster, an absolute marvel of practical engineering, opened at the center one. The chute was constructed of large, heavy rubber trash barrels with the bottoms cut out, stacked one just inside another, and held in place by chains looped through the handles and bolted above the inside of the window. The three-story drop to the Dumpster was a modest arc rather than a straight shot, and the overall appearance of the green barrels was that of a giant caterpillar.

"Remarkable," Nick said, calling Jillian over to see.

"How did you know how to do this?" she asked, amazed.

"How else?" Noreen replied. "The Internet. I just drop that canvas flap down over the window when I leave. It took a few trips to a few hardware and Home Depot stores to get enough barrels, but it wasn't that expensive or that hard to build."

Nick closed the blinds and dropped the canvas over the window opening. With the room sufficiently dark they gathered in front of the television. Nick and Jillian were both feeling too anxious to sit.

"Well, I hope this disc is holding what you're looking for."

"We hope so too," Nick said.

"In that case, I think we should get on with this." Noreen slipped the DVD into the slot and with a nod of understanding to her guests, pressed Play.

# CHAPTER 40

"You ready for this?" Nick asked as the screen lit up with static.

"Dunno," Jillian said grimly. "Are you?"

"I'm not sure. We've come so far."

"I can't believe I'm going to see Belle alive."

"Want me to stop it?" Nick asked, holding up the remote, given to him by Noreen.

"No, but I want to sit down, I think."

Jillian inhaled deeply and took Nick's hand in the darkness. They were six feet from the screen, about to watch a video that included the death of a patient. It also was probably going to include shots of Jillian's younger sister, subsequently murdered in a manner that every police-man involved with the case believed was suicide.

Saul Mollender and Noreen Siliski sat next to each other, behind and to the right of the others. The tension in the room was high.

In half a minute, the static gave way to a set of standard legal notices, yellow on black, that included a summary of the HIPAA laws surrounding patient confiden-tiality, an outline of who was allowed to view the recording and for what purposes, and the name of the editor, Annette Furst, Department of Medical Records. Finally came the hospital name, date, and operating room number. Jillian was rigid in her seat, squeezing blood from Nick's hand.

The introductory information was in the same yellow print.

**PATIENT:** Aleem Syed Mohammad
**Hospital ID:** 881-83-7782—Karachi, Pakistan
**Condition:** Cardiac rhabdomyoma
**Procedure:** Cardiopulmonary bypass;

excision of rhabdomyoma; cardiac
reconstruction

Present in the Operating Room:

**Surgeon:** Abigail Spielmann, M.D.
**Asst. Surgeon:** Lewis Leonard, M.D.
**Cardiac Surgical Resident:** Yasmin Dasari-
Olan, M.D.
**Anesthesiologist:** Thomas Landrew, M.D.
**Perfusionist:** Roger Pendleton, CCP, Cert.
ABCP
**Scrub Nurse:** Kimberly Fox
**Circulating Nurse:** Cassandra Browning-
Leavitt
**Medical Student:** Yu Jiang
**Nursing Student:** Belle Coates

Nick felt the energy in Jillian's grip increase at the sight of her sister's name.
He froze the picture.

"Do we know who Dr. Abigail Spielmann
is?" he asked.

"I think she was brought in from another
hospital," the Mole replied. "Probably an
expert in cardiac tumors like this one."

"She must be big stuff if the cardiac surgical chief would allow it," Jillian said.

Nick undid the pause.

The printing gave way to a gleaming operating room. Three cameras, according to Mollender—one of them straight down into where the patient would be placed on the now empty table; one up from the foot; and the other giving a wide-angle shot of the entire operating room. The video editor's job, Mollender explained, was to mix the various camera angles into a cohesive and useful presentation.

The opening sequence was shot from the wide-angle camera and showed the perfusionist, wearing scrubs, a mask, and hair cover, but set back from the sterile field where the surgeons would be working. Seated behind the long heart-lung bypass machine, he looked like a concert pianist preparing for a performance. He was chatting with the scrub nurse.

"Need anything?" the perfusionist said. "Cassandra's right outside."

The audio and visual feeds were excellent.

"As a matter of fact, yes," the scrub nurse replied. "The only thing from Dr. Spielmann's instrument list that I don't have here is a LocNess tissue stabilizer. Could you ask Cassandra to get one for me, please?"

"Will do. Have you met Spielmann?"

"She came by to see me a little while ago. She seems terrific."

"I thought the same thing. Be right back."

The scrub nurse was positioned just above and behind where Dr. Abigail Spielmann would be working. She was ready for the case—gloved, gowned, and masked, with intense dark eyes looking out from beneath her blue hair covering as she checked through a huge tray of instruments.

At that point there was some obvious editing—eleven minutes according to the running digital time in the upper right corner. The perfusionist was back at his post, and the circulating nurse had appeared and was helping one of the surgeons, a dark-skinned woman, it appeared, into her gloves and gown.

It felt stranger to Nick than he had expected to be viewing OR drama after so long. Between his internship, residency, fellowship in trauma surgery, private practice, and the military, he had been a surgeon for more than nine years before the explosion that took Sarah—nearly as long as he had been away from his specialty.

Suddenly, Jillian's grasp on his hand intensified. Two people, a man and a woman, both in scrubs, mask, and hair covers, entered through the main doors and took a position against the wall, well away from the table.

"That's her," Jillian whispered loudly. "That's Belle."

Nick was able to make out a tallish, slender woman with very attractive eyes.

"If Dr. Spielmann has no objections," the circulating nurse told Belle and the medical student, "we'll get you up on risers so you can see more than people's backs. Either way, the procedure will be on that screen. Have you both read up on cardiac rhabdomyomas?"

"Yes," the students said in unison.

Nick felt Jillian stiffen at the sound of her sister's voice.

"Great," the circulator went on, "so you know it's not a cancer that spreads to other parts of the body, but it arises from the inner heart muscle and just keeps growing and taking up space until cardiac function becomes severely compromised."

There was another lengthy edit, leading to the sudden appearance at the head of the table of the anesthesiologist and, on the left side of the table, another surgeon— the first assistant, Nick assumed, actually remembering Lewis Leonard from the list of players because of a grade-school classmate in Oregon with the same name. At that moment, the main doors burst open and Aleem Syed Mohammad was wheeled in by two men in scrubs, surgical masks, and hair covers. In a short while, the infamous murderer and terrorist lying so peacefully on the stretcher was going to be dead.

Mohammad, eyes closed, probably in a pleasant swoon from his pre-op medication, had a sheet draped across his body from the midchest down. He was a swarthy, rather handsome man, with high cheekbones and narrow features, including a striking aquiline nose. Nick got a brief, clear view of him as he was transferred onto the operating table.

One of the two transport men remained in the room and was posted to Belle's right, on the other side of the main doors. Nick recalled that such a person was not identified in the roster of those observing the procedure, and speculated that he was a security presence, probably from the CIA. He was a stocky man, of average height, and although only his eyes and throat were exposed, there was something strangely familiar about him.

The door to the scrub room opened and the principal medical player in the scene, Dr. Abigail Spielmann, backed into the room, her hands up in front of her, palms in. She was a surprisingly slight woman, with light blue eyes that sparkled with intelligence despite the distance from the camera. The hand drying and nurse-assisted gowning of the cardiac surgeon was edited out.

"Dr. Landrew," she said to the anesthe-siologist, every word tinged with authority, "anything I should know about in his pre-op examination?"

"His history and examination were done with the help of an interpreter. The patient had not received any medication that would alter his mental status, but he still seemed a little groggy."

"Despite the grogginess, you trust his

signing of the consent form?" Spielmann asked.

"I do. There were three witnesses—two nurses from his floor, and his interpreter."

"I actually spoke with him after you did," Spielmann said. "I have been using some tapes to learn a little Arabic. Mr. Moham- mad seemed to know what I was saying, which made me very pleased. I was able to pick out a few words he said, but just a few. At the time we spoke, he seemed tired but in command of his faculties. So I agree with you, Dr. Landrew."

"Excellent."

"Then are we ready to get this show on the road?"

"Ready."

"Mr. Pendleton?"

"Ready, Doctor," said the perfusionist.

"Okay, then. We'll put him to sleep and prep him as a team according to the method I have distributed to each of you. Those of you observing can take your places on the risers after he is asleep, prepped, and draped. Questions?"

There were none. The anesthesiologist adjusted his position to inject what Nick felt certain was succinylcholine to paralyze Mohammad before inserting a breathing tube into his trachea.

But at that instant, Aleem Syed Mohammad began to move.

First he stirred. Then he groaned. Then he reached both hands up and squeezed them against the sides of his head. Next he began to moan, then he cried out loudly and suddenly he screamed.

A moment later, he sat bolt upright, flailing his arms and screeching at the top of his lungs in what Nick assumed was Arabic. Instantly, everyone around the operating table seemed to be speaking and moving at once. The surgeons and the circulating nurse tried to force him back onto the table. His flailing arms caught one of the assistants on the side of the face and sent her sprawling. His IV tore from his arm. Blood instantly began oozing through the gauze that had been holding the large cannula in place.

His cries of pain grew louder still. His eyes seemed twice their natural size.

He violently snapped his head from side to side as if trying to dislodge a parasite.

Then, with his arms waving wildly, he

flung himself off the table, sending the circulating nurse and a surgical assistant crashing into the heart-lung perfusion pump, which rose up on two wheels and toppled over.

The camera angle switched to the one looking from the foot of the OR bed toward the head—the only view that could show the utter chaos on the operating room floor, where three people struggled amidst the fluids from the IVs and the perfusion machine.

"*Sa'edoony, sa'edoony!*" Mohammad shouted out.

"I'm sure that's Arabic," Nick said. "But I don't know what it means."

Despite the noise and commotion, Mohammad's words were clear.

"**Sa'edoony . . . ahderoo lee ed-Doctor Fury . . . ahderoo lee ed-Doctor Nick Fury! Sa'edoony . . . ¡Socorro! ¡Ayúdenme! ¡Búsquenme al Doctor Nick Fury!**"

"Oh my God!" Nick exclaimed in a strained whisper. "That last bit wasn't Arabic, it was Spanish. It's Umberto! That's his voice. I swear it is! He's calling for me!"

"**Sa'edoony! . . .**"

Umberto's screams echoed through the room.

The camera angle was switched to the overhead view.

Then, as suddenly as it had started, the thrashing and screaming ended. The surgical assistants stumbled to their feet and lifted the lifeless body of their patient back onto the table.

Nick felt ill as the man's head flopped back. His face was absolutely that of Aleem Syed Mohammad.

*Plastic surgery!* Nick realized. *Lots of it.*

"Pump!" Abigail Spielmann ordered.

"Endotracheal tube is in."

"No pulse," someone called out.

"Both lungs aerating."

"EKG is hooked up. Flat line. Absolutely flat."

"Pupils are blown, fully dilated, and fixed on both sides."

"Keep pumping."

"BP zero."

"Looks as if he blew an aneurysm in his head," Abigail Spielmann said with seasoned calm. "A huge one, I suspect. Could I have two ccs of epi on an intracardiac needle. I think we should see what this does and then make a decision about opening his chest for manual compressions."

"BP still zero."

Spielmann took the long cardiac needle and drove it down beside the patient's sternum, keeping suction on the plunger. There was an immediate jet of dark, almost black blood into the syringe. She injected the contents into the left ventricle of the heart.

"Nothing. Straight line."

"BP zero."

"Pupils fixed."

"I cannot see anything to be gained by going to the final level and opening this man's chest. Anyone feel differently?" There was only silence from the room. "Okay, then. Time of death ten thirty-one A.M. Thank you, everybody. I appreciate your efforts. I'm very sorry this happened."

The overhead camera showed the deceased man's face, staring sightlessly upward at the saucer lights. Nick hit Pause and held the image in the center of the screen.

"My God," Nick said. "While they were doing all that work on Umberto's face, they must have taught him Arabic so he would be ready for the pre-op interviews."

"It's just like when I heard Manny speak in Arabic. Billy Pearl said that Manny had been brainwashed. I bet the same thing was done to Umberto," Jillian said.

"Did your sister speak Arabic?" Mollender asked.

"No. But as Nick said, the Arabic Umberto spoke was mixed in with Spanish."

"Okay. So, did your sister speak Spanish?"

"She was almost fluent," Jillian replied. "We both were."

# CHAPTER 41

Nick was dazed when he shut off the TV. Witnessing Umberto's gruesome death held him spellbound, capable only of staring at his own reflection in the black television screen. He ached at the irony that Umberto's final words had been a chilling cry for help—a cry to him.

**¡Búsquenme al Doctor Nick Fury!**
**Get me Dr. Nick Fury.**

With the man's agonized screams echoing in his head, Nick tried to make sense of the almost inconceivable events that had occurred in the operating room three years ago. First, though, he had to begin to deal with the fact that his search was finally over. Don Reese had been right. The reason Umberto's and Manny's captors had not bothered issuing them new Social Security numbers was that both men were slated to die. Manny Ferris's escape had spoiled their plan. The secret mission that was to be Umberto's passage out of his PTSD hell had been anything but that. It had been the doorway to another, more ferocious nightmare, and ultimately the invitation to his grave.

"Umberto," Nick murmured, feeling intense anger searing the back of his neck.

He stared at the screen as if the ghost of his friend was trapped inside it, marked for eternity by a video epitaph. Jillian placed her hand gently upon his shoulder.

"Nick, I'm so sorry."

"What was it he said, Jill? I mean exactly."

"Just what you would imagine—for the Spanish part, anyway. 'Help. Help me. Get me Dr. Fury. Get me Dr. Nick Fury.' Even though the words were jumbled in with Umberto's screams and with the Arabic, Belle heard and understood them, although not the meaning behind them. Later on someone must have told her about the comic book character, and she set out to understand more. Belle was all about understanding—getting to the bottom of things."

Jillian's voice sounded distant—barely audible. Nick could not respond. He was already weighed down with guilt over Sarah's death. Now this. Was there anything he could have done? It didn't matter. The line between grief and guilt was often a very fine one. As long as the two didn't paralyze his life, he thought now, there was no reason he couldn't live with them.

Eventually, the fog enveloping his thoughts began to lift.

"Now we know," he managed to say.

"Now we know," Jillian echoed softly.

She wrapped her arms around him. At first, Nick thought he was trembling, but soon he realized that it was she. Jillian pulled away, her hands still on Nick's shoulders.

"I am so sad and so damn angry," he said.

"I know what finding Umberto alive meant to you. But you didn't let him down. Something terrible is going on here—a secret that somebody desperately needed to keep hidden—a secret Belle paid for with her life."

*Belle.* The mention of the name jolted away what remained of Nick's self-pity. He had to stay strong and be there for Jillian, and for himself. *Of all the perils on the road to truth,* one of his favorite Buddhist teachings read, *the truth itself could actually prove the greatest peril of all.*

"Who would have done this?" Nick asked aloud. "It's hard to believe his death was unexpected. There was no damn cardiac tumor. What we witnessed was an execution—a lethal charade that amounted to the ticket to freedom for Aleem Mohammad. I'll bet that bastard was thousands of miles away when Umberto died."

"A very public execution," Mollender said. "The ultimate witness protection hoax."

"That's horrible," Noreen said.

"Belle must have been unable to let matters lie," Jillian said. "Maybe she's the only one who heard and understood what Umberto was screaming. Maybe she said the wrong thing to the wrong person."

"What we just saw ties Umberto to the

Singh Center," Nick said. "Poor Manny Ferris, too. Maybe Manny was the one who was supposed to be on that operating table, but something about his plastic surgery didn't work out. They couldn't make him look enough like Mohammad to pull off the switch."

"Possible," Nick said. "If he were partway through a sequence of surgeries, that would explain Manny's appearance. Listen, I know it's painful to watch, but we might have missed something important in the initial viewing. I need to watch the operation again and maybe again. You guys don't have to."

"I'm in," Jillian said. "I'm feeling stronger than I have since Belle died."

"Noreen?" Mollender asked.

"I don't know what help I could be, and I'm really shaken up," she replied, "but if the solidarity will help, I'll try."

Noreen and Mollender stood beside Nick and Jillian, forming an arc in front of the television. Then they took their seats and Nick pressed Play. Out of the corner of his eye, Nick observed Mollender take hold of Noreen's hand as the first images of the operating room appeared. They watched the video twice through, until Jillian broke down crying and Nick felt his own eyes begin to well. Finally, Jillian excused herself from the room—to clear her thoughts, she explained. Noreen decided to go with her. Of the four of them, Mollender seemed to be the most composed, although it was clear that he too was affected.

"You okay to see it once more?" Nick asked.

"It's easier to take if I keep telling myself it's only a movie."

This time, at the moment just before Umberto's death, Nick paused the disc. Using the remote control, he advanced the video a single frame at a time, then back and forward once more.

"Umberto grabs his head here," Nick said, tapping his finger against the television screen. "It's as though something erupted in his brain. I haven't actually witnessed an aneurysm bursting in someone's head, but a rupture like that is accompanied by a sudden, massive increase in volume within the skull. The victims experience a blinding headache, which he showed signs of having, but he wasn't vomiting from the huge increase in intracranial pressure. A seizure is typical, too, but he didn't have one of those either. The whole thing with Umberto took no more than a couple of minutes from beginning to end. I don't know what else it could have been besides a ruptured aneurysm, but something seems off to me."

"Are you suggesting that someone might have done this to him?" Mollender asked, just as Jillian and Noreen returned.

"I don't know. All I keep thinking is that the surgeon could never have been allowed to open Umberto's heart to operate because he didn't have anything wrong with it. No tumor. Nothing. If their plan was to have it look like Aleem Mohammad died on the table, it had to happen before his actual operation. That means someone had control of the situation the whole time." Nick turned to Jillian. "I think Umberto was killed right there. It looks like an aneurysm, but I don't believe it was. Someone did something to him—to his brain. Otherwise, they would have operated on his heart and found no tumor."

"But what about the tests?"

"Tests can be faked. The surgeon could

have been brought in to do the case on the basis of someone else's MRI. The people who did this are no amateurs, and I would bet they have technology available to them that the average man or even doctor knows nothing about."

"So, who do you think is responsible?"

Nick's anger was pulsing through him now, driving his thoughts. Pieces of the mystery surrounding Umberto were falling into place almost too rapidly for him to integrate them.

"You mean what person is responsible," he said. "Or what government agency with three letters beginning with a *C*, that just happened, at least according to the papers, to be pumping information from one Aleem Syed Mohammad.

"Noreen," Nick asked, more energized perhaps than at any time since Sarah's death, "do you have a large piece of paper and something to write with?"

She left the room, returning moments later with a flip chart and several markers. Freezing the list of those in the OR, Nick transcribed it to the flip chart in a two-column format.

| Dr. Abigail Spielmann– Surgeon | Dr. Yasmin Dasari-Olan–Surgical Resident |
| Dr. Lewis Leonard–Asst. Surgeon | Cassandra Browning-Leavitt– Circulating Nurse |
| Dr. Thomas Landrew– Anesthesiologist | Yu Jiang–Medical Student |
| Roger Pendleton– Perfusionist | Belle Coates– Nursing Student |
| Kimberly Fox– Scrub Nurse | |

"What are you doing?" Jillian asked.

"These are the people who were in the OR that day. I noticed something on that last viewing, but I need to confirm it first. Jillian, I have to play some of the video again."

"It's okay. I can handle it."

He located a shot that contained a full view of the room.

"There are ten people in the OR, not counting the patient," Nick said. "There are nine names on this chart. I noticed the tenth man when he helped wheel Umberto in. There were two of them, actually. One left, and he stayed."

"I remember," the Mole said. "The one who left was quite a bit taller."

"Exactly. I thought maybe the two of them, or at least this guy, were from security. That made sense at the time. But take your eyes off of Umberto and keep them fixed on the tenth man."

Once again, Nick had the strange feeling of having seen the heavyset man before. He appeared quite a bit in the view from the camera above the foot of the narrow table. Not once during the terrible commotion surrounding Umberto's death did he move from his spot—not so much as an inch to get a better vantage point or to help. This time through, Nick also noticed that, unlike Belle, the medical student, the perfusionist, or the anesthesiologist, the tenth man was wearing a surgical gown. In addition, he kept his hands inside the gown throughout the grisly ordeal.

Nick's pulse was hammering. He ran the DVD again, and then once more. His eyes remained fixed on the man. At the instant the team finished transferring Umberto from the gurney to the operating table, Nick paused the playback, backed up a few frames, and then walked it forward again, his focus intensifying with each advance.

"There!" Nick exclaimed. "Did you see it? His hands stay underneath his surgical gown while Umberto is going through whatever it was that killed him. And look at his eyes. He is like dead calm."

"You think he has some sort of device under there?" Mollender asked. "Something that could fry Umberto's brain or burst an artery?"

"Maybe they had implanted some sort of radio receiver in there. Poor Umberto had multiple procedures done at the Singh Center. One of them certainly could have been that."

For a time, there was only silence as each of the other three—Mollender, Noreen, and Jillian—mulled over the awesome possibilities. Finally, Jillian spoke.

"So, why did they kill Belle?" she asked in a near whisper.

Again there was silence. Then the color drained from Nick's face.

"Oh, God," he breathed.

"What?"

"Belle wasn't the only one who heard Umberto. She may not have been the only one who could understand that he was speaking Spanish in addition to his Arabic."

"What are you suggesting?"

"We're assuming that Belle was murdered because she said something to the wrong person. What if she wasn't the only one who spoke up? What if it's not just Belle they killed?"

Noreen took a few steps backward.

"I'm not sure I can handle this anymore," she said. "Do we need to call the police?"

"I don't know yet," Nick said. "But I do know we need your help, Noreen. If Belle is the only one who has died, then I'm way off base. But we need to check on the rest of the people on that flip chart."

Noreen was beginning to hyperventilate.

"Look around," she exclaimed. "There are reasons I work with computers and not people."

Mollender took Noreen by the hand and walked over to her desk, where she had two computers already set up and running.

"We'll do this together," he said. "Noreen, I'll work off your laptop, you take the desktop. We'll start searching each of the names on the Web and see what comes up."

"I'm scared, Saul."

"We need to do this. Lives may be at stake. Nick, listen, in addition to the other nine who were in the OR, maybe you should put down Annette Furst, the video editor who works for me. She's very much alive. I saw her yesterday."

"That might be a good sign. Maybe I'm completely off base here. Or maybe they just haven't thought to include her. They make mistakes all the time. Cover-up is their middle name."

"All right."

"Okay. Start with the surgeons," Nick directed them. "Saul, take Spielmann, and Noreen, look up what you can on Leonard."

Noreen sat in her chair, while Mollender had to hunch over the desk to access the laptop. They both opened Web browsers and in near synchronized movements began scouring the Internet. Mollender struck first.

"Jesus!" he exclaimed. "Spielmann's dead. She died just a couple of weeks ago in her apartment in New York, apparently from an anaphylactic reaction to a bee sting."

"I think I just found something on Leonard," Noreen added a few minutes later. "This is just too freaky. I think I might get sick. Leonard was riding his motorcycle when he was killed in a collision with a tractor-trailer. According to this report in the *Chicago Tribune*, the driver of the truck said it looked to him as though Leonard lost control of the bike and went into a skid across a lane and right into his path."

"It could have been an accident," Jillian said.

"Or somebody could have sabotaged his motorcycle," Nick countered. "Keep going."

Another tense minute passed. The only sound in Noreen's office was of fingers tapping on keyboards. Nick added the location of each person's death next to their names. Chicago. New York. North Carolina. There was no longer any doubt in the room.

Mollender was next to speak up.

"Dr. Thomas Landrew drowned," he said grimly. "'Avid sportsman and prominent anesthesiologist drowned while kayaking on the Chesapeake.'"

"When?" Nick asked.

"Just three weeks ago. April eighteenth. This is terrible. I actually knew about his accident. Landrew did the anesthesia on me when I had a hernia fixed a few years ago. He was a terrific guy. I just glossed right over his name."

Nick wrote "Maryland" next to Landrew's name.

Mollender continued.

"Kimberly Fox is dead too, assuming she's the same Kimberly Fox on the board here. She was killed near her family's home in Utah. Skiing accident, it says here. Broke her neck. No details. No mention that she worked at Shelby Stone, but it does say she was a nurse."

"She could have moved," Jillian said. "Nurses, especially younger ones, are constantly changing hospitals. Like Belle."

"Mass murder, one by one," Nick muttered.

"Oh, no, I've got another hit," Noreen said shortly. Her voice quaked with a raw mix of fear and anxiety. "Cassandra Browning-Leavitt. Killed here in D.C. Shot from the woods while she was jogging along Rock Creek. No witnesses. Believed to be a random event. No suspects."

"I remember Cassandra now," Jillian said. "She was still working at Shelby Stone when she was killed. They sent a notice around after it happened warning people to be careful. That was a while ago. Maybe back in February."

For a minute, two, nobody could speak. Nick felt a band tightening around his chest.

"Washington. Chicago. New York. North Carolina. Utah. Maryland. Somebody is killing these people and doing it in such a way that it doesn't appear to be murder," Nick said, "or at least not deliberate murder, and certainly not serial murder."

"I knew it," Jillian said viciously. "I told them. I told them all she'd never kill herself."

"With these deaths so spread out across the country," Mollender said, "who would think to link them?"

"We would, that's who," Nick answered. Then he drew a line through the names of those they had confirmed dead, including

Belle. "That leaves us four people we haven't accounted for yet. Roger Pendleton, the perfusionist; Yasmin Dasari, the surgical resident; Yu Jiang, who was a medical student at the time; and Saul's video editor, Annette Furst."

Noreen nodded. She kept her gaze fixed to her computer screen, her fingers sweeping across her keyboard, while her computer mouse remained in a state of constant motion, expecting to find death notices posted online for at least three. Mollender continued his search for other victims as well.

"I'm not getting anything on Dasari or Jiang. But I logged in to our intranet at Shelby Stone," Mollender said. "Pendleton is listed as still being an employee. I have an address for him. Phone number too. According to this, he lives in Alexandria, Virginia."

"Let's hope that's true," Nick said.

"What, that he's in Alexandria?"

"No. That he lives."

# CHAPTER 42

"There are three possible reasons Pendleton's not answering his phone," Nick told Jillian. "Either he's not at home, he's busy, or he's already dead."

Jillian grimaced at the notion.

"Why are they doing this after so many years, Nick? It's pure evil. Could a branch of our government really be responsible?"

"I wish I knew. I really do. Maybe people from Mohammad's terrorist organization are finally exacting revenge for his death. Even though we know he wasn't the one who died that day, maybe they don't."

"It's a thought, but terrorists usually go

out of their way to take credit for acts of vengeance like this, and we haven't heard a word."

"Six people dead."

"At least."

Nick gripped the steering wheel with white-knuckle force, frustrated that so many answers still eluded them. Before they left her office, Noreen had handed Nick two leather cases, each containing a copy of the operation that she had burned to DVD. Now, Jillian held them in her lap, a reminder, she said, that Umberto and Belle were with them on this journey until the end.

The traffic was moderately heavy, and Nick estimated they were still ten minutes away from Roger Pendleton's address in Alexandria. The Mole had volunteered to stay behind with a still-shaken Noreen, and to continue searching for information about the surgical resident and the medical student, neither of whom had proven that easy to find.

During the drive, Jillian wrote a note for Pendleton, begging him to call either of them as soon as possible. Twice she had tried to reach him at home and through the page operator at the hospital. Nick had also phoned Don Reese, but his call to the detective went straight into voice mail.

"Maybe we should call nine-one-one," Jillian suggested, "let the authorities take it from here."

"Remember what Reese told us? We're in deep here too, Jill. If the police are going to get involved now, better if it's Reese's call how and when. In the meantime, we need to warn Pendleton to be careful."

"I just hope that we're not too late."

"Me too," Nick said with a heavy sigh. "Me too."

Pendleton's modest split-level ranch was the last house on a tree-lined dead-end street. The idyllic, family-friendly setting made the reason they were there even more disturbing. Nick pulled up along the grassy tree belt and had opened the driver's side door when Jillian grabbed his arm and pulled him back inside.

"We can't just go rushing in there, Nick," she said. "We have no idea what we're up against. I don't want to see any more death, and I . . . don't want anything to happen to you."

Nick took hold of her hands. "Nothing's

going to happen to either of us. Trust me on that, Jill. We'll knock on the door, we'll leave the note, and then we'll look for Pendleton at the hospital."

"I'm sorry to sound like such a baby. That video really got to me—the thought of that man in the surgical gown calmly standing there, murdering Umberto. It's as if he had no soul."

"Well, thanks to you I'm reconnecting with mine," Nick said. "I have an EMDR session later on. I intend to work at it the way I used to when I was studying organic chemistry or training for a climb."

Jillian squeezed his hands, then caressed the stubble on his face.

"Are you ready?"

"Ready."

Side by side they proceeded up the flagstone walkway to Pendleton's red-painted front door, with Jillian clutching a copy of the DVD. All was eerily quiet save for the crunch of loose slate and the white noise of birdsong on the warm afternoon breeze. The yard was small, but well maintained, with no toys to suggest Pendleton had kids.

Nick peered into the living room through

a small opening between the drapes, but could see only a few feet inside. There was no movement. He rang the bell, then tried the door. Locked.

"Maybe he's at work," Jillian said. "I don't trust Shelby Stone's page system."

Nick pressed the doorbell a second time and they listened to a cascade of chimes reverberating inside the house.

"Let's try around back," he said, growing more anxious.

Suddenly the door swung open.

The man standing there was dressed in hospital scrubs and had a cell phone pressed between his ear and shoulder. He was hopping around in a circle, trying to wiggle on a sneaker.

*Just untie it!* Nick wanted to shout.

As Pendleton wrestled the sneaker onto his foot, he lost hold of his phone, which dropped to the hardwood floor with a sharp crack.

"If you're recruiting me for your church, I'm going to be really pissed!" he snapped, bending down to retrieve the phone. "Jerry? Jerry, you still there? Shit, that's just great."

"We're sorry to bother you."

The man hesitated, taking in a deep breath.

"Don't worry, it's not your fault I'm a klutz. I'm running late and the guy on the phone was telling me where I needed to have been twenty minutes ago. Sorry if I raised my voice at you guys. Phone still seems to be working, though, so I'll call him back. Just hang on, or else leave if you're going to try and cost me money."

His composure regained, Pendleton placed his call and learned what he needed to about the emergency case waiting for him at Shelby Stone. The perfusionist was a trim, balding man in his early thirties, and struck Nick as an athlete.

"Roger Pendleton?" Jillian asked.

"Yeah. That's me. Look, I'm really in a hurry, guys. There's a transplant going down. So if you're selling something, especially God, just assume I've got one already, okay?"

Nick stepped forward.

"Roger, I'm Dr. Nick Garrity, a surgeon working with the Helping Hands medical van. This is my friend, Jillian Coates. She's a psych nurse at Shelby Stone."

Pendleton seemed to soften at that.

"Okay, what's up? Not often a tech like me gets paid a house call. Not ever, actually."

"I know you're in a hurry, but we need to talk. It could be a matter of life or death."

"Yeah? Alas, so is the operation if I don't make it in to the hospital. I'm on backup and the guy on duty is tied up, and word is a heart's come in."

"When we say matter of life or death, we mean yours," Nick said. "We really need to talk. Can you get anyone else to go in for you?"

Pendleton studied Nick's face and his expression darkened.

"No, I can't get anyone to go in," he said. "How many backups do you think we have? Okay, okay. I'm sorry to sound snippy. I can't imagine what you're talking about, but I can give you two minutes."

Standing just inside the open doorway, Nick relayed what they knew of the identity switch in the OR three years ago, and the fact that over recent months, six of the ten people who were there for the disaster had died suddenly. Then he handed over a copy of the DVD recording the events.

When Nick finished, Pendleton stared down at the disc, a deep furrow across his brow.

"So you're saying that I'm on somebody's kill list?"

"There's nothing else to believe, Roger," Jillian said.

"Well, I stopped in and met Mohammad the evening before the case. I try and do that with all my patients. His photo had been all over the papers. I promise you that was him in his room that night, and him on the table the next day, and him who went berserk and flew into my equipment, and him who died."

"Six out of nine medical personnel are dead, including my sister, Belle," Jillian said patiently. "We believe the man responsible for the OR death, if not all of them, was number ten—one of the two who wheeled the patient in. We are absolutely certain that the victim in the operating room that day wasn't the man you thought he was."

Pendleton checked his watch.

"Look, I don't know whether you two know what you're talking about or not, but I do know I've got to finish getting dressed and get to the hospital."

"You sure you don't have just a few minutes to watch that video?" Nick asked. "It will convince you."

"I don't need to watch anything to remember that day. That sort of thing you don't forget. All I can tell you, and I probably shouldn't even be doing that, is that after it was over, I was called into my boss's office. There were a couple suits waiting there to speak with me. They told me what had just happened was a matter of national security and that I was to tell nobody about anything I had seen. They made me sign a paper stating just that, and warned that if I spoke about the case, I could lose my job or even face prison time. They gave me a name to refer any reporters to, but I have no idea where that is. Otherwise, I'd refer you to them. Look, just give me your card and I'll get you the name. But I gotta leave."

Jillian shot Nick a concerned look. "That would explain why Belle never told me much about the operation."

"Look, I appreciate the warning," Pendleton said, "but I have to get to the hospital right away. I'm not sure I can even talk with you about this case without risking my job and God only knows what else. Why don't you tell me quickly what you think I'm supposed to do now, and I'll think it over?"

"Just please give us your cell number and pick up if you see it's me or Jillian calling. Also, stay very aware of your surroundings and remain extra vigilant. We're trying to contact a detective we know in D.C."

"I appreciate the visit. I'll pick up if you call."

"We tried to reach you a bunch of times on the way over here, but you didn't answer. You had us a little worried."

"Long night last night. I was sleeping with the ringer off. That's why the hospital called me on my cell."

Nick and Pendleton quickly exchanged numbers.

"Call me if anything comes up," Nick said. "Otherwise, I'll call you as soon as we have more information to share."

"Sure," Pendleton replied, his tone still tinged with disbelief, "do that. One last thing."

"Yes?"

"Why has it taken three years for all this horrible stuff to start happening?"

Jillian and Nick exchanged looks and shrugged.

"We don't know" was all they could say.

Roger Pendleton hated rushing into a case—especially a transplant. Experience had taught him that mistakes happened when protocols were shortcut or skipped altogether for the sake of expedience. Often, there wasn't enough time to review the patient's medical record properly. Certainly today, time was a luxury that a twenty-year-old kid, his heart failing rapidly, could not afford.

Instead of contemplating the shocking revelations about the Aleem Syed Mohammad operation from three years ago, Pendleton was thinking about his cardiopulmonary bypass setup. This operation would mark only the sixth time he had used the new machine that featured a centrifugal pump, an advance over the roller pump he had used for so long.

Not many knew the stress involved with being a perfusionist. Keeping blood out of the surgical field was one part of the job. In addition, he was the patient's lifeline, controlling oxygenation and balancing any number of fluids. For all his world-be-damned, carefree attitude, Pendleton was almost maniacal about maintaining his equipment.

He trotted up the carpeted staircase to his bedroom to grab the gym bag he would need for his ritual post-op workout.

He wondered if his surprise visitors could be anything but kooks. Doubtful, he decided. When they could explain the three-year gap from the operation to the killings, assuming they were killings, he might take them more seriously.

He was on his way back down the stairs when they rang the bell again. Pendleton really didn't have any more patience for them, even if they had thought of something more persuasive.

"Listen, we'll have to talk later," he was saying as he swung open the front door. "Right now I really have to—"

A tall, uniformed man from his gas company smiled politely, said his name, and held out his ID.

"Oh jeez!" Pendleton said, holding his hand over his hammering heart and laughing at himself. "You startled me. I thought you were the people who just left here."

"Sorry about that," the man said, his eyes shadowed by the bill of his cap. "I actually think I saw them go. I startle lots of folks when I have to make a house call."

"Well, I was a little jumpy. The people who just left were telling me I had to be careful."

The man chuckled. "Actually, that's why I'm here," he said. "It's about your gas leak."

Pendleton sniffed the air. "I think you have the wrong place. I don't have a gas leak."

"No, not yet you don't."

That was when Roger Pendleton looked down and saw that the man was holding a gun.

# CHAPTER 43

Jillian suggested they use the time before Nick's EMDR therapy session to grab a drink and something to eat and plan their next steps. They settled on Kilkenny's Irish Pub in the Adams Morgan section of D.C., arriving there just after noon. The cozy tavern, paneled in dark barn siding, was crowded with businesspeople enjoying a Guinness with their lunch, along with those Nick pegged as regulars, some of whom sat at the bar watching an international soccer match on TV, while others were engaged in an animated game of darts. The jukebox was off and traditional Irish music, piped through an impressive sound system, provided a pleasant background.

Relaxed.

Simple.

Life.

They sat down beside each other at the end of the bar, where two of the dozen worn and scratched wooden stools were empty. Passing on the lunch menu offered by the bartender, Nick ordered a Glenlivet neat and Jillian an Amstel Light in the bottle. Their lives at that moment were as far removed from those of the folks in the homey pub as the Earth was from Mars.

Nick took a sip of the single malt scotch whisky from a reasonably clean tumbler, letting it linger in his mouth until the taste demanded that he swallow. Then he stared numbly ahead at the liquor bottles, housed inside cubbies built into the wall behind the bar. Jillian touched his hand and he turned slowly to meet her gaze.

"A bar snack for your thoughts," she said, smiling as she nudged over a black plastic dish filled with pretzels.

Nick took one, but offered only a thin smile in return.

"What do you think these people would

say if they knew the depravity of what we're confronting?" he asked finally.

"If they believed us, and that's a big if, they'd probably say something like, 'As long as it doesn't affect me directly, and I can go on tossing my darts and drinking my stout, do whatever it is you need to do.'"

"We've come so far from when we first met, Jill, and yet I feel so incredibly helpless. You know, Pendleton thought we were crazy."

"I know. He seems like a good guy, though."

"Yup. Maybe we'll hear from Reese before something happens to him."

"Do you want to try the Mole again? Maybe he's come up with something on the resident or medical student."

"Nah, he said he was going to stick around with Noreen at her place and keep looking. He'll call if he comes up with anything."

"I know what you mean about feeling helpless. What did Junie say when you told her?"

"She was stunned, naturally. I don't think it's hit her yet that Umberto is dead and that somebody killed him in such a horrid, self-serving way."

"Has it hit *you*?"

The question pulled Nick's head down until his eyes met the gritty floor. He looked up long enough to take a hard swallow of his drink, which he downed in a single gulp. Then he closed his eyes tightly, clenching his fists against the burn of the alcohol spilling down his throat, and against the evil.

"None of this is your fault," Jillian said softly.

"Believe it or not, I've come to grips with that. What I'm angry at now is my own rage. I was put together to care for people, regardless of who they were or what they might have done in their lives. Now I want to kill someone. Maybe anyone. I really do."

"Which would you take at this moment, your rage or the total lack of feeling you've had for so long? It's all changing for you, Nick."

"Maybe. Maybe you're right."

"I'm going to tell you something that scares the bejesus out of me."

"Yeah? What's that?"

"I think you may be the most amazing

man I've ever met. Somebody I'm really capable of falling for. Someone I think I would have fallen for in a heartbeat before . . . before what happened to you in Afghanistan. But I want the next time I fall in love with a man to be the last. I don't need you to have arrived at the person—at the doctor—you're capable of being. I just need to know you're committed to making the journey. You can't go on hiding your emptiness behind your charm. A doctor loses a patient. Do they quit being a doctor?"

"I'm going with no."

"Damn straight. Even if they believe it was their fault. Sick patients force doctors—and nurses—into having to make decisions. If we had more time, less pressure on us to act, the choices we made might have been different. Continuing to help others with our talent and skill is actually honoring the memory of the patient who died. I don't blame myself for Belle's death. I blame the person who killed her. Same way as losing Sarah and Umberto isn't on you, Nick. It's on the people who killed them. We can't bring them back, but we can still do more for them."

Nick looked up at the dark rafters.

"Here's the thing with PTSD," he said. "Some people think it's in your head and that you can just snap your fingers or crank up your willpower and come out of it, or like MacCandliss keeps insisting, that it's all manufactured for some secondary gain. But that's not the case at all. It's a chemical change where the thinking takes place, like an internal depression, or a cancer eating away at you. Much as you want to just shake the symptoms off, sometimes they won't let go. So you end up walking around in circles, holding yourself hostage to the places and people where you feel most comfortable and safe, because the alternative means facing an unknown. I used to love the unknown. I was a pure adrenaline junkie. Rock climbing, skiing, you name it. But after watching Sarah get hacked apart by that truck moments before Umberto saved my life under that refrigerator, lying there, covered with broken bags of blood, that rush lost its appeal. I retreated into what was safest for me."

"I know you're hurting, Nick . . ."

Nick held up a hand, cutting her short. The scotch was settling in, doing what he wanted it to.

"No, let me finish," he said. "Since losing Sarah, I know I've been a walking shell. But then you came along. And now, each day your strength is becoming my strength. You just have to be patient with me, Jill, and believe that I really do want to become the man—the doc—I once was. This struggle is a war, not a battle, but I feel the tide turning, and more important, I feel I want to work at it."

"And I'll help you as best as I can. I swear I will."

Nick swung his legs around to face her.

"It makes all the difference," he said, no longer able to keep his lips from hers.

As they were kissing, the bar erupted in a huge cheer. They quickly pulled away from one another, thinking for an embarrassed moment that the applause and shouts were for them.

"Back to your smoochin'," the totally amused bartender said, pointing up at the TV. "Chelsea just scored the tying goal against Manchester United."

"Maybe I'll skip therapy," Nick whispered in her ear.

"Maybe you won't. We have time, baby. Step by step, we have time."

"Let's plan on meeting up with Saul, either at the hospital or at Noreen's place, after my session. If I haven't heard from Reese by then, we might have to find somebody else. I'm sure Junie knows who we can contact. She's connected with everyone."

"But you said yourself, we don't know who we can trust or how deep this whole thing goes."

"That'll be a chance we have to take."

Just then, Jillian's cell phone rang. Nick perked up, thinking it might be Reese, but she let him know she did not recognize the caller ID. Her expression brightened, though, as soon as she answered. Over the din of the pub, Nick picked up only fragments of her brief conversation.

"Hi there, I'm so glad to hear from you. . . . You do? Oh, my God, that's fascinating. As I told you, I've been suspicious of the timing from the get-go. . . . No, it's not a problem. This is a good time. . . . Sure, I can. . . . Where? . . . Yeah, I know the place. I'll meet you in an hour. . . . Okay. See you there." She set the phone down and turned to Nick. "Talk about things coming together."

"What was that all about?"

"That was my condo's insurance company. Now they're thinking the fire was arson. Apparently, they actually have information about who might have set it. He wants to meet with me in an hour and go over their findings."

"Is this the same fire inspector you told me about?"

"Exactly," Jillian said. "His name's Regis, Paul Regis."

# CHAPTER 44

Nick's ninety-minute eye movement therapy session was especially intense, but he was ready for it. Dr. Coletta Deems, his therapist, a tall, formal scarecrow of a woman, was impressed, and said so.

"You seem exceptionally focused today, Dr. Garrity."

*Well, uncovering a conspiracy of serial murder has that effect on me*, he thought about saying, *especially when combined with finding out that the woman of anyone's dreams might be in love with me.*

"I'm visualizing better," he said instead.

"Maybe today's like the fifty-foot putt that keeps you coming back to the golf course."

"Pardon?"

"Not worth repeating. I have a lot on my mind today, which makes my ability to control my thinking that much more surprising and satisfying."

"So, where would you put your SUD score at this moment?"

Nick looked up at the Subjective Units of Distress chart on the wall of the tranquil therapy room. Ten was defined as "unbearably bad." Zero was "absolute peace and serenity."

Four, he decided, and said so.

**Four: Somewhat upset to the point that you cannot easily ignore an unpleasant thought. You can handle it okay, but don't feel good.**

"Yes, I believe I'm under five."

Deems was as delighted as she seemed capable of being.

"Progress is what we're after, Dr. Garrity," she said, adjusting her wire-rims. "No more or less than progress."

"Progress," Nick echoed, excited to share the news of his SUD triumph with Jillian.

"Oh, by the way, Doctor, you asked not to have our session interrupted for any call other than one from Don Reese."

"Yes?"

"Well, he didn't call, but a"—she checked a small slip of paper—"Mr. Mollender called about twenty minutes ago. He asked you to call him in the office. I have the number here."

As soon as he could, Nick called Noreen Siliski's office. The Mole answered on the first ring.

"Saul! Sorry I wasn't able to take your call. You got anything?"

"I do. But I think we need to meet in person to discuss it. I'm still at Noreen's office."

"I . . . know. That's the number I dialed. Did you find them?"

"The med student and the resident?" Mollender said vaguely. "Yes, yes, I think so. But I'd rather show you. Can you make it down here?"

Mollender sounded tense and exhausted, hardly like a man with any good news to share. Nick looked across at the SUD chart and decided he had drifted up to a five: *Unpleasant feelings still manageable with some effort.*

"It's getting on rush hour," he said, "but I'll be down as soon as I can."

"And Nick, do you still have the DVDs of Andy's death?"

"Andy? You mean Umberto. I have one and I left the other one with Roger Pendleton, the perfusionist. I'm pretty sure I already told you that."

"I'll see you soon," Mollender said.

The line went dead.

On the stop-and-go drive to Sutton, Nick tried unsuccessfully to reach Jillian and Junie. He did manage to catch Reggie at home, who told him that both his foster mother and the RV were gone, although he hadn't seen her leave. Strange, Nick thought. Junie almost certainly was in the RV headed for D.C. to pick up the Professor, as they referred to this particular covering doc. There should be no reason why she wouldn't answer her phone.

Maybe she had already arrived at the Professor's and stopped in for coffee. . . . Maybe.

Jillian, he figured, was bogged down in dealing with what had now become an arson investigation. But she had a caller ID. Why hadn't *she* answered his call?

His SUD score had spent a nanosecond in the fours and may now, he realized, be approaching six: *Feeling poorly or anxious to the point that you begin to think something ought to be done about the way you feel.*

Nick pulled into the same space where he had parked earlier that day, to the left of the Dumpster and alongside a red Corolla, the only other vehicle in an otherwise deserted lot. He peered up along the ingenious two-story telescoping trashbarrel chute snaking down from Noreen's window to the center of the half-filled Dumpster. There was no light coming from the window surrounding the upper end of the tube, and he assumed the canvas shade had been dropped down.

His uneasiness increased.

What had earlier been a bright afternoon, had, during his drive south, progressively given way to dense clouds. Now a light rain had begun to fall, plucking rhythmically against the leaves of the dense woods that bordered the parking lot.

As Mollender requested, Nick had dropped the DVD into his well-worn leather bag, alongside the research on Aleem Syed Mohammad that Reggie had compiled. Now, glancing about, he took the disc out of his bag and slid it onto a metal support beneath the Dumpster. He felt increasingly unsettled about the Mole's nervousness and use of his dead brother's name rather than Umberto's. Perhaps he was being paranoid, but with all they had uncovered, he felt he had good reason to be.

He heightened his own tension by trying Junie, Jillian, Reese, and Mollender once more.

Nothing.

Moving through a burgeoning sense of unease, Nick entered the building and took the stairs up two floors. He tried the door, assuming it would be open. Locked. He knocked several times. No answer.

"Saul? Noreen?" His voice reverberated off of the stairwell walls. "You there?"

He tried the knob again, and was only slightly surprised when it turned. He pushed the door open and stepped inside Noreen's partially renovated office.

The first thing he saw was blood.

There were pools of it on the floor, soaking several of the white sheets red, and mixing with sawdust to form nauseating clumps. The scent of freshly cut wood, so pleasant earlier that day, was overtaken by the hideous, bitterly metallic stench of blood and death.

Nick's mouth went dry and he felt his stomach lurch. Then he saw Noreen. She lay spread-eagled on the floor, several feet to the right of her workbench in roughly the center of the room. Her throat had been widely sliced open, drenching her white work shirt with blood, now in the process of drying. She appeared to be staring right at him. Instinct made him check her carotid pulse, though he knew her gray eyes and milky, nearly colorless skin meant she was looking only into oblivion.

Nick turned his head to the right to look away. That was when he saw Mollender. The Mole was directly opposite Noreen on the other side of the room, nearer the windows. He, too, was spread-eagled, but facedown on the polished oak floor. Two feet away was a heavy, eight-inch kitchen knife, covered with gore. The right side of Mollender's head had been blown apart—an exit wound. From his years of dealing with gunshot wounds, Nick knew there would be a bullet hole on the opposite temple. Blood continued seeping from the gaping hole and fragments of bone and brain tissue dotted the floor like tiny islands of death. Nick took a few cautious steps forward, his eyes now transfixed on the dull steel of a pistol resting next to Mollender's outstretched, lifeless hand.

A guttural, primal scream exploded from Nick's throat as he crouched by the body. The odd little record room librarian had killed his one-time lover and then shot himself. That conclusion seemed obvious. But why? The two of them had held hands. They appeared to be doing wonderfully. He did not know Mollender well, but on the surface at least, the man hardly seemed capable of such violence.

It was then that Nick heard the click of the door closing behind him. Startled, he whirled around, rising to his feet. His leather bag, still slung over his shoulder, swung in an arc across the front of his body as he confronted a tall, well-built man, dressed head to toe in black. He was wearing latex surgical gloves. The heavy pistol held loosely in his right hand was pointed at the center of Nick's chest.

Nick's gaze traveled upward, until he met with the coldest pale blue eyes he had ever seen. Pure evil.

"What have you done?" Nick shrieked. "Why?"

"Pipe down, Doctor," the killer said calmly. "What I've done is the non-kill that I do better than any other. Murder-suicide. I'm a master at it if I do say so myself. What do you think?"

He gestured to the grotesque pair of corpses.

This was the man. Nick knew immediately. This was the man who had sat by and watched Belle Coates die. He wasn't the stocky killer in the OR, but he was probably responsible for some of the other deaths, if not all of them. Nick could barely keep from charging him. In fact, fueled by rage, he actually took a half step forward.

"Easy, Doc. This thing could get ugly for you quick. You brought the DVD?"

The man spoke with utter confidence, and his soulless eyes actually flickered with a hint of joy.

Suddenly, Nick was certain that he had Jillian.

"Where is she?" he demanded.

"She?"

"Jillian Coates. Where is she? If anything happens to her, I swear I'll kill you."

"Relax, Doctor. Isn't that what you tell your patients before you take your index finger and ream them? Just relax. From what I can see, you're not really in a position to demand or threaten anything. Besides, as chance would have it, I stopped by Roger Pendleton's place right after you left and retrieved one of the discs. It had this lovely woman's business sticker on it. That's what led me here. With a little prompting, she told me you probably had the second of the two discs she gave you. I had our friend Mollender over there summon you here. So, give me the DVD."

"What DVD?"

"DON'T FUCK WITH ME!"

Nick recoiled from the ferocity of the killer's outburst. As quickly as that explosion came, the emotion drained from the man's face until he was once again a steely evil. In an unhurried voice he said, "You know what I'm talking about, Doc. That cute little nurse died rather than expose her sister to the pain I had in store for Jillian. Don't make the mistake of thinking I won't do it to her now."

Nick's heart beat wildly. He could feel his blood pressure rising, releasing beads of sweat across his brow and down the back of his neck. Instead of reacting irrationally, though, he closed his eyes, willed his pulse to slow, and began taking charge of his emotions.

His only option, for himself and for Jillian, was to buy some time. To that end, he had two possible tools: the DVD, and the monster's gigantic ego.

It might be too late for him, too late for Jillian, but he had to do what he could to take charge of the PTSD that had controlled his life for so long. He had to act intelligently, rationally, and with force.

"Why are you doing this?" he began, searching for an opening—any opening. "Who are you?"

"Hey, slow down. I have the big gun, so I get to ask the questions. Now where's the disc? In your sack, there? In the glove compartment of your car? Don't make me tie you up and torture you, my friend, because if I have to do that, after you're bloody and dead, I'm going to settle up with that girl of yours. And I mean settle up in every sense of the words. Now, the disc."

"Just tell me. Tell me how you managed to kill all those people from the OR without having anyone know."

It looked as if the killer was about to answer him. But before he could, Nick heard the haunting first notes of AC/DC's "Back in Black." The man pulled a cell phone off of his belt clip, never for a second lowering his gun or averting his soulless eyes. For several seconds he held the phone to his ear and listened.

"No, he hasn't given me the DVD," he said. "I think I can convince him, but it may require more pain than he's equipped to endure."

He listened again, then took a step toward Nick, the pistol an accusatory finger now pointing steadily at Nick's heart.

Then he grinned.

"It's for you," he said.

# CHAPTER 45

"Who is this?" Nick shouted into the killer's phone.

"Mr. Koller there intends to torture you, until you give us the disc, or you die," a man's gravelly voice said. "I don't want you to die. I have great respect for you as a man and a patriot who has served his country with honor."

The voice sounded familiar, Nick thought, but from where? It was unhurried and composed, with an edge of power and entitlement.

"Who are you?" Nick said. "Why are you having these people killed?"

"Dr. Garrity, I believe if you were in my position, you would do the same thing."

Again Nick tried to connect with where he had heard that voice before.

"That's insane," he said. "You're insane. It was you in the operating room, wasn't it? You're the one who killed Umberto."

"You'd be better off letting me drive this conversation," said the man. "So I suggest you listen and try to understand what this is all about."

Nick's eyes met Koller's. The gun in his right hand was rock steady and pointed straight at his head. The self-confident smirk etched across the killer's face had Nick envisioning kicking him full force in the teeth.

*Easy*, he told himself. *It's going to happen. Somehow it's going to happen. Just be cool.*

"At least tell me who you are," he said, his composure now largely regained.

"All you need to know is that you have become involved in business that is of the utmost importance to our country's national security. The danger we are facing is very real. We need you to act like the soldier that you are."

**Ramsland.**

Nick caught his breath. He felt his chest tighten. The room seemed to be spinning.

The man's ads had been all over the media. Alone and with moderate presidential candidate John Greenleigh.

Ramsland the patriot.

It was all starting to make sense. The ads portrayed the man as the consummate American, whose promise to protect every citizen against the threat of terrorism was resonating loudly with voters of both parties.

What in the hell had the man gotten himself into?

"The solider that I am, the doctor that I am would never take an innocent life. Why don't you come over here and see what you've done. Look at the people you've murdered, Mr. Ramsland."

For a time there was silence.

"The people who have died are heroes."

"No, they're victims. I'm going to bury you, Ramsland. Just like you buried them."

**Easy . . .**

"An understandable reaction given the circumstances. But Doctor, before you go making any more threats, it's best we have a little talk."

"I mean it, Ramsland. I'll find you, and when I do, you'll wish our paths had never crossed."

*Easy does it*, Nick warned himself again. *You need to understand more of where he's coming from.*

"I didn't want this to happen to these people, Nick. There was no choice. Do you think I'm against peace in this war-weary world?"

Nick hated that the man was now using his first name so casually.

"I think you're a murderer," Nick said. "Simple as that."

"No, sir. That is not any more true than saying that the men in your unit in Afghanistan were murderers. You see, what I am, Nick, is a patriot, just as they are, and you are. The people from that operating room, and lying there now in front of you, are casualties of war, just as were all those blown up in your hospital in FOB Savannah."

Nick's sense of the man and his motivations was coming more into focus. Whether it was guilt or zeal, Lionel Ramsland needed to have his actions justified. He was looking for understanding and even praise for the choices he had made and the lives he had taken. And Nick, a decorated soldier and a surgeon, as well as a friend of several of the casualties, was the perfect subject from which to earn such absolution. If Nick had agreed and cooperated by turning over the DVD, he might have been offered a position in Ramsland's inner circle. But as things were, he was going to die.

"We're nothing alike," Nick said.

He turned his back to Koller, who continued blocking the only exit. Keeping the phone pressed tightly against his ear, he stepped farther into the room, trying unsuccessfully to avoid looking at Noreen's lifeless body to his left, and Saul Mollender's to his right. His insides quaked with rage as he wondered what their last horrible moments were like.

**Patriots, indeed!**

"You're wrong there, Nick," Ramsland was saying, "you and I are far more similar than you think."

Nick was eight feet away from Noreen's workbench now. Many of her impressive array of tools were resting on top in a tool bucket, and in the heavy work belt that surrounded it. Wary of drawing Koller's attention to the setup, he quickly broke off his gaze.

*Maybe*, he was thinking, as a plan began to materialize, *just maybe I have a chance.*

But he also knew it would be one chance and only one. He needed to stall and to continue composing himself for a single, definitive move.

"Yeah?" he said. "You and your friend here kill people and I save them. How is that alike?"

Pacing in front of the workbench, Nick wanted his movements to appear random. It was doubtful Koller missed much, so he had to move carefully. Powerful jolts of adrenaline were coursing through him, bringing the sort of heightened awareness he often experienced during an intense triage or operation.

"You and I are both soldiers, Nick. A guy like you could have made a bundle in private practice. But no, you sacrificed that earning potential for something much more important. Your country."

"I did what I felt was right."

"My point exactly. Your devotion to finding your war buddy, Umberto, is in a soldier's DNA. Never leave a man behind. Am I right?"

"I guess."

"That's loyalty."

"Go on."

"All I'm saying, Nick, is that you have a very rare opportunity to serve your country in a way few Americans can. You can make a difference."

"How? Murder?"

"No, Nick. By saving lives."

"Check again. I don't see any lives being saved here."

"Of course you don't. That's just my point. You think you know everything about what's going on, but you haven't the slightest clue what's really happening."

"Yeah? Why don't you enlighten me?"

Nick glanced over at Koller. The killer stood just a few feet away, like a big cat, lean and sinewy, poised to launch himself at the slightest hint of trouble.

*It isn't time yet*, Nick decided. *But soon. Keep stalling.*

"This wasn't how we wanted things to

play out," Ramsland was saying. "Mohammad wanted out. He was weary. He had a price on his head, and one of his sons was killed while someone was trying to collect it. We wanted Mohammad to give us information—information that would save American lives. And he did. The Sears Tower in Chicago. The American Embassy in Paris. Grand Central station at rush hour. Thousands and thousands of lives. Attacks against innocent civilians, women and children, who might have been blown to bits."

"I never heard a word about any of those attacks," Nick said.

"You didn't hear about them in the news because they never happened. The information we . . . extracted from Mohammad kept them from happening."

"You didn't extract information from him, Ramsland. He gave it to you. We didn't capture him like the news said. He gave himself up. He gave the information to you in exchange for my friend's life. You cut a deal with him. Public, high-profile death— the ultimate disappearing act."

"You know as well as I do that the United States does not negotiate with terrorists.

We capture them and learn what we can through due process of law, abiding by whatever protection the Geneva Convention grants these monsters."

"That's bullshit and you know it, Ramsland. You don't play by anybody's rules but your own. It was a trade—pure and simple. If you want me on your side, then at least tell the truth. That's the best starting point."

Again Nick made a cautious glance over at Koller. The killer appeared as though he were enjoying the banter, despite his hearing only half of the conversation. The pistol was no longer pointing at the center of his chest.

**Good. Lower your guard just a fraction. That's what I need.**

"Rules are what keep men like me from making a real difference in the world. We're all walking contradictions, Nick. In Afghanistan you patched up soldiers just so we could put them back in theater again. We don't torture prisoners. All we do is use every means to make them give us information they don't want to share. If promising them something they want will get that information out quicker and more

completely, that's a road worth considering. Don't you think?"

"I suppose so."

"Do you think we enjoy trading soldiers
like your friend Umberto? Of course not.
But men like us know our duty as patriots
is to act. We do so to save lives, just as
Truman traded one set of lives for another
when he sent out the *Enola Gay*. That's
the nature of war, Nick, and you know that
as well as I do."

"I'm beginning to understand."

"I hoped you would. You've suffered a
great deal for the cause."

Nick continued to shake on the inside.
His stomach was churning. Still, with Koller
watching his every step, gun at the ready,
he managed to keep a calm demeanor.

Nick marched back and forth in front of
the workbench, willing himself to look on
occasion at Mollender's and Noreen's bodies, now using that emotion to help fuel his
resolve.

*Soon*, he thought.

"What is it you want from me?"

"I want you to cooperate. Give the DVD
to my associate. Forget about Umberto.
Forget about your friends here. Focus on

yourself for a change, Nick. How involved is Ms. Coates?"

Nick felt a new flash of anger rip through him.

"You leave her out of this!"

"Maybe we will. Maybe; it all depends on you. You see, I can trust you if you say you'll do something. Know why?"

"No, tell me."

"Because I know everything. I know what people think. I know what they say before they even say it. I know when they break with my program. You could have asked your friend Phillip MacCandliss."

"MacCandliss? What's he got to do with this?"

"Nothing, now. You see, he went against his country. That's when we had Mr. Koller pay him a visit."

"You're a sick, sick man."

"Don't feel sorry for MacCandliss, Nick. You can thank him for bringing us Umberto. And true, your friend was the right profile for our mission, but I also knew how much MacCandliss despised you. Umberto was his pathetic little way of beating a man that he couldn't beat on his own."

Nick clenched the phone, wishing he

had the strength to crush it into tiny pieces. He closed his eyes, counting backward to slow his pulse. Turning his back to Koller, he leaned up against the workbench. For his plan to succeed, he had to get the killer even closer to him. Keeping his hands out of the assassin's line of sight, Nick hoped it would be enough of a lure to get him to move for a better angle. In seconds, Koller had changed position, crossing the room and moving diagonally toward the bench.

"I don't believe MacCandliss had anything do to with Umberto's death," Nick said.

"And I don't care," Ramsland replied. "Believe what you want. Both are dead. But you still have a choice. Give us the DVD and your pledge to be a patriot, and we'll see about letting you move along with your life. Ms. Coates, too."

"By patriot, you mean silent."

"Call it what you will. We're soldiers, Nick. You and I. I felt I owed you a chance."

Koller was in the best position possible, directly to Nick's right. Nick had served Ramsland's purpose by even considering going in with him. There was absolutely no chance he was going to be allowed to survive this day.

*Now! Do it now!* Nick thought.

His senses were heightened by another intense surge of adrenaline. The pungent, coppery stench of blood, noticeable before, was now overpowering. Koller's empty left hand was the target. There was no way to get at his pistol.

*Panic is not an option,* Nick was thinking, remembering his days in the OR. *Panic costs lives.*

He silently repeated the mantra, while praying Koller had not noticed his hand inching closer toward the tool bucket.

With Ramsland still on the line, Nick set the phone down on the middle of the workbench. His pulse was hammering in his throat. Chances were he was about to die.

"He wants to talk to you," he managed.

Koller kept his weapon level. As his left hand moved to pick up the phone, his eyes left Nick for perhaps a second. It was just enough time.

The nail gun's bright orange handle stuck out of the tool bucket holster like an outlaw's six-shooter. It was a cordless model, not the compressor type Nick had used in his early teens to help his father frame a modest addition on their house.

The magazine on the Paslode gun was designed to be easily visible. Nothing upset a framer or roofer more than running out of nails mid-job. Nick had already noticed that the tool was full with what looked like three-inch nails. If the battery was charged, he had a chance. If not, he hoped it would be over quickly.

Koller's gun hand dropped several inches as he looked down to locate the phone. In that moment, Nick went for the nail gun. Koller saw movement, but turned his head just before he raised his pistol. In that instant, Nick snatched the nail gun out of its holster and in a continuous motion drove the tip into the back of Koller's hand with all the force he could muster.

There was a sharp pop, followed by a geyser of blood from the spot. Simultaneous with the sound, Nick heard the cracking of bone as the nail plowed through skin, then metacarpal, then nerves and muscle, and finally through skin again. The shaft shot down its full three inches, exiting the palm and entering the wood, impaling the killer's hand onto the workbench.

Koller's feral scream was more surprise and rage than agony.

Nick dove for the floor, clutching the nail gun with both his hands as he hit. He was positioned directly beside Koller, and hoisted the nail gun again, this time driving the steel nail into the top of Koller's shoe. Koller's scream, louder this time, reverberated throughout the office.

*Run!* Nick yelled to himself. *Run now!*

Koller remained cool enough to work his hand free and turn to shoot. The bullet tore through Nick's upper right arm with the sensation of touching a hot stove. A second shot missed.

Crouching, Nick charged toward the windows, zigzagging sharply. He had considered the stairs, but those were to his back and turning around would have cost seconds he didn't have.

**Three feet.**

Nick closed his eyes and lunged for the canvas flap hanging in front of the Dumpster chute, barely aware of the pain in his arm. The flap gave way, and in an instant, he plunged into darkness, flying downward three stories inside Noreen's makeshift trash-can slide.

The trip down was bruising. The hard rubber of the barrels gouged at his face and chest as he sped toward the disk of evening light at the bottom.

The Dumpster itself was hardly a sanctuary. It was half filled with splintered boards, broken glass, jagged metal, and nails.

Nick shot headfirst from the end of the tube, dropping two feet into the potentially lethal trash, shielding his face from the impact. When he hit, it was into a blanket of pink fiberglass insulation. Glass fragments embedded in the insulation tore at his skin. He rolled to the right as he landed, gashing his scalp just above one eyebrow on a strip of rusty metal. Blood began pouring into his eye.

His thoughts were fogged and his vision blurred from the combination of pain, blood, and what he had endured in Noreen Siliski's office. Partially by feel, he found the Dumpster's edge and began to climb out, jamming an exposed nail through his sneaker and into his foot. He cried out, but kept on scrambling.

He hit the asphalt of the parking lot heavily, and immediately toppled over, pawing at the blood that was oozing down into his eye. Closing that eye, he looked up for any sign of Koller and saw him ripping down the canvas covering the window. It was too gloomy to see if the nail that had pierced through the man's hand was still lodged there. But then, with a warrior's pride, the killer held it out for Nick to see that it was.

"You look bad, Doc," he called out. "Real bad."

*God, he's smiling!* Nick realized.

Koller hoisted his gun and Nick took off running. Two shots snapped harmlessly into the asphalt several feet from him. He clambered for the woods, blood continuing to blur his vision, and reached the tree line knowing that although he was still alive, he was not in the least safe.

Koller would follow.

# CHAPTER 46

Weaving awkwardly, Nick hobbled across the parking lot. The impact of the asphalt on his injured foot sent jolts of pain up his leg. His upper arm was afire, and any number of lesser injuries were also making themselves known. Blood continued to flow down into his eye. It took most of a minute to reach the woods. He tangled with a wall of saplings and thick brush that lined the forest perimeter and lost his balance, falling face-first onto the rain-soaked ground. The damp leaves turned red with his blood. His face was muddied and bruised.

Keeping low to the forest floor, and running clumsily ahead, Nick ripped a strip of fabric from his shirt and tied a makeshift bandage around his head. Even with pressure in place, blood from the cut still oozed down into his eye. With branches snapping across his face, he risked a glance over his shoulder, but could not see his pursuer through the rain and mounting gloom.

Veering to his left, Nick tried to gauge where the road might be. The building housing Noreen's office was an odd one, and quite isolated, as if a developer had bought a lot of land, built the first building of a planned office park, and then simply stopped. Nick sensed that he was heading not toward the highway, but deeper into the dense woods.

He thought about trying to find the road but rejected the notion and plunged ahead.

Another thirty or forty feet and he stopped and listened. The rain was continuing steadily, and he was breathing heavily, making it difficult to hear anything else. He held his breath and risked a furtive glance behind him. It took several seconds for him to make out the soft crunching of brush. Koller had traversed the parking lot and was moving stealthily but steadily toward him.

**Hide or run?**

Through the dark, he thought he saw the man's silhouette. He cast about, trying to get a sense of his position. There really was no place to hide.

The darkness was his ally. His injuries were his foe. But Koller was hurt, too, he reminded himself.

Crawling forward on hands and knees, Nick waited until the trees grew taller and denser before rising to his feet again. His only chance was to push deeper into the darkening woods. The predator was closing in.

Ignoring the burning from his gunshot wound, and sacrificing his forearms to the whipping branches, Nick shielded his face and barreled ahead. Here, the forest floor was uneven, and decaying leaves hid sinkholes that with one unfortunate step could break an ankle. He accelerated toward a small clearing. That was when the ground dipped unexpectedly. He failed to see an exposed rock directly in his path. His foot caught the solidly embedded stone and he tumbled down a steep embankment, landing heavily on his back in the middle of a slow-moving stream. His head snapped against a rock with dizzying force.

The water instantly soaked through his shirt and jeans, weighing him down when he tried to stand. Again, he paused and listened. Again he heard branches breaking somewhere up the embankment behind him.

**Damn.**

For no well-conceived reason, he decided to let the bank of the stream be his guide. His lungs were burning now with each labored breath, and a painful stitch had developed in his right side.

Soaked through, he began following the stream as it widened and snaked its way through the forest in what seemed like an east-west flow. Dusk had given way to a deepening darkness. The going was slow. Twice the muddy bank gave way, dropping him into the water. Despite his intense exertion, he quickly began to chill. Now, though, when he stopped, he heard nothing except the spattering of rain and the white noise of insects.

**Have I lost him?**

Twenty feet . . . thirty . . . forty. Oblivious to the pain, Nick dove ahead.

Suddenly, from behind and to his right, he heard the crack of a gunshot followed by the hum of a bullet cutting through the heavy air. At almost the same moment, a small tree to his right splintered. Whirling, he saw Koller's silhouette, perhaps a hundred yards away, climbing over a fallen log. Given the distance, the accuracy of the shot was astounding. Driven by new, intense urgency, he pushed forward.

Another shot zipped past, this one slicing into a tree, only inches above his head. The thought of hiding from the killer, even in the mounting darkness, vanished with that near miss. His only chance was to somehow get out of the woods to a neighborhood and call for help. It seemed, though it was probably totally irrational, that continuing to follow the water was his best chance.

Once again the storm intensified. Rain pelted his face, washing away the mud and blood. His injured foot ached with every step, sending hot needles up into his calf.

"Give me what I want and I promise your lady won't be hurt."

Koller's taunts seemed to echo from every direction. Nick kept his vision focused forward as he thrashed ahead. He would have sacrificed himself for Jillian without hesitating, but if Koller even had her, he was bluffing about letting her live. Ramsland could never leave survivors now. Despite his bluster, he had never really intended to. There was too much blood on his hands to chance putting his patriotism to the test. He might believe in the horrible things he had done or authorized, but it was doubtful the electorate would.

Nick forged on for what he guessed to be a quarter of a mile without slowing down. His eyes stayed fixed on the ground in front of him as he dodged treacherous rocks and heavy roots. He had done well to avoid going down as the last fragments of light seeped from the forest. Several checks behind showed no sign of Koller, and Nick began allowing himself to believe he might have somehow lost the man.

The forest landscape began to change. There were fewer trees here, more low brush. It was as though the woods were disappearing. Then the brush, too, gave way. He lifted his head just in time to see the stream fall away. He dropped to his knees and inched forward, peering down into the darkness. A thin, shallow water-fall disappeared beneath him. Fifty feet straight down? Seventy-five? It was impossible to tell. The gorge, formed by the river below, cut the forest in two. It was a hundred or two hundred feet wide, and ran ahead as far as he could see. The sound of rushing water reverberated off the cliff walls. From behind him, Nick heard dead branches and leaves crunching.

How could he have made such a mess of things?

To travel the ridge of the gorge in either direction would leave him totally exposed from lack of cover. Going down beside the narrow falls was an option, but not a desirable one.

Years ago, before Nick traded in his adrenaline addiction for EMDR therapy, his skills as a rock climber hovered just below expert. In his heyday, Nick could engineer the three most common rope systems blindfolded. He knew the right knots to tie in for most climbing situations.

Abseiling down a rock wall such as this was always a favorite maneuver of his. He did some rappelling in the Army and always excelled at it. But free-solo descent was a different beast entirely, especially in the rain.

There were no ropes here to provide him a quick trip down. He had tried bouldering before, but that hardly qualified him as more than a rank novice at free-solo techniques. Still, with Koller getting nearer, he had no options.

"Necessity is the mother of insanity," Nick muttered to himself.

Lying flat on his stomach, he inched over the cliff's edge. Forty feet down, there appeared to be a rock overhang. If he could descend the top part of the drop and reach the overhang before Koller spotted him, there was a chance he could hide out underneath it until it was safe to move again— until dawn if necessary.

More rustling to his back.

There were no options.

He would have to on-sight this route— figure out his holds on the fly as he worked his way down.

Turning around and dropping his feet so

he was facing the rock, Nick eased himself over the ledge. He located his first foothold five feet down. Moss and the rain had turned every rock and crevice slick and treacherous. There was no sure footing here, no dependable handholds. He kept his hands just past shoulder width, digging around the loose stone until he found what seemed like a reasonable grip. His left leg was shaking, perhaps from the tension of the tiptoe hold, but probably from exhaustion as well.

The first twenty feet down passed fairly easily. The rocks jutted out like jagged teeth, making the holds painless to feel out, even in dim light. Nick was gaining on the overhang, ignoring his fear and the pain from the gunshot wound in his right arm, and focusing all his intensity on the goal.

**Almost there . . . Keep going . . . Easy . . . Easy . . .**

A voice called out to him from above.

"Hey there, Doc," Koller said. "Haven't you read about the dangers of climbing at night without ropes?"

The monster was only a silhouette, but even in darkness, Nick thought he could see the white of his Cheshire Cat grin. He hurried his movements, inch by inch working his way down.

"You made this very easy, Doc. Set up a perfect non-kill, actually. Watch out for falling rocks. Those can be a bitch."

A small boulder clattered past, just two or three feet from Nick's face. He sensed the miss might have been on purpose.

"What about the DVD?" Nick yelled up into the blackness. "You don't have my copy."

"Yes, it's a shame your death will make it harder to find. But I know it's not far from where your friends Siliski and Mollender are napping. The good news is you'll be dead so I won't have to send you my medical bills for the hand and foot you impaled with that fucking nail gun."

"I hope they really hurt."

Nick's right foot hungrily sought out a new hold. The tips of his fingers began to burn from fatigue. Koller dropped another rock, missing by no more than a foot. The overhang was too far away for Nick to reach in time to get cover. Another rock clattered down, then another—this one glancing off his left shoulder.

"Once you fall and hit bottom, I'll amble down myself and make sure if you're still alive that you die slowly. You stuck there?"

The next rock, a foot or more around, smashed just above Nick's head, spraying a cloud of loose stone and dust into his face. The river continued to churn some fifty feet below, and he began peering down, searching for a pool. There was one. He felt certain of it. But there was no way of guessing its depth. Even if it ran deeper than six feet, a drop from this height could still be fatal, or at least leg-breaking, which would be the same thing.

Still, his options had all but vanished.

*Where did I screw up?* he wondered. *What could I have done differently?*

Koller's next drop hit Nick squarely on the shoulder. Startled, he lost his footing and for several seconds his body swung out over the river like a hinged door, with only the fingers of his left hand sustaining him. Teeth clenched, he held on and waited to swing back.

Staying there was suicide, he decided. He had to jump.

"And Doc," Koller's voice rang out, "I'm going to do your girl before I kill her."

Driven by the demon's words, Nick found the grip he needed. His footing felt solid enough. The handholds were in long fissures of the rock, which provided him with surprisingly good leverage. He visualized the move he was about to perform. There was no time to work up the needed courage. No matter what, he was going to jump. He flattened against the rock, feeling the cool moisture on his skin. Then, with every bit of power he could generate, he pushed himself away from the crag, and flew.

**Am I far enough out?**

His arms and legs flailed against the rushing air as he plummeted downward.

**Please, God . . . Please . . .**

Nick hit the water with the force of a thunderclap. Air exploded from his lungs. His head snapped forward. His legs hit bottom, then gave way. Immediately, the current pulled him under, grinding his body against rocks and sand before spitting him back to the surface again. Nick choked and sputtered on the musty-tasting water.

A bullet slapped into the river mere feet from where he was being carried downstream. It was followed by another shot, but there was no sound of impact. Nick took one stroke, but again was pulled under. His lungs burned. His strength was all but gone. Panic had replaced fear, and he was desperately hungry for air. Back on the surface, Nick gagged and coughed out the water threatening to fill his lungs. His arms windmilled wildly, searching for anything that would hold him on the surface. Each time he submerged he felt it would be his last. The sense of dying one moment, living the next was a cruel joke. Finally, the churning water slowed, and the turbulent river became a placid stream once more. Nick floated on the surface, completely spent.

**Don't give in, Garrity. . . . Stay conscious. . . . Stay alive. . . .**

Everything went black.

Nick had no idea how long he'd been out. He was faceup in the stream, and he was still alive. His shirt had caught on a branch that was jutting out over the water, and might have been what had saved him. He was chilled to the core, and unable to stop shaking. The first sound he heard besides the rippling water was Koller, calling his name. The killer was somewhere up-stream, but moving in Nick's direction.

It wouldn't be long.

"I know you're out there. I hope you're suffering. I hope I don't find you dead. I owe you. I owe you for the holes in my hand and my foot. And I owe you because I'm getting cold. Please don't be dead."

Nick freed himself from the branch and sank to eye level in the chilly water, which was only two or three feet deep at this spot. Bit by bit, details of his flight from the killer came into focus.

Hesitant to leave the water despite his chill, he pushed himself downstream. The rain had stopped, and moonlight had broken through the clouds in places. Thirty or forty feet ahead were the roots of a huge fallen tree.

He let go of his hold and guided his body toward it. The tree was hollow. The opening was barely big enough for him to fit through, but Nick managed to squeeze his body inside. No sooner had his feet disappeared into the moss-lined opening than he heard Koller pass by, at most five feet from him.

"I'll find you, Doctor. And I'm going to

make you watch what I do to your pretty girlfriend. You hear me? I'm going to make you watch!"

Nick breathed fresh air using a rotted-out hole in the trunk. He could hide out inside the log, but hypothermia was now a serious concern. Nick closed his eyes. He listened. Then he waited.

Thirty minutes was probably too long to survive in this cold. There had been no sign of Koller for at least the last ten. Nick shivered violently. He had to move soon, before his body began to shut down permanently. Another five minutes and he slipped out the other end of the log. He floated with the current, praying that Koller had abandoned the search. The water slowed considerably. After another ten minutes, virtually helpless and barely conscious, he saw the lights of passing traffic.

It took every bit of his will and remaining strength to crawl toward them.

Waving his arms on the side of the road, he watched with growing dismay as car after car zoomed past.

**Why aren't they stopping?**

His teeth continued snapping together like a jackhammer.

**Please, stop! I'm in trouble!**

Every muscle in his body ached. He no longer had the strength to stand. Suddenly a Ford pickup truck slowed and then pulled to a stop in front of him. Responding to a burst of adrenaline, Nick rose and ran over to the truck. The old man behind the wheel sized him up.

"You okay, son?" the man asked.

"I . . . could use a blanket and a ride," Nick said, through chattering teeth. "But first, do you have a phone I can borrow? It's very urgent."

The man considered the request, then tossed Nick a blanket he fished out from behind his seat, and handed Nick a cell phone.

Jillian was probably in Koller's control. But he could still reach Junie. With his hands shaking, he could barely dial her number. On the third ring, he gratefully heard his call being answered.

"Thank God you're there," he said, not even waiting for her to say hello. "Junie, we've got big trouble."

"That we do," Koller's voice responded over Junie's phone. "Big trouble indeed."

# CHAPTER 47

"Goddamn you, Koller! If you've hurt Junie, I swear . . ."

"Zip it, Doc. I'm nowhere near the woman. But obviously, I had calls to her cell forwarded to me, so I do know where she is. She's unharmed . . . for the moment at least."

"The RV has scheduled stops all over Baltimore and D.C. Police will be looking for her when it doesn't show."

"Actually, the whole evening's been canceled already. Dr. Saunders, that's who's listed for tonight in the log book, knows all about the mechanical problems you're having with the RV. In fact, you yourself told her—at least she thinks it was you. As we speak, that woman is visiting each stop to break the bad news to your patients."

"This isn't over, Koller. Not by a long shot."

Nick could no longer tell if he was shaking from cold or rage. The old man, as easygoing as his faded denim jeans and button-down cowboy shirt, sat patiently in the front seat of his pickup, keeping a watchful eye on his cell phone and Nick through the open passenger door.

"You know something," Koller replied. "I sort of wish that were true."

"Believe me. It is."

"No. It is over, Doc. And you've lost. You just don't realize it yet. But I must confess, you've impressed me."

"I hurt you, too. A big hurt. And I'm going to do it again. Next time it'll be a hammer to the mouth. I have a score to settle with Ramsland, too."

"Now, don't you start naming names there, Nicky. Or whoever's phone you've borrowed will be none too pleased to have helped you out."

"This is between you and me, Koller."

"You bet it's between you and me. Do you know how many contracts I've executed in my career?"

"I know what you did to Saul and Noreen. Belle Coates too."

"The answer is, I've lost count. But suffice it to say, it's an impressive number. And do you know how many of those marks have managed to hurt me?"

"A monster like you has no feelings."

"Oh, wrong again, Doc. I have plenty of feelings. The point I'm making here is that after all those people I've taken out, you'd think at least a couple of them would have left a scratch or two behind. But there you'd be wrong. Turns out you're the first to, how should I put it, nail Franz in any way. For that I commend you."

"Where is Junie? Do you have Jillian too? Tell me, you bastard!"

The old man slid across the cab and poked his head out after hearing the commotion.

"Everything all right out there? I'm afraid you have to be moving on before long. My daughter's got dinner waitin'."

"Tell whoever that is you'll only be a

minute," Koller instructed. "You and me have some business we need to discuss."

"Everything is okay, sir. Thank you. Just another minute and I should be all set."

"No worries, son," said the man. "At my age, time is something I might not have in bulk, but I got no trouble giving away."

"Now, Nick," Koller said, "I want to offer you a deal."

"No deals."

"Really? Even when I have something precious that you want? Two things, as a matter of fact. And you have a couple things that I very much want, too."

"Which are?"

"The DVD . . . and your life."

"You won't get either."

"I think I will. Let's get down to business, shall we, because you don't have much time."

"Nobody else dies, Koller. I won't let it happen."

"I'm afraid that's an option that is well out of your control. It's not *if* you're going to die, Doctor, or your two friends . . . it's *how*."

At Koller's words, much of Nick's bravado faded.

"What are you saying?"

"Give yourself over to me, the last DVD, too, and I promise that when I kill you and the ladies, it will be instant and painless. A single shot to the base of the skull. Oblivion in an instant. You won't even know what hit you. But should you refuse me, should you give me any further trouble, I will torture Ms. Coates and Ms. Wright in ways so horrible you couldn't possibly imagine. And I'll enjoy it. I always do. Then I'll burn them alive, Nicky. But I'll take my sweet time doing it. Piece by piece until they're nothing but cinders. That bus of yours will be their incinerator."

Clearly, Koller was relishing the description.

Nick began to shake. "You wouldn't dare," he managed, with no authority whatsoever.

"You're a doctor. You know the degree of pain I'm talking about. And the ladies' miserable, agonizing deaths will be on your head, too. I'll make sure you have souvenir photos of the aftermath and give you ample time to think about what you did to them before I do something similarly creative to you."

Nick froze at the words. Tears of helplessness and sheer anger blurred his vision.

**This isn't happening. No, not like this.**
Nick's index finger hovered just above the phone's red-lettered End button, but he could not bring himself to disconnect the call. His mind was filled with the imagery and hideous screams of Jillian's and Junie's horrifying final moments. He pictured their blackened bodies in some landfill. He smelled their deaths.

"This offer has a limited shelf life, Doc. You know how Belle Coates died. I cut her a similar deal. A painless, peaceful end for her, and in exchange, sister Jillian got to live. I'm a man of my word. That you should know by now."

Nick was hesitating, stalling as best he could, desperate for the sudden brilliant flash of an idea. Each turn in the maze led quickly to another dead end. Beaten, he bowed his head.

"The location of the DVD only after I know for certain that nobody suffers. I have to see their deaths for myself. I can handle it so long as I know mine is next."

It was Koller's turn to think.

"My, my," he said. "You are a source of constant surprises. I can always torture the information from you if you try and hold out on me. Okay, it's a deal. You get to watch, I get the disc."

Nick found it strange, but he believed Koller would keep his word. There were aspects of the monster that he had come to understand, including a twisted code of keeping his word, testified to by Jillian's continued presence on the planet. What other option did Nick have? At least if he gave himself up, Jillian and Junie would be safe a while longer. Meanwhile, he would spend every moment searching for an opening. And in the end, if there was any chance, however small, of defeating Koller before he killed the women, he would take it.

"What now?" he asked.

"Give the phone back to the man you borrowed it from. Allow me to speak with him."

Trembling, Nick handed the old man back his phone. Exhaustion, his wounds, and the battering his body had absorbed had him bracing himself on the front seat to remain upright.

"He wants to talk to you," he said.

"Who is it?" the man asked.

"Better if you don't know. But I really need you to talk to him."

The man pressed the cell to his ear.

"Yes? . . . That would be exit thirteen, sir. . . . Yes, I can do that. . . . Okay, two and a half minutes, then. . . . Yes, I understand."

Nick could feel panic tightening his throat.

"What did he say?" he asked.

"I have two minutes and thirty seconds to get you down the highway and to drop you off at exit thirteen, or the deal's off. That's what he said."

Nick leaped into the truck's cab.

"Drive! Please drive! Two people's lives are at stake."

"Anything I can—?"

"Nothing! Just drive and drop me off, and then get as far away as possible."

The old man's weathered face blanched and he hit the gas pedal before Nick had even closed the door. His tires squealed on the wet pavement and the pickup skidded into oncoming traffic, nearly broadsiding a minivan.

"We got two minutes, but the exit ain't that far. What sort of trouble are you in, son?"

"I'm dealing with a very bad, sick, dangerous man. It won't concern you as soon as I'm gone, but take this card." Nick worked his sodden wallet from his back pocket and fished out Don Reese's limp business card. "When you're far enough away, and I mean several miles down the road, call this man. He's a detective. Tell him that Nick's been taken somewhere. Leave a message if you get his voice mail."

"Nick's been taken. That all?"

"The less you know, the safer you'll be." **As it is he's probably going to get a look at your license plate number.**

Nick set Reese's business card on the truck's dash.

"We got a minute and a half," the man said. "I ain't got no wife anymore. Died some years back. Nowadays, I live for fixing up old trucks, driving new ones, and watching NASCAR with the boys. But I sure wish I could help you out more."

"That makes two of us," Nick said.

"Almost thirty seconds to spare."

"Nice going. I really appreciate it."

The man pulled the truck off the highway just past the exit thirteen cutoff. They peered out through the rain-dotted windows for another vehicle, but saw none that were parked.

"Doesn't seem to be anybody here," the old man said.

Suddenly, the driver's side door flew open as if blown by the wind. Koller leaped inside, shoving the driver over as if he were a doll, sandwiching him between himself and Nick. Then, without uttering a word, Koller grabbed the man's head between his hands, and in a single, powerful twist, snapped his neck with a sickening crack of bone. The cab instantly filled with a foul stench as his bowels and bladder let go.

"You fucking bastard!" Nick screamed.

Koller leveled his gun on him.

"Nothing you can do will save him now. But a deal's a deal, Doc. And you just cut one with me you don't want to go back on. That's a promise."

With the dead man riding between them, Koller eased the truck into the flow of traffic. The rain was falling harder now.

# CHAPTER 48

"If you light up in here, young man," Junie said, "I promise you I'm going to throw up."

"Even with the door and windows open?"

"You could cut the roof off this bus with a giant can opener and I'd still vomit. It's like an allergy. A person smokes around me indoors, I throw up. Just go outside. You'll be looking right at us through the windows while you give yourself cancer and emphysema and heart disease. But what you won't be looking at, darlin', is this old lady getting violently ill."

The guard, a handsome, well-built African-American man in his thirties, glanced about the RV, clearly pondering what problems could possibly arise from leaving the two women handcuffed to the supports of the dining table while he smoked outside. Finally, he unfolded his six-foot frame from the passenger chair and stepped easily down to the dirt-covered floor of the barn.

"I've seen you smoke, Junie," Jillian whispered.

"Only one a day. It's a deal I made with Sam when we got married. I've never broken the deal, not once, but God, does that one Marlboro taste fine."

"Junie, we can't just sit here waiting for them to kill us. We've got to do something."

"We're not going to be as easy as I was when they hijacked the RV. The guy was already behind the curtain in the exam room, waiting for me when I left to go pick up Nick's replacement for the night. Let's vow right now we won't go down without a fight."

"Any sense of where Nick might be?"

"I'm worried, that's for sure. But I'm also worried they might be using us to get at him."

"All the more reason to fight. The question is, how do we deal with an armed guard while we're handcuffed?"

"You may not be able to tell yet, but I'm softening him up. I remind him of his mother."

"How do you know that?"

"I remind every man of his mother."

"What do we do after you've got him softened?"

"I'm counting on you for that one, sweetie. You're the psych nurse."

It had been five uncomfortable hours since Paul Regis, or whatever his name was, had led Jillian to his car on the pretext of getting some papers for her to sign. Over coffee, he had been charming, worldly, funny, and complimentary, even after she had told him she had met someone, and so she was totally unprepared when he grabbed her wrist and viciously twisted her arm behind her back. In almost the same movement, he shoved her facedown onto the passenger side floor, hoisted her into the car by her belt, and demanded she hold her hands together behind her back. By the time they arrived at the farm—somewhere north and west of D.C., she guessed—her forehead and one cheek were rubbed raw by the carpet.

It was late afternoon when the car finally stopped and Regis opened the passenger's side door. They were parked in a broad field, flat and verdant. Facing them, in parallel, were four large, weatherworn barns, the sort used for storing and curing tobacco. Some distance behind the barns was a small whitewashed house, but there was no farming equipment anywhere, and no corrals or other signs that livestock was about.

Parked in front of the second barn from the right was a black pickup truck, and beside it was a man in dark slacks, sunglasses, and a white shirt, wearing a shoulder holster. It bothered Jillian greatly that Regis had made no attempt to keep her from viewing the setup or from gazing around. Apparently it didn't matter to him what she saw because she wasn't ever going to leave the place alive.

At the second barn, Regis spoke briefly with the man on duty, turned her over to him, and left in something of a hurry. She was handcuffed and led through the side door into a surprisingly vast raftered space, two stories high, poorly lit by three widely spaced naked bulbs. There were dozens of boxes and crates of all sizes stacked along the walls, and a small Jeep parked at the rear. In the center of the barn, beneath one of the three hanging lights, was the Helping Hands Medical RV. She was devastated but not completely surprised to see Junie through the windows, sitting calmly at the table. A minute later, Jillian was sitting across from her, also handcuffed to the table leg.

"Looks like he's almost done with his smoke," Jillian said. "Any ideas?"

"I feel certain I can get out of these handcuffs, at least temporarily."

"How?"

"No man wants to sit around and watch while an old lady wets herself. In fact, I'm not going to have to act very hard to convince him of that threat."

"What comes after that?"

"Coffee," Junie whispered urgently, as the guard stubbed out his butt and turned to mount the stairs.

"I gotcha," Jillian replied as the man settled back wearily into his seat.

"Hey, thanks for doing your smoking out there," Junie said.

"No big deal."

"You really shouldn't be doing that at all, you know."

"Thanks for the advice."

"My name's June—Junie, everyone calls me. This here's Jillian. We're both nurses. We know about smoking."

"That's nice."

"You got a name?"

"Call me Butch."

"This can't be much fun for you, Butch, holding two ladies prisoner like this."

"I do what I'm told."

"I have a son your age. He never did what he was told."

"That's nice."

Jillian sensed that she was watching a master at work—a queen of swaying people to her point of view.

"He's a lawyer now—a public defender. You some kind of cop?"

"Why would you ask that?"

"I don't know. Just something about the way you carry yourself. I been around for quite a while. I know people. For instance, I know that underneath that gruff exterior, you're a good guy—sort of a John Wayne type. You got kids?"

"Enough! All you need to know is that I'm very good at my job, which right now is watching over you two."

"I understand. Tell me something, Butch, did your boss or bosses tell you what to do if your sixty-two-year-old captive's bladder was about to explode?"

The man chuckled.

"You can go to the bathroom. You just got to keep the door open."

"If you wanna watch, that's not my problem."

"Door stays open, even though I don't see you as much of a threat."

"You're right there, Butch. Hey, I don't want to push my luck, but after I get this bladder business straightened out, any way I could make us some coffee? It's instant, but you'd never know it."

"Well, we'll see. First things first."

Butch removed the small brass key from his pants pocket and unlocked her cuffs.

Junie managed a sideways glance at Jillian, who immediately picked up the ball.

"Me next?" she pleaded.

"Like I said, first things first."

Junie rose with no small difficulty, groaning mightily as she did.

"Someday, someone's going to handcuff you to a pole, Butch, and make you sit in just that position for a million hours."

"Sorry. Orders are orders."

"I can barely move."

"You'll loosen up."

"Maybe and maybe not. About that coffee . . ."

"What is it with you two? First things first. How many times do I have to say it?"

"Let me just get some water simmering while I use the bathroom. Like I said, you'll love this stuff."

Junie had already taken a large saucepan from beside the sink, run in some water from the tap, and set it on the propane stove.

Jillian was astounded watching the woman operate. It was just as Junie had said—as if Butch was responding to his mother.

"There's a box of matches right here," Junie said. "I just have to light the—"

"Okay, enough! Put those down and get into the bathroom."

"Sure. You take cream in your coffee?

Sugar? I'll bet neither. You look like a neither type of guy. My son is a neither guy, too. Here, I'll light the burner and you can take charge. Then I'm off to the restroom. The coffee's in the refrigerator right next to the cream. I take both cream and a couple of sugars."

By the time she had turned around and headed up the aisle to the small washroom across from the shower, the propane burner was on and the water was beginning to heat.

"In and out," Butch insisted, adjusting the gun in his shoulder holster for emphasis. "I don't have much patience."

"My son doesn't have any patience either."

*Deception . . . diversion.* The woman was good, Jillian was thinking. *Incredibly good.*

She risked a glance over at the stove, where the saucepan had begun to rattle on the burner. That they had gotten this far was a miracle, but they couldn't stop or even hesitate now. These men were professionals, committed to learning how much the two women knew and then eliminating them. Unless they did something about it, they were both going to die. It was as simple as that.

Jillian swung around as much as she could. Junie had maneuvered her way into the tiny bathroom near the rear of the RV. Then suddenly she closed the door. The guard raced past the stove and pounded on the bathroom door. Jillian noticed that the saucepan on the stove was beginning to clatter as the water approached boiling.

"I told you not to close the door. Open it up now, or I'll kick it in."

"I can't go with somebody watching me. Two more seconds."

"Now!"

The door flew open and Junie stepped out with both her hands in the air. "I'm done. Don't shoot."

Junie lowered her hands and began moving down the narrow aisle as Butch backed up two feet in front of her. With all the commotion, Jillian wondered if he even remembered the near boiling water just a few feet behind him. With luck, if gentle, loving Junie wasn't tentative in anything she did, he was about to get a fearsome reminder.

*Three feet*, Jillian estimated.

Suddenly, Junie reached one hand behind her back and brought it out holding an aerosol can of disinfectant. Butch was reaching for it when she sprayed him in the face. It was a feeble effort and the guard swatted the can away after only one blast. But some of the chemical had stung his eyes. His hand shot up and grabbed her by the throat as his other hand wiped the aerosol away.

"Please don't hurt her!" Jillian screamed. "She's never harmed anyone. Junie, don't be foolish."

Butch hesitated, then loosened his grip.

Junie dropped to one knee, gasping for air, but Jillian noticed that she had moved the guard backward another two feet. Butch, still rubbing at his eyes, was paying no attention to the saucepan of water, which Jillian felt certain was boiling now.

"That was a damn stupid thing to do," the guard said.

"You're going to kill us anyway, aren't you? I had to try something."

"Shut up and get back to your seat. There's not going to be any killing here."

Inch by inch, Junie moved ahead, purposely keeping her gaze down.

"Thank you, Butch," Jillian said. "Thank you for not hurting her."

Butch glanced behind him at Jillian. The distraction had lasted only a fraction of a second, but it was enough.

Junie's moves were quick and deadly accurate. She grasped the saucepan handle, cried out Butch's name, and as he turned back, splashed the boiling water into his face from just a few inches away.

Before the guard had even hit the carpeted floor, screaming and pawing at his eyes, Junie was pounding him again and again with the saucepan—powerful strikes that sounded like rifle shots. It took just two blows for him to become limp, but Junie landed half a dozen more, each more forceful than the last. At some point, Jillian thought she heard bone crack.

She stared wide-eyed at the woman.

"I grew up in a dog-eat-dog neighborhood," Junie said, breathless. She reached down first to check Butch's carotid pulse, then removed his pistol, and finally fished inside his pocket for the handcuff key. "Sometimes just making it to the corner grocery store was a serious adventure.

He's still got a pulse. But I don't think waking up is in his near future."

"Just remind me never to ask you for any coffee," Jillian said.

# CHAPTER 49

Koller exited the highway, pulled to a stop on an unlit, deserted street, and cut the engine. He had been using only one hand to steer. The other he rested on the dead man's lap, pointing the gun he held there at Nick.

"Move this guy into the truck bed back there," Koller said, motioning Nick out of the Ford with the gun barrel. "He stinks. And don't get any ideas. I've left instructions with my people that if we don't show in thirty minutes, to start scalding the ladies with hot oil. You understand me?"

Nick nodded and slipped out of the passenger door and onto the grassy roadside. He was desperate to get to Jillian and Junie, and believed that as long as he did what Koller asked of him, that would happen soon enough. There was nothing he could do to help the old man now, except to add that guilt to the guilt he was already dealing with. He felt terrible about indirectly being the cause of his death, but he forced himself to remember that it was Koller who killed him—Koller and fate.

Cold, hurting, and tired, Nick struggled to lift the body, relying essentially on his one good arm. Then he laid the old man down gently on the truck's muddy bed and covered him. One more score to settle with Koller when the time came.

"What will you do with the body?" Nick asked, as soon as they were traveling again.

"My clients have the means to dispose of bodies. I just provide them."

"You don't feel a thing for that man's life, do you, Koller?"

The killer smiled. "Think of me like an animal put on earth to hunt for food," he replied. "I've been put on this earth to use my considerable skills to kill people. That's just what I do."

"Somebody might report the truck stolen. Aren't you afraid of getting stopped by the police?"

"Do I strike you as a man who's afraid of anything?"

Nick did not answer.

"We have plenty of time to get where we're going without speeding," Koller added.

"You really think of everything, don't you."

"You think of a lot yourself, Doc. I'm curious. Why didn't you bring the DVD with you up to Siliski's office?"

"Saul tipped me off," Nick said, gritting his teeth against another wave of pain, this one centered in his belly. "He used his dead brother's name instead of Umberto's."

"So you knew exactly what he was doing," Koller said with a laugh.

"I picked up on it, yes."

"Well, I did, too. That's why I made him suffer before I killed him. I don't like people messing with me or thinking they're smarter than me."

Even with the truck's heat on high, Nick could not stop shivering. The bullet wound was throbbing more intensely now, perhaps irritated from his efforts moving the body. Chatting with Koller disgusted him, but it seemed like the only thing keeping him conscious at the moment. He was afraid that if he closed his eyes for anything longer than a blink, he might never open them again.

"Don't worry. I won't do to you and the women what I did to your pal Mollender," Koller said, breaking a brief silence. "After all, a deal's a deal."

Nick dug his index finger into the bullet hole in his arm, and discovered that the intense pain caused by the maneuver made him feel more alert and even more determined. From now on, he decided, he would repeat the action again and again for as long as he could stand it. Until this was over between him and Koller, he wanted to feel the hurt. He wanted to feel the hatred.

By the time the killer eased the pickup to a stop in a wide, grassy field, Nick doubted he had the strength even to stand.

**How can I help anyone if I can't even walk?**

Once again, he dug his finger deeply into his wound.

With his gun drawn, Koller crossed in front of the truck and dragged Nick out, letting him drop to his knees on the ground. They were at a farm of some sort, reached by a road that had no traffic. Outside lighting was minimal, but Nick could see a number of barns, none with any windows, and another pickup truck. Koller hoisted him up by what remained of his shirt, and dragged him to the closest door. A man wearing a shoulder holster was standing guard.

"This the doc?"

"Yeah. Open up the door. You might not want to stick around in there for what's going to happen."

"I signed on to die for my country or to help someone else die for theirs. Whatever's going to happen I can handle."

They spoke as though Nick were not present, which in his current state was not that far from the truth. Nick again pressed his finger into the bullet hole, and was a bit dismayed that the pain he generated seemed less. Still, his alertness was enhanced. As his eyes adjusted to the dim light, he began casting about for anything he could use as a weapon, while at the same time testing his limbs.

The barn door slid open on a track and Koller pushed Nick inside. Nick's heart sank at the sight of the Helping Hands RV parked in the center of the space. The interior of the barn was poorly lit, partly because the bulb hanging over the van, one of three dangling on cords from the rafters, was out. Then he realized that the RV, itself, although the passenger door was open, was dark.

**Could the women be in there?**

Once inside the barn, Koller hesitated, then stopped.

"Where's the other guard?"

"Butch?" the guard called out. "Butch, where in the hell are you?"

"Does he know what he's doing?"

"He's the best, sir. The very best."

"Call him again."

"Butch. Hey, buddy."

Nick was awake now. Wide awake. Something was going wrong.

Koller was tense.

"Shit," the killer muttered, scanning the barn, which was stacked with cartons, crates, and any number of places to hide. Violently, he pushed Nick down so he was leaning against the rear tire of the bus. Then he turned to the guard. "Gun out. Watch the door and stay here with him. If he opens his mouth, if he says one fucking word, shoot him in the balls. Don't kill him."

Nick was fully with it now.

Pistol ready, Koller cautiously approached the open RV door. Then he dropped down to one knee and peered inside.

"Jesus Christ!"

"What?" the guard called out.

"Your pal, Butch, the very best, is on the floor unconscious. There's water everywhere, and unless I miss my guess, his prisoners are no longer in this bus."

"Yes!" Nick whispered.

He could see that the killer's face was contorted with anger.

"This door is the only way out," the guard said, "and I was out there on duty every second, just like you ordered. I swear I was. If they're not in the bus, then they're still somewhere in this barn."

A determined smile crossed Nick's face.

He had enough circulating adrenaline now to hold his head up and survey his surroundings. Dark corners, tall rafters, mountains of crates and boxes would give the women ample places to hide. Despite their being trapped inside, they were smart and resourceful and had the advantage of surprise on their side, as well as the fallen guard's gun.

*You go girls*, Nick was thinking. *But for God's sake be careful.*

On red alert, Koller spun in a circle, his gun aiming wherever his eyes traveled. He walked backward a few feet, moving away from Nick, to scan areas of the barn that were obscured from his view by the RV.

"Do you have a flashlight in that truck?" he asked the guard.

"Um . . . I'm afraid it's Butch's truck, so I don't know."

"Of course. . . . Come on now, ladies. I've got your friend Nick here. Do you really want to see him die?"

Koller's voice was less commanding, Nick noticed, his confidence not as evident.

*He absolutely can't stand being at a disadvantage*, Nick was thinking.

"Nobody else has to get hurt. But only if you come out from wherever you're hiding. I'm going to get you, ladies. If I have to burn this barn to the ground, I'm going to get you."

Nick dug his finger deep into the bullet hole in his biceps again. It was time to get active.

"Stay where you are!" he shouted. "Make him come to you. He can't kill us. He needs—"

His words were cut short as the butt of a gun whipped against the side of his head, dazing him and knocking him over.

"I thought I said shoot him if he talks!" Koller screamed. "Disc or no disc, shoot him."

Nick pushed himself to his feet as Koller took up a position five feet away.

"Sorry pal," the guard said, stepping forward.

"Wait," Koller ordered. "Ladies, you have three seconds to show yourself, or we kill him. One . . ."

"Don't come out!" Nick yelled, loud enough for his voice to fill the barn.

"Two . . ."

"I'm sorry, buddy," the guard said again to Nick, "but this is war."

"Three!"

Nick clenched his jaws. There was a loud gunshot, but remarkably, no pain. Nick looked up just as the guard reeled past him and Koller and slammed into the RV, smearing a broad crimson stroke on the white wall as he slid to the ground. Another shot rang out. They were coming from somewhere among the crates to Nick's right.

Koller whirled in the direction of the first shot and fired a rapid spray. The second shot was accompanied by a muzzle flash that both he and Nick saw. The killer needed no more. He snapped off a four-shot volley aimed precisely at the spot. Junie cried out and pitched forward, face-first, collapsing a tower of crates and boxes on top of herself.

Slowly, agonizingly, Nick pulled himself to his feet.

At that instant, there was another scream, this one from the shadows overhead.

**Jillian!**

Koller spun around and peered up through the gloom at the roof of the RV. He was still raising his gun when several gallons of gasoline were poured down into his face. Nick was close enough to be splashed a bit, but Koller was doused. Nick scrambled away as the killer, screaming and pawing futilely at his eyes, stumbled and fell. In the dim light, he could see Jillian, kneeling on the roof of the RV, hurl a now empty metal bucket down on the man. The bucket hit Koller squarely on the top of the head, but the pain had to be nothing compared to the agony he was already experiencing.

"I'LL FUCKING KILL YOU!" he was screeching, though his words were barely audible through his violent gagging. "I'LL KILL YOU."

Koller was on his feet now, spinning wildly, coughing, and rubbing fruitlessly at his eyes. Jillian, on her feet as well atop the RV, had one more surprise in store for the monster, whose thick, black hair was matted with gasoline.

"Paul Regis or whoever you are," she screamed, "you killed my sister. Her name was Belle Elizabeth Coates, you son of a bitch!"

Nick was backing toward where Junie lay motionless when he saw Jillian light a match and drop it into the small cardboard box she held in her other hand. The matches within the box flared, illuminating her face and the beams above her.

At that instant she released her grip and let the container drop.

Nick felt as if he were watching the fireball descend in slow motion. It landed a foot away from Koller, but that was close enough. There was a moment of silence, and then an explosion of fire that lit every corner of the expansive barn, along with a tremendous sucking sound as oxygen rushed to fuel the flames. The pungent odors of gasoline and smoke were overpowered by the stench of Koller's burning hair and flesh, carried skyward inside a towering pillar of fire. In seconds, flame swallowed his face and his skin charred off before it could even blister.

Koller's saturated clothes were consumed as one, incinerating the flesh beneath them, which melted in places down to the bone as the killer continued to stagger around the floor of the barn.

Nick had to shield his face and turn away from the blast of heat. From somewhere within the pillar of flame, he thought he heard Koller screaming.

Then the cylinder of fire collapsed, as the flames receded. Darkness began to recapture the recesses of the barn.

Nick raced past the smoldering mound that had so recently proclaimed itself the master of the non-kill. He moved the crates aside and gently rolled Junie to her back. He knew the moment he touched her that she was alive. The bullet had entered her left chest just above her breast. There was no exit wound that he could discern. Her eyes were closed, but she was breathing, albeit shallowly. Her carotids were still reasonably strong.

Jillian, having scrambled down the ladder at the rear of the RV, had raced to Nick's side. Blood was forming an expanding circle across Junie's shirt.

"Pulse?" Jillian asked, taking the woman's hand in hers.

Nick shrugged. "Not so bad, actually," he said. He leaned over, made a tube of his hand, and used it to check each side of her chest. "She's moving air."

"Hey, Junie Wright, it's Nick and Jillian. Can you hear us?"

Junie moaned, and tried to open her eyes.

"Just lie still, sweetie," Jillian said. "We'll take good care of you."

"Good thing she brought her van," Nick said.

"Good point. How about if I go and get you some equipment?"

"I know where everything is in there. You keep pressure on this wound and a couple of fingers on her carotid, and I'll get my black bag and some stuff for an IV. We've got a neat little crash kit, too."

"You going to make it? You don't look so good."

"I can do it."

"Find a phone in there and call nine-one-one," Jillian called after him. "I'll bet the guard inside has one."

"Got it."

"Flashlights, too, and turn on the head-lights."

Nick passed what remained of Koller, and paused long enough by the guard to affirm that he was beyond fixing. Minutes later, he had the RV's high beams on, and was lugging the crash kit and some other equipment over to where Junie lay.

"Hurry, Nick," Jillian called out, "her pressure's dropping."

"I called nine-one-one," he said, breathless from his exertion, "but I had no idea where to tell them we were, and I didn't want to spend too much time talking to them. The dispatcher said she could barely hear me, but she'd try to locate us using our cell phone signal."

Working amidst the smoke and the stench, nurse and doctor kneeled side-by-side, establishing an IV, and then another, getting a blood pressure cuff in place, and finally hooking up some oxygen. They spoke little.

"Pressure's eighty," Jillian said.

"I'll add some dopamine to the drip."

"Nick, she was the real hero. She saved us all. She's got to make it."

"She's going to make it. Come on, lady, enough of this. Deep breaths, deep breaths."

"Did the dispatcher say how long it would take to find us?"

"All she said was that it would take time."

"Pressure's seventy, Nick. We don't have time."

"I'm doing about all I can do. The dopamine and the fluid are wide open. All this smoke isn't helping. I wish we could get her the heck out of here into some decent air." He snatched up the cell phone. "Any luck? Well, keep trying. Keep trying."

"Nothing?" Jillian asked.

"Nothing. She needs an OR and she needs it fast. I think we should try and get her into the van, and see if we can find a hospital."

"Do you have the strength to move her?"

"If I need it, I'll have the strength."

"Would it hurt her if we have to drag her over to the RV?"

"Maybe."

Jillian checked Junie's pressure again and clenched her fist in frustration.

"Still seventy," Jillian said. "Come on, God. Don't you let this happen. We need her. We all need her. I've been at least willing to discuss Belle and my faith with you, but if you take this woman, I swear, you've heard the last from me. Get it?"

At that moment, the still night was pierced

by the faint sound of sirens. Less than a minute later, with the sirens rapidly closing, strobes appeared across the field. Many strobes.

"They found us!" Jillian exclaimed.

"Looks like an invasion from outer space."

Nick picked up the cell phone and talked for a few seconds. Then he looked at Jillian curiously.

"The dispatcher lady says she's sorry they haven't been able to find us. They're still trying to track us."

Several police cars and an ambulance pulled up at the barn door.

"I think it's safe to say there's a surprise or two waiting in here for them," Jillian said.

The first to enter the barn was Don Reese, followed by the paramedics, who immediately set about performing their magic, praising Jillian and Nick as they worked.

"Reese!" Nick called out.

The detective hurried to Nick's side and stared about in uncharacteristic disbelief.

"The police report on this scene should make for some interesting reading," Reese said. "Who got torched? I sure hope he's a bad guy."

"The worst," Nick said. "How the heck did you get here? Nine-one-one said they couldn't find us."

"Remember after you, um, helped me out, I gave you that magnetic GPS logger for your RV?"

"Of course."

"Well, twenty messages of distress from you freaked me out, Doc. I always thought you were a pretty cool customer. When I couldn't reach you, well, let's just say I chose action. I made a quick call to the company and we tracked your position here."

"Nice going. Now I guess we can call us even," Nick said as the paramedics gave him a thumbs-up.

"I don't think so," Reese responded.

"Oh, come on, Don," Jillian said, taking his arm. "If I can settle the score I just settled, you guys can settle yours."

Junie was up on a stretcher. Nick and Jillian kissed her on the forehead as she was rolled past them to the waiting ambulance.

"Do you want to ride in the ambulance with her, Nick?" Jillian asked.

"If they'll let me."

"Looks like you'll need some medical attention too," Reese said. "We'll meet you at the hospital. They'll be taking you to County General. It's a good place and only five miles from here."

Jillian and Reese supported Nick and helped him to the ambulance. The rain had stopped. Overhead the clouds had parted, revealing a bright crescent moon.

# CHAPTER 50

The white stretch limousine eased its way down Constitution Avenue toward the Hart Senate Office Building. It was the twelfth day of September, a sparkling clear Wednesday, and it would be no under-statement to say that there was more in-terest in the hearing scheduled to resume in half an hour than in any Senate inquiry since Watergate.

"Answer me true," Reggie said from the center of the backseat, "are we going to get us one of these limos or not?"

"I wouldn't bet on you not getting one of your own someday," Junie said, pausing to cough and take a breath, "but only if you do your homework."

"Hey, Dr. Nick Fury here told me that when I move in with him and Nurse Jillian, I won't have to do any homework."

"You wish," Jillian said. "You haven't seen the nasty side of either of us yet. Junie, you okay?"

The older woman cleared her throat and nodded. She hadn't done that well following the removal of the upper lobe of her left lung, and seemed to have aged considerably over her months of recovery. Still, it was no surprise to anyone who knew her that she had managed to parlay her growing celebrity into massive donations to Helping Hands, as well as the promise from Winnebago of a new, deluxe, fully equipped RV.

"Have you looked outside?" Don Reese asked. "We still have a ways to go and it's already wall-to-wall photographers and reporters."

"Let's hop out," Reggie said. "I want some more pictures of me in the papers. There's this girl at school I want to impress and—"

"Enough!" Junie said. "I've spoken to

your civics teacher, and she's expecting at least a five-page paper on these hearings. That should be more than enough to impress any girl that's worth impressing. Nick, honey, the humidity's getting to me a little. Could we please have the driver take us right up to the door?"

"Yes, ma'am."

"There are a few stairs," Reese said. "But there's a ramp. Do you need a wheelchair?"

"I can handle it," Junie said.

Reese had not only been a lifesaver during the drama in the CIA-owned barn, but afterward as well. It was he who first began to put the pressure on William Conklin, the director of the CIA, whom he knew personally, to do what he could to restore public trust in the agency. Given Ramsland's stature and power, Conklin had for years turned a blind eye to the activities of the Jericho vigilantes. Now, Conklin's job was on the line. The nasty publicity the agency was garnering around the globe was unlike anything since the Senator Frank Church hearings in the midseventies, which focused on CIA political assassinations and other excesses.

This afternoon, Reese's work with the CIA chief was hopefully going to come to fruition.

Following a morning of testimony from Paresh Singh, officials and surgeons from Shelby Stone Memorial Hospital, and relatives of the seven victims from operating room ten, Lionel Ramsland had begun what to Nick and the others was an utterly frustrating denial of any direct wrongdoing.

Soon, after the man completed the remainder of his testimony, it would be Conklin's turn. The final testimony, although it would be only hearsay, would be from Nick.

"Don't expect to be called if they run out of time," Nick's attorney told him. "They may reconvene tomorrow or they may delete you because your story is unsubstantiated with objective evidence."

The reporters crowding the curb and spilling over into the street seemed to have been tipped off about the occupants of the approaching limo. There had been lengthy articles on Nick, Jillian, and the others in the *Times*, the Washington papers, and *People*, as well as on all the networks and CNN. *The Ten Little Indians OR Murders*, *People* had headlined their cover story.

David Bagdasarian, the group's attorney, and one of the legal team representing Nick and Jillian before the boards of medicine and nursing, had arranged for the transportation. Now, he met them at the curb, opened the door for them, and led the group into the modern Hart Senate Building. Nick's and Jillian's licenses to practice had been suspended, but then the suspensions were stayed pending further investigation.

"Ramsland's real good," Bagdasarian said as they passed through the nine-story atrium and by the massive Alexander Calder metal mobile, *Mountains and Clouds*, and ascended to Room 216. Today, the legendary hearing room was the home of the Senate Select Committee on Intelligence. "He admitted to being the tenth man in the operating room video the senators saw, but he denied doing anything illegal. And of course, even with the plastic surgeon's testimony, no one can figure out definitively who was on the operating table that day three years ago, or what happened to the body. Supposedly, an autopsy was performed, but no one has produced the results. God bless 'em all."

"Hey, don't press that panic button just yet," Reese said as they took their seats in the third row behind the witness table. "As Yogi Berra said, the opera ain't over until the fat lady sings."

Reese had admitted to Nick and Jillian that, for weeks, he had been working with William Conklin at the CIA, but he had shared few details until this morning.

The six of them were all seated except for Nick. Thanks to his flight from Franz Koller, his shoulders and knees still balked at being kept in one position for very long. Physical therapy had helped, but his joints continued to feel a decade or two older than the rest of him. His PTSD was another story altogether. His ultimate triumph over the killer, his continued EMDR therapy, and his new life with Jillian and Reggie were working wonders with his condition. His SUD score was now consistently between three (*Mildly upset, worried, bothered to the point where you notice it*) and two (*A little bit upset, but not noticeable unless you take care to pay attention to your feelings and then realize, "Yes, there is something bothering me"*) with an occasional one (*No acute distress and feeling basically good*) thrown in.

Nick was massaging the muscles at the base of his neck when Lionel Ramsland entered the packed hearing room. He had lost some weight, and almost certainly was wearing expertly applied makeup. But in general, he appeared as cocky and confident as ever. And as Bagdasarian said, he had strong reason to be.

Nick had taken great pleasure in the man's announcement two months ago that in the interest of not being a distraction to his party, he was stepping down as a vice presidential candidate before being nominated.

Now, as Ramsland approached his seat, his eyes and Nick's met. For a few frozen seconds, neither of them moved. Then, never releasing his gaze or altering his expression, Ramsland raised his right hand and saluted. Nick, swallowing a jet of bile, shook his head derisively and took his seat between Jillian and Reese, facing the panel, and behind them, the massive marble wall with the seal of the Senate.

Ramsland's continued testimony was

gaveled to order by the chairman, a wizened senator from Missouri named Blackstone. Over the next hour, under oath, the man who might have been a heartbeat from the presidency lied again and again about his relationship with Franz Koller, the electronic device under CIA contract that could stimulate portions of the brain or cause the electrical pathways of the brain to short-circuit and stop functioning altogether, his role as creator and mastermind of the black ops Jericho unit, and his relationship and dealings with Aleem Syed Mohammad. He also swore that he had never had a cell phone conversation with Nick, and that records of the calls made from his personal cell phone showed absolutely no calls made during the time period Nick had stated in his deposition.

Nick's fists were clenched throughout the barrage of dishonesty. At one point Reese leaned over and whispered, "It's all just rope, Nicky-boy. Every lie is just more rope."

"Well, he's almost finished," Nick said, "and I don't see any noose."

At that moment, as the final senator was finishing his five minutes of largely redundant questions, Reese looked over his shoulder. His expression, which had been getting somewhat gloomy, brightened considerably. Again, he bent over close to Nick.

"Let the games begin," Reese whispered. "The fat lady has arrived."

Nick turned around to see CIA chief William Conklin standing by the rear doors between what appeared to be two lawyers. Minutes later, with Ramsland now seated to the side of the room, Conklin, in his midfifties with thick white hair, the body of an obsessive athlete, and heavy bags under his eyes, was called forward, sworn in, and asked by Blackstone to identify himself.

"I notice that you have not been present for the early portion of these hearings," Blackstone said, clearly prepared for this witness.

"No, I just flew in. The flight was delayed."

"You were traveling alone?"

"No, I traveled with deputy CIA chief Arthur Senstrom."

"Lionel Ramsland's successor to that post."

"Yes, Senator."

"And where did you fly in from, Mr. Conklin?"

"From South America, Senator. I cannot disclose the country."

"The purpose of your trip?"

"We spent two days with the terrorist Aleem Syed Mohammad."

The hearing room erupted. Everyone, it seemed, was speaking at once. In an instant, Blackstone's gavel was pounding.

"Nice going," Nick whispered to Reese.

"Conklin's scrambling to keep the Agency together. I helped him to see that this was his only chance. I just didn't know if the trip was going to accomplish what we hoped. Now it appears as if it did. Tell Jillian she can take out that photo of her sister she's got in her bag."

Nick did as Reese asked. Jillian set the photo on her lap. It was a five-by-seven black-and-white candid of Belle, in a spring dress, seated with her back against a tree. She was reading a book. Her shoulder-length hair framed a porcelain face that was at once beautiful and transcendently serene.

Nick had seen the photo a number of times before, and knew Jillian had taken it.

He reached across and squeezed her right hand with his. A single tear broke free from the corner of her eye, and landed on his wrist.

Gradually, order was restored to the chambers.

"You have come back with evidence pertaining to this case, Mr. Conklin?" Blackstone asked.

"Yes, Senator."

"Objection," Ramsland's lawyer shouted, leaping to his feet. "I demand the right to review this evidence before it is presented."

"Mr. Dietz, this is a hearing to gain facts. Your client is not on trial here, just under oath. I am going to permit the presentation of any evidence that will help us expeditiously get to the truth. Please proceed, Mr. Conklin."

The CIA chief set two tape recorders on the table before him and turned the first one on. A man's deep voice filled the room. He spoke in Arabic.

"Rather than play the full recording, I'm going to read you the translation," Conklin said, shutting off the tape as he began. "'Voice prints will confirm that I am Aleem Syed Mohammad. You will also find my fingerprints on this and another tape. I am speaking to you from a concealed location in South America. In exchange for my co-operation here, as well as for any further information Mr. Conklin may require, I have been given permission to continue living my life in secrecy.

"'Some years ago, after the death of my oldest son, I grew extremely weary of war and of the jihad. For reasons that will become clear to you, I sought out Mr. Lionel Ramsland of the CIA, and he agreed to meet with me.

"'My capture by U.S. forces was arranged, and I was transferred from the American military to the CIA. Over the next year, my appearance was totally altered by a number of plastic surgical procedures performed by Dr. Paresh Singh. At the same time, two men with bone structures similar to my own were chosen to be made to look exactly as I did before my surgeries. In the meanwhile, medical evidence was created showing that I was dying from a rare cardiac tumor.

"'It is my understanding that my doubles were brainwashed with very sophisticated methods, and taught to speak enough Arabic to converse with people, and in particular with the physicians who would be caring for me.'"

Nick glanced behind him to the second row from the back, where Bill Pearl, wearing his trademark black suit and dress shirt, was sitting next to Manny Ferris, who looked remarkably well in a tan sports coat and tie. Thanks to Jillian, Manny had begun a series of plastic surgery procedures designed to reverse the disfiguring that had resulted from his escape from the Singh Center. In addition, a team of therapists from Shelby Stone had been deprogramming him and treating his PTSD. According to Jillian, progress was slow, and there was some doubt among his treaters as to how far back Manny could make it. But no one was inclined to stop trying.

"'After a year,'" Conklin continued, "'my perfect double was sent to the operating room at Shelby Stone Memorial Hospital, where he died before the operation could be performed. By that time, I was safely ensconced in the country and the home where I am living now. In exchange for my life, I fed a great deal of legitimate information to Mr. Ramsland regarding various

activities of the groups you refer to as terrorist.

"'Mr. Ramsland came to see me every
couple of months and pumped me with
more questions. After three years, Mr.
Ramsland resigned to pursue his political
ambitions. His replacement, Mr. Arthur
Senstrom, began visiting me. But on the
second visit, he made the mistake of telling me that the operation in which I alleg-
edly died had been recorded. I, of course,
demanded to view the recording. As you
will learn, I had the leverage with Lionel
Ramsland to make such a demand.

"'The recording showed me sitting
up before my surgery in great distress,
screaming in Arabic and in Spanish for a
man named Dr. Nick Fury, then collapsing
and dying from a device that I am certain
was triggered by Lionel Ramsland, who
was in the room. Clearly, the others in the
operating room that day heard the same
thing I did. It was my feeling that so long
as they were alive, my safety and security
would be in jeopardy. I met with Mr. Ramsland, and he assured me he could and
would take care of the matter in such a
way that no one's attention would be called

to the operation. Further, he promised that all copies of the recording would be destroyed. As far as I know, Mr. Ramsland kept his promise in that regard.'"

William Conklin set the transcript aside and folded his hands. The packed hall was deathly silent. All eyes were fixed on Lionel Ramsland, who sat rigidly erect and looked to Nick as if he were going to launch into a tirade of self-justification and patriotism, similar to the one he had spewed at Nick in Noreen Siliski's office.

This time, the silence held. There was no need for Blackstone to gavel for order. There was one unanswered question, and the room was waiting for the senator from Missouri to ask it.

"Assuming what we have heard is true, Mr. Conklin, this is a terrible, terrible revelation, and I am sure that all who have heard it are as stunned as I am."

Ramsland could stand matters no more. He leaped to his feet and shouted, "There are two sides to every story! I saved lives, hundreds of lives! Thousands of lives. This is war, Senator! War! Young American soldiers are being killed every day!"

Blackstone's gavel thundered down again

and again. Bailiffs rushed over to silence Ramsland, who had lost all composure and was now an apoplectic crimson. His lawyer whispered harshly into his ear. Meekly, he sank back into his chair.

"Mr. Conklin," Blackstone said finally. "Is that second tape going to further enlighten us as to just what this so-called leverage was?"

"It will, Senator, but it is more than an hour long."

"Can you paraphrase it for us?"

"I can, sir." Conklin adjusted his notes. "It is a conversation that occurred six years ago in Karachi, and was secretly recorded by Aleem Mohammad. The meeting was instigated by Lionel Ramsland. In it, Ramsland promises Mohammad the delivery of a large cache of untraceable weapons, mostly Russian in origin, as well as five million dollars in untraceable cash in exchange for the death of Mr. Ashai Bayoumi, the Egyptian foreign minister, who was openly anti-American. Ramsland then promises to inform Mohammad of the precise time and place when Mr. Bayoumi would be at prayer. Our intelligence shows that a month later, that small mosque was blown up, killing Bayoumi and a dozen others. Neither I nor anyone else at the Agency had any knowledge of such a deal being made.

"It was Mohammad's possession of that tape that led him to contact Lionel Ramsland regarding his desire to pass on vital information to Jericho, and then to have his death staged. That tape, which we have here, has been the leverage—the dead man's switch if you will—that Mohammad has used to insure his own survival."

Again, Ramsland was on his feet, screaming. "Dispensing of Bayoumi kept Egypt from forming alliances with several terrorist groups! Thousands of lives were saved! Thousands."

This time, the chambers were in chaos.

Helpless, Blackstone gaveled the session to a close. But few heard him. Everyone seemed to be running at once, wedging through the double doors.

Ramsland was surrounded and led away.

As Ramsland and the bailiffs neared the exit, Nick felt certain the man turned and glared at him.

At last.

For a time after the room was nearly empty, the six of them—Nick, Jillian, Reese, Junie, Reggie, and Bagdasarian— remained silent in their seats.

"I thought it would feel better than it does," Nick said finally.

"How could it?" Jillian replied. "Dead is dead. Ramsland will go to his grave believing that what he did, the good, innocent people he had killed, was in the best interests of the country."

Again, there was a pensive silence.

"Well, I think we've all heard enough for one day," Reggie said suddenly. "Can we go home?"

"Not only can we," Junie said, "we should."

"In the limo?"

"In the limo, my friend," Nick echoed.

# EPILOGUE

Thanksgiving dinner at the new headquarters of the Helping Hands Foundation was at once joyous and bittersweet. The broad rented table in the waiting room was piled high not with food but with boxes of food, prepared by volunteers and supervised by Jillian. Board and staff members set up a human chain to pass the boxes to a waiting line of patrons. Sam Wright and the Levishefsky twins worked alongside members of the Washington and Baltimore professional sports teams handing out the turkeys. The mayor was there, shoulder to shoulder with Reggie, and Nick's PTSD students were there in force and unusually good humor.

"Hey, Nick," Matthew McBean called across the room. "I think my SUD score is a three today. Seeing all these people outside makes me so appreciative of what I have that I'm having trouble feeling lousy."

Nick smiled at his friend. Since the death of Phillip MacCandliss, a number of the former enlisted men had gotten the benefits that had previously been denied. Several more had gone back to work and one, Eddie Thompson, had actually gone to work for the VA.

David Bagdasarian, Nick's attorney, entered the crowded room carrying two huge boxes of pastry.

"Breaking news, Nick," he said. "Yesterday evening, Ramsland's latest bail appeal was denied. Too great a flight risk. The guy is going to stay locked up until his trial. His lawyers argued that without Aleem Mohammad, the prosecution doesn't have much of a case, but the judge disagreed."

Jillian, who was standing nearby, gave the lawyer a thumbs-up.

"I guess the judge knows a mass murderer when he sees one," she said.

The fallout from the government cutting a deal with Mohammad in exchange for his statements and cooperation had not fully dissipated. There had been demonstrations, and an organization called No Deals was agitating the CIA to disclose the terrorist's whereabouts and to begin proceedings to bring him back.

"Anything new on Paresh Singh and the money-laundering charges?" Nick asked.

"Not since he jumped bail and vanished. India is a big country and he has more than enough money to bribe anyone. Nobody thinks they're going to find him."

Junie came in from where she had been arranging the equipment in the new Helping Hands thirty-nine-foot Winnebago.

"Do you want me to take you home?" Nick asked.

"What do you think?" Junie said. "This is more physical labor than I'm used to, but the doctors say it's good for me to start pushing myself a bit more. And now that I don't have to worry about this guy every day since you're adopting him"—she put her arm around Reggie—"I'll be back to a full schedule in no time."

"Remember," Reggie said, "you promised

I could go with you on the first run in the new RV. It's not exactly a limo but, like you said, I plan on having my own one day."

"Mr. Mayor," Junie said. "Things are slowing down a little now. Would you like to come out and see the new RV you helped us raise money to purchase?"

"I'd like that very much," the mayor said.

Together, Jillian, Junie, Reggie, and Nick guided the mayor to the street where the two vans were parked. Second Chance, leashed to the steering wheel, greeted them proudly.

"This is my dog, Chance," Reggie said. "Chance, this is the mayor."

The mayor toured the new RV briefly and thanked them before heading off. For a time the four of them stood quietly, looking at a glass-enclosed display on one wall. In it was a poster-size version of the picture of Umberto Vasquez that Nick had carried from street to street for four years, and beside it was the photo of a beautiful young woman reading a book beneath a tree.